PIECES

MICHAEL ALOISI & REBECCA ROWLAND

www.DarkInkBooks.com

First Published by *Dark Ink Books*, September 2019

www.AMInkPublishing.com

Dark Ink Books is a division of *AM Ink Publishing*. *Dark Ink* and *AM Ink* and its logos are trademarked by *AM Ink Publishing*.

Contents

For the *chosen few*

Prologue
A suburb near Springfield, MA

<u>Tuesday</u>

Survival of the fittest, he thought. *Natural selection.*

He had watched the sandy-haired girl walk unaware from the convenience store to her car, a rusting black Volkswagen two-door with a frayed ragtop. To him, she had been nothing. Now, as she lay before him, her skin beginning to pale and emit a waxy sheen, she was still nothing. She was not Julie Piedmont as her ID stated. She was not twenty-one and just about to graduate college. She did not have four brothers and two loving parents. She was merely an object for him to use for his game.

She was a puzzle that he had to take apart so that society could try to put it back together again.

Abducting her had been easier than he thought it would have been. He followed her beaten-up convertible for three blocks until it teetered into the parking lot of the coffee shop. He sat, patient as a cat in front of a goldfish bowl, while she worked her evening shift; he watched her swim about the diner, back and forth, filling and refilling cups and serving perfectly cut triangles of pie, sweeping into her apron the pittance of tips left by customers who had spent hours sitting and sipping, sitting and sipping, until finally—finally—the digital clock on his dashboard read ten o'clock and he saw her gather her coat, wave goodnight to the evening manager, and step back into the early fall air and walk towards her car.

It was over before she knew what happened.

He supposed this thought would be a comfort to her friends, to her four brothers, to her mother with the gray roots peeking out from her scalp, and to her father, who pursed his lips and did his best not to break into tears as the ravenous media carved out their pounds of flesh.

With one crack to the back of her head with a tire iron, she dropped to the ground in the shadow beside her car. He had worn sneakers because he knew they made him stealthy, silent. He had worn black clothing, but nothing too obvious. There was no use skulking around in a black-hooded sweatshirt if it made suspicious passers-by look twice at his face or his Buick. Just as he had practiced in his garage using bags of cement innumerable times, he quickly tossed her limp body into his trunk and quietly closed the door.

Natural selection. Philosopher Herbert Spencer had coined the phrase first, long before Darwin ever explained the concept, decades before humans regularly produced gaggles of offspring only to watch them thinned by disease and misfortune. The grey tree frog camouflages itself against predators; the Galapagos finches develop beaks to fit the types of food they eat. England's peppered moth, for instance, once appeared with equally light colored wings and dark ones. Once the coal-burning factories began to dot the nation, however, the dark-winged version easily concealed itself in the soot and ash residue that stained every surface. By the time the twentieth century began, nearly all of the peppered moths possessed dark wings. Dennis had taken—and excelled—in biology, botany, and human anatomy courses in college. He understood that, more than anything, the game known as survival of the fittest only worked when a substantial amount of the players died. Those who were left standing were the strongest, the smartest—the ones who would endure. He was a dark winged moth. Julie, with her Hallmark Channel movie family, her Saturday morning cartoon social life, and her complete oblivion regarding the predators around her, was a white winged moth.

Her time had always been cursory.

He had planned this night for months, noting where each and every security and traffic camera was posted. He had taken his time selecting his victim, and when he narrowed the prospects to Julie Piedmont, he spent six nights in his car parked at various locations within sight of the diner. He followed her home, witnessed the interactions with her middle-class family framed by the wide bay window. He tracked her commute to and from the small college two towns away. He watched her, studied her movements, drank in her naïveté. *Twenty-one years old with a university education and a lifetime of growing up nearly surrounded by men and you don't know enough to carry your key between your first and middle fingers when you walk at night?* Dennis rolled his eyes. It had almost been too easy.

While he had killed before—seven times, in fact—it wasn't the killing itself that excited him. Exterminating the person was merely a necessary initial step in the process. The seven kills before Julie were solely for practice. When he had finished with the seventh girl, he had decided he was ready, for he finally could dismantle a body with the surgical precision imperative to his mission.

He had been choosier when he selected Julie Piedmont as his final oblation. He knew she would have to be striking enough to glean the rapt attention of the media but wholesome enough to melt the hearts of avid viewers. She had to be feminine and fair and preferably blonde. Men, dark-haired women, dark women, period: they might catch a wink of interest here and there, but no one would remember them a week later. Their stories fell further and further into the recesses of the newspaper's back pages, and often, follow-ups on their misadventures never even made it into the digital press. This one would be different. This one would get their attention.

Because he would use her body for something greater, Dennis Sweeney killed Julie Piedmont gentler than the others. While she was still unconscious on his sterile worktable, he suffocated her using a rag soaked in the formalin he'd procured from the lab where he worked. When he placed it over her mouth and nose, he made certain the cloth was dripping with the solution so that it trickled into her throat, poisoning her while it preserved much of her wet tissue.

He removed the new blade he'd purchased and attached it to his reciprocating saw. He'd gone through ten blades in the past five years—three of them when he had to cut into the steel oil tank four years ago. Then, he took out the rest of his instruments and went to work.

Friday

It was so early in the morning, only the first slips of purple and orange whispered along the horizon in the dark sky. Dennis sipped his coffee. It had begun to cool and the creamer he'd drowned it in was beginning to separate and pool like scum on the surface of a pond in the summer. He'd been up for nearly two hours already, too excited to sleep through the night and anxious to begin his long journey.

Thirty white packages lined up like pale soldiers on his kitchen table. Most were the small or medium-sized, like standard flat-rate boxes; six outliers were of the larger variety. All were addressed neatly in even typewriter font and marked Priority Mail, and he knew that he'd have to bring each one personally into a post office to pay for the postage. This alone caused Dennis some anxiety, but his excitement far outweighed any trepidation.

He counted his cash, rechecked his duffel bag, and itemized, for the fifth time, his assortment of hats, glasses, jackets, hairpieces, and wigs. The stars were aligned in his favor: the weather forecast predicted a cold spell for the next few days; he'd be able to wear the gloves and hats without arousing suspicion. The gloves weren't really necessary—he'd made the proper precautions— but they added an ambiance of additional security. The plan called for him to drive 1,233 miles round trip to locations all over the Northeast, sticking to rural routes when he could, and mail each of the packages at random post offices along the way. He knew the boxes would eventually be tracked back to their shipping locations and that he'd be on camera, so he developed a repertoire of postures, gaits, and mannerisms to further disguise himself. He'd even packed theater padding to add weight to his frame at times.

The media and their investigative journalism. Dennis scoffed. They might as well write an instruction manual for burgeoning murderers with the degree of detail they offered each time a perpetrator was caught. Just a year previous, a right-wing lunatic who'd had the insane idea of mailing letter bombs to prominent liberals around the country was nabbed after forensic investigators lifted his fingerprints off of the packing tape used to seal the shipments. He had left traces of his DNA all over the address labels. Dennis had not made that mistake. Dennis was blessed with a genetic gift that had made it his destiny to achieve this masterpiece. Dennis would not be caught.

It would be a long journey, and he hoped the dry ice would keep long enough to adequately preserve his precious cargo. He took one last look around his kitchen, double-checked the timers on his lights, and dumped the last of the tepid liquid from his cup down the drain. He dug gently around the duffel bag's interior and pulled out the single envelope encased in a Ziploc bag. This would be the last item he'd ship, the one he'd toss in a mailbox just before ditching the stolen Buick and hopping a series of buses to return home.

And then, his work would be over, and the game would begin.

The Letter
Milwaukee, WI

Get the Facts With Jax! With a sigh, Jax rubbed his face, staring at the blinking cursor at the end of the title. Over two thousand of these damn articles in the past eighteen years as a reporter. They used to be so full of life and passion, he couldn't stop writing them; hell, the first ten years he wrote more than he was required every week. Now, writing one was like trying to make a gallon of lemonade with a teaspoon of lemon juice. No matter how much sugar you added or how you stirred it or marketed it, in the end, it was just that: sugar water, empty calories with no flavor other than the overpowering sweetness trying to trick your brain into thinking it was good.

One more year. One more year was all he had to get through and then he could start over. It was that mantra that made Jax's fingers do what they always did, move across the keyboard, pouring out mangy words that were the equivalent of empty calories. His readers would tell him how good it was, but his editor would shake his head and Jax would know it was just more fluff for the sake of having fluff. *Wisconsin's daily milk consumption has dropped thirty percent in the last year. This week, Jax will get you the facts as to why the milk drinking is drying up!* The journalist wanted to throw up on the computer.

Seven hundred and fifty words later, Jax hit send. He didn't even bother reading the crap over anymore; the days of fifteen drafts were over. On the way out of his office, he glanced at the pile of mail on his desk he had been ignoring. He paused for a second, but he wanted to get home, so he snapped the lights off and headed out of the dingy little paper's office. Three young reporters were still at their desks banging out stories the way he used to, and it made him smile in nostalgia. The days when his career was skyrocketing seemed so long ago. From when he first exposed the Mob connections in his hometown of Chicago, to his peak in New York when he took down a famous media personality for lies and claims she made, Jax had a hell of a career and he had let it slip away. If someone were to draw a chart of his notoriety as a journalist, it would look like Mount Everest. It was straight up, with a few stops at base camps, and then hit a peak that took him to national attention. But, just like Everest, you can't breathe at the top, so you have to come down quick. Now he had fallen all the way down to Milwaukee where his readership in print was one fifth what it was in Chicago, but his online readership had pretty much always stayed the same, which is why he got the highest salary in the office all while doing the least amount of writing. Unlike everyone else, Jax didn't care that his career brought him to the bottom of the Midwest media; he was happy with his star fading because he was getting ready to live the life he truly wanted.

Pulling into his modest two-story colonial, Jax didn't realize he was smiling, which he did every day at this time. He parked outside of the garage, rushed inside, threw his keys in the bowl by the door, and searched the rooms to find his wife, but before he could get through the kitchen, he saw the sticky note on the counter. *Went to store, be back around seven.* Jax's smile grew bigger. He loved that she left notes instead of texting his cell phone; it reminded him of a simpler time, when going to the store was not something a spouse needed to instantly know. He felt a bit disappointed he did not get his customary fifteen second hug (*hugs need to be at least ten seconds because that is when the endorphins are released and it becomes a hug. Anything shorter and it's a greeting.* That was Maggie's rule and since they first dated ten years before; all of their hugs had lasted at least ten seconds, and to be safe, they bumped it up to fifteen when they moved in together), but he knew he'd get it when she came home.

After getting changed and going to the bathroom, Jax headed downstairs to the garage as if he were on a mission. Inside, he flipped on the lights, grabbed a blue apron that appeared Jackson Pollock had thrown up on, and took a big breath; he loved the smell of pine, varnish, paint, and sawdust: this was his happy place. Walking over to the drying table, he checked his work from the previous night, making sure the glue and epoxy had cured enough to be moved to the large rack where it would wait for Maggie to take it to the photographing area. There, she would work her magic to make his "unique" wooden art pieces look stunning.

Before the age of nine, Jax had whittled wood; by ten, he was shaping crude figures; by fifteen, he was making wooden cars and buildings for fun. There was a deep love for woodworking inside of him, and it always calmed him, but he never thought of it as something that would make money or that anyone would love. When he was in college, he stopped whittling because having a knife and wood shavings on a dorm floor wasn't the coolest thing in the world. It wasn't until he was thrust into the spotlight when he cracked the "Media Molester" case wide open, when the stress poured over him, that he found himself in a woodworker's shop buying supplies. It was as if he did it on autopilot: he hadn't even known where he was going or what he was getting until he got home and put the bags down on the counter in his Chicago apartment. Being older and having more life experience and needing more creativity than building model cars, Jax started making…things.

Jax had no names for his things; they were just that: things. Pieces of perfectly smooth wood with beautiful varnish that shone like precious metal, stuck together at odd angles and making shapes that made no logical sense yet had such a beauty that they were stunning. At first, he kept them hidden, not thinking anyone would understand or care for his odd creations, but when he started dating Maggie, it was hard to keep them a secret. When she saw them for the first time, a tear fell down her cheek; she brushed back her red hair, looked up at Jax and said, "Now I see the real you and I love it." The next day, his pieces came out of hiding, were placed around the apartment on end tables and shelves, and by Christmas that year Maggie had talked him into giving them out as presents. He had been shocked at the reactions: people loved them.

After almost twenty years, a small online shop, and one gallery showing in Chicago, Jax was almost ready to open up his own permanent gallery in New York City, funded by some rich art lover who had stumbled across his work online and became an angel investor on the terms that Jax supply enough to keep a gallery in stock. The man would buy the location and run it; all Jax had to do was supply the art and make the occasional appearance. There were meetings, flights to NYC, visits to spaces for the permanent shop, and countless other business aspects. It was legitimate and it was happening.

Jax and Maggie agreed that they would wait for the shop to stay open for one year. If it was successful, they would quit their day jobs and move to the suburbs of NYC where they would live out the dream life they never allowed themselves to dream. With the gallery opening seven weeks away, that dream was about to begin. For the next four hours, Jax cut and sanded and painted, hugged his wife, had dinner in the shop with Maggie (chicken pot pies, homemade) and then made love in the shower with her like they were twenty-somethings on a first date. Life was damn good.

In the morning, Jax got up, made breakfast for the two of them—omelets with farm fresh eggs and organic, locally grown peppers and tomatoes—and the two smiled and laughed about how they looked like an ad for happy newlyweds. They often joked that they shouldn't be this happy or excited (their friends said it was only because they didn't have kids) since something could change or the shop wouldn't work out, but they couldn't help it: the moment was too intoxicating. After cleaning up, he put on his business casual outfit (never a suit anymore) and gave a sad look to Maggie as he kissed her and walked out of the house.

"Our new lives start soon: no frowns," Maggie said, and she watched as the smile reappeared on his face.

At the office, Jax did his rounds of saying good morning and getting coffee. As he did this, the editor, who was twenty years younger than he, pulled him aside, like he always did, and asked if he could find something a little more hard-hitting than a milk controversy. Jax just nodded. His contract allowed him to write about "any" topic he saw fit each week, but Jax knew the editor of the paper regretted that decision, so he threw him a good piece now and then to make him happy. That week would have to be one of those weeks.

Sitting down at his desk, Jax rubbed his eyes and started his typical process of figuring out what story to go after next. There was always a long list available: readers writing in about scams they thought were happening, the "grab" list that his editor compiled each week that was open to all reporters looking for extra scoops, and his own folder of leads and stories to pursue when he was ready. Picking the next story, unless something was urgent and topical, was always a pain in the ass. Jax had a system of figuring out what appealed to him that particular week, but mostly, he selected what he could exert the least amount of effort on. With a shake of his head, Jax realized the coffee had not kicked in enough for him to start looking for his next topic, so he decided to open his mail.

He waded through a deluge of junk mail and a smattering of readers' letters. Jax was quickly bored until he got to one particularly crisp looking letter that seemed a bit thick. His stomach turned when he looked at his name neatly printed on the white envelope. He had not had that feeling in a long time. It was the gut feeling he used to have on big projects. He had even tried to explain the feeling when he was being interviewed about his reporting techniques on *60 Minutes*. The famous interviewer called it his "gut instinct," but Jax didn't like that term; he called it his *oh shit meter*, but he couldn't say that on air. He assigned it this moniker because he knew some shit would happen when his stomach turned that way: good shit, bad shit, dangerous shit, or deep shit. His meter had not gone off in ages and it made him nervous, so he set the envelope aside and opened all the letters and junk mail first.

When nothing was left but the ominous thick letter, he debated just throwing it away. His deadbeat brother had a theory: if he didn't open his mail, his bills didn't exist. Maybe if he didn't open the letter and threw it away, he wouldn't have to deal with whatever was inside. He held it in his hand above the trash, wanting, needing, to drop it in, but instead, he picked up the letter opener and slipped it through the seal with the ease of a butcher through a prime cut of beef.

With the letter open, he once again got the feeling that he should just throw the piece away. He rubbed his eyes, sat back in his chair, took a deep calming breath and lifted the flap. He spied the edges of a few Polaroid pictures inside. Seeing this, he sat forward and opened the small side drawer of his desk. Four seconds later he had rubber gloves on. Later that day, he would try to explain to the police why he used the gloves and that he had suspected the package to be sinister. He knew they wouldn't believe in his *meter* so he told them that ever since he had been sent anthrax a decade ago, he had used gloves for anything other than plain letters. Jax was right to use the gloves that day. He set aside a pristinely folded piece of paper and looked at the edge of the three pictures inside. That was when his gut flipped and every damn alarm possible went off in his body. Jax took out his phone and snapped a picture of the envelope, the letter still folded and the pictures still inside. Then, he gingerly removed them.

Jax knew without a doubt that the pictures were not going to contain anything he would want to see. Maybe a dead mob boss, maybe some meeting of a politician and his secret lover, maybe nudes of some crazed fan. Deep down, he knew it was going to be something bad. He set the envelope down, trying to delay seeing whatever was inside, but a moment later, he picked the letter back up and opened it carefully. He slowly and carefully read the typed letter contained inside:

Jax! Want some facts?

I'm a life-long fan of yours, a die-hard reader you might say. Your reporting had always kept me on the edge of my seat. I'd wait day after day for the next edition to see what you'd uncover or what you'd expose to the light. But recently, you seem to have lost your edge. You only report on fluff and not the big-time things that once got you on national talk shows! I still have all your appearances on tape, by the way. Now you report on lazy, inconsequential things. Well, no more! NOW you must cover a story so grand and so great, it will certainly thrust you in the national spotlight again.

A girl has gone missing. Truth be told, she is not really missing: I know exactly where she is, but her family does not. You see, not long ago I took her and killed her, very humanely, I think. Since her death, I have been rather busy, cutting her body up into precise pieces and ever so carefully packing them up in boxes to be delivered by our great postal service to thirty people across the country. These thirty were chosen entirely at random: aren't they lucky? I'm sure you can tell by the photos that this is real and not just some hoax. And if you still think it's a hoax, by the time you read this letter, all of the packages will have arrived on the doorsteps of these unsuspecting civilians.

How do you factor into this? Well, to me, Jax, we have a bond, one that is so strong, I can't explain in a letter, but maybe one day I can explain it to you over coffee, perhaps with Maggie? Our bond has made me choose YOU to be the voice of my actions. You will be the one who covers the story. If all thirty pieces are found within a month, the poor girl's family can bury their daughter, and then, and only then, I will turn myself in. If ALL of the pieces are not found, well, as the nursery rhyme goes: All the King's horses and All the King's men, will force me to start all over again.

You can bet that within the next twenty-four hours, your brethren at the various news circuits around the country will be splashing their individual stories about a mysterious body part turning up. Start the first article, come up with some clever name for me, use what you can of this letter before the police ask you not to and try to examine it for all sorts of ridiculous clues they won't find. If I don't see an article by you within three days, then I'll assume you are not accepting my gracious offer to bring you back as one of the greatest journalists of our time, and I won't be happy about that, because we have a bond and bonds should not be broken.

Good luck!
You'll be hearing from me soon,

Your Biggest Fan.

Jax's head swirled. He read the letter four more times, making sure to memorize it, but then he remembered his phone and took a picture of the text, including some close-ups for printer font analysis. Quickly, he uploaded all the pictures he had to his Cloud in an encrypted folder, then deleted all the pictures on his phone, because the police would check it and he needed copies for himself just in case. There had been hoaxes in the past: crazy letters, threats and all sorts of insane things, like the guy who once sent him a vial of his own semen with a letter asking him to consume it so they could be one together, but all of that was just that, the lunatic fringe. *This* was real, he knew it and all he had to do was look at the pictures to confirm it. His stomach burned with fear as he picked up the envelope, hoping that it was obviously fake or a picture of a doll, but he knew it was not that lucky and that what Maggie said this morning was too good to be true.

The pictures.

Pure horror, madness and gore. Jax had seen dead people

up close and personal: mob hits, people beaten to death, one corpse damaged so badly, nothing was left but liquid and bone fragments, but this, this was a sweet girl, in pieces. There was no way it was faked. Jax did an article once on a scam artist who was using special effects make-up to scare people into paying him money not to sue them. The guy would pretend to get hit by their car, then run over and show a bone sticking out of his arm and blood pouring out. He'd scream about suing and then shake them down for as much money as he could. Jax caught the guy himself after consulting with an effects expert who was working on a movie shooting in town. He knew what was real now and what wasn't. Certain colors and globs of fat that oozed out of the skin when cut were not things an effects artist could do; no, what he saw in those pictures, that was real and he had to shut off his brain and swallow hard over and over again to not throw up. Jax hated it, but he took pictures of them as well and sent them to the encrypted online storage. The second he hit DELETE, he called Maggie.

"Tell New York we won't make the deadline and pack a bag," he said before she had a chance to speak. "I need you to initiate our ghost plan. Hopefully not for long…I can't say anything now." Jax's voice was stern, and he bit his lip as he listened to the silence on the other end of the line. He could hear Maggie thinking.

"You sure?" she finally whispered. "We are so close, Jax."

"Your name was mentioned, so yes, you need to go," he answered. He didn't want to say any more than he had to, didn't want to revisit the images in his head while talking to her. "It's beyond my control, but you know I'll fight my damndest to stay on track."

She acquiesced, and with that, they said *I love you* and hung up. No more questions, no further instructions.

When he wrote articles about milk, it never crossed his mind that they would have to put their emergency plan into use. They had agreed years ago that should he ever be in danger, she would relocate to a safe location that he did not know about in case any nut bags came after him. Back in the day when he took on organized crime, a "go bag" was in each of their cars along with a few licensed weapons in case anyone came after him, but in the last few years, those bags got moved to the closet, then to the basement. He had been so close, so damn close.

"Alright. You want to play?" Jax said out loud, staring at the letter. "I have one last game in me."

He picked up the phone and called the police.

Piece #3
Phoenix, AZ

The doorbell rang during the final showcase showdown on *The Price is Right*. This aggravated George. *No one, no one should interrupt The Price.* That was the one damn upside about his wife dying: she no longer talked over the amounts the contestants bet, making it impossible for him to make his own educated guess. More often than not he would have won the showcase over the idiots on the show.

Today, the doorbell ensured he'd never know the true price of the Hawaiian trip and pontoon boat. More than missing the showcase, he hated getting up in a hurry. At eighty-three, getting up was hard enough; trying to get up in time to not miss the person at the door? Forget about it. Aching and wobbly, he shuffled towards the door, trying to keep an eye on the TV to see what the actual price was, but his eyes were no longer good enough to see the tiny numbers. *Son of bitch better be the Publishers Clearing House with a check to make getting up like this worth it.*

The doorbell rang a second time just as he turned back to the TV and saw a woman jumping up and down. *He missed it. Fuck.* With his attention back to the door, he grasped the knob, swung it open, and found himself face to face with a sweaty mailman. George looked him up and down, disgusted that the man's shirt was untucked and that he was wearing shorts. That would *not* be tolerated in his day. *Goddamn shorts are for kids and only a damn hobo has an untucked shirt.* As he thought about this, he checked his own shirt, making certain it was tucked in properly. It didn't matter if most days he didn't even leave the house: every day at six-thirty, he ironed his slacks and shirt and got dressed after showering and shaving. You would never catch him in pajama pants like his neighbor always wore. *That damn queer even wore them doing yardwork and even goes shopping in them. Goddamn world.* Shaking the angry internal rant from his head, he looked at the mailman again.

"What?" George said, even though it was a dumb question, since the mailman would probably be delivering mail.

"Package for you, sir!"

The chipper voice irritated George. If the man were dressed properly, he wouldn't have cared. "You interrupted my damn show…" Just as he was about to finish his sentence, he noticed a thumping noise. "What is that sound?"

The mailman, who George now saw couldn't have been older than his mid-twenties, smiled and grabbed the large black circle around his neck. "My headphones. Can't get through the day without them, know what I mean?"

George almost slammed the door shut in disgust. Not a damn day in his life had he listened to music at work. "They let you do that?"

The man nodded while shuffling a small package in his hand. "Oh yeah, we can pretty much do whatever we want as long as we get the mail delivered. Speaking of which, package for you. I was going to leave it in the mailbox, but with the heatwave we've been havin', I figured I'd see if anyone was home so it wasn't left out in the heat. Could be perishable. Crazy temps for September, right?" The mailman thrust the package toward George and smiled, seemingly proud of his forethought.

George purposefully stared at it for a solid ten seconds just to make the man uncomfortable, then slowly grabbed the box, took a step back, and shut the door without another word.

Instead of looking at the package, which was suspicious since it was the first delivery he had received in over two years that didn't contain medication, he watched the mailman walk back down the small stone path through the narrow window in the door. The guy put on his headphones and started nodding his head. *Motherfucker*, George thought. *I'm sending a letter to his boss. How the hell could he hear anything coming or if a customer needed help. Someone should teach that kid a lesson. If I was young again, I'd be happy to.*

As the little white truck pulled away, George let out a sigh and walked back to his recliner. The stupid soap opera that ran after *The Price* was already starting, and this made George even madder. At noon, he always switched over to the local news, and now he had missed the opening story, which was always the most important one. Shaking his head, he grabbed the remote and switched the channels until he saw the familiar man in the suit. *That's how a man should dress in public.* As the man spoke about the recent hundred-plus temperatures, George found himself growing annoyed again. *They lived in a desert: of course it's fucking hot.* Then, George remembered the package in his hand.

Staring down at the small white box, he wondered what the hell could be inside. He hadn't ordered anything, his birthday was months away, and his daughter didn't care about him and sure as hell wouldn't send him anything out of the blue. Curious, a bit of excitement seeped into him as he examined the box. *No return address?* He couldn't have won anything: he wasn't one of those suckers who entered contests, unlike his wife who would enter a damn contest to win a piece of chewed gum just to say she won something. Turning the box over in his hand, he realized that he was just taking his time to have, well, something to do. After a solid three minutes of looking at the creases, the clean and crisp black letters of his typed address and name, and the tight clean lines of the clear tape, he got up and headed to the kitchen to get his scissors.

He pulled the gray handled, tiny, rounded edged scissors out of the drawer and felt a bit of anger bubble up in him. The scissors always did that. He hated the damn things. *Fucking safety scissors, I'm eighty-three!* After his wife died, his daughter, *the little bitch*, came over and took out everything sharp, because her mom was always worried about him getting a cut while on the blood thinners. Kim took pretty much anything and everything that could cut him, even his gardening tools. When she started to put child safety bumpers on sharp corners of the furniture, he'd lost his shit and they got in the biggest fight they'd ever had. If he wasn't on the thinners, he would have hit her too, like in the old days. He kicked her out and they have never been the same since. She went from visiting weekly and calling twice a week to calling once a month and visiting on holidays and birthdays only. George told himself he didn't give a shit, but the anger he felt every time he used those fucking scissors told him something different.

He angled the rounded edge under the tape, cursing the entire time, and sliced the dull blade across the seal. When the box was finally open, he threw the scissors in the drawer and slammed it shut, glad to be done with them. Opening the two flaps, the first thing he saw was a small folded note sitting on top of some waxy looking white paper wrapped neatly, the way the butcher used to do. He looked at the note and squinted; he hated getting his glasses, so he just squinted harder as if it would improve his eye sight. It took a few times, but he figured out the words to be a short poem.

> A girl whose status is unknown
> Pieces sent to a chosen few
> Action is yours; her destiny own
> Will this poison tongue entice or disgust you?

George hated poetry more than he hated workers who listened to music and wore shorts. It was a stupid waste of time and for faggots and women who thought they were fucking smart, which they weren't. Instead of reading it a second time or even putting it aside, he took the piece of paper and tore it into ten little pieces and threw it into the trash without a second thought. Before he closed the trash drawer, he sniffed hard through his nose, sucking all the mucus and snot to the back of his throat, and spit on top of the tiny pieces. The poem reminded him of the time his wife told him she wanted to go back to school for writing. It was cute how nervous she was to ask, but he put a stop to it by burning all of her books in the back yard and banning all fancy-shmancy literary crap permanently from the house before using his belt over forty times on her. She never once brought up writing again, nor did she bring anything into the house other than housekeeping and cooking magazines. *That is all women should read, after all.*

Knowing that this package, whatever the hell it was, came with a poem, George considered just throwing it away. He could put it right into the trash, just like he did whenever his wife had gotten letters in the mail. She hadn't been allowed to get the mail: that was his job, and anything he deemed unfit for her, into the trash it went. That old side of him was coming out, the side that didn't give a shit and was never curious to see what the letters were; it was the side that just followed the house rules he created. By those very rules, the package should be garbage, but the what the hell was the use of rules when it was just him? Hell, the past few years he hadn't even followed half of his own rules anymore. He sure as hell wasn't wearing shorts in public, but if once in a while he had one beer over his three limit, or he stayed up past the evening news or forgot to lay out his clothing the evening before, who gave a shit anymore? No one was watching, no one cared. Realizing this, he dug his wrinkled, arthritic fingers into the box and pulled out the carefully wrapped delivery.

The feel of the butcher paper brought back memories of when he was first married. Back then, you had to buy your meat at the butcher; the supermarket didn't have shit for good meats then. The butcher was where you went, two, sometimes four times a week to get fresh cuts and ground beef for dinner. That was back when things were good, before it was all chemicals and processed. Hell, the last time his daughter had him over to dinner, the entire meal came out of boxes and bags. The girl didn't do a damn lick of cooking and her mother, who could cook like a fiend, taught her every damn thing she knew, yet she wasted that knowledge and instead opened packages. A woman was meant to cook, and not having a home-cooked meal on the table, piping hot, at exactly 5:30 was blasphemy, pure and simple. That was the one thing he missed about that damn woman: the food.

George shook his head, partially at his anger at the world again, but mostly for letting his mind wander so damn much. It seemed lately that was all it was doing, taking a damn walk when it was supposed to be marching.

George set the neatly swathed, four-inch long, three-inch wide package down on the counter, pulled out its contents, then flipped it over to get to the start of the paper so he could begin unwrapping it. Again, curiosity, like the old days, had not overtaken him: this was simply a task. There was no wonder as to what was inside. *Why bother wondering, just open it and you'll find out what it is*, he used to say to Kim and his wife over and over again on Christmas morning, until he finally got bored of their rowdiness and walked away, dispensing no punishment on that *one day* only.

Two flips and pulls of the paper and what was inside finally started to show itself. It was a pinkish slab with a slightly purple and graying hue to it. Instantly George knew it was a tongue, just like the ones he used to get from the butcher as a child for his mother to make for dinner. God, he hated eating tongue back then. The one time the wife made it for him, he destroyed half the kitchen and instructed her, with his hand around her throat, to never make it again.

George's realization that it was a tongue was rather nonchalant. It was a tongue, plain and simple, but it took a solid thirty seconds of staring before he realized it was not a cow's tongue, which was thirty or forty times this size. It wasn't any other animal's he had ever seen either, so...*Jesus fucking Christ.*

Seven minutes later, George sat at the kitchen table with a glass of water, the nitroglycerin pill starting to kick in and calm his weak heart. George was never one to get flustered in a situation; hell, he had seen war and gotten a front row seat to so much gore and body parts that the little damn tongue did not freak him out. What did scare the shit out of him was *why* was the tongue in his kitchen, sitting neatly on the butcher paper, ten feet away on the counter.

George had been an asshole his entire life and he knew it, but it was who he was and he was never ashamed of it, though his attitude and fearlessness of anyone and anything including the law got him into trouble more than a few times over the years. Look at him the wrong way, he'd knock you the fuck out; cut him off driving and he'd chase your car down and smash every window out of your car. He could remember forty-seven fist fights; who knows how many he could not. He had slept with countless married women, even the ones who hadn't wanted to sleep with him. At one point, he had more enemies than allies, so much so, that he had been certain he would be murdered at some point, but fuck, if he had been wrong, well, he was alive and kicking longer than most everyone he knew. He might have stopped knocking strangers out twenty years ago because he was getting too old, but that didn't mean he didn't have enemies.

George got out a pen and paper and started to make a list of the people he'd severely harmed, the ones he stole from, the ones whose marriages he'd ruined, the people he'd put in the hospital. The list was getting long and he was becoming certain that he was missing countless others when the house phone rang. He ignored it and let it go to the machine, but as soon as the irritating BEEP sounded, it started to ring again. He shuffled to the phone on the wall and answered it with a bark.

It was his daughter and he was not happy to hear from her.

"What do you want? I'm busy," he spat the words with such hate, even *he* thought it was a bit much.

"Christ, Dad, nice to hear from you too. Did you get anything in the mail today? I got a letter about your mortgage and…" George didn't hear anything after "mail," he simply saw red for the first time in years. It was the sort of red anger and fire behind his eyes that made him go blank. The times when he got this angry, he would completely blank out and often did not understand what he had done until his fists were covered in blood and raw from whoever was the recipient of his wrath.

"You fucking no good ungrateful cunt. You goddamn kids today and your sensitivity and gender equality shit. What is this, some sort of therapy lesson you have for me, teaching me to be softer? What, because I called you names and said the truth, that you were fat and ugly growing up, I have a…what did you call it? A poisoned tongue? Am I supposed to learn something from this?" He didn't pause to listen to her reply. "You are dead to me and out of my fucking will, you fat fucking piece of shit." George slammed the phone down so hard, the receiver cracked into two pieces and landed on the floor.

Without even thinking, he raced over to the tongue, picked it up with his bare hand, marched over to the sink and crammed it down the disposal. With a flick of the switch, the machine jumped into action with a horrible thumping, grinding noise. He turned the faucet on, and the counter vibrated as the old disposal tried its best to break down the gummy tissue. "I'll give you a fucking poison tongue!" George screamed at the sink.

As if in response, the sink screamed back with a loud shrieking noise that indicated its blades had become stuck. Without even thinking, George stuck his hand down the narrow drain, past the decaying plastic barrier, and reached around in the hole. For a time, he had been a plumber and he understood that disposals didn't have giant sharp blades like the horror movies proposed. Instead, they have flat flappers that push the food against the textured outer wall: *that* was what broke down the food. The flappers might sting, but they sure the hell weren't going to grind your hand into hamburger.

Within seconds, George felt for the mutilated tongue with his fingers, grabbed it, and moved it to the center of the disposal.

As he pulled his hand out, he laughed and heard the machine start to chug along again. He was going to have the last laugh, not his smartass daughter. Then, he felt a small trickle on the back of his hand. Thinking it was water from the sink, he wiped it on his shirt. Looking down, he saw it was red. There, on the back of his hand was a two-inch long, thin scratch. George closed his eyes and screamed a guttural yell. God, he hated being old. In his youth, he could have put his hand in that sink a hundred times without even a red mark. The thumping, grinding noise made George think the machine was laughing that it could slice his paper-thin skin on the old cracked plastic.

Anyone else would have washed the blood off and put a bandage on the scratch, but George was on the highest dose of blood thinners there was. The last time he had cut himself shaving, a nick a quarter this size, he ended up in the ER for two hours.

He wrapped the kitchen towel around his hand, and the rage came back in full force. This was *her* fault. He couldn't stop himself: his fist flew out and punched the cabinet in front of his face. Before it even made an impact, the rage disappeared and fear set in. As his knuckles splintered the wood and two dozen cuts and lacerations covered his knuckles and fist, he knew once and for all his rage had finally done him in. Only, instead of meeting the business end of a gun or the tip of a steel toe shoe to the face, it was a cheap cabinet he had refused to replace when his wife wanted new ones thirty years ago, *because there is nothing wrong with them.*

When he pulled back his hand, it looked as if he had just pulled it out of a bucket of blood: the skin up to his wrist was soaked and the blood was pouring from the wound at an unnatural rate. George lifted his hand above his head, like he had learned to do in the military, and shuffled to the phone, leaving a long blood trail behind him, but when he reached it, he saw that the receiver was shattered and broken, *When the fuck did this happen?* His rules and everything leading up to this point in his life crashed down on him like a comical piano from the sky. From the day he'd bought his first house, there had been only one phone in the house, a landline, in the kitchen: that way, he could make sure no one had any privacy or talked to anyone without him knowing or being able to listen, so they couldn't talk about him. He briefly pictured the cell phone with the oversized buttons that his daughter had given to him that he'd thrown away. *Because who needs stupid shit like that, I lived almost eighty years without one.*

This thought process took longer than it should have, and the puddle on the floor grew massive where he stood. The entire side of his body was covered in blood, as it slid gleefully down his sleeve, through his arm pit, down his side, through his nicely ironed slacks, and right onto the floor.

As spots started to dance in front of his eyes, he made his way to the front door. It felt as if he were walking through a marshmallow: his legs stuck to the floor, and he had to push hard to move each limb in order to make it to the door handle. Using his clean hand, he fumbled with the lock but finally got it open. The door swung wide and the heat hit so hard that he felt as though he were walking into a furnace or opening the door to hell, *maybe the anchor was right to talk about a heat wave.* He stumbled outside, tripped on the first step and fell straight to the ground, his face hitting the stone walkway with a wet THUNK. Instantly his skin started to burn, but he couldn't lift his head.

He could hear his name being called by his idiot neighbor. He could smell his skin burning. It wasn't unpleasant, though; in a way, it reminded him of his wife's cooking he missed so much. Everything started to get blurry and George couldn't focus on much, but the one thing he could see was his neighbor's legs in front of him: the man was wearing fucking pajama pants with rubber ducks splattered all over them. As the last of the necessary blood left his body, his vision faded completely. All George could think of were those fucking rubber duck pants and how anyone could wear them outside of the house. They were certainly worse than shorts.

The Reverie

Dennis cringed as the sharp edge of the plastic top on his Dunkin' Donuts coffee scraped against his upper lip. His engine ticked as it cooled; he was certain it was a sign it would shit the bed soon. The Subaru dealership had assured him that the sound was normal, but he was wary.

He stayed in the driver's seat of the car and watched the dry leaves swirl in tiny vortexes around his driveway. He knew he had to rake: hell, he was becoming *that* house on the block: the neighbor who didn't keep his landscaping up, the one who waited for the snow to melt instead of shoveling after each storm. He didn't want the added attention.

Soon it would be time to turn on the heat, a task much less worrisome since he'd switched over his furnace to gas. When he first moved into the modest Cape Cod home nearly ten years ago, he'd had to shell out nearly nine hundred dollars to fill the empty oil tank the previous owners had left empty. Three winters later, he'd used up every drop he'd filled that year, then financed a brand-new gas heating system; now, he could pay for fuel on a monthly basis instead of being hit with a large bill all at once.

Four years ago, when his mother stopped going outside, a few people on the street dropped by to inquire about her health. He hadn't adequately prepared for their interest, and his explanations came out jumbled and fuzzy, prompting a few of the neighbors to stop waving at him when he drove past them on his way home from work. From that point on, he was "that guy," the strange man who lived with his agoraphobic, aging mother. He didn't bother turning off his porch light on Halloween to dissuade trick-or-treaters; no one ventured up the walk to his home anymore. He was lucky the postal carrier still left his packages on his screened-in porch.

Dennis pulled the keys out of the ignition and climbed out of the orange SUV. A pimply teenaged boy in a navy hooded sweatshirt was lumbering uncomfortably along the sidewalk nearby. When he made eye contact with Dennis, he turned away immediately, quickening his pace, but Dennis saw the kid side-eye his car door as the alarm issued a tidy beep. *That's right, you little prick. Keep walking. Nothing for you to swipe here.*

The day after Dennis had returned from his trip around New England, his next-door neighbor had discovered his sedan burglarized. Dennis only knew this because he overheard the man on a cell phone call berating his wife for leaving the doors unlocked. He lived in a nice neighborhood, a "good part of town" by all accounts, and so far, he hadn't experienced any issues with theft or vandalism, but he was pro-active just the same: he always locked his doors, those both of the house and car, and he had programmed timers throughout his home to keep the lights on when he went out at night.

People, Dennis believed, were just too damn trusting these days. Julie Piedmont had been the last, or at least the most recent, in a series of encounters with young, healthy women whose lives he'd watched drain from their eyes just a few hours after leaving the sanctity of their family homes, boyfriends' apartments, or college dormitories. All of them had been in decent physical shape with no impediments, ambulatory or otherwise, that could have prevented them from escaping him, or at the very least, fighting more ferociously for their survival. The third girl, a curvy coed with strawberry blonde hair who'd spent the afternoon window-shopping at Thornes Market, a multi-story emporium in a nearby suburb that peddled hipster clothing, eclectic housewares, and unusual gifts, never surveyed her environment for potential threats during his entire reconnaissance. He followed her for hours and watched as her eyes darted back and forth exclusively between store inventory and her cell phone screen, the two places engaged in a vapid tennis match for her attention.

Finally, he became so overcome with irritation at her carelessness that when she made her way outside to the small municipal lot by ducking out of the back exit, he tapped the girl on the shoulder and confronted her. "Excuse me, but I couldn't help but notice that you were looking down at your phone almost the entire time you walked through the mall," he said, staring into her eyes for the first time. They were pale blue, and for a moment, the Velvet Underground song covered by R.E.M. that his mother used to play when he was small—*Dead Letter Office*, that was the name of the album, he suddenly recalled—echoed nostalgically in his head. He had been very young, perhaps only five or six, and his mother Karen, a hungry prosecutor in New York City, worked nearly incessantly, and any quality time spent with her son was spontaneous and fleeting.

For most of his childhood, Dennis had been mothered by teenaged babysitters, by daycare attendants, and (when Karen was physically home but researching and writing briefs and organizing cases,) by the television in the den, the room farthest away from the enclosed pantry Karen used as an office. However, on a rare occasion, his mother would spend the morning in her worn pajamas and stocking feet, playing the stereo loud enough so that it could be heard in every room of the apartment. During these ephemeral moments, Karen would carry her son in her arms, pretend they were skating at Rockefeller Center, and sing along to Michael Stipe at the top of her lungs, unconcerned with the subsequent banging on the wall and ceiling from nearby neighbors. Dennis remembered nestling his face in the crook of her neck, seeing her thin, gold necklace scintillate when it caught the light, and smelling the remnants of her drugstore perfume as he listened to the *whoosh-whoosh-whoosh* her thick wool socks made along the dark hardwood floorboards.

His reverie was broken, however, when the girl shook her shoulders slightly and stepped around Dennis, saying nothing, essentially ignoring him. She walked directly to her car in the lot without accelerating her pace, her head tilted downward and her eyes resuming their adhesion to the screen.

It was her sole car key that broke off in the door lock when Dennis wrestled her quietly to the ground. He searched her pale blue eyes again as he cupped his gloved hand over her nose and mouth, silencing first her screams of panic and then her life completely. The fog of warm breath escaping from the slits between his fingers thinned and then dissolved entirely. A half hour later, as he peeled the winter gloves from his hands and dropped them in a nearby trashcan in front of a Walmart three towns away, he cursed himself for the impromptu assault; he had promised himself that each target would be used as rehearsal for the *big event*; every girl was a learning experience, an opportunity to hone his craft to perfection because the game *itself* would be perfection. Her body was found two days later, shoved beneath her car in the lot where she'd parked it, her dead cell phone placed gingerly in the breast pocket of her coat.

"The goddamn radio keeps going to static every few minutes. Change the channel! Do you know what it's like to have to listen to that all day?" His mother's voice drifted up from the basement like a wildfire being goaded by a gust of wind.

Dennis closed the front door carefully and turned the lock. "I'll get to it in a minute," he called back. "I just walked in the door."

"No shit you just got home," the voice responded. "I'm old, I'm not deaf."

Dennis pulled his windbreaker over his head and draped it over the back of the living room couch. His hair sizzled a bit with static electricity, and he absent-mindedly smoothed it down with the back of his hand. The antique Victrola radio on the mantle vacillated between bars of a Glenn Miller orchestra tune and a snowy rustling of static. He turned the dial until finding the signal from an alternative rock station; an early Nirvana song played, Kurt Cobain's vocals echoing like they were emerging from a closet lined with tin. Not bothering to hang up his jacket on the coat rack, Dennis proceeded into the kitchen to start dinner.

Out of sheer habit, he opened the cabinet above the stove to retrieve a can of cat food, and then he stopped himself. His cat, John Boy, a black and white short-hair who Dennis had adopted when he showed up in his backyard the previous winter, gaunt and shivering, had not been seen since Dennis had returned from his trip. The feline sported a few unusual markings in his fur, including a brown spot to the right of his nose, a blemish Dennis mistook as caked dirt until he tried unsuccessfully to rub it away. It was this marking that prompted him to name the cat John Boy Walton, a reference to actor Richard Thomas, whom Dennis had recently seen on a particularly riveting rerun of *Law & Order: Special Victims Unit*.

He'd left plenty of food in the automatic feeder, and even if the sensor on John Boy's collar that unlatched the small cat door he'd constructed to provide unfettered access to the outdoors to his pet had malfunctioned, he had to believe that the cat would have turned up on the patio at some point, as needy and persistent as he'd been when Dennis first discovered him.

Dennis shut the door and leaned against the stove. Although he didn't crave human companionship as much as other people did, and if he was honest with himself, he saw his mother's presence as more of a burden than a blessing, he had to admit, he missed John Boy. Although he pestered his owner for attention from time to time, John Boy was relatively independent and asked little of Dennis; he was the perfect companion.

Dennis had tried dating. He wasn't a bad looking man: he was of average height and build with good teeth and, at 34, a decent amount of hair on his head. People often had told him that his best physical feature was his eyes. They were large and hazel, *soulful*—that's what one woman had said to him. He had soulful eyes. But eyes only took you so far, he soon discovered. Women—hell, people in general—wanted so much more from him. Too much, he realized.

The previous winter, he'd taken an intern named Suzanne to dinner after work. She'd asked him on the date, and her brazen invitation taking him off guard, he'd been powerless to decline. They exchanged polite conversation over the meal, and when it came time to drop her off at her apartment, he'd pulled over and placed the car in PARK but left the engine running. The night was over, he thought. She would open the door and leave.

She didn't. Instead, she turned her upper body to face him and leaned her face toward his. "It's still so early," she said. "Why don't you come up and hang out for a while?" A faint whiff of amaretto drifted around the car, an afterthought from her last drink with dessert.

He glanced at the digital clock on the dashboard. It was 9:30. "Yeah, okay," he answered. "Sure." He turned off the engine and climbed out of the car, then followed Suzanne as she unlocked the front door of her building and began to walk up three floors to her apartment.

Before they had reached the final landing, she spun around, nearly knocking Dennis backward down the stairs, and grasped his face in her hands. "I just can't wait any longer," she said, and brought her mouth to his, kissing him aggressively. He kissed her back, and the two of them stumbled awkwardly up the rest of the steps and to her door, pawing and necking the entire way. When they were at last inside, Dennis unbuttoned Suzanne's dress and then his own pants, and without waiting to move into the bedroom, began rubbing himself against her panties and exposed skin. Her thighs and stomach were soft and smooth, like warm satin cloth.

"Hold on," she whispered, and unwrapped her arms from Dennis's body in order to ransack the purse she'd thrown onto a nearby accent table. Her hands reemerged with a condom, and once she had opened the package, Dennis snatched it from her grasp, rolled it quickly onto his erect penis, and pushed her against the wall. She reached down and pushed her underwear aside, and he entered her, thrusting only four or five times before achieving orgasm and withdrawing. He carefully dislodged the latex sheath from his body and without a second thought, wrapped it in a discarded tissue in the pocket of the jacket he was still wearing.

It wasn't until he had pulled his pants back to his waist and was re-tucking his shirt that he looked at Suzanne's face. She hadn't moved to replace her clothing and was staring at him. He didn't understand why she was looking at him. "Thanks," he said quickly. "See you at work tomorrow."

"Yeah," she said in a small voice. "Uh, you don't want to stay? I have a king-sized bed. We could…" she began.

"No, that's okay," he interrupted. And with that, he fished his keys from his pocket and left.

The next day, Suzanne stopped by the lab to drop off some samples. Dennis was logging test results into the computer.

"Did I do something wrong?" she said immediately.

He paused before looking up. This was always the case with the women he met. He didn't go out with them for the sole intention of having sex, but they were adults, after all. They weren't looking for canasta partners. To him, sex was a biological need, like eating. When he was hungry, he ate; when he was full, he put away the food. The same was true for screwing. When he was aroused, he had sex. After he came, the activity was over. There was nothing more to it. He never understood the movie scenes where sex partners lounged in bed together naked long after the act was over, stroking one another's skin and having long, intimate discussions where they revealed their inner-most secrets.

"No," he answered, not bothering to turn away from his computer. "I had a great time. Let me know if you want to do it again." He continued to type, and after a minute of silence, Suzanne spun around and walked away without a word. From that day on, another intern delivered the samples.

The song on the radio changed to one by the band Radiohead, their biggest hit. "Peter Peter Pumpkin Eater," his mother's voice called incongruously over the music from below. "He put his mother in a pumpkin shell and there he kept her very well."

He ignored this outburst. She was always complaining about having to live with Dennis, but it hadn't been her son's decision to make this living arrangement, at least not in the beginning. Karen had lost everything: her job, her posh condo in Manhattan, and most of her friends and acquaintances. For the first few years, she had lived off of her savings, refusing to accept employment outside of her field to make ends meet.

When she called Dennis, a bimonthly occurrence that Karen utilized to purge her frustrations all over her son like an emotional bulimic, it was always to complain that she was running out of money. "Why don't you register with a temp agency?" he suggested. "There are a million in the city."

"You want me to prostitute myself?" she yelled into the receiver. "I went to goddamn law school. Less than a decade ago, I was one of the most powerful people in the borough, and now you want me to fuck people for rent money?"

"I want you to get a job typing or filing or answering a phone, Mom," he answered, trying to keep his voice even. "Jesus, enough with the hyperbole. It's a perfectly honest living."

"If you suggested I walk on the moon, I'd ask you if I looked like a fucking astronaut," she said. "You're 28 years old, for Christ's sake. Grow the fuck up," she added, her voice becoming shrill like a siren at the end. Three months later, he was moving her belongings into the house in Western Massachusetts he had purchased just a year earlier.

He continued to lean his back against the stove, listening to the music echo from the next room. He rubbed his fingertips along his upper mouth, tracing the roughness of the beginnings of chapped lips.

Over the span of his lifetime, Dennis had surrendered more things to the woman who'd given birth to him than he had gleaned from her mothering. However, she had given to him one thing of value: a genetic mutation of adermatoglyphia. Instead of his fingertips having ridges, Dennis' were perfectly smooth; while the remainder of his finger skin was wrinkled and worn, the tips of his fingers were smooth as polished porcelain. According to Karen, his father, a man Dennis knew in name only, had suffered the same mutation, and scientists had traced only four familial lines around the world who carried the disease.

This slight altering of chromosome four was a gift Dennis had tried to keep hidden most of his life. As he grew up, the spotlight had been hot enough, as he was the only child of media darling Karen Sweeney. It wasn't until Dennis applied for his job at the state crime lab that the oddity posed great difficulty: he had to be fingerprinted as a prerequisite for the position, and although he was hired eventually, he had to admit, the obstacle his printless fingers posed nearly guaranteed he'd never seek employment elsewhere—it was too much scrutiny for his comfort.

Dennis glanced out of the kitchen window and onto the back patio, hoping to see John Boy. The cat was nowhere in sight. It was just as well. Every relationship had a purpose, and it appeared that his and John Boy's had run its course. His relationship with Julie Piedmont had also been brief but it had a purpose, and that purpose would come to fruition any day now.

Dinner could wait. He sat down at his laptop on the kitchen table and opened an incognito internet window for the Milwaukee *Sentinel*.

Piece #18
Philadelphia, PA

It was just like that postal carrier to leave her boxes strewn carelessly across the stoop, not even bothering to make the effort to open the screen door and shove the damn things onto the three-season porch and out of the rain.

Kristin Daniels readjusted her purse strap on her shoulder, pushing the hard leather stitching into the skin just beyond the edge of her collarbone, and lowered herself into a half-squat, doing her best not to expose her underwear to the gawking neighbor next door who always seemed to be watering his lawn—even as rain poured from the sky—when she was outside. She grabbed the two boxes and the large, white plastic mailing envelope off of the cement steps and piled them into an awkward heap on her left arm. She reached into the mailbox that was nailed to the white vinyl siding and pulled out the handful of bills and junk from within and with her one free digit, pushed the button on the black door handle to let herself inside. She nodded a half-greeting to her omnipresent spectator, who was drowning a pot of fuchsia geraniums as he stared at her, maneuvered the screen door open with her bare knee, and slipped out of his view. She dumped the pile of deliveries onto the wicker loveseat and fiddled with the contents of her purse to find her house keys. Kristin had made it a habit to separate her car key from the rest of her keys—the rest of her belongings, really—ever since she began her almost daily visits to Brad's home during their lunch breaks and occasional early release. She never knew if she'd have to escape quickly, and it was better to travel light.

Once she was inside her quiet living room, the early dinnertime sunlight illuminating the Roman shades she kept perpetually closed, Kristin rustled through the pile of mail. Three of the small envelopes were addressed to former roommates; the remaining pieces with her name on them consisted of a promotional mailer for the local supermarket, a postcard pleading with her to consider a candidate for reelection to the city council in the fall, her American Express bill, a Chanel skirt she had won after a bidding war on eBay, and her small Subscribe and Save monthly delivery from Amazon. The third package, a nondescript, postal service flat-rate carton no bigger than a shirt box, listed no return address, but her name and mailing information had been typed neatly in capital letters and taped onto the front. She flipped the box over to yank the pull-tab and open it when her cell phone issued a muffled ring from the bottom of her purse.

She placed the box carefully on the coffee table, looked at the caller screen, and hit SILENT. It was her sister Addie, probably calling her on speaker, the phone propped up next to the sink as she scrubbed her husband and children's dinner plates, yelling above the din of tiny voices, obnoxious toys, and a too-loud television her brother-in-law sat comatose in front of every evening. Addie called her twice a week, sometimes just to remind Kristin that she was getting older and that the time to marry and reproduce was quickly running out, or at least, it always seemed like that was her intent. Kristin didn't need reminding. She was thirty-eight, and all of her friends had gotten, or were soon getting or *re-getting*, married. She had long since stopped buying new cocktail dresses to wear to their events; if she wasn't one of the bridesmaids—an embarrassment at her age on its own, she was seated at the back table of pathetic nomads and out of the range of photographers. The Island of Misfit Toys, as Kristin liked to refer to it. *So, did you meet anyone interesting?* Addie would ask hopefully the evening following her latest nuptial attendance. *Just a factory worker who dreams of becoming a dentist*, was Kristin's pat response. After the fourth or fifth go-round of this, Addie stopped asking.

She didn't live alone, though; not really. To supplement her income, she shared the house with other singles: mostly women, a few men here and there, and their rent paid her mortgage while she padded her nest egg with the salary she made as a bookkeeper at Fox Chase Cancer Center, a position she had landed and maintained since graduating from Temple. She didn't mind living alone, per se: she could take care of herself, having obtained her license to carry at the age of twenty-five. She had a Smith & Wesson M & P 22-caliber compact loaded and ready in the top drawer of her nightstand, and although keeping it unsecured was definitely against the law, she would rather be prepared.

Her most recent roommates, strangers when they moved in just the previous year, had fallen in love with each other and eloped in early April, buying a condo in Puerto Vallarta and securing jobs as nannies and private tutors to rich expatriates. Kristin had been grateful for the reprieve from attending a wedding, but now she was faced with finding their replacements. With so many roommates shuffling in and out of her home in the past decade and a half, she ought to forgo the annual lock changes and install a revolving door instead.

She picked up the package. It couldn't be junk mail: junk mail mandated its sender to put forth the smallest amount of investment for the slightest possibility of a hook; this was a package: the postage alone must have cost a few bucks. Perhaps a special delivery from Brad? She had been hinting that the novelty was wearing off: there was only a handful of months when the newness of an illicit affair held the participants' attention; after that, they might as well be dating like traditional people. *Netflix and chill*: isn't that what the kids were calling it these days? I mean, come on: Brad had made it very clear from the get-go that he would never leave his wife— the public shame would simply be too much. He couldn't bear to be classified as divorced, never mind an adulterer, a *philanderer*, for Christ's sakes. People talked. They gossiped. Word got around. And if nothing else, Ashley men were not such common trash. I mean, Kristin knew the score when she signed up for the game, didn't she?

Bradford Ashley was a research supervisor at Fox Chase, a former Rhodes Scholar with a bowl of alphabet soup after his name. They had met innocently one afternoon when Kristin had forgotten her lunch at home, and too lazy to drive to the local Cheesecake Factory or Famous Dave's to pick up a to-go order, she braved the staff cafeteria. Two weeks later, she was shirtless with her skirt pushed up to her waist, his big arms hoisting her ass as he fucked her against the wall behind the closed door to his office. She hadn't gone into the relationship with even one eye closed. Sure, there had been a part of her, maybe a small part, that wished deep down, Brad would find her so addictive, he'd rather die than be without her. As she lay in her bed at night, the sounds of her newly amorous roommates slamming the headboard against the shared wall, she fantasized about his wife discovering his transgressions, withdrawing every cent of their bank accounts, and fleeing with the children to some faraway country without extradition agreements, but even that stray hope was dashed when, over a greasy dinner at an Applebee's one afternoon when Brad had come immediately and they still had an hour to kill, he admitted to her spontaneously, "You know, Jennie told me once that she'd forgive me if I ever cheated."

Kristin stared at him, speechless, her fork still holding a wad of sad-looking Caesar salad in mid-air. He took a big bite of his sandwich and continued, his mouth oozing grease and mayonnaise remnants as he spoke. "Well, specifically, she said she'd forgive me the first time. After that, it would be *hit the road, Jack!*" He smiled as he chewed, staring off into space for a moment. "And I haven't been caught yet, so I still have that Get Out of Jail Free card in my pocket."

Kristin shoved the Romaine lettuce into her mouth and forced herself to chew, feeling the grains of garlic scrape against her tongue. After she swallowed, she took a deep breath and forced a believable grin across her face. "That's super, Brad. Guess we shouldn't waste it then, huh?" She winked, hating herself. She hated herself even more as she bent down to give Brad the requested blow job in the front seat of his car before he delivered her back to her vehicle. *That's a twenty-two dollar fellatio*, she thought to herself, estimating the cost of her lunch and martini in her head. *I'm a goddamn bargain. Target better watch its back.*

Kristin picked up the mysterious package again and shook it. There was something inside, something not of significant weight, but something nonetheless. Whatever it was, it was wrapped securely with tissue paper or those annoying bubble sheets her brother used to pop incessantly anytime they appeared in their childhood home. The object inside shifted slightly in response to her movement, but it was securely tethered in its coffin.

She stroked the pull-tab with her index finger. Brad did say that he had a big surprise planned for her. Was this a gift? He had presented her with a small assortment of things over the past year they'd been together (if *together* were even the appropriate word; *fuckbuddies* was the more fitting moniker, she thought): a dozen roses on her birthday, emerald stud earrings at Christmas, an obnoxiously large stuffed whale—her favorite mammal—on Valentine's Day, but none of them were ever true surprises, and none of them, except the whale tangentially, were personal to the two of them. Just that afternoon, as her body sank deeper and deeper into his marital bed's down-filled mattress topper, her bare skin caressed by brown and green Laura Ashley sheets worn and unwashed into milky softness, her eyes darted around to the array of framed photographs plastered about the walls and stacked neatly like dominoes on the nearby nightstand. As she lay there, Brad occasionally biting her shoulder and burying his face in her dark brown hair as he pounded away on top of her, his family's eyes stared blankly at her from their tableaus. Brad and Jennie wearing matching Eagles jerseys, waving foam fingers at the sky. Brad and Jennie in wedding garb, locking hands in the air to form an upside-down V for Victory with their arms. Brad and Jennie gathered around a mall Santa Claus, their two small children, one boy and one girl, each balanced precariously on a red velvet knee. One long ago afternoon after work, Kristin and Brad met downtown. They downed a few too many drinks in a bar across JFK Plaza before stumbling over to the iconic LOVE statue. Spontaneously, Brad scooped her into his arms, his barrel chest and baseball mitt hands swallowing her tall, thin frame, and kissed her—openly, in broad daylight, in public— and Kristin had wanted so badly to take a selfie of the two of them embracing. It would have been a single snapshot just for her, never to be printed and displayed, but she knew Brad never would have allowed it. Get Out of Jail cards were a rarity. He wouldn't have wasted one on such a frivolous moment of weakness.

She grasped the pull-tab between her thumb and forefinger and pulled it along the length of the box, exposing its red string underbelly. Inside the cardboard frame was a swaddle of manila paper; Kristin pulled out the rectangular mass and turned it over, looking for an edge to begin unwrapping. The consistency was familiar. It felt slightly waxy, like the paper had been covered with a thin protective gloss to waterproof it. She stroked her finger gently along the surface and finally, it hit her.

It was butcher paper. He had wrapped her present in butcher paper?

Had he sent her meat?

She located an edge of the paper and began to unroll the contents. The gift, whatever it was, must have been cold at some point, as the more layers she unfurled, the cooler the paper felt. Finally, her living room rug awash with a sea of off-white crumpled packing material, she held a narrow, white box about six inches long in her hand. It looked too short to hold a bracelet and too thin to house a necklace or cameo pin. She sniffed the box. A slightly sweet odor emanated from inside. Not flowers, not fruit... sweet and somewhat metallic, like the brown sugar-glazed ham her mom used to serve at Easter every year.

They always fucked on his side of the bed, the side closest to the bathroom. Kristin used to think it was because Brad wanted to smell her later that night when his face lay on the pillow; she knew now, it was to keep his wife from discovering any strange body fluids on her menopausal sweat-soaked sheets. Kristin's only knowledge of Jennie was from their bedroom photos and the occasional anecdote Brad recounted. She was a loan officer for a local bank branch and worked ten to six, weekdays. Every now and then, she'd call Brad at work and ask him to meet her for lunch downtown, throwing a wrench in Kristin's plans to see him. His wife used to be a runner, he told her, but after they married, she had stopped. She was doughier than when they had first met, but weren't all couples? he argued, more to himself than to Kristin. After having the second of their two children, she had lost interest in sex completely, at least with Brad, and he had to beg her for an obligatory shag every month or so to which she complied, often with a roll of her eyes or a pat on his shoulder when he was done. That was how Brad portrayed her. Kristin couldn't imagine putting up with such humiliation.

The one thing Brad missed the most in his marriage, he told Kristin, was his wife's perfume. It seemed like an odd thing to choose, especially with Brad's insatiable sex drive and general athletic prowess— he played racquetball with the other executives twice a week without exception—but it was true, he insisted. Jennie had stopped wearing any fragrance after their first child had been diagnosed with a wicked case of asthma. The kid was twelve now and had long since grown out of his use of a nebulizer or even an emergency inhaler, but his wife still refused to wear anything with a scent. Kristin asked him for the name of the perfume, intending to wear it surreptitiously to please him, but he refused to tell her. "If I smelled it on you…" His voice trailed off for a moment as he thought how best to complete his sentence. He never did, he simply shook his head. Kristin never inquired further.

Therefore, the last guess to cross her mind before she opened the small white box was of a vial of perfume. An expensive vial, an aroma found only in Europe or Saks or the duty-free shops at the airport. She had psyched her mind up for seeing a carefully padded glass cylinder of some exotic scent, so when her eyes fell upon the detached finger lying in the center of the white cotton batting, her rationale skipped like a needle over a deep scratch on a 45 record.

This wasn't perfume. No, it wasn't perfume at all.

Most women would have dropped the box out of fright. Some would have screamed, maybe even run from the house dramatically, pushing the button on that fight or flight instinct on reflex. Kristin held tight to the box and simply stared at its contents for a long minute.

And then, the only question that popped into her head was, which finger was it?

Still holding the box face up in her left palm, she brought her right hand alongside the finger and eyed the comparison between it and her own digits. It was most definitely a woman's hand, long and lithe; the skin, where it hadn't become slightly necrotic, was pale. The fingernail was not painted, but it was slightly longer than the fingertip, a sliver of white underbelly peeking through at the top. *It could be the pointy finger*, Kristin thought, *or maybe the ring finger. Too short to be the middle finger, and too wide to be the pinky*. More importantly, whose finger was it? And who had sent it? And why?

She placed the box carefully on the coffee table and rummaged through the discarded packing paper. She must have missed a note, some sort of explanation. A card? What would one write on a notecard accompanying a discarded body part? She thought back to the card attached to her roses from

Brad. "Roses are red, but my outlook is blue, when I don't see your brown eyes. Happy Birthday to you!" it had read. Terrible. He would have been better off stealing something cheesy from the inside of a Hallmark, but Brad fancied himself a poet, so Kristin had pretended to like it.

After carefully searching the butcher paper remnants and finding nothing, Kristin picked up the box once again. When she turned it slightly sideways, she saw the corner of the note sticking out from under the cotton; she carefully pressed her own fingertip against it and slid upwards, pulling the tiny sheet into view. It was folded in half, and when she opened it, she saw the same meticulously typed lettering that appeared on the delivery box.

```
        A girl whose status is unknown
           Pieces sent to a chosen few
        Action is yours; her destiny own
  As this ring finger points directly to you
```

Kristin couldn't help but giggle. The whole thing was absurd. Sending a body part in the mail? It couldn't be real. She poked the digit resting silently on its pillowy bed. It felt like a real finger, just harder and colder. The action brought back the memory of accidentally pushing up against her grandmother's folded hands when she had adjusted the woman's corsage as the old woman lay motionless in the funeral casket. At the time, she had thought to herself that the body felt like a mannequin's body, only slightly squishier, more like the "real dolls" they sold in sex shops.

That was it. Brad had cut this off of a sex doll, a pretty high-end one from the realistic quality. She had complained to him that the excitement, the mystery, seemed to have leaked out of their relationship, and here he was, rekindling it. It was a creepy approach, to say the least, but it was original: she had to give him that.

Kristin reread the note trying to decipher its riddle. *A girl whose status is unknown. That could be me*, she thought. A reference to her being single: no family, no husband. *Pieces sent to a chosen few.* He'd chosen her. *Brad's chosen me... but for what?*

She scratched her head. She had always heard of people scratching their heads when they were deep in thought, and now, here she was, doing it for real. *Action is mine*, she thought, *the ring finger points to me?* A ring could mean only one thing: Brad wanted to marry her! Kristin's mind raced. He had realized the error of his ways, had finally decided that it was she, not Jennie, whom he loved. *Her destiny own.* She was going to take Jennie's place. He wanted her to take Jennie's place. Finally, she would sink into that mattress topper and be able to relax. At last, her eyes would dance over photos of Brad and *her* pasted everywhere within their sprawling, six-bedroom home in Gladwyne. Brad and Kristin at the beach, holding an inflated plastic ball between them. Brad and Kristin on the slopes of Colorado, wearing matching pom-pom hats. Brad and Kristin. Brad and Kristin.

Brad was signaling that the jet was ready for take-off; Kristin just needed to push Jennie off of the runway. She thought for a moment more, then replaced the cover on the white box and placed it gently on the end table. She refolded the note and shoved it in her purse. She would reread it if she lost her nerve.

Kristin retrieved the gun from her bedside table, placed it next to the note in her purse, grabbed her car keys, and closed her front door. As she walked down the cement steps to her car on her way to Gladwyne, the finger poem ran on a loop in her mind.

Action is mine, action is mine, she repeated in her head.

She winked at her watering neighbor and he turned and looked away.

The Detective

When Jax showed Declan the pictures, the young editor's face lit up like he had won the lottery. There wasn't even a second of hesitation before the little man started to rant and ramble about doing research and starting an article before calling the police. When Jax told him he already had contacted the authorities, the man frowned comically, then waved in the air as if getting rid of a smell. Instead of acquiescing, Declan simply changed gears and offered new ideas on how the paper could benefit from Jax's disturbing letter.

The journalist watched the editor's excitement, but his eyes drifted down to the pictures and onto Julie Piedmont's face of sheer terror on the Polaroid. Over Declan's rambling, Jax simply said, "I quit."

The next two hours were a whirlwind of naggings from his editor to not leave, of interviews from the police who didn't take the situation that seriously—likely because they knew the Feds would take over soon since the postmark was out of state—and of packing. During all of this, Jax kept cool, ignored everyone he could, and answered requisite questions from both the police and Human Resources, who wanted to know about his departure.

With six file boxes in his trunk and back seat, he sat in the driver's seat with both hands on the wheel and thought. Jax's mind was clear, as empty as it could be, so much so that he stared at his wedding ring; the thin gold band that was bought at a pawn shop needed a polish and he made a mental note to make use of that little jar of solution Maggie kept under the kitchen sink. From there, his thoughts wandered to how dry his hands were; he had that green tube of cream Maggie gave him, but he never used it; he really should get in the habit before his skin started to crack. His thoughts finally wandered to the color of the leather steering wheel, the gray that was fading to a charcoal color and starting to crack. It was a nice color, he could use that on a piece…THUD, THUMP!

The slamming on the window made him jump and his heart do a back flip. The scare was so sudden and intense that his hand actually shot up to his chest and his eyes squinted shut for a solid five seconds, assessing if he was going to have a heart attack. Only then did he bother to look to see if someone were attacking him. Once the tingling around his heart had settled and he could breathe normally again, he turned and looked at the man in the suit leaning over his passenger window, glaring at him with a smile of confusion and concern.

"Are you alright, sir?" the man said in a friendly tone.

"You're Jackson Matthews, right? Detective Connor. I just showed up, wanted to talk to you real' quick if you didn't mind. Glad I caught you."

Jax heard the long rambling greeting in a muffled echo through the glass. Taking a deep breath, he reached for the handle but realized the man was so close he'd smash his face if he opened the door. He hesitated, then had to make a gesture to show the detective he had to move, which he did with a brief laugh.

As Jax stood up, his legs felt a bit like mush, but the air was soft on his face, refreshing him a bit and balancing out the rush of adrenaline that overtook him. Jax forced a smile and offered a hand to the baby-faced man, who couldn't have been more than twenty-five. With his mind clearer, Jax looked the man up and down; the clean-cut and perfectly pressed plain suit reminded him more of a Mormon on a mission than a detective. "Detective, if you don't mind, can I see some ID please?"

The young man's face went slack and a bit of what Jax determined was rage flashed over the boy's eyes, but it was quickly replaced with a smile and nod. A second later, Jax was looking at the folded leather holder with the man's badge and ID; it checked out, as far as Jax could tell. "It doesn't matter that I was top of my class or that I was in the military for six years or solved sixty cases in my first two years on the job; my youthfulness always leads to doubt—I get it."

Jax wasn't in the mood to apologize, so he simply asked how he could help.

"I'm going to take on this case. I know you were already interviewed, but I wanted to ask some questions myself first," said Connor.

Jax sighed before responding. "Look, I just sat through two

hours of interviews. I got a letter and I opened it: that is the extent of my involvement or knowledge. No, I have no clue who this fan could be; I have readers all over the world and the postmark is from half a dozen states away." Something about the way Connor smiled during Jax's rant irritated him and made him a bit nervous. "Look, I have done this job long enough to know not to mess with the crazy ones and when not to get involved. I was retiring at the end of the year. I'm not taking chances with this crazy ass. I'm heading out of town and starting a new life. I have nothing to hide and will be available via phone for any further questions. Now, I have to get to my wife. We've had threats in the past, so I made her take off as well and I'm sure she is panicking as much as I am, so I'd like to get to her and comfort her if you don't mind," Jax said as nicely as he could.

Connor took a step back and nodded. Jax started to get back in his car when the boy spoke. "You know he won't stop. He chose you and he'll ask for you and no one else, no matter where you go."

With one hand on the door edge and half a leg still in the car, Jax stopped and turned back to the man. "I know: that is why I'm leaving. If I don't work here anymore and I leave, the letters won't go to me and he won't find me, so I won't be involved and won't be thrust into the spotlight. I just want to go home and start my new life, Detective." Jax wanted to get in and shut the door just then, but the years of being an investigative journalist wouldn't let him. "Connor, why do you think he won't just pick another journalist? You don't even know if the murder was real yet or some sick joke. And if it is real, the FBI will take this away from you before dinner anyway. So why do you care so much?"

The young man licked his teeth for a second as he thought of his response. "Sorry to have bothered you, Mr. Matthews. I have your number if I need anything. Be safe and good luck in your retirement." He began to back away from the car, a polite grin plastered across his face.

Jax felt a chill run down his spine as he climbed back into the car. Just as he started to shut the door, Connor yelled. "Oh! One more thing!" He jogged back so that he was within arm's reach of the journalist's car again. "I feel awkward saying this, but I'm a big fan of your work. While not the best of situations, it's an honor to meet you." The man smiled again and offered a half-wave before turning and walking away.

Jax shut the door without a word and drove away, his body feeling like melting putty.

The next morning, Jax used a burner cell to call Maggie's burner to check in with her. She was fine but stressed out, just like he was. It was an overboard precaution, but after finding out that Connor was not a detective, a fact revealed after a simple call to the police department, Jax had gone into full panic mode. The very same night, he had grabbed a few articles of clothing and his own "go bag" and gotten a hotel room under a fake name using the fake credit card that he used to use for undercover investigations (nothing too illegal—he made sure the bills on it were paid through a third party), and tossed and turned through a fitful night of sleep. After calling Maggie, he paced the dingy orange carpet of the motel room that had not been updated in decades. He had learned early on that if you stayed in nice hotels, you got noticed; in seedy ones, everyone kept their eyes down.

Jax knew he had to go back to the police to give the full description of the fake detective. Even if his gut told him he was not the killer, there was still something wrong with a man posing as an officer of the law, and it was a felony after all. The most concerning issue, however, was how did the guy know so much detail about the case already? Jax stopped his nervous pacing, his sock-covered toes just touching the edge of what looked like an ancient blood stain on the carpet. When he looked down at it, pictures of Julie Piedmont's dissected body flashed in his head. He squeezed his eyes shut, clenched his fists, and felt his body start to tense up; every fiber of his being was fighting against what was creeping up in the back of his mind and he started to argue with himself. *Just leave, you already quit, go to the cops, report the guy and head out of town and you're done.* Then the other side would jump in: *That girl is dead, there could be more victims, you can find this guy, he already chose you and no one can investigate and bring someone down like you can, you can save lives, don't let more innocent people die.* Standing frozen in that spot, he realized how crazy he looked if anyone saw him, so he loosened up his tension, took a breath, and opened his eyes.

He sat back down on the bed, grabbed his shoes, and put each one on slowly, tying each lace as if he were giving a demonstration to a child. Just as he finished, the burner phone rang, and with a sigh of relief, he clicked the answer button and said, "Hey Mags: I miss you." There was no immediate response on the phone, which made Jax's stomach drop like a disconnected elevator. "Honey?" he asked cautiously. He could hear her sniff on the other end.

"Jax, this is not the end of our dream, it's just a bump on the road, but we'll still get there. I know you, I know you are arguing with yourself…" Maggie sounded tired. "Look," she said with more insistence, "if you ignore this, it will bug you forever, I know that, you know that. Take care of it, cover the story, find this asshole, and then get your ass back to me."

Jax smiled and rubbed his face. "What prompted this, Maggie? We talked an hour ago and you were fine with me heading out to you this afternoon."

Jax heard another big sigh before she responded. "Because this morning I was hoping it was just a hoax, but I just saw on the news that a body part was delivered to a soccer mom in Warwick, Rhode Island. Her poor kid opened the box, thought it was something from Amazon. The police are not saying what the part was, just that a 'piece of human remains' was delivered. It was a quick story on the news, but it can't be a coincidence."

It was Jax's turn to sigh heavily. "Honey, this could take months, years—hell, most serial killers are never caught." Jax laid back on the bed.

"Jax, this one is reaching out directly to you: it's different," said Maggie. "Chase it down. If you get nowhere after a few weeks or it goes cold, let it go and move on. You weren't going to leave the paper for another year anyway." They were both silent for a moment. "It's alright," she said finally, as if answering his anxious thoughts. "We'll get through this."

After talking for another five minutes about the logistics of keeping her safe and how long she had to hide to be safe (reassess after one week was the agreement), they said their goodbyes and Jax sat back up. A wave of excitement and fear raced over his skin like a team of lady bugs trying to trace the outlines of his body in a hurry. It had been a long time since he had the rush of taking on a serious story. It was a bit exciting yet terrifying as he had shut off all of that toughness in his life to focus on Maggie and his art, but he was sure he could get it back and face whoever and whatever he needed to in order to track down this killer. It wouldn't be his first case, but it would be his last. To punctuate this thought, several cheesy lines from movies popped into his head. *Just when he thought he was out, they pulled him back in.*

Settling on a decision made Jax feel like a new man. The nerves were gone and the obsession with a juicy, hard-hitting story was setting in. There was going to be a lot of traveling, long nights of research and interviews in the next few weeks, and he had to be prepared. After a quick call to his editor, he was back on the books, but Jax made Declan swear that no one in the office would know he was going to be investigating the story. As far as everyone was concerned, he had quit and left, period. He would give the paper only the final exclusive story and not a series of filler articles that just recounted police statements: that fluff would be for someone else. Jax would give them the full story when it was time. The editor was to receive his mail every day and call and notify him about it. After the call, Jax checked his bag and made sure he had enough clothing and items to get him through the next few weeks. There wasn't much, but he could make do and buy what he needed, for he couldn't risk going to the house. Someone could be watching it: the police, the killer, or whoever the hell the fake detective was, and that was something he didn't want to risk.

With his bag repacked, he checked the room quickly and headed for the door, ready to stop by the police station before starting his day. His hands full, he nudged the door open with his knee, then he felt the elevator line in his stomach snap again. There, standing hunched over ten feet away and peering inside of the windows of Jax's car was "Detective" Connor. It was less than a second before Connor noticed him, but when he did, the kid stood up straight and smiled.

Piece #21
Salt Lake City, UT

Alaea, Black Lava, Flank, Fluer de sel, Himalayan, Jukyeom, Kalahari, Kala Namak, Khoisan Pearls, Malden, Maras, Murry River, Namibian, Persian, Sal De Tavira, Sale Marino Di Trapin Sea, Sal de Guerande and lastly, the most important: Utah Salt. By the ripe old age of six, Emily could rattle off this list of edible salt without prompting. Considering her father changed the family's last name to Salt when she was four, saying salt was her life was an understatement. No one thought this obsession was odd: after all, they did live in a city with salt in its name, and her father—"Old Salty" as the tourists called him—ran a salt flats tour company.

The fact that he was called Old Salty always made Emily giggle as he was the complete opposite, as he was one of the happiest people on the earth and truly loved both what he did and salt. Every day at 9:30, Old Salty would load up a bus full (well, sometimes it was) of tourists visiting Salt Lake and he'd take them on a four-hour adventure to the Bonneville Salt Flats an hour and a half away. The tour made several stops along the way and gave the local gawkers plenty of time to visit and experience the massive open salt desert that always put everyone in awe.

When her father died of salt poisoning at fifty-seven, Emily was shocked — how could the thing Daddy loved kill him? No one else was surprised: he ate salt like candy, mostly to show tourists how good his souvenir salt tasted. The particular day he died it was over a hundred degrees; he'd been sweating profusely, drinking beer and eating enough salt to kill a horse. He had four tours that day and in each one, he did his dog and pony show where he showed the tourists how much salt he could eat in one sitting. Usually his little trick and spiel would result in countless sales (the Himalayan Pink rock salt with grater was a favorite with ladies, and the black Hawaiian salt was the male favorite. He always tried to push the local stuff, but people loved colors so he sold every salt he could), but that day, his sales pitch ended in his death. Emily was only twelve at the time and to say it destroyed her being would be putting it lightly. Her father was her everything.

Two months later, her mother sold the tour company and moved them to Texas. A year later, Mom changed their last names back to Prescott and forbade any salt, even table salt, from being in their house. Emily never forgave her mother for this decree and fought daily with her. The day she turned eighteen, she changed her name back to Salt, waited three months to finish school, and then headed back up to Salt Lake City where she took classes at Salt Lake Community College, or SLCC, as everyone called it. The day she got there, she applied to every salt tour company there was; there were only about five left, but she was sure to offer her services to all of them and in her interviews, delivered an impressive pitch about knowing every fact possible about the flats. All five offered her a job, but each hardly paid anything. Emily didn't care, though: salt was back in her life.

Ten years, one pointless college degree, four kids, and one marriage and subsequent divorce later, Emily was finally able to start her own Salt Flat Tour Company. The kids were all in school full time by then. The pride she felt when she saw the logo on the tour van, "Old Salty's Tours," was unparalleled by anything she ever felt: even seeing her first child emerge from her womb paled in comparison.

Truth be told, she had to fake her emotions when it came to her children. All of her friends on Facebook did nothing but post cute pics and talk about how much they loved their kids; hell, she did it too in order to keep up appearances, but what she really felt inside, she was scared to share with anyone. She hated every one of her damn little brats. They were nothing but whiny, needy little assholes who did nothing but suck the life and money out of her. Sure, once in a while, they said something cute and gave a good hug, but she wished every damn day she didn't have them—and those were the kind thoughts. The other thoughts, the ones she really relished and thought of over and over again: no one could get those out of her; not even Jack Bauer waterboarding her could release those secrets.

With these dark thoughts swirling around in her head, she focused on the one thing she had that she loved: the salt flats and her tours. Once, she thought about her father and wondered if he ever had such thoughts about her, but she pushed that thought out; her father had been the one true person who loved her and the one person she truly loved in her life: not her ex-husband, not her kids, not her new boyfriend whom she kept around mostly for babysitting duties; no, she never loved anyone except Daddy. She hoped that her kids never realized she didn't love them, but not because she was worried about hurting them. *Fuck them*, she thought. She was more worried about appearances and making sure everyone thought she was super mom, the single mother of four and business owner who could do it all. The praise she got from that, especially after the article that showcased her company in the local paper, got her off and gave her a warm feeling she hadn't had since her father hugged her. It was that intense feeling of attention and praise that planted the seed of her plan.

In the tour bus, she kept a big picture of her and her kids: Joanie, who was seven and the littlest, sitting on her lap; Tina, who was nine; Joey, who was ten; and Becca, who was twelve, all knelt in front of her on the salt flats ground. Each held both hands scooped together and filled with salt and of course, beamed huge smiles on their faces. A single mother would naturally have the picture there so she could look at her kids all day; Emily had it there so paying customers could look at it and compliment her on what a good-looking family she had. When she got a compliment, she'd smile warmly, look back at the picture and say, *Yes, yes I do: thank you.* Sometimes, she'd add a wink and if she were really in the mood, she'd conjure up some tears to show them just how damn much she loved those kids.

The tears were part of her practice for when she killed them. She was going to have to sob intently for a long, long time to pull it off. Every night for two months, after all of the kids had gone to sleep, Emily locked her bedroom door, turned up the television and practiced sobbing. Looking in the mirror (and some nights she recorded herself on the phone to play it back and critique herself), she'd force herself to break down, mumbling things about her kids and wailing about not being able to go on without them. At the end of the two months, she felt ready and was able to focus on phase two.

The second part of her plan was just that, the plan. How could she kill *all* her kids and get away with it? Doing extensive research (using a free Wi-Fi address at the local Starbucks and a burner laptop she bought for two hundred in cash), she looked up every instance of a mother killing her children. Of course, the only cases you'd find were the ones who got caught, but that is why she studied them: to see what they did wrong so she wouldn't make the same mistakes. She made extensive notes and read every article and watched every cheesy hour-long documentary show about killer mommies she could find. In the end, like all killers, she figured she was too smart to get caught. All of the others had been stupid and hadn't planned well enough. Not her: she was a fighter. Hell, if she could run a company and raise four kids at the same time, she could easily kill them and get away with it as well. The best part was she was financially sound, so the police would never suspect money was an issue.

After four months of researching ways (*God, there were a lot of ways to kill people!*), genius struck her, or more so, the obvious: salt poisoning. Mothers had done it in the past and gotten caught as the salt level needed to be astronomical and for that to happen naturally is almost impossible, but Emily ran a salt tour business. Salt was their lives; there had to be a way to come up with some reason why they would have ingested that much salt. It took a while, but a plan was hatched that she found very convincing and that the media would find tragic, meaning they'd spend a lot of time on it. The first step would be to increase their sodium levels, not by a ton, but enough to where when the day came, she didn't have to force them to eat too much. Since she made all their meals, it would be simple to increase their intake a few days before, a few extra grams of sodium in each meal and *voila*!

The actual tragedy, that would require a bit more work, but basically it was simple. During summer break (it had to be hot so they'd sweat more), she'd take the four of them alone out to the flats to "find a new area for their tours that they could show their returning customers." In the chaos of wrangling four kids, the cooler with the ever-important waters would be left at their office, *by accident*.

Then, as they drove around the remote parts of the flats (and she sure knew the most remote areas), they'd happen to break down. Cell phones didn't work out there, but the radio in the van did. That part would be tricky. Emily used the ancient device to call back to the office and give updates on tour times because the signal still transmitted in the flats, though not well. The good thing was that no one would be in the office as they close one day a week, the day she picked to go scouting. If she drove far enough out, the service would be weak and if she let the kids play with it on the way (making sure it was not plugged in to charge), the battery would run out once the car was dead. It would be a lot of coincidences. She practiced saying, "It was a perfect storm of events that caused my…my…" and breaking down and not being able to finish the interview. It was going to be so wonderful.

Once stranded (oops, the engine overheated: it took a lot of research to figure out how to rig this so it wouldn't look purposeful), the radio would have spotty reception and die quickly. The heat in the van would be unbearable and force them out into the sun, which would pound on them at over 100 degrees. With the salt already high in their system, the children would overheat and dehydrate quickly. She, however, would have ingested a no salt diet for the previous week and have drunk over a gallon of Gatorade before leaving that day. When thirst started to set in, she would tell the kids the old story about how Old Salty believed that eating salt could cure hunger and that it contained water molecules. In fact, he did tell a story about a man who was stuck in the flats alone and survived on doing nothing but eating salt for days, and the kids knew this story. They'd be just desperate enough to start to eat a handful or two of the salt that surrounded every inch of them. In order to show she was dehydrated, she'd have to eat some as well. This was fine, because if she was not in rough shape by the time Search and Rescue found her, they'd be suspicious. Emily planned on having severe sunburn and dehydration… and to be clinging to her dead family when help arrived.

If everything went as planned, they'd break down around nine a.m., giving them a solid eleven hours to bake in the sun, panic, eat salt, and die. She just had to last until the next day around eleven, when she estimated that help would come. She'd make sure of this by having her office manager arrive early the next day. Sandy would see the van missing and the cooler by the door. She'd try to contact them for an hour, panic, and then call the police and ask for a search team. Unlike the woods, they'd find them rather quickly out there as a fly-over would spot them miles and miles away in the vast desert. Emily's only concern was that one of the kids might survive. She wasn't worried they'd blame her or have anything against her; she just wanted them all dead. If one of them didn't die by midnight—probably her oldest one since she had more body mass to fight off the dehydration and salt—she would have to kill them another way. Preferably by hand, but it couldn't be that obvious. She'd love to strangle the shit out of them one by one, but that would be foolish. No, if one didn't die, she'd suffocate the child and make sure it looked like he or she hyperventilated. It wasn't ideal, but it was plausible. And if that cause of death was caught, she could again break down and say, "The others had all died, I couldn't make her suffer anymore, I put her down and was going to kill myself, but I just, I just…"

With her plan set, all Emily had to do was wait until the forecast predicted the hottest Monday of the month because they were closed on Mondays. It was September 23rd and the temps were supposed to rise to 98 that day, unheard of for that time of year; in the flats, that number could jump by thirty degrees with the heat reflecting off the white salt fields. It was going to be perfect. *Why did they pick a day that was so hot? It was the only day they could all go together, of course, besides, they get so few Mondays off like that during school, they just had to take advantage of it.* The police would believe that and she filled up her calendar to show just how busy the kids were the rest of the summer. The few days beforehand, she was so excited and chipper that she had to keep reminding herself to not show her enthusiasm as she was usually a bit of a curmudgeon with the kids.

That morning, all the kids were fine with getting up early and going (she bribed them with the idea of ice cream and a movie when they got back), and she packed the cooler and left it right by the door and took off just as planned. On the drive, she offered the kids the chance to talk to the truckers on the radio, which they gladly did. Looking at their smiling and laughing faces as she drove, she mentally picked out each of their funeral wardrobes. She'd have to go shopping and get a new dress for herself, though. It was going to be wonderful.

On Tuesday morning, September 24th, at eight in the morning, Sandy Frank, who had been working the booking desk at Old Salty's for over two years and had become good friends with Emily, arrived at work ten minutes before her early start time, just like she was raised to do by her single mother. *On time is late, early is on time.* She heard that damn saying a thousand times growing up, and it sure as hell stuck. She walked up to the doors, the heat already reaching ninety, and was wiping the sweat from her forehead when she noticed a small package leaning against the door. This was odd, as the mail usually came around two. Figuring it was left the day before, Sandy picked up the white box and entered the office like normal, placing her purse in the desk drawer, her water bottle on its coaster next to her mouse, and the package to the left of the computer. There was a cooler next to the door, which was odd, but Emily and the kids must have left it there when they had returned the night before. However, Sandy remembered that the van was not in the lot. Why would the cooler be there and the van nowhere in sight?

She walked over and double-checked the lot; sure enough, the van was nowhere to be seen, but Emily's car was parked in the back. Odd. Sandy shrugged her shoulders and decided that Emily must have just been tired after the trip and had decided to drive it home instead; she'd return it when she came in. Sitting back down, she pushed the package aside and went about her normal routine of checking emails and making sure the schedules and tickets were all set for the day. This took just over two hours. At that point, she grew a slight bit concerned that Emily wasn't in yet, but on days when they had tours starting late, she typically took her time coming in. It wasn't until she was fully caught up that she bothered looking at the package that sat on her desk.

With a sigh, she looked at the white box with mild curiosity. It wasn't like anything they normally received. She picked it up, took her letter opener and went at the strips of tape. There was no return address, which was strange, and the address was labeled neatly and with Emily's name. Even though it was for Emily, it was Sandy's job to open all of the mail, and Sandy sent anything personal to the house. She popped the box open and pulled out the contents with a casual ease she'd later regret.

There was a small note and something about the size of a softball wrapped in what looked like butcher paper. *Must be another salt from a distributor in some far-off land that wants it to be sold in the gift shop*, she thought with a bit of annoyance, since she'd have to do all the paperwork if Emily wanted to carry it. Setting the note on the desk, she pulled back the waxy paper, picked up the package in her left hand, and shook out the contents into her right. There, sitting in her palm was a human knee cap, or more so, the entire knee of a person. The skin surrounding the body part was shriveled and cracking, the raw meat on the edges was dried and reminded her of the time she went to a fancy steak restaurant in Las Vegas where you could pick the finest of the "aged meats" on display in a big case. It looked as if it was cut off with a rusty saw right above and below the knee. Bone parts, ligaments and other rotted material she could not recognize was smashed together in a rancid puck-like shape. The smell that hit her nose a few seconds later made her puke right on her desk, on top of the note. Later, she'd regret not aiming for the trashcan, as the vomit smeared the message enclosed, making it illegible to the detectives.

Exactly four seconds after the knee slapped into the palm of her hand and a mere one second before her vomiting, she tossed the knee with a spastic movement as if it were a spider, with no rhyme or reason. It went into the air, hit the edge of the desk, and rolled three feet away from her. After puking once more, followed by some whimpering, Sandy ran to the small bathroom in the back where she rinsed her mouth, washed her hands, and splashed water on her face. It took her a full ten minutes to calm down before she called 911 and tried in vain to explain what the hell she meant. She managed to spit out, *Just get the hell out here*, and they did just that, thirty-three minutes later. During that wait time, Sandy called Emily's cell fourteen times and sat far as she could across the small office, not taking her eyes off the knee cap for a second. It was as if she thought it was going to come alive and attack her like in some horror movie. Instead, it sat there, still as could be, like some forgotten malformed baseball that rolled under a bush to be forgotten by a child.

It wasn't until almost two hours later when the detectives showed up that Sandy's heart really sank, because they were the ones who suggested it could be one of Emily's knees, since she wasn't responding to any attempts to contact her. When one of the detectives opened the cooler by the door and saw it was full, he suspected foul play. Sandy broke down at this point. Why hadn't she checked the cooler, why hadn't she called the police right away when she saw that the van wasn't there? These two decisions would haunt her.

It wasn't until weeks later when the whole story shook out that Sandy started to not blame herself; though the blame was gone, Sandy was never the same after losing her job, her friend, and the children she considered family; plus, there was that added horror of having held a human knee. The medical examiner assured her that all of the children had died long before she could have called for help, that noticing and calling the police earlier wouldn't have changed anything for them. Emily on the other hand, might have lived as they put her time of death in the early afternoon of that day. Sandy's husband made her realize that Emily wouldn't have wanted to live, so it was meant to be. Emily would have never, never been able to handle losing all of her children, he told Sandy. She loved those kids too damn much. Maybe it was a blessing in disguise that the box distracted her from checking on Emily earlier, because now she could be in heaven with her kids, the most important thing in her life.

The Lullaby

Twenty-five years earlier

Karen leaned closer to the mirror to examine her eyebrows. "Do you think my brows are too thin, Denny?" She frowned, then feigned surprise, watching her forehead wrinkles fold and ripple like an unsettled ocean. "That Drew Barrymore has some thin eyebrows...maybe to make her eyes seem wider," she continued, more to herself, to vocalize her train of thought, than to her son, who wasn't really listening anyhow.

She rifled through a pink satin cosmetic bag and pulled out a dark brown pencil. Holding her palm against the underside of the upper lashes of her left eye, gently resting her wrist against her temple, Karen carefully traced the underside of her left eyelid with the pencil in her right hand. She continued the mark into her bottom waterline as well, then pulled both hands away and blinked furiously, her eyes tearing slightly. After a moment, she refocused her gaze on the mirror, glancing down to catch her son's expression from his position in the bathtub.

Dennis was staring blankly into space, his arms crossed awkwardly across his pre-teen body, stretched gawkily across the small tub. When he looked up and caught his mother's glance in the reflection, eyeing him, he pulled his bent legs up to his chest and hugged his calves. His knees stood high above the waterline like volcanic islands.

"What?" he scowled at her. He hated when she stared at him like that. Even more, he hated that she continued to stroll anywhere he might be in their apartment without bothering to knock; he was nearly ten and not a little boy anymore. He deserved a space of his own, even a small one; just a modicum of privacy would suffice every now and then. Bath time was a particular bone of contention between them, as she had taken to finding excuses to invade his private bathroom musings with petty errands into the room. She insisted that he bathe nightly, stating that he was beginning to stink like dirty teenaged boys do. It was true: he could smell the sweat on his own skin; it was a rank, sour smell, a mixture of fresh dog doo and musk brushed with a hint of ocean salt water. It was hormones, it was anxiety, it was fear and growth and excitement and lust, and it was coming from inside of him, growing like a fungus. Part of him wanted to wash it from his body, to bleach his insides so that he was squeaky and bright again like a starched white dress shirt waving on the clothesline that crossed their tiny side balcony. But another part of him, he had to admit, wanted to snuggle up with the smell beneath the sheets of his small twin bed. He wanted to embrace the stench, roll in it like a pig in mud, cover himself with it like a sniper in reconnaissance, and each time he took a bath, he felt his protective shield slip from his body and ooze down the drain.

Karen finished lining her right eye and turned from the mirror, still blinking wildly. "What?!" she mimicked. She sat daintily on the edge of the tub and dipped her hand in the warm water where his feet had been a moment earlier. When his expression did not change, she playfully splashed a handful of water at his bony shins. "What's the matter?' she asked.

"Piggy got your tongue?"

Karen had replaced the traditional cat in this idiom with a pig in reference to a particularly painful incident from three years earlier, one in which Karen, in her empty-cradle approach to parenting, tucked her son into bed with one of her special retellings of a traditional nursery rhyme. That year, she had been called by Dennis's first grade teacher and asked to meet with the woman and the school principal about the boy's vivid depiction of the scourge of London by the Black Death following a schoolyard game of Ring Around the Rosie.

This night, which would forever be engrained in his memory, she began her wish goodnight with a tickling of her son's neck until he giggled. Then, she pushed the blanket from his body, exposing his bare feet.

She grabbed the big toe that was closest to her body as she sat on the edge of the bed. "This little piggy went to market." She paused a moment, then looked seriously into her son's eyes. "Do you know what that means? It means that the farmer, who owed the pig, decided to sell his prized pig to the butcher in town." She wiggled her son's toe between her fingers and smiled.

Dennis did not smile back. This was the first he had heard of such a thing. "What? What do you mean?" he asked.

"You know what a butcher is, right?" asked Karen.

"Remember the butcher at the supermarket? What does he sell?"

Dennis imagined the big glass case in his head; the big, dark-haired man with the wide, white apron standing behind it. "Steak?" he replied weakly. He could see the rows and rows of bright red slabs of beef, the white veins of fat and grizzle and bone snaking through each one. "Pork chops?"

Karen smiled wider. "That's right! Pork chops! They come from those little piggies." She tickled the bottom of her son's foot and he laughed instinctively. As she continued to wiggle her fingers along his pink skin, she added, "Chop-chop-chop: the butcher takes his big knife and chop-chop-chops up the little piggy until he is in little pieces for people to eat."

Dennis could not stop laughing as the tickling grew stronger, more insistent. Karen moved her fingers to the second toe on the foot, finally offering him a reprieve. "This little piggy stayed home," she said.

Dennis hesitated. "No chopping of the piggy?" he asked.

Karen stared at her son for a second, then burst into laughing and began to tickle his foot again. Dennis tried to kick away from her grasp, but she held his ankle with her other hand. "No chopping today. That piggy is too skinny to eat. The farmer will keep him home for now." She moved her hand back to his toes and grabbed the middle one. "This little piggy had roast beef. Now, why do you think the farmer gave middle piggy a big delicious sandwich?"

Dennis thought a moment, grateful for the moratorium in her torture. "Um…" he stalled. "Um…he was hungry?" he offered. He liked roast beef sandwiches, especially those with extra mayonnaise and slices of tomato from the fruit stand down the block. When Karen had taken him on a Saturday to Orchard Beach the previous summer, the only Saturday she had spent a whole day with him without stopping to work, she had packed roast beef and tomato sandwiches on rye bread in her cooler alongside two cans of orange soda. The day had been hot, one of the hottest that season, and by the time the two were hungry and had taken a rest from splashing in the cold water of Long Island Sound, the sandwiches were not cold anymore and the mayonnaise was warm and gooey and dripped from between the slabs of lunchmeat like grease, but that made them even more delicious.

Karen made an exaggerated expression of surprise with her face. "He sure was hungry, and the farmer wanted to fatten him up,"—she grabbed her son's foot hard with her hand—"so the butcher could chop chop chop him up for the market!" She reached her other hand over to Dennis's stomach and tickled him there. He cackled uncontrollably in response until his throat began to ache.

His belly was starting to hurt from all of the laughing, and hiccups had begun to force their way violently from his chest and out of his mouth. "Stop," he begged. "Stop, it (hiccup) hurts, Mommy." Dennis tried to turn onto his side and hide his extremities from his tormentor, to no avail. "Stop, pl-(hiccup)-ease," he pleaded.

Karen removed her hand from his stomach but maintained her grasp on his foot. Ever so gently, she held her son's fourth toe between her thumb and forefinger. "This little piggy," she whispered conspiratorially, "This little piggy got none." She looked around the room nervously as if checking for onlookers, then leaned dramatically into her son's face. He could smell the night's dinner on her breath. "Do you know why farmers stop feeding their pigs before selling them off to market?" Her eyes were wide and darted back and forth between Dennis's.

Dennis said nothing. He held his breath. All he could feel was her hand on his ankle.

"Do you?" she repeated. A fetid cloud of sherry-soaked chicken wafted over his face.

He slowly shook his head, trying his best to muffle the hiccup shuddering from his lips.

"Because," Karen said, backing her head away, "when you slaughter an animal, it poops whatever is left in its stomach and intestines. They poop it all over the ground. Humans do it, too. When someone dies, they pee themselves and poop their pants. Pretty gross, right?" she asked rhetorically. "So the farmer, he decided to make sure there was nothing in the piggy's tummy before the butcher chopped him up. That way, chop-chop, no poop!"

She was silent and still for a moment and simply stared at

her son, waiting for his reaction. When he said nothing, she smiled and suddenly brought her other hand up to tickle Dennis's foot again. He erupted with uncontrollable laughter tempered with cries of pain. A few more hiccups escaped in the process.

"Sssssstop!" he screamed between gasps for breath. "Stop! Sssssttop!" He kicked his leg as hard as he could, finally breaking free of her clutch. He continued to kick until his heel struck her shoulder and in response, angry that he had dared to hit her, even by accident, Karen leaped forward and threw her body across his, pinning his legs and shoulders to the bed with her torso. Her left forearm pressed against the bottom of his neck. With her free hand, she aggressively tickled the underside of his neck, though the force of her fingers were more like pitchfork prongs than feathers, and he pulled his head back in agony.

She grabbed her son's face and turned it to the side and held it there so that he had to look as far as he could to the left to catch a fuzzy glimpse of her expression. "Don't you EVER hit your mother: do you hear me?" When her son did not reply, she squeezed harder, felt her manicured nails push into his small, doughy face. Then, for emphasis, she pulled back then pushed Dennis's jaw as hard as she could into the pillow, not once but three times, and he felt a sharp pain on his tongue. "Ever." With this, she let go of his face and slid backwards until she was standing upright by the side of his bed. Now unencumbered, Dennis opened his mouth and felt a thick puddle of drool escape onto the pillow. It was singed with red.

"Serves you right, hitting your mother," Karen said.

Dennis was silent. He knew that the less he said, the faster she would leave him alone for the evening. His tongue stung with pain, but he held his jaw tightly closed and willed himself not to cry.

"Piggy got your tongue, huh?" Karen laughed to herself. She walked to the doorway and flicked the switch on the wall, turning off the light. "Sleep tight, Denny," she said, and quietly shut the door behind her.

Three years later, as Karen smiled at her son across the bathtub, Dennis could feel the ache in his tongue as freshly as he had on the night of the incident. She splashed his shins again. "Quit it, Mom," he said, and scowled. He felt helpless and vulnerable, his prepubescent scrotum pushing against the back of his ankles, the downy brown hair on his legs adding only a hint of color over his pale skin. He could do nothing to fight her: any act in defense, even a playful splash back, might be taken as rebellious behavior, a gesture of defiance. He had taken his share of punishments from Karen over the years. She never did anything in her life half-assed, and she wasn't about to start with her child's discipline.

When her son refused to react, Karen had no choice but to withdraw. She removed her hand from the water, shook it slightly, then leaned backward to rest her spine against the corner of the wall, her buttocks balancing precariously on the edge of the tub. She placed her right foot on the floor and her left squarely on the tub's edge in front of her.

She smiled dreamily at Dennis as if she were reclining comfortably in an easy chair. "I know I told you a lot of scary stories when you were little, but I did it for your own good," Karen said. "I see what soft men grow up to be, every day in my job. They become these weak, spineless jellyfish who can only dominate by ambush: raping and stealing and terrorizing and killing other people... sneaking up on their prey and paralyzing their lives, just like those damn jellyfish. Remember, we saw a dead one on the beach that one summer in Rockaway? You've never been stung by one, but they hurt like crazy, and often, you don't even see them in the water before they sting you."

She paused and looked at her son's knobby knees, then back at his face. "You know, the word 'lullaby' comes from the Hebrew term *Lilith abi*, which people used to say to shoo Lillith away. Lillith was a demon, a female demon, sent to men while they slept to suck away their health and livelihood, so parents sang lullabies to their children to protect them from the evil of the world." Karen smiled at her son but he said nothing, so she continued. "I mean, most lullabies and nursery rhymes are based on real events from history: they aren't these rock candy mountain tales where everyone ends up happy in the end. That's what makes them real; that's what makes them helpful and why we sing them to children in the first place: to teach them."

Karen swung her left leg over the tub so that both feet were again on the floor. She stood up and smoothed the back of her pants with her palms to check if they were wet. "Life is hard, Denny. Really hard. You have to look out for yourself because no one is going to look after you." She reached down and placed a hand on his knee and squeezed.

As she exited the bathroom, closing the door behind her, Dennis exhaled an audible sigh of relief and took another breath. Then he allowed himself to slide downward into the water. He turned his knees to the side and folded his body as flat as he could against the bottom of the tub, feeling the smooth porcelain caress his skin, until every inch of him was submerged. When he felt certain Karen was not standing just outside of the door listening, he screamed into the water until his lungs ached.

Piece #13
Wells, ME

Someone was killing townies.

There were twenty-two officers staffing the Wells Police Department— twenty-three, if you counted the patrolman stationed permanently at the local high school after a series of fruitless mass shooter threats and a barrage of demands from anxious helicopter parents at the subsequent emergency city council meeting— and Daniel Defoe, one of only two detectives on the force, was assigned to the case. It wasn't anything to make national news, mind you: the small, coastal town had been plagued with a wicked meth and opioid problem since the '90s, but now that the summer season was winding down and a tourist had died, it was time to get serious. It was one thing for the local junkies from Sanford or a nomad or two from Hampton Beach to o.d., but when a vacationer, southern Maine coast's bread and butter, kicked in a posh, beachfront hotel room, the case needed to be closed quickly and quietly.

The victim's name was Tristan Saunders. Daniel didn't have to do the research to know the kid's background. He was likely in his early twenties, garrulous and mop-haired, from Connecticut or maybe the Berkshires, on break from graduate school or a year of "finding himself" while roaming rent-free around his parents' spacious Colonial. He was white, in decent shape save for a rounding microbrew belly, with either a meticulously-groomed but completely nonsensical facial hair design or a faded, dirty Sox cap backwards on his head. Or both. Sure enough, when he arrived at the scene and took a quick look at the body, Daniel wasn't surprised. The only error he had made was the cap: the kid had been a Yankees fan.

"Coroner places the time of death as sometime early this morning, between one and two," Mary Stewart, Daniel's on-again, off-again partner said. "The lab will run it, but I'm guessing it's the same stuff." She gestured to the small bag of white powder and miscellaneous drug paraphernalia on the coffee table nearby. "What is this, the fifth this summer? Makes you wonder where the rest of the batch went, though. I can't imagine we've seen the last of it, or of this mess." She patted her jacket pocket and pulled out a small notepad and pen. "I mean, *fuuuck* me if we're trudging through three feet of snow at Christmas to do more of these."

Daniel glanced around the room. It was a spacious suite with a sprawling king-sized bed, a small bistro set, and a microwave cart with a large dorm refrigerator. Clothes were strewn about the bed and over the sand-colored recliner, most of them pastel or white in color. A wide sliding-glass door opened to a small balcony overlooking the Atlantic. Late morning sun warmed the room even as the air conditioner hummed tirelessly in the background. On the light grey carpet where Tristan lay sprawled on his back, staring languidly at the ceiling, was a hard, dry puddle of brown vomit. A drizzle of the same substance was caked on Tristan's chin and along the top of his pale pink Polo shirt. Daniel thought he saw a chunk or two of undigested shrimp in the mix.

Mary poked one of two water glasses on the table with her pen. "Looks like he had company. Maybe a hook-up? Maybe the dealer himself?" She made a note on her pad. "You up for canvassing solo? I have court at one."

Daniel's mind was somewhere else. "What? Yeah, no problem."

Mary searched his face for a moment. "Everything alright with you? You look tired, Willy."

Although Daniel Defoe shared his name with the author of *Robinson Crusoe*, his friends never made castaway jokes or any literary puns when addressing him. Guys called him Willem instead, after the actor. Daniel guessed it was because he was unnaturally skinny and had both a prominent space between his two front teeth and an unnerving tendency to stare wide-eyed at people longer than was socially acceptable. But what Mary said was true. Daniel hadn't been getting much sleep lately. After the incident in August, he hadn't slept more than two hours at a time, often basking in the glow of early morning infomercials and sitcom reruns while he prayed for his digital clock to hurry up and clatter for him to get out of bed. He rubbed his bottom lip, a habit he'd picked up recently to keep himself alert.

"Yeah, 'got sucked into a *Breaking Bad* marathon on AMC

last night," he said, smiling weakly. "'Lost track of time and now I'm paying for it. Go ahead: I got this."

Mary patted him on the shoulder and walked cautiously around the tiny number tents the forensic tech was placing around the carpet. "We didn't find any empties in the room, so the kid must have come from the bars. Puke smells like it. Maybe try Captain Jack's downstairs?" Mary called over her shoulder before stepping lightly out the door.

A uniformed rookie walked past Daniel in the same direction as Mary, and Daniel caught him by the arm. "Hey, did you find any ID for this Saunders guy? Something with a photo?" The rookie passed him a clear plastic evidence bag with a wallet inside. Daniel stuck his gloved hand into the leather billfold and leafed through a handful of metallic-themed charge cards until he found the driver's license, then used his phone to snap a photo of the kid's picture.

With its rugged, icy winters, cerulean water, and greying rocky coast, Maine could not have been more antithetical to the Caribbean, but Captain Jack's was clearly suffering from wishful delusions, or at best, an identity crisis: on its roofed patio facing the sea, table after table was covered in bright pink and orange and green cloths topped with centerpieces of hibiscus and fern. Plastic parrots hung from the rafters, and here and there, a cardboard palm tree leaned against a support beam. Although it was not yet noon, the bar was full of patrons drinking tall, fruity cocktails through bendy straws. Steel drum music drifted from the speakers. A skinny blonde hostess greeted him with a wide smile. "How many?"

Daniel showed her his badge. "I was wondering if I could speak to the manager," he said, smiling back. He had discovered a long time ago, especially in a small town, that everything was easier when you topped it with a toothy grin.

The hostess was a townie, he could tell, although she was definitely a new hire. Daniel had come to Captain Jack's a few nights himself after work, but usually only when his staple watering hole on the beach, Mally's, had closed for the season in mid-October or he just didn't feel like staring at the same arrangement of whiskey bottles against the mirror on the back wall of the bar next to the cash register. Then again, he hadn't been to any of the shore bars since the incident.

He didn't recognize the hostess, but he didn't frequent the festive theme-bar with enough regularity to know her anyway. No, it was more in her manner, the way she nervously glanced about the room that clued Daniel in on her still-acclimating status. After glancing behind and to the side of her, the girl looked slightly confused for a moment, then spoke. "Oh, that's Big Mike. He went down to the Shop N' Save off Mile Road for a few supplies. Our delivery doesn't get here until mid-afternoon, and we're running low on pineapple."

Daniel kept the smile on his face. "Do you know if anyone working now was on last night? I just have a few quick questions."

The hostess glanced around the room and onto the patio, then returned her eyes to Daniel. "Josh, maybe? He's the bartender. He works the closing shift most nights and is just covering for the day shift guy who called and said he'd be a few hours late." She paused. "He's got a newborn at home, ya know how it is."

Daniel didn't know: he'd never been married, never procreated anything that he knew of, but he suspected the hostess might have a kid or two at home. She was young, twenty-two at most, but her skin looked tired. Daniel tipped his hand to his forehead like he was giving her a tiny salute, then wandered over to the heavily shellacked bar and sat down on an open stool. On the other side of the counter, a squat, large-armed man with wet blue eyes and thinning sand-colored hair walked towards him. He looked familiar to Daniel, but so did most bartenders. "What can I get ya?" he asked, placing a cheerful cardboard coaster in front of him.

Daniel nodded and pulled out his phone. "Josh, right?" The bartender nodded back. Daniel showed him the picture of Tristan's driver license photo. "Was this guy in the bar last night?"

Josh placed his hand on Daniel's phone and turned the screen slightly, a move Daniel found a little unnerving but he said nothing. The bartender squinted. "Yeah, he was here. Parked himself at the corner there, drank a few on his own and kept looking at his watch," he said. His accent was thick, old New England, elongating the vowels in *pahked* and *cornah* and *wahtch* in a way Daniel always thought existed only in Stephen

King movies. Josh lightly tapped the phone's screen with his finger. "I think he had one of those Apple watches though. Probably playing Words With Friends or something."

Daniel replaced the phone in his breast pocket. "So, he was alone all night?"

Josh leaned forward a bit and lowered his voice. "No, not all night." He paused. "After the sun went down, maybe nine or ten o'clock, I looked over and saw one of our resident sleazes cozying up to him. Jody is his name. Always suspected he was dealing, you know, but I never saw him move any product in the bar, and he always paid his tab and added decent tips for the girls, so I never had a reason to shoo him outta here." He held a finger up in the air to signal that he'd be back in a moment, then shuffled off to help another customer.

Daniel pulled his fist over his mouth to stifle a yawn and used the reprieve to glance about the patio and assess the clientele. All tourists, from what Daniel could guess. Despite living in a heavily-trafficked vacation destination, townies didn't frequent bars like this. They didn't go to the ten mini-golf attractions that dotted Route 1; they didn't walk the Marginal Way in Ogunquit every morning or shop for trinkets in Perkins Cove. No, from Memorial Day through Columbus Day, the year-round residents of the southern Maine coast were held hostage by the bombardment of noisy, brightly-colored, money-spending visitors from out of town: annual prisoners of Vacationland.

A lanky, tanned man wearing a wrinkled Hawaiian shirt unbuttoned and a tank-style undershirt underneath walked past him and behind the bar. "Thanks for covering, Josh," he called out, sticking the corner of a bar rag into the waist of his jeans. "I'll stay later, man—come in when you're ready."

Josh didn't need to hear the invitation twice. He ducked under the server passway and walked over to Daniel. "That guy, Jody: he's here just about every night," he said to Daniel. He rubbed the stubble on his cheek with the back of his fingers. "I gotta get some shut-eye, but I'll be back tonight myself if you have any more questions."

Daniel slid down from the barstool and fished his car keys from his pocket. "I gotta catch a few winks myself," he said. "And yeah, I'll swing by. Thanks."

Late that afternoon, as he slid the key into the lock of his modest ranch-style house on a cul-de-sac a few miles inland from Moody Beach, Daniel saw it: a white postal service box pressed up against the black iron railing. He picked it up and saw that it was addressed to him, but there was no return address. He shook it lightly as he walked into the kitchen, tossing his keys and badge on the table and unhooking the snap on his waist holster. He didn't remember ordering anything, but that wasn't unusual. The lack of consistent sleep was starting to take a toll on his memory and rote activities. Twice this week he had poured orange juice into his coffee, and last Saturday, he had taken out chicken breasts from the pantry chest freezer to defrost for dinner only to forget he had done so, later seeing the half-thawed meat and recalling his plan on his way to answer the door for pizza delivery.

He brought the box to the counter and stood it on its side, examining the address. His name and address had been typed carefully onto a white label. There was no return address anywhere, and the red postmark was smudged; Daniel thought he could make out a D at the end of the city name, but the state was completely illegible. He picked up the box again. It weighed about three or four pounds, give or take, and when he shook it to assess the material, nothing inside of it seemed to move.

He ripped the pull-tab sideways and jammed his fingers under the cardboard sleeve to open the top, then turned the box upside-down and jiggled it back and forth to dump the contents onto the Formica countertop. An off-white rectangle of packing paper spilled out, formed to mimic the exact shape of the box like a sculpture emerging from a mold. Daniel shook the box again, then peered inside to see if anything else remained. He could see a small piece of white paper taped to one of the longer sides of the box, and he stretched his hand inside, removed the note, and unfolded it.

```
               A girl whose status is unknown
                  Pieces sent to a chosen few
              Action is yours; her destiny own
       You can love her or liver, it's now up to you.
```

"What the fuck?" Daniel said out loud. His voice echoed

slightly in the quiet house. He tossed the note aside and began to unwrap the package, which was cool to the touch. *It must have been kept in a refrigerated delivery truck overnight*, he thought. They'd been enjoying an Indian summer the latter half of September, and he'd had to turn on his central air more than once in the past few weeks. Anything cold these days didn't get that way naturally.

After he had peeled seemingly endless layers of the paper packing away, he found himself holding an oblong shape a little over three inches long. It, too, was wrapped in the off-white paper, and Daniel tore a bit of the covering away, then proceeded to pull the rest off quickly, like an eight-year-old unwrapping a Christmas present, until his fingers touched something damp and meaty. He pulled his hand away in revulsion, then examined the small sack of deep red flesh on his kitchen counter. It was pillow-like with a strip of white membrane running vertically off-center and shaped somewhere between a right-angle triangle and a rectangle. With this thought, Daniel cynically congratulated himself on finally being able to apply one item of knowledge from high school geometry class.

A faint smell of decay wafted up to his face, and he turned his head in an attempt to avoid it. The scent reminded him of a crime scene he and Mary had visited last January; the two had entered a modestly-decorated efficiency overlooking the marshes and immediately had been accosted by the stench of the slowly rotting body, knocking both of them backwards two steps. The heat had been off for weeks, and when the pipes froze, spilling water into an adjoining rental, the landlord was prompted to investigate and discovered his tenant on the floor of the kitchen, dead of a possible overdose. The cold had staved off decomposition for a bit, but nature had begun its process just the same.

It was a smell you never forgot.

Daniel snatched the note and reread it. *Love her or liver.* Now he got the pun. He picked up a piece of packing paper from the discarded pile and ripped off a corner, a piece just large enough to cover his finger, and poked the organ. It was denser than he imagined. In all of his visits to the coroner's suite, he'd never seen a human liver before, but surely this had belonged to a cow or pig, a butchery discard. He tossed the makeshift finger shield aside and opened the cabinet under his sink, searching for latex gloves, something he should have done before opening the box in the first place: but how the hell could he have known that he'd be handling a gift-wrapped organ?

Once he had pulled gloves onto both of his hands, he gently picked the liver up and turned it over. There was nothing hidden underneath it, nothing else to see.

He replaced the organ on the countertop and sat down at the table. The box had been addressed to him specifically. No return address. No name inside. Someone sent him a liver. A liver. And that poem... *A girl whose status is unknown.* There was something about the line that nagged at Daniel. What girl was he talking about? *Action is yours; her destiny own.* What action? What did the sender want him to do with the organ? With the poem? With any of it? And why? The answer was there, he knew it: he was just too tired to see it right now.

He started to put his hand, still wearing the soiled gloves, on his face to rub his eyes in exhaustion, then stopped himself. He needed sleep. He rewrapped the liver in as much of the packing paper as he could salvage and placed the bundle in his chest freezer, then peeled off the gloves and slipped the folded poem into his shirt pocket. After setting an alarm on his phone, he curled up on the couch and pulled the green cotton throw—an often-used Christmas gift from Mary—over his lower body. His last thought before he drifted into fitful sleep was of an image of a girl with blonde hair on an autopsy table, her abdomen sliced open to reveal slippery intestines and gobs of red and black blood coagulating between meat-like organs.

She had tire tracks across her forehead.

When Daniel sauntered back into Captain Jack's at nine o'clock that evening, he did his best to not look like a cop. It wasn't that difficult, actually: he hadn't shaved in days, and he had awoken from that afternoon's nap covered in sweat from a nightmare he couldn't quite remember. Since he had been running late, he hadn't bothered to shower or even change his clothes before leaving for the beach. He looked, and smelled, like a heavy drug user, or at the very least, like someone who did not have his act together.

Daniel slid past the empty hostess stand and past the covered patio, which was brightly lit with a scattering of multicolored Christmas lights. The steel drum music was absent; in its place was an aging hippie sitting in the corner of the room, singing into a stand microphone and strumming a ukulele. Daniel caught Josh's eye as he approached the bar, and the bartender cocked his head subtly toward a pale man with dark hair and eyes sitting alone at the far corner. Leaving an empty seat between him and Jody, Daniel slid into a nearby stool and rested his hands on the bar.

"What can I get ya?" Josh asked, placing the cheerful cardboard coaster in front of him exactly as he had earlier that day. He gave no hint that their conversation had ever occurred.

Daniel beat his palms on the wood like a percussionist accentuating a comedian's punchline. "Jameson on the rocks. Double, please," he said. Josh turned his back to make the drink, and Daniel looked over at the basket of shelled peanuts sitting halfway between Jody and him. "Do you mind if I grab these?" he asked the pale man.

Jody shook his head. "Nah—all you, man," he said. He paused. "Kitchen's open until ten. Standard pub fare."

Daniel began breaking the shells and tossing the nuts into his mouth. "Thanks. I may just have to order something. I'm not much of a seafood guy, you know? And my luck: we went to a fish place for dinner." He had devised this backstory in his head on the drive to the beach. He was a single guy, up from New Hampshire for the day to visit with his sister and her family who were staying at one of the hotels down Atlantic Avenue. It seemed plausible and might explain why Daniel, who looked like neither a tourist nor a townie, was a disheveled mess and looking to score smack from a stranger. For once, his alarming thinness would work in his favor. He pushed his shirt sleeve up to his elbow and scratched his forearm absent-mindedly the way he had seen junkies do in the station house when they were being questioned.

Jody smiled into his beer. "Up with the family for vacation, huh?"

"No, no: I'm up to see my sister. She and her husband rented a few rooms down a-ways," he pointed toward the door, "with my nephews, and I drove up from Portsmouth to go to dinner with them." He laughed. "Guess I should've known it would be seafood, being Maine and all."

"Next time, pack a snack," Jody laughed as Josh set the short glass of amber liquid on the bar. Daniel fished in his pants pocket for his wallet but Jody put his hand up. "I got this, Josh," he said. "My new friend drinks on my tab tonight."

Daniel raised his glass and nodded to his new companion. "Very kind of you to take pity on me, thank you." He swallowed the whiskey in four gulps, letting the ice cubes rest for a beat against his teeth. When he replaced the glass on the bar, Jody reached over and pushed it toward Josh, who hadn't moved.

Josh raised an eyebrow at Daniel, who gave the bartender a tight-lipped grin. "Sure, another sounds good to me." Josh poured more Jameson into his glass, not bothering to freshen the ice, then walked quickly to the other end of the bar.

Daniel took another big sip and resumed cracking the peanut shells. After a minute or two of silence, he turned to Jody. "So, you live in this town? Must be a pain in the ass dealing with all the out-of-towners each summer. Traffic alone was a bitch getting up here, and it's after Labor Day!"

Jody smirked. "Yeah, you get used to it. I live in Berwick, next town over. Grew up in Bangor but drifted down here with some friends after college and never left." He finished his beer and pushed the glass to the edge of the bar to indicate he wanted another. "Area's a ghost town off season. Feast or famine, right?" Josh returned and replaced the empty glass with a full one. Jody continued to talk. "I may relocate to Portland one of these days, but only time will tell. What do you do for a living?"

Daniel finished the second drink in two swallows. "I'm between jobs at the moment. You?"

Jody smiled. "I get by on my charm, you could say." He winked.

This took Daniel by surprise. Maybe Josh has misread this guy. Maybe he wasn't a drug dealer: maybe he was a prostitute. Maybe the bad batch of heroin hadn't come from Jody at all; maybe the kid had brought it with him from home, or maybe he had scored it from someone on the beach.

He pushed the glass of half-melted ice toward the inside of the bar. He was starting to feel the numbness rolling over him. He loved this feeling, the progression, how one by one, the dull aches in his muscles muffled, his spine softened, and his jaw relaxed. He knew that soon, a gossamer veil would drape over his thoughts, pulling them just out of focus like a portrait photographer's lens. Soon, the air would hug him warmly like a tightly knit shawl and he would escape, if only for an hour or two.

A memory clicked into his brain. Darkness in front of him through the windshield. The long stretch of pavement banked on each side by marshland. His headlights suddenly illuminating the thin figure in the grey hooded sweatshirt, holding tightly to the leash. The girl's face when she turned and saw—

"So what do you say we order some food, yeah?" Jody stretched his arm away from Daniel and grabbed a small menu from the edge of the bar.

Daniel shook his head in an unconscious attempt to shoo the memory away. "Yeah, yeah," he agreed. His voice sounded slightly hollow, further away than before.

Josh returned and removed the rocks glass and placed it in his sink. "Another?" he asked matter-of-factly. He had done his part in helping Daniel; the cop was on his own. If he wanted to get plastered and fuck up his investigation, that was his business. He poured another double over fresh ice in a new glass and set it on the bar.

Daniel nodded, a delayed response to the bartender's rhetorical inquiry, and fingered the remaining shelled nuts in the basket. "You got any more peanuts?" he asked.

Jody didn't give Josh a chance to respond. "My new friend here needs some food in his stomach. How about a burger for, er, uh…" he paused. "I just realized: I don't even know your name."

It seemed too much effort to lie on this front, so Daniel stuck his hand out. "Dan. It's Dan."

Jody accepted his hand and shook it. He had a firm handshake. His hands were large but soft. "Mine's Jody. Nice to meet you, Dan." He turned back to the bartender. "Dan here will have a Beachbum burger with everything, including the fries. And I'll have a double order of shrimp cocktail. Extra sauce." He tossed the menu sideways, and it landed only an inch or two from where Jody originally had retrieved it.

"How'd you like that cooked?" Josh asked Daniel.

The thought of eating a burger made Daniel's stomach lurch, but he knew he had to put something in his empty stomach. He hadn't been lying about that: he hadn't eaten anything since breakfast that morning, a sad egg and cheese bagel sandwich from the local chain doughnut shop drive-thru. "Uh, no, no burger. Maybe mozzarella sticks or something. You got those?"

Josh made a note on his order pad. "Yep, one order of mozzarella sticks and a double of shrimp cocktail, extra sauce. Be right out." He disappeared to input the order for the kitchen.

Jody sipped a full glass of beer and Daniel realized, he hadn't seen the man order a new one, and he couldn't remember Josh bringing it over. Had he passed out for a moment? The thought made him panic slightly. It was one thing to wake up on one's living room floor still holding the car keys; it was quite another to be napping in public places.

"It's not so bad living in New England, especially near the shore, you know?" Jody said out of nowhere. Daniel couldn't tell if this was a non-sequitur or if he was continuing a conversation the cop hadn't been conscious to hear. "There's something about the smell, that smell of ocean air, that makes all the bullshit with the tourists and traffic and stuff worth it." He took another sip and looked at Daniel. "My family always went camping—there's a shit ton of camp grounds right around Bangor—but sometimes we'd drive up north, near Moosehead Lake. Never the ocean, though. Did you go to the beach a lot with your folks when you were a kid?"

Daniel thought for a moment. He'd grown up in Wells, not far from his house now, as a matter of fact. When he was little, his parents would drive out to the beach on Saturdays. His mother covered herself in Coppertone and dozed in the mid-day sun while his father, always wearing a fishing hat and cut-offs, sat in a folding chair and consumed Robert Ludlum novels and Pabst Blue Ribbon, so Daniel was left to his own devices. When the tide retracted, giant rocks that dotted the beach in clusters sheltered shallow pools of ocean water. Eight-year-old Daniel sought shelter between the stone walls, sitting in the sun-baked water that had trapped itself in shallow pools and digging for crabs and abandoned sea shells. He pretended he was a shipwrecked sailor looking for treasure, hiding from the native cannibals that lurked behind the boulders. One afternoon, he had misjudged the timing of the incoming tide, and a particularly ambitious wave barreled through and over the rocks, finding Daniel and knocking him onto his side. He had panicked as the salt water covered his nose and mouth and filled his eyes. The wave pulled backwards as suddenly as it had come, and Daniel sputtered and coughed, rubbing his eyes so hard, they were bloodshot for the rest of the day. He had caught a glance of himself in the car's rearview mirror on the ride home before dinner: not a trace of white was visible. The ocean had transformed him into the walking dead.

"Yeah…" he finally answered. "Yeah, my parents took me to the beach a lot when I was a kid. The 80s, you know? A dab of sunscreen and kids were free to play as they pleased." He took a sip from his glass. The whiskey was making his tongue numb, and he had to concentrate to keep from audibly slurring his words. He glanced about the room. The patio was only half full, but almost every seat at the bar was filled. He wondered self-consciously if he should move into the empty seat between Jody and him, if only so that a stranger wouldn't intrude on their conversation. Daniel still had investigating to do, and he was resolute on doing it, despite the slightly hazy vision.

Across the bar, a woman wearing a bright pink tank top over enormous breasts got up from her seat. As she drifted away, another woman appeared and took her place. She was blonde and seemed young—too young to be drinking at a bar, Daniel thought: at least, not without a damn good fake ID. The hood of her grey sweatshirt partially covered her hair and face. Daniel's view of her was obscured when Josh's wide chest stepped in front of him and the bartender placed a plate of hot mozzarella sticks and a side of marinara sauce in front of him.

As the detective drained the last of his drink and offered up the empty glass, Josh lowered his voice and leaned forward. "Listen, if you want to get plastered, that's none of my business. But you can't do it here in my bar, not when you still have car keys in your possession." He paused and his eyes searched Daniel's. "I'll bring you a water to chase down that next Jameson. After that, if you don't surrender your keys, I can't serve you another. If nothing else, man, it'll give your liver a rest." He shifted sideways and walked over to another waiting customer to take his order.

It'll give your liver a rest.
You can love her or liver.

Daniel looked at the eight logs of breaded cheese on the plate in front of him for a long minute. When he looked back up at the young girl across the bar, he noticed she had taken her grey hooded sweatshirt off. She was turned sideways, looking somewhere towards the exit, and Daniel saw there was something odd about her head. It was her hair. It wasn't blonde, it was a dark maroon from the top of her ear back and black in some places. No—he realized as his focus shifted—it wasn't hair he was looking at. It was her scalp. Her scalp was exposed, a pulpy mess of grey brain matter oozing out through the cracks in her skull, the back slightly concave and covered in dried black blood and yellow puss. She turned and looked Daniel straight in the eye. The whites of her eyes had disappeared, swallowed by massive hemorrhages. She blinked once, and dark brown liquid seeped from her lids and onto her cheeks and lips. She reached her arm out toward Daniel. She was gripping a broken dog leash in her hand, the end frayed and—

"How is everything?" Josh asked, stepping in front of Daniel's field of vision once more. He placed a tall glass of ice water and a fresh whiskey in front of the detective.

Daniel craned his neck to attempt to look around the bartender but found the action was useless. He rubbed his bottom lip with his thumb. Was he dreaming? Had he fallen asleep? Awake, asleep: it seemed like he didn't know the difference these days. "Good. Good—thank you." He pushed the glass of whiskey and ice away from him, his vision clouding. "I don't need this, but thank you."

Josh took the glass away without a word and disappeared.

Daniel turned to Jody, who was dipping chilled shrimp into bright red cocktail sauce and shoveling them into his mouth. "I… I appreciate your company and charity." He wrestled his wallet from his pants pocket, pulled out two twenty-dollar bills, and placed them in front of the pale man. "But I have to be on my way. It's a long drive back to Portsmouth." Before Jody could protest or offer him an incentive to stay, Daniel was on his feet and walking, with great effort on his part, toward the exit. When he finally found himself outside, breathing in the cool, salty night air, he closed his eyes and fished around in his breast pocket, fingering the folded note. He pulled it out and reread the poem.

Her destiny own.

He finally understood why he had been sent the mysterious package in the mail. He didn't know who had sent it, but it didn't matter, really. All of those sleepless nights had prepared him for what he had to do.

Daniel slid into the driver's seat and started the engine. The rumble echoed in the hush of the still parking lot. Keeping his windows shut tight, he placed the gear in drive and turned out of the lot and onto Mile Road, the dark strip of road through the marshes that led to Route 1, just a few miles from his house. As the darkness swelled around him on all sides, his headlights stabbing two slits in the emptiness in front of him, Daniel pushed his foot on the accelerator until he felt the floor beneath his foot. When he saw the shadows of the marshland appear in his peripheral vision, he cut the wheel suddenly to the left. As he crossed the double yellow line and drove off the road and into the dark green water, he closed his eyes and gripped the enigmatic poem in his fist. As his car sank deeper and deeper in silence, Daniel peered out of the driver's side window until the last slice of faded moonlight was swallowed by the marsh.

Finally, he'd get some sleep.

The Suspect

Jax despised weapons and this was a well-known fact. One of his most famous reports was an undercover exposé of the NRA and their corrupt methods. In fact, it was such a big deal, Jax received over a thousand death threats from Second Amendment enthusiasts. *Attack Jax!* people ranted in unison outside his office for weeks; it was a terrifying period in his career.

The irony of it was that the gun nuts' constant threats were what forced him to get a gun. Taking gun safety classes and bringing home the small Glock 26 and a box of bullets made him sick; he even cried on numerous occasions, though after he found his car full of bullet holes on three separate occasions, he felt he had no choice but to get a firearm. *Sometimes you have to fight fire with fire*, his editor at the time (a tough old lady who simply shrugged at the need for the office to have a security guard on staff for the six months following the article) had said.

The worst part about the whole ordeal was when an investigative reporter hired by the NRA found his carry permit on file. The next day it was national news: *Anti-Gun Activist Owns a Firearm!* There were articles, interviews, and protests, and both sides made demands; the anti-gun lobby demanded he give up the gun while gun nuts demanded he denounce the article he wrote. In the end, Jax ignored everyone and wrote an editorial about people not being able to make their own choices in today's society without harsh outcomes. It was beautiful and poignant and reflected all sides of every argument and made such an American statement about freedom that both sides backed off and disappeared (the media did, at least; the nuts on both sides kept it up for some time). To this day, Jax thought the article was his best work. It did get him his highest award of his career, the Edward R. Murrow award for journalism, which now sat in the box in the back seat of his car. Jax carried the gun faithfully on his ankle for over a year, then it went to his belt for half a year, then his car, then finally, to a lock-box in his house, where it sat at the very moment Jax stared at Connor's smiling face in front of him.

Jax stood, frozen, cursing himself for not going to get the gun earlier, but also for not figuring out what to do. Should he play it normal as if he didn't know the man was not a detective or jump inside the room and slam the door shut and call the police? The latter was the smart decision, but it was not the best for a story.

All at once, Jax felt the excitement of his undercover journalism days flood his nerves like electric fireworks and it felt good. It reminded him of the time he had a gun to his head during a meeting with the Roberto Mafia family head. At one point, one of the henchmen stuck the cold, tangy-tasting barrel half way down his throat, cocked the gun, and threatened to shoot. It was a test to see if he was a rat, but Jax was able to keep his cool. After the gun was pulled away, Jax spit on the ground, told the *goomba* that if he ever did that again, he'd cut his balls off, then laughed and shared a salami sandwich with the crew. After that, no one ever questioned him; that is, until they all had cuffs on their hands. Remembering that victory and how he helped to take down ten of the biggest mob bosses in Chicago history, Jax smiled and realized a kid pretending to be a detective was nothing in comparison.

"'Morning, Detective Connor. How may I help you?" Jax said with an enthusiasm that was noticeable but not uncalled for, given the situation. He watched as Connor straightened his tie and gave a fake smile back.

"I was looking for you. 'Got a few minutes to talk?" Connor motioned to the room but Jax knew that was too private, and he did not want to add to the blood stain on the carpet.

After carrying his bags through the threshold, Jax shut the motel room door and said, "Already past checkout time, we can chat here or go to a diner if you'd like?"

Connor looked around as if to see if the parking lot were a private enough place to get away with murder. This made Jax a bit nervous as he had no defense, coverage, or back-up like he normally would, but it was much better than in a private room. "Sure, this works. Just a few questions, anyway," Connor said, still playing the detective role.

Jax took a step forward to judge Connor's intentions. He

had taken countless body language classes, read books, and even studied with a few experts, so at this stage of his life, he had become rather good at assessing someone. Jax took that step forward to see how Connor would react. Connor made no movements; he did not flinch or recoil in any manner, making Jax understand Connor was not on edge or planning his own attack: he *was* there to talk. This loosened Jax up a bit as he hoped he wouldn't have to fight, defend himself, or run. The question now was, should he straight out confront the man or play along with this little game of detective? He decided to listen to the first question before making a decision.

"So, what can I help you with?" Jax said, trying to put forth an air of relaxation.

"The letter you got, did you feel there were any clues as to who the man contacting you was?"

Jax pursed his lips and shook his head. "No, not at all. I've worked with a lot of seedy people in my life, but none that screamed *crazed killer.*"

Connor just nodded slowly. When the young man, who Jax noticed had on the same suit from the other day, took too long to fire back another question, Jax grew tired and continued. "Look, I've done this a long time. I used to let things play out and let people hang themselves by their own rope, but I'm tired, I don't really want to be doing this, so let's jump like five steps, ok? Who the fuck are you?" Jax watched Connor's face carefully. It hardly registered any emotions, but he could see that the young man's breathing had doubled into quick, short breaths.

"I, I'm Detective Connor for…" he began.

Jax took a step closer. "Cut the shit, no Connor works for the Department. Who are you, why are you looking into this? You have two options: tell me the truth and leave or be arrested; the police are already looking for you, it's a felony to impersonate law enforcement." Jax emphasized the last clause and let it sit in for a moment, waiting for the kid to crack or run. He counted in his head slowly, with a Mississippi in between each number. When he got to seven, the kid cracked.

Conner let his arms go slack next to his body, sighed heavily, then lifted them up and ran his fingers through his hair. "I, I didn't mean any harm. I…I run a serial killer website.

Shit…" Connor, turned around, facing away from Jax, his hands on his head as if practicing for his arrest. The next time he spoke, he did so over his shoulder.

"Look, I don't want to get in trouble, I was just trying to save my company by getting a scoop on a serial killer before anyone else gets it. We are going bankrupt. There are too many competitors; information is too easy to steal. I have people who work for me, and I need to support them." Connor finally let his hands down and turned around, then, angering Jax a bit, he stepped forward and sat on the hood of the car. His entire demeanor changed. He was no longer the tight-walking detective; he was just some twenty-year old punk.

"See, we started this new part of the site called the Kill Tracker: every time a murder, attempted murder or dead body is called into 911, *anywhere* in the country, it pops up on our virtual map. At the end of the day it resets and that day's information gets logged, documented, and updated with the outcome of the murder. You can go to any day in the past year and find out who killed who in what state. One day we hope to make it world-wide. Last year alone there were over 17,000 murders in the US, and people get off on that shit. If we went global we—"

Jax put his hand up, the information was interesting, but he wanted Connor to stay on track.

The kid nodded. "Okay, sorry. Our site was kicking ass until someone ripped off our software. Now they are getting our traffic, so we are starting new, 'exclusive killer' updates." Connor made the air quote motion with his fingers. "We are sending out journalists, well, new writers, to investigate murders as they are unfolding and writing our own reports on them; it's much more in-depth and dark than standard cut and dry reporting. No offense. It's picking up and we have been hoping to be the first on a serial killer case so we can get back in the market. When we heard the details of your call, I came running."

Jax was a bit disappointed that the kid was not connected to the case personally, but he was interested in the technology the kid had. He took a few steps back and leaned his head against the wall of the motel. "How do you listen in to 911 calls? They are encrypted and it's illegal."

Connor's face beamed at hearing this question. "Technically, they are a matter of public record, so we found a few loop holes. Yes, we are 'hacking' into a nationwide system, but the information we are getting is of public record. Our lawyers say we have a great case if we get caught to say we are merely providing public information, just faster."

Jax wanted to ask more questions on that, but he really didn't need to know the technical aspects of how a computer program worked, so he shifted gears. "Well, look, kid…what is your real name, by the way?"

The kid looked confused. "It's Connor."

Jax raised an eyebrow in incredulity. He wanted to go on a rant and tell the kid to never use his real name if doing something under the radar, but he didn't think it was worth it. "Alright, Connor, what you are doing, playing detective, can put you in jail. Get the hell out of here, go home, and focus on the site. Don't go into the field: it's too dangerous. If you leave now, I won't tell the cops about you and you should be able to get away without any issues. Just promise me you won't do something stupid like this again. It could get you killed." Jax picked up his bag and made a motion to get into his car, but Connor still sat lazily upon it.

"Mr. Mathews, I can help you more than you can ever imagine. I have a network of intel that runs every single town in this country. I can see and find things that would take you months to even get a second's glance at. I can get you access to any location, I can make being a reporter easy as cake. I don't think I have to do anything to prove myself. I already went into the police station: I walked right in, went through every report, saw the pictures and made copies of every file they had on the case… *and…* erased all evidence that I was there. Not a single video or record of me being in this town, let alone in the state or precinct, will ever exist. This is the new age of reporting, Jax. Let me help you."

Jax was intrigued. He had always worked alone for numerous reasons, but this… this job he didn't even want. Hell, he was being forced to work on it. Maybe a little help could get it done more quickly and get him back to Maggie. The problem was what it always was: trust.

"How could I trust someone who has already broken ten

laws and lied and tried to trick me? This isn't some chat room game. A girl is dead. More will be soon and you can go to jail or get killed yourself. Hell, your actions could put me in harm's way and I'm not willing to risk that. Sorry, kid." Jax said this knowing the man was holding his ace in case he needed it, so he pushed politely past him and threw his bags in the back seat and waited for Connor to blurt out what he could really offer. As he grabbed the driver's side door handle, it came out.

"Jax, my team has already narrowed down where the killer lives. We've gotten it down to three two-mile radiuses and we have a list of forty possible suspects within those areas that we are whittling down and looking into. You'll have this done in a fraction of the time with me and you'll be able to get to your installation in New York before you know it."

At this, Jax felt his face flush, no one knew about his art, only Maggie and the dealer. Connor saw this and kept speaking. "You do this and I can erase any part of your life you want from the internet and create you a new life. I can help Jax disappear and the real Jackson live the life he wants."

Jax stared at the suit on the kid. Suddenly, it irritated him. "Get rid of that damn suit and meet me in an hour to discuss our terms. But the bottom line is, I'm in charge." Connor's face lit up like a little kid's as he nodded and started to walk away. Jax yelled at him, "Kid, I didn't tell you where to meet up."

Connor turned around and laughed, "You don't have to, I'll be there." That comment shocked and confused Jax, but mostly it made him hate technology, for the kid had to be tracking him through something: there was no other way he would have found him this morning. His gut tightened as he got into the car, not from nerves of the kid, but from both the excitement that he might get through this more quickly than he had anticipated, and the relief that he was getting out of this industry before it became something that scared him.

The Report
Omaha, NE

Quantico Forensic Laboratory
Marine Corps Base, Quantico Station, VA, 22134

FORENSIC REPORT

Client: FBI Field Office, 4411 So. 121st St., Omaha, NE

Client contact: Dylan Burakiewicz, SAIC

Police Reference   No.19/060658

Laboratory Reference No.   314-2874-767

Order Reference No.   495-5317

Forensic science lead: Anthony Santiago, M.D., D. Crim.

Number of pages: 2

RE: Unidentified disarticulated right thigh bone

A DNA profile was obtained from the reference samples of Eileen PIEDMONT (79826115) and Daniel PIEDMONT (79826116).

A second DNA profile has been obtained from an unidentified disarticulated right thigh bone with musculature and skin intact (JD257/1).

A third DNA profile has been obtained from the hair root sample provided by Eileen PIEDMONT from her daughter Julie's hairbrush (JD257/2).

All of the DNA bands present in the profile obtained from thigh sample are also found in combined profiles of Eileen PIEDMONT and Daniel PIEDMONT. This leads me to believe that thigh sample originated from a natural child of theirs. It is 25 times more likely that the DNA profile obtained from the thigh sample originates from a natural child of Eileen PIEDMONT and Daniel PIEDMONT rather than someone unrelated to them.

All of the DNA bands present in the profile obtained from hair root sample (JD257/2) are also found in the DNA profile obtained from the thigh (JD257/1). This leads me to believe that hair root sample and the thigh originate from the same individual. It is 53 times more likely that the DNA profile obtained from the thigh sample originates from the same individual from which the hair root sample was obtained rather than from someone different.

It is my opinion that the results detailed above provide extremely strong support for the view that the disarticulated thigh belongs to Julie PIEDMONT, the only female child of Eileen and Daniel PIEDMONT.

Comparison of DNA profile of sample from thigh through the National DNA Index System (NDIS) positively identified a match with five active investigations in Billings, MT; Monroeville, AL; Lexington, KY; Cleveland, OH, and Leavenworth, KS.

Piece #5
Branson, MO

Brent's smile snapped off the second the stage lights did. It was his twentieth performance of "A Miracle in Branson" that week alone. After grabbing the towel he had strategically placed off stage, he mopped his face and sighed heavily into the scratchy cloth: *Cheap bastards make him sing and dance countless hours a week for fucking peanuts and they won't even pony up for nicer towels?* In his dressing room, which was a glorified janitor's closet, he stared at his face. The red, white, and blue sequins caused a patriotic glimmer to shine across his scowl. Shaking his head, he ripped off the vest as if it were burning his chest.

Fucking Branson.

Sitting in the tiny, non-air-conditioned room, Brent went through the same thought process almost nightly. How the hell did he end up doing twenty shows a week that contained ten cheesy costume changes and enough sappy patriotic songs to make an Alabama-born Republican sick? He had a goddamn degree from Juilliard; he had done residencies at the Met, studied under the best vocal and movement coaches in the world, and won season two of *The Talent,* and yet now, he was performing in a show where attendees could use a coupon to get a free corn dog to munch on during the first act, drinks came in plastic cups, and the median age of the audience was 81.

A new performer would eat up the raucous applause from the audience who genuinely loved the show, but at forty-two, Brent was in the twilight of his song and dance career, and this applause did little more than depress him, especially when it was coupled with the pain in his knees and the nodules in his throat. That crap scared the hell out of him. One blown out knee and he was an unemployed has-been with no hirable, real-world skills other than a killer smile and the ability to recite over three hundred songs from memory. Popping a few pain pills, he finished his routine thought process and started to get changed. *Goddamn it, why doesn't this place have a shower?*

At his apartment, which was nicer than most he had had over the years (but only because it was Missouri and the prices were a tenth of those in NYC), Brent showered and then dropped onto the couch in a dramatic fashion. He snatched the remote and flicked on the television; *The Talent* popped on, showing a robust teenager belting out a tune like a young Mariah Carey. Brent threw his head back as if in shock that the show was on, even though he knew exactly when it was on and had purposefully tuned to the channel before leaving for the show, but for some reason, even alone, he needed to put on a show of disgust as if it were some crazy coincidence.

"Don't be stupid, kid," Brent said to the two-dimensional image on the screen. "You win it and think the world is going to love you. You'll do two U.S. tours with the rest of the cast, with you, of course, as the lead. They will try to market you, then force you to record an album you hate, which will bomb, and you'll end up in Branson as my understudy. Go at it your own way, not through a stupid reality show, kid." Once he had finished his monologue (which he had performed every time he had seen the show in the past eighteen years), he looked around the room as if waiting for applause, but he was met only with the beep of the microwave telling him that dinner was ready.

Throwing away the small plastic tray in the kitchen trash, Brent took a big sigh and walked out of the sliding door to his tiny balcony. He had picked the third floor to force him to use the stairs and strengthen his knees, which were starting to hurt more and more, but he also wanted a pleasant view as well. Instead, he got a view of the back of a Wal-Mart. Only a few sickly trees separated the small yard from the barren and boring back docks of the store, making it clearly visible and the only thing in his field of view. When he first moved in, he made the mistake of telling a friend it was the apartment complex next to the Wal-Mart. Little did he know, Branson has three Wal-Marts. *Got to love the Midwest!*

Brent held tight to the rails around the balcony. A soft whisper came from the broken trees: *Jump, jump, just do it, jump, the press will eat it up... former Talent star dies in suicide, it would make it on the front page of Yahoo, maybe even the crawl on the bottom of E! News or TMZ.* Gripping the railing tighter, feeling the chipping paint dig into his flesh like small flecks of shrapnel, Brent started to rock back and forth as if he were working up to a jump, but then he stopped and stilled himself. If he were going to jump, he'd want to leave a note or at least a Vlog to say goodbye to his fans, the ones that had stuck around, at least. He let go of the railing and brushed his hands together, and the microscopic flecks of white fell off and fluttered lightly to the ground on which he had just imagined himself smashed and broken.

Twenty minutes later, he sat at his computer and went through Backstage.com to look for any shows he could audition for—the ones he liked, which was pretty much anything back in New York City. He copied and sent five of them to his half-assed manager Nick, who had done nothing for him but get this embarrassing gig in the past two years. While he saw himself as a perfect fit for the five he sent, Brent knew Nick would respond with an excuse as to why each one wasn't right or wouldn't take him on. His excuses were tiring and if he were back in the city, he'd go and wait in line and audition like all the other nobodies. His fantasy was that he would be waiting in line for a new Broadway show and someone would recognize him, usher him inside, say he was perfect and then rush outside to tell everyone to *go home, we've found our lead!* In the back of his mind, however, Brent knew he was doomed to shuffle from dinner theater to dinner theater until he could no longer dance or sing.

After his searches were over, he logged on to his favorite social media site, Random, and checked his followers. When he discovered that his number had gone down by over a hundred from the day before, he snapped. Brent slammed the laptop onto the table before throwing it across the room (though purposefully at the couch, so it wouldn't be harmed yet have the same effect), stood up, and marched back onto the porch. He grabbed the small chair he kept out there, pushed it against the railing, and took a step up onto it. With one foot on the chair, the other cautiously on the railing, he closed his eyes and took a deep breath.

Because he was alone, social media was his family. His real family didn't give a shit about him and his string of lovers were just that, quick fucks here and there that never lasted more than a few times. His fans on social media were all he had and now he was losing them by the hundreds, daily.

"JUMP!" Brent suddenly heard loudly, and the voice was unlike the soft whispers of the trees he normally heard; it startled him and he almost lost balance. As he slowly brought his foot down to the floor, he looked over the railing in a panic. No one was ever out back, but there below him was a scruffy man smoking a joint and looking up at him.

"I'm just…changing a light bulb," Brent yelled down.

"Ah, shit, that sucks," the man replied. "I'm bored and was looking forward to some excitement tonight." The stranger's voice instantly sent a rush of blood down to Brent's dick. Before he could stammer a response, which would have been some sort of awkward line about coming up to hang out, the man smiled, nodded and walked into his own apartment on the first floor.

Sitting down, Brent felt his heart slamming. The man had gotten him so excited he didn't know what to do. Part of him wanted to run down and knock on his door and throw himself on him, but he looked like a tough guy, the type that initially seemed fun and nice but soon as you tried to find out if he liked men, he kicked your ass, spit in your face and called you names that would haunt you forever. Unfortunately, that tough ass attitude was what Brent was attracted to and it had more than once earned him a few lumps.

Not willing to risk a beating that night, Brent pulled out his phone and opened up Grindr for the umpteenth time while being in Branson, totally forgetting that he had been about to jump off the balcony a moment before. The quality of men sucked, but quantity-wise, there were more than he ever thought there would be in a religious mecca like Missouri. However, the vast majority were men on vacation with their families who had found an hour or two to get away from the wives and kids for a quick blow job or screw. This always amazed him, but he didn't look a gift horse in the mouth and if he believed in God, he'd thank him for all the married men who secretly wanted cock, because they fuck hard, were grateful, and wanted to get the hell out the second they finished, and if they ever saw you in public, they'd walk by as if they had never seen you.

One hour and fourteen minutes later, Brent was back in his apartment after a quick rendezvous in an animal-themed bar bathroom with a father of six who was also a pastor several towns over. Brent only knew the last part because the man dropped to his knees when they were done (not that he wasn't on them earlier) and asked Brent to pray with him. When Brent laughed, the man begged and told him he was a pastor and he could absolve them from their sin…as long as they promised God they'd never do it again. Brent, in his typical post-sex, pissed off mood, replied, "You're fucking gay and no matter how much praying you do, you're going to keep sucking dick in bathrooms until you die. Just come out to your family, they will accept you."

Brent turned and was walking to the sink to rinse out his mouth when the man screamed behind him, "Being gay is a sin! You'll burn in hell! You'll see, you'll repent, or God, or someone else, will make you one day."

Brent rinsed his mouth, spit, and casually turned around and said, "Guess we can suck each other off in hell then, because you'll be burning right next to me." The man started to cross himself and go on some sort of rant, but Brent wasn't having it and left.

Back in his apartment, Brent was fuming, ready to jump again, and this time, he even opened the hidden word document in his laptop labeled *Cheeseburger Soup Recipe.* Inside that was an extensive suicide note he had written over a year ago and edited over sixty-three times since. It was sad and sweet in places, and other times, the overall tone was vindictive and mean. Tonight, he was editing it from mean to nasty. As with every time he typed in this document, when he hit the last key, he planned on leaving it on the screen, getting up, and using the balcony to jump, but he never did. He didn't know why. Most nights he'd fall asleep drunk in his bed crying about how much of a pussy he was. That night was no different.

The next morning, just as he was about to open his car door he heard, "So you didn't jump?"

Turning around, Brent instantly fell in love. Matt. His name was Matt and he looked like a lumberjack from a high-end porno. Brent felt his throat dry up and he couldn't think of a witty comeback, so he smiled, trying not to look too effeminate. "I just moved in. My name is Matt. 'You lived here long?" There was something about Matt's smile that instantly made Brent melt and then feel at ease. The conversation started up quickly and didn't end until Brent suggested they have drinks that night after he got out of his show. That evening, for the first time in ages, Brent put everything he had into his performance and his smile was genuine.

In less than two weeks, Matt was spending most nights at Brent's apartment and Brent was happier than he could ever remember feeling. It was true love, love unlike he had ever experienced. Matt was a lighting technician on one of the Cirque shows in town and the two quickly bonded over old theater stories. They slept together that first night. Brent worried at first that Matt was in the closet and wouldn't want to be seen with him in public, but he was surprised when the next day, they went out for brunch and Matt kissed him in front of everyone in the restaurant. While Brent had been out since he was a child, he was still nervous to do such things in certain places…like Missouri. However, for some reason, Matt made those worries disappear, and besides, Matt was big and tough enough to beat down any guy who spoke up.

As things progressed and weeks turned into months, Matt moved into Brent's apartment and Brent had no memories of when or how he could ever have been suicidal. He still might have hated the smell of corn dogs while belting out a tune, but life was good with Matt. They even talked about moving back to NYC together if one of them could get into a show first, but deep down, Brent knew they were happy there and he could see them staying forever, maybe even running or starting their own show.

Everything was perfect, but then the sore throat started.

At first it was just a regular cold, then it turned into the flu and vomiting, but nothing out of the ordinary. At most, a flu would stop Brent from singing for a week, two at most, but he always bounced back. Not this time. This time, two weeks after his last vomit, he still couldn't speak. The panic was awful and he could say with certainty that it was the first time since meeting Matt that he was truly upset and worried about his future. Without his voice, he was nothing. Matt was more than supportive and did everything from getting him flowers and making fresh tea every ten minutes to giving him neck massages and driving him to doctor's visits. While the fear of not singing made him cry, the love he felt from Matt made his heart melt and made him think that even if he lost his voice, maybe he still had a future.

It was on his third week out of work, when the sick leave stopped and the pay ceased, that the package came to the door. Matt was at his show and Brent was sitting wrapped in a blanket, sipping tea and watching crappy daytime talk shows when a knock came at the door. It startled him so much he spilled his organic Throat Ease tea all over the soft throw Matt bought him last week to "cuddle and recoup" in. A string of swears came out of his mouth as he sopped up the tea and stumbled his way to the door. The last time someone had come to the door, it was a Jehovah's Witness that Matt got to run away quickly by grabbing Brent's crotch in front of him. The thought made him laugh as he grabbed the handle and pulled without looking out the peep hole.

There was no one there. Stepping outside, Brent looked both ways and caught a flash of someone going down the stairs. Realizing it was the mailman, he looked down and saw a small box between his feet. Brent instantly felt a warm tingle sail over his body. The package had to be from Matt: no one else had ever sent him things (to the apartment at least; a few fans had sent stuff to his P.O. Box). He picked up the small package and quickly walked back to the couch and plopped down.

It was the size of a jewelry box, like one for a set of earrings. Brent smiled wide: God, Matt was good to him. His name and address were neatly typed, but there was no return address; why would there be? They lived together. With a happy sigh, Brent slid a nail behind the four strips of tape and lifted the small box lid. Inside was a small note, folded neatly, typed in the same font as the address.

<pre>
         A girl whose status is unknown
           Pieces sent to a chosen few
             You now have her voice:
  Will you give it an audience or silence her too?
</pre>

The poem, or whatever the hell it was, took away the anticipation that Brent was feeling. It made no sense to him and it certainly was not romantic. He might have been slightly effeminate, but Matt would never call him a *her*: they were men and proud of it. Was it not about him? Not for him? Either way, he didn't care; now he was angry and going to open the package just out of curiosity.

Carefully unwrapping the tiny object inside, Brent noticed it was incredibly light and soft, if not squishy. When the last crinkly paper flipped open, Brent saw what he thought was a halved grape at first, but then he noticed it was more of a teardrop shape. The coloring was almost purple and it was dry and slightly wrinkled. *What the fuck is this?* As soon as the thought crossed his mind, he recognized the object from the countless hours he spent looking down his throat. It was a uvula. Brent did not panic nor freak out; he merely took his right index finger and touched the small piece of tissue lightly. In that moment, he instantly knew this was meant for him. It was a taunt-—it had to be—from a fan who knew he was too sick to sing.

Years back at the peak of his so-called "fame," Brent had a half a dozen instances of crazy fans: obsessive ones, weird ones, and down-right dangerous ones. Some sent him wonderful, expensive gifts (a lot of which he still had in storage), others sent homemade baked goods (that he never ate out of fear), art work featuring his image, and boxes and boxes of his favorite cookies. Then there were the countless letters, so many he had to hire an assistant to send form letter responses with a computer printed copy of his signature. It was wonderful and made him feel loved. But the dark side of that was the crazy people, the ones who would send him baggies of body hair they wanted him to consume so they could be "a part of him." The scariest were the hate mail. The anti-gay nut bags at the local mega church selected Brent as their poster boy for hate during the season finale of the show. They protested outside of the theater and threw pigs' blood at him as he entered (that clip made it to TMZ).

Fame was a crazy ride, but the good usually outweighed the bad. The worst part was, Brent could complain about all the attention, but once the adoration stopped, it was like a drug withdrawal: he craved it again. When he didn't get it…well, he became a miserable wash-up holding a human's uvula in his palm.

Theories and fears started to run through his head, one after another, about who sent it, why, and how the hell they got it in the first place. The little voice in his head started to scream to him again: *Railing, Just jump, So easy. You'll never sing again, it's a sign.* The depression kicked in hard and fast, this time mixed with fear. However, for the first time, he had a safety net: Matt. After slipping the uvula back in the box, he darted up, grabbed his car keys, and raced to the door. A phone call would not do and he knew Matt would lose his job if he left during the middle of a show. If he rushed, he could be in his arms in the lighting booth in a mere ten minutes. Matt would make it better.

Thinking of Matt's arms and his gruff voice telling him it would be alright, Brent smiled and raced down the concrete steps, the box in one hand, the keys in another. On the last step, he looked out at the parking lot towards his car. He instantly knew then that he would not make it to Matt. Four burly men, three of whom were wearing plaid lumberjack-looking jackets (oddly similar to the ones Matt wore), stood by his car. Two had baseball bats, another a small pipe, and the fourth wore a small white collar around his neck and held a Bible. If the last man had his pants around his ankles, Brent would have recognized him as the one he was in the bathroom with the night before he met Matt, but that realization did not come until the third hit of the bat. Of course he tried to run, but the men were big and faster than him, and yelling was useless, as he had no voice. Brent had survived more than his share of lumps from people who didn't like "gays" over the years, but nothing that required medical care. He had believed that something this bad would never happen to him, that America was changing and becoming more accepting.

He was wrong.

As Brent was lying on the ground, a whispering sob leaking from his mouth, he could feel something was broken in his right arm. The four men stood over him.

One asked, "This is him?"

The pastor nodded with sadness, then spoke. "Gentlemen,

I want to pray for this man, to help him see that his ways were wrong." Brent let out a hissing laugh—he couldn't help it—but the preacher ignored him and continued. "When I recognized you on a billboard outside of town, I knew I had to make an example out of you. I had to show you that our church and I could bring you back to God. Let us show you the light, son." The last line was said with gentle caring, as if the men surrounding him hadn't just hit him numerous times and weren't standing above him with weapons.

Brent couldn't help but smile; he was not going to fake shit for this man. Swallowing hard, he did his best to speak. "You loved my cock, Father. Just admit it: you're gay. Shit, I bet the four of you probably sucked each other off as you waited for me." Brent knew that whatever was to follow was going to be bad, but he didn't care anymore. A TMZ ticker exclaiming, *Former Talent Contestant Killed in Anti-Gay Beating* sure as hell beat a suicide report. His fans would come back, flood his funeral, post thousands of messages on his page, his album sales would skyrocket. He smiled, imagining this, and then, the bats came down fast and hard.

Brent had forgotten the uvula until he saw it there, spilled out of the tiny box a mere few inches away from his face. Staring at the tiny piece of flesh, he finally understood. The uvula was a trap. It represented the deep throat actions they did on each other in the bathroom. They put it on the doorstep to make him come out as they knew he would not answer the door for three scary looking men and a pastor. As the blows broke bones, he tried to recall the note and how it related to this, but his brain was not working anymore. Instead, he thought of Matt holding him and he softly prayed to a god he did not believe in…and asked that it be a slow news day, so that the media scrolls would be saturated with reports of his murder.

The Punisher

Dennis pulled the sliding bay window open, pushed his nose to the screen, and inhaled. The weatherman had predicted a "temporary return to summer" for the weekend, what Dennis in his younger years used to call Indian summer, and while brown leaves discarded from the maple on his tree belt tumbled gently along his still-green front lawn, the sun was already bright and the air felt warmer outside than it did in. His neighbors in the large blue house across the street had strung orange holiday lights and obnoxious, plastic spiders along the bushes that traced their front walkway: creepy seasonal decorations that appeared incongruous in the balmy New England air.

He plopped himself onto the worn sofa and nestled his Macbook in his lap. He had read somewhere that men shouldn't rest their laptops so close to their junk, that something about the heat or the Wi-Fi would damage their prized organs, but Dennis didn't plan on procreating, and at the age of 34, he was relatively unconcerned about cancer. He was content to spend most Sunday mornings like this: surfing the internet news, sipping his coffee, and eying from his vantage point near the wide window an occasional pedestrian. He had placed the box of Entenmann's doughnuts on the side table within reach but had forgotten both a napkin and how disgustingly messy the damn things were, but he was too settled to get back up. Instead, he tilted his head back to try to gather all of the wayward powdered sugar into his mouth and brushed his smooth but sticky fingertips on the chest of his sweatshirt before fingering the touchpad on his computer.

It had been two weeks since he'd placed the letter to Jax Matthews in the mailbox. Dennis had threatened to take action if the reporter hadn't acted within three days, and yet, the *Sentinel* site had been void of any mention of the pieces. Even the few AP stories about body parts popping up on Yahoo and Apple News hadn't trickled their way into the Milwaukee paper's website, and Jax's byline hadn't appeared on any story in the past week, which seemed not only odd but purposeful. Was Jax calling his bluff? Had he been fired from the paper?

His work as of late had been vapid and mediocre at best, so it was a possibility. Dennis scanned the trending story headlines, then clicked on one from the *Anchorage Daily News*.

```
The Point MacKenzie Sheriff's Office is
asking for the public's help in identifying
the individual who sent an unsolicited
package to a 75-year old man, calling the
crime both "gruesome" and "disturbing."
Sources close to the investigation state
that Tuesday, Bill Jensen of South Dairy
Loop received a nondescript U.S. Postal
Service box containing a pair of what
appeared to be human kidneys. Police
spokesperson Danielle Bailey refused to
verify if the package is the work of the
person wanted in connection with a series
of shipments of human remains to various
regions of the country. Dubbed The Hangman
by law enforcement, the individual is
believed to reside in the continental
United States but no further information
has been released about his or her identity
or motive. Anyone with information about
the package sent to Point MacKenzie is
asked to call the Sheriff's Office with
```

A shadow skulked by his window, and Dennis closed his laptop quickly and craned his neck to follow the figure with his eyes as it walked quickly across the street and toward the driveway of the blue house. It was the shifty-looking teen from the other afternoon: he was wearing the same navy-blue sweatshirt and walking unusually slowly toward Dennis's neighbor's white Honda. Dennis took another careful bite of his doughnut and ignored the shower of white powder that sprinkled onto his computer case. The boy subtly glanced around then pulled a long silver rod from his back pocket. He carefully slid the slim jim into the well of the driver's side window, popped the lock, and folded his body inside. After a minute of fumbling, the car engine started and the car quietly backed out of the driveway, pulled forward, and sailed down the street. It was out of sight before Dennis had swallowed.

The Hangman. He wondered whose clever idea that moniker had been. He imagined the group of agents gathered together around a large SmartBoard in the center of a bustling situation room, all of them sporting those dark blue windbreakers with bright yellow F-B-I letters printed on the back and one holding a big electronic pen and drawing a rudimentary gallows on the board. As each receipt of a body part was confirmed, the corresponding space on the stick figure hanging from the crude crossbeam would be added. With his index finger, Dennis traced the image he'd manufactured in his mind into the fine covering of powder on his laptop's silver case.

"Your little asshole media friend gone AWOL, eh, Big Man?" his mother yelled from the downstairs. "He probably doesn't even read his own mail, dipshit. Some lackey or undergrad intern is likely in charge of that." She paused. "Or maybe he's so washed up, he doesn't even GET interns anymore: he's gotta do his own grunt work and your sad, pathetic note is at the bottom of a pile of political mailers and coffee-stained napkins on his news desk. I mean, who the fuck writes paper letters anymore?"

Dennis quickly brushed the powder from his laptop case, erasing the image he had drawn. "Shut up," he whispered under his breath. "Just shut the fuck—"

"What was that?" Karen's voice interrupted his seething. "You have something to say to me?"

Dennis stood up quickly and tossed his computer aside; it bounced lightly on the cushion of the couch but did not topple onto the ground. "I said SHUT THE FUCK UP!" he said loudly, with enough volume that his voice echoed slightly off of the silent walls of the house. He stomped angrily into the kitchen and snatched a small plate from his dish drain and a handful of napkins from the holder he kept on the microwave.

And then he heard it. A soft but insistent giggling was tinkling from the bottom of the stairway, drifting from below and wafting throughout the room around him. "Oh, Denny," his mother laughed. "Denny, you shouldn't speak to your mother that way. You know better than that. And you also know what happens when people lose their tempers. Spontaneous decisions only breed problems."

Dennis stood silently for a moment and considered her comment. He weighed the delicate plate in his hand, then threw it as hard as he could against the refrigerator door. He was unsatisfied to see it break into only a few pieces, not shatter as he had hoped.

<u>Twenty-one years earlier</u>

Dennis arrived home from school as the sun was setting; he'd lingered a while at the soccer field to watch a game before making his way home on the IRT. As soon as he had let himself into the quiet apartment, he began his search. Dennis checked the countertops and peered into the refrigerator, scanning the shelves for any sign of a cake. Karen couldn't have forgotten, could she? She'd been reminding him that he was becoming a teenager for a whole month now. Admittedly, there were a lot of shelves to check: he was still getting used to the cavernous, stainless steel behemoth in the new apartment in Lenox Hill, the lower part of New York's Upper East Side. They had moved into the spacious home just a few blocks away from Central Park only two months earlier, and while his mother had slipped into her new role as media darling on an ever-expanding track to the national spotlight as easily as she might relax into an overstuffed recliner, Dennis was still adjusting: adjusting to a new school, to a new neighborhood, and to a new lifestyle.

Everything had happened so quickly. Karen had been assigned to prosecute a case against an armed robber who had held the convenience store clerk at gunpoint before panicking and shooting a hapless customer who just happened to saunter into the Duane Reade at the wrong time. It had been a slam dunk win for the state, but what pushed Karen into the forefront of the public's attention was what began as a random "slice of life" piece by an ingénue *Times* intern that was picked up by the AP and reprinted across the country.

Readers learned that Karen had been the only child of a middle-class, working couple who grew up living the all-American dream: she had a canopy bed in a pink-tinted bedroom on the second floor of a brick home surrounded by a gleamingly white picket fence Tom Sawyer might have crowd-funded to paint. As she recounted her most painful memory to the girl writing the story, Karen's eyes welled up with tears.

"I had just turned seven," explains Sweeney, "and my parents had gone out to dinner and left me with a babysitter for a few hours." The strong-willed lawyer pauses to collect herself, suddenly vulnerable and emotional, a side of the cunning prosecutor those in the courtroom never see. The next thing she remembers is being whisked away to a stranger's home, her clothing and a handful of her stuffed animals shoved into a few suitcases and pillowcases. Her parents, she learned years later, had been mugged on their walk through the restaurant's parking lot. Both were shot and left for dead, eventually bleeding to death on the blacktop. The criminals were never caught. It is because of this traumatic experience that Sweeney chose to study law and joined the district attorney's office. "It sounds silly to say it out loud, but I think a part of me hoped to someday discover the culprits and bring them to justice," she says, running a finger beneath her eye to catch a falling tear.

Sweeney understands that many perpetrators are at the mercy of their upbringing and home lives, but she doesn't think that excuses bad behavior. She says she herself was shuffled from foster home to foster home for a decade. "Some of the families were very nice: kind and generous. But not all of them. I understand what it's like to be hungry, to be so ravenous that when you finally have the opportunity to eat, you wolf your food down and make yourself sick… then you curse yourself for wasting the food you were lucky enough to have been given. Yet that's not justification to steal food from others," she points out. Sweeney has made it her mission to bring wrong-doers to justice and advocate on behalf of survivors because, as she explains, she's "one of the latter." This crusade has earned her the nickname The Punisher around the office, and with this latest successful prosecution, it is certain to be a designation not to be forgotten anytime soon.

The Punisher. The nickname always bothered Dennis, as he thought his mother's backstory seemed to align better with Batman's, but he supposed that her being a woman prohibited the media from tacking that one onto his mother lest the public be confused. The Punisher seemed gender-neutral, though Marvel fans might rabidly disagree. In any case, Dennis had never heard anyone from Karen's office call her that name, at least not until long after the news story had gone viral, and he questioned whether the title had originated with Karen herself. It didn't matter: just three days after the story appeared in the *Times*, their telephone rang nearly continuously for a full week. Journalists, television anchors, even a handful of movie directors—big names even Dennis recognized—wanted to meet with Karen and tell her story. Her winning streak elongated and the headlines exploded: *The Punisher Successfully Pummels Another, Prosecution Serves Just* Punish*ment for Repeat Offender...* instead of the criminals rubbernecking viewership, Karen was the celebrity and readers were regaled with her victories.

Being a public figure didn't translate into a lucrative salary, however; that is, until Karen sold her story to a network producer for a savvy price and watched it premiere as a made-for-TV movie in primetime. Before long, she and her son were mobbed by people in the corner market, accosted with case questions on the subway, and Monday-morning quarterbacked by neighbors in their drafty apartment building. She finally had the means to move into an air-tight—and sophisticated—place in the heart of the city, but her success came at a price.

Dennis shut the refrigerator door and on a hunch, opened the freezer. Sure enough, there was an ice cream cake, delicate and pristine in its clear plastic casing, sitting on an eye-level shelf. Without warning, a set of hands covered his face from behind. "Snooping on your birthday?" his mother's voice accused.

Dennis wiggled out of her grasp and turned around. Karen, still in her gray suit and ivory blouse, raised an eyebrow at him but her mouth was smiling. "Go get washed up for dinner," she commanded. "Quick, quick: I brought a pizza home, and I hate eating it cold."

In the bathroom, Dennis took his time washing and drying

his hands. He had closed the door, an action more out of habit than anything else, though he knew by now that a closed door meant nothing to his mother. She still entered without knocking, but at least the obstacle granted a two-second window of warning. He could hear her playing the phone messages from the answering machine in the hallway.

Karen, this is Doug. I was wondering if you still wanted to—
((BEEP))

His mother had erased the message before listening to all of it, a sure sign that it was from an unlucky suitor who had displeased her, or at the very least, hadn't kept her waning interest. The machine continued its roll call of appointment reminders and other dribble, but there was something about the strange, deep voice of the man who began leaving the final message that piqued Dennis's interest, and he shut off the water and stood very still so that he could listen to all of it.

Mizzzz Sweeney. Listen, you skanky cunt bitch. You think you're The Punisher? I'm gonna show you what punishment is. I'm gonna cut you hands off and shove them up inside your twat so that you're fucking your own dirty hole. I'm gonna cut off your lips and your tongue so you finally silence that bitch mouth. I know where you live and where you work. Don't try to run: I'm gonna cut off your feet so you can't run. You dirty, fucking—
((BEEP))

Dennis had heard his mother press the STOP button on the machine, but he was too engrossed in his own thoughts to notice her footsteps padding down the hallway. When she opened the door and saw him standing at the bathroom mirror, his pants open and his cock in his hand, rubbing it furiously, she erupted into a rage and began to scream. He shuddered as the thick, warm liquid sprayed onto the bathmat. He was still smiling as she began to hit him over and over.

Piece #7
San Francisco, CA

Everything had a smell. Lucille knew this now, even though the infomercial for the five-hundred-dollar air purifier she watched, mesmerized for a full thirty minutes before finally drifting off to sleep the previous evening, insisted differently. As she ran her same route at five A.M., passing the same regulars—the blonde woman with the knee brace half-jogging, half-wincing her way up 18th Street, the salt and pepper haired baby boomer riding his bike on an endless loop around The Castro, the aging hipster with greying dreadlocks and Beats headphones walking his tiny terrier—she drank them in through her nose. The salty aroma of the blonde woman, the garlic-tinged sweat of the cyclist, the mellow Sour OG hangover of the hipster: they had become, after five months of running, her security blankets.

As she passed Midnight Sun, the iconic video bar sleeping off Friday night's rush of sweaty patrons, and approached Hartford Street, a broad-chested man about her age walked toward her. He was wearing grey gym shorts and a faded navy t-shirt with an insignia Lucille didn't recognize, and as their unavoidable passing neared, she swallowed, clearing her throat for the obligatory *Good Morning* that friendly neighbors exchanged. He was younger than she had estimated, Lucille realized as their shoulders nearly brushed, and as he drifted behind her and she further away, she found herself surrounded by the scent she most closely associated with her freshman year of college. Her dormitory floor had been co-ed, and although gender-specific bathrooms were designated, more mornings than not, she'd encounter a naked man or two emerging from the showers. When the man in the grey gym shorts passed her, she had an instant sense memory: the dorm shower potpourri of Irish Spring, beer sweat, and testosterone. It made her feel young again, if only for that moment.

She crossed 18th and turned left onto Hartford, feeling the pull in her calves and hamstrings as the incline of the pavement increased. You had to be slightly crazy to be a runner in San Francisco; she knew that from the day she began the hobby two years ago. Although the area near her apartment wasn't as hilly as say, Cow Hollow or Russian and Nob Hills, where even a leisurely stroll could deliver shin splints in a matter of an hour, it certainly wasn't like running in Des Moines, where she grew up. In Iowa, the weather was fickle but the sidewalks were neat, even stretches of flat, smooth concrete; in Silicon Valley, the air was staid and constant, but every lap was an adventure in flat-track stair-climbing, with the occasional hop over a hurdle of uneven curbing. She turned left again onto 17th Street and circled back onto Castro, breathing in the stale vanilla and burnt toffee smell of Hot Cookie; it lurked like an awkward morning exchange following a mistaken one-night stand. The iconic bakery, squeezed tightly between the Castro Theater and a handful of restaurants, sold cookies and sexy men's underwear and was open until eleven at night; Lucille and Dave had often roamed there when they first moved to Eureka Street, and on one occasion, giggling, she'd bought him a skin-tight pair of red briefs trimmed with white piping. Of course, they didn't eat late night cookies anymore.

Lucille loped across the street and continued onto Harvey Milk Plaza toward Market Street. She spotted the silver trash receptacle on the corner and ran toward it; when she was within arms-distance, she casually dumped the folded paperwork from her back pocket inside as she passed, then looked up and continued across the open concrete. A bright yellow bumper sticker announcing *You only live one life! Do it!* pasted across a passing white Honda sedan irritated her: it seemed like an irresponsible proclamation, a billboard advertisement for hedonism. She had married, sensibly, right out of college at the age of 22, and as her 30th birthday rounded the corner, she regretted nothing. Sure, a few years immediately following her nuptials, she'd been out with her closest friends, all unattached and still reveling in the carefree single life, and she'd wondered, if only for a moment, what her life would have been like had she not met Dave. If she had not married Dave. If she had fucked Dave on the first date, realized he was Mr.-Right-Then and not Mr.-Forever, and moved on to more adventurous and therefore interesting cocks. But then she had returned home, and Dave was snoring peacefully under the goose down comforter on their ostentatiously broad king bed, and Lucille breathed a sigh of relief. She'd never have to put forth that awkward and slightly self-deprecating mask for the singles bar again. Dave was her permanent date to the movies, her slot-machine wingman at the casino, and someday, the father of her children. Stability was the ultimate goal, and Dave was her partner in the pursuit. They were like two police officers, sharing a patrol car, hoping like Christ that they wouldn't get called in to anything more serious than a drunk-and-disorderly.

Dave worked in marketing at a rising-like-a-rocket software firm in Chinatown. Lucille, luckily, had managed to land an anchor job at one of the local affiliates soon after they moved to the city. However, she was stagnating: without the freedom to chase down positions in another market around the country, she had no bargaining chip to wager a better shift than the lunchtime/weekend rotation. No one watched television news anymore; even fewer watched it at weekday noontime. Channel 8's midday edition's chief demographic was stay-at-home parents. A distant second were the all-night ravers waking-and-baking.

The format of the show was always the same: breaking news, weather teaser, three or four local news stories, another weather teaser, a sprinkling of world issues, a human-interest story or two, still another weather teaser, the traffic report, and finally, the full weather forecast. She never understood the unnecessary drama with which the station dragged out delivering the weather report: this was northern California— the temperature rarely dropped colder than 60 degrees or rose higher than 70, and despite the almost constant overcast skies, it rarely rained. But, Lucille—*Lucy Pedro!* as the announcer would proclaim while the camera zoomed in to her airbrush makeup-ed face each weekday—didn't complain: at least, not out loud. Dave made three times the salary she did. She'd likely be behind that anchor desk until she was too jaded to care or too wrinkled for the producer's liking.

With this thought, she raised her thighs extra high as she climbed the three flights to her apartment. She didn't look her age, she knew that, and she didn't intend to anytime soon; thus, the daily ritual of three mile runs and early evening yoga. She and Dave had found a lovely two-bedroom on the corner of

Eureka, a sprawling Art Deco multi-unit building painted mint green and grey with picture window views of Market Street. It was close to everything and best of all, provided plenty of opportunities to get additional exercise and walk to each and every necessity: the hair salon, the yoga studio, the market, even the doctor. They planned to start house-hunting as soon as they started trying for a baby, but Lucille was in no hurry, for the baby nor a new abode.

She shoved the key into the lock and turned. Dave had left early for work that day, and the apartment was silent. She clicked the remote on the television just in time to catch the last five minutes of Channel 8's morning edition. The peppy brunette who fancied mod-style dresses and hairstyles was reporting on a store robbery in the well-known, affluent neighboring county of Marin. She pronounced the name *MAY-rin* not once but four times during the report. "It's muh-RIHN, you idiot," Lucille said under her breath. The brunette smiled into the camera, oblivious of her gaff. *If you're not from this area, the least you can do is run your pronunciation of its proper names past your director or fellow anchorman before saying them for the camera*, she thought, and sighed.

It would have been easier for her to accept her career plateau—her *station* in life, no pun intended—had she not been surrounded by idiots. There were some days Lucille was incredulous at the thought of one of her colleagues having written a basic college essay, never mind graduating with a degree in journalism or communications. One girl, a morning anchor with wavy hair named Joya who sometimes stayed late at the editing desk to repackage her own pieces for the evening edition gave Lucille her graduate school essay to read over; Joya had earned her bachelors in English from some small state school in New England but wanted to attend Stanford for their prestigious journalism program. Lucille read the first page and honestly believed her colleague was pulling her leg: the document was full of misspellings, malapropisms, and grammar mistakes; in fact, it had more incorrect sentences than correct ones. Joya, crestfallen at Lucille's flabbergasted reaction, snatched her essay back and never spoke to her again, but that fall, she was accepted to Stanford on a full scholarship.

In her seven years working for the program, first as a

roving reporter and then on the noontime show, she had seen twelve other co-workers move up and away to more lucrative positions: in Atlanta, Los Angeles, Denver, even New York City, and all of them had had the combined vocabulary of a twelve-year-old. And yet, they were all know-it-alls, convinced that Lucille had no idea what she was doing or talking about. She didn't understand how a seven-year age difference could create such a disparity in education, attitude, and class, but it did. Her current partner at the desk, a smarmy frat boy with tousled hair and one perpetually raised brow, had chastised her at a company social four months ago when she balked at a comment someone made about having to pay back their student loans.

"If everyone just got together and, like, refused to pay back the money in a unified protest against the Man, colleges would be forced to lower their tuition, maybe even offer free attendance to in-state students," Frat Boy's tightly-bunned wife who had been resting her hand on her enormous pregnant belly suggested. Everyone in the small circle nodded their heads and sipped their martinis.

Lucille, who wasn't even a part of the conversation, just a passer-by, laughed uproariously. "Yeah, and the next time someone applies for a student loan, the rates will have tripled or quadrupled to make up for the loss deadbeats created 'in protest,'" she snorted.

To her surprise, Frat Boy whirled toward her and thrust a finger in her face, his cheeks purple with either anger or too much liquor, she didn't know which. "It's sheep like you who stop the world from changing," he said, waving the finger up and down like he was shaming a dog who had peed on the living room carpet. "Get woke, Lucy." He turned his back on her, and the five or six people he had been standing with laughed, not bothering to disguise their patronizing looks.

Lucille was flustered by the unexpected reaction and kept to herself for the rest of the party, but she played the incident over and over again in her head as she rode the subway and trolley home. She thought about it all day the following morning, and the next, and the next. How dare this twenty-four-year-old idiot condemn her, publicly dismiss her like she was an uninformed simpleton when he was the moron. She pictured Frat Boy's wife in her mind. She was young, like him, with soft features and a cherub face scrubbed squeaky clean. An angel. She, too, had been laughing when her husband had shamed Lucille. Suddenly, she was overcome with an irresistible urge to make them both pay. She had to teach them, those self-righteous imbeciles, that they were the fools, not her.

And then the idea came to her.

When she was a senior in college, she had been doing her best to study for a final exam in the library when she overhead two students talking behind one of the nearby shelves. "Dude, it was easy," one of them was saying. "You wouldn't believe what I saw." Her interest piqued, she put down her highlighter and craned her neck to listen.

"Wait: you used your own picture and stuff?" another voice asked.

"Nah, guy," answered the first. "I just grabbed one off the web, opened a fake email account, and added all this crap under a fake name. I can't believe it was so freakin' easy. And there's like, a million dating sites on there, and you can specify a certain area where you live and stuff."

The two men paused for a second, and Lucille was sure she'd been caught snooping, but when she turned to look at the shelf, she didn't see either of their faces, and the conversation continued.

"You know that secretary in Financial Aid? The one with the big tits and wicked butter face?" the first voice asked excitedly. "She's totally on there. And her profile's all like, *I don't mind a one-night stand with potential.*" Both men laughed and the voice continued. "So I hit her up, asked her to email me, and I've been sending her all these bullshit messages, like, *can't wait to meet you, what's a pretty girl like you need a dating site for?*" The man laughed. "I mean, so fucking pathetic: I can't take it!"

The second man chimed in. "So, you gonna hit that thot or what, son?"

"Faaaack, no," the first replied, drawing out the first word like he was pouring it with molasses. "That girl is nasty. But I'm gonna see if she'll send me some bank shots."

The two men drifted to another section of the shelves, and Lucille returned to her studying, vowing that if Dave suddenly disappeared off the face of the earth, she would never enroll in an online dating site or use a hookup app. She knew now that she would never be able to be certain she wasn't being catfished. It would be much too humiliating.

The day after the party, she opened up her laptop, and carefully opened a private window on Safari, she googled Frat Boy's name and clicked *images*. Of course, his network headshot popped up, along with a few candids from promotions the show had done over the past year. She scrolled down the page. As a public figure, Lucille was careful to make all of her social media accounts restricted and private; it was one thing to be recognized as a television celebrity at the grocery store, it was quite another to be stopped in CVS by a stranger to be asked what was served at the barbecue she had attended and posted pictures of the previous Saturday. Frat Boy, however, was not as savvy. His pages and their contents were open for the world to see.

At the bottom of the page of results, she spotted two photographs that were more casual and personal than the ones commissioned by the news public relations team. One was of Frat Boy with a long-haired dog of some kind— a collie, maybe—on his lap. Her co-worker was wearing a San Diego Chargers t-shirt and an unbuttoned flannel shirt and was smiling at the camera, his bottom half almost completely devoured by the cushions of a puffy easy chair. Another photo showed Frat Boy in a tuxedo: he was part of a wedding party, and his wife, dressed in a short black cocktail dress, hovered nearby. Lucille right-clicked her mouse on each of the pictures, selected "Save as" from the drop-down menu, and named the photos FB1 and FB2. Then, she opened another private browser window to perform another search.

Her inquiry of "dating sights for sex" brought up a slew of advertisements and pages of results. She opened and surfed through the ones on the first page: Ok Cupid, EasySex, DateMe, HookingUp, Seeking Arrangements, until finally settling on Ashley Madison, a website geared specifically for married people looking to have affairs. She scrolled through the basic instructions on adding a profile, open a new TAB and created a simple faux email account using Outlook, and clicked back to the site and created a lengthy and salacious profile for Frat Boy, complete with her pilfered photographs. When she was done, she leaned back in her chair and smiled at her work. She knew she would have to be patient.

That week, she was extra warm to her co-anchor, taking care to laugh at his jokes, smiling a *Have a good afternoon!* when they parted ways after the broadcast: somehow, the very thought of the profile and the public shame he would soon endure buoyed her enthusiasm. Frat Boy responded as he usually did, with a sarcastic, superior grin and dismissive wave. Lucille checked the account every evening before Dave came home and saw the responses grow in its mailbox. Just as she suspected, a number of the local respondents recognized Frat Boy from the news; his minor fame only fueled their interest. There was a sprinkling of barely-veiled prostitution offers as well. Lucille placed all of the emails in the profile's SAVED folder, and each day, she spent the better part of her evening, posing as Frat Boy, virtual chatting with women from all over the country. She carefully preserved each and every conversation, starring the ones that were particularly salacious and detailed. Her plan had proliferated, like a virulent bacterium left to fester in a warm Petri dish.

It had been fifteen weeks since she'd open the faux dating profile in Frat Boy's name. She began printing out photographs of the women with whom she'd conversed, jotting down details on the back to help her keep each girl straight in her mind, then filing the pictures in a manila folder in the bottom drawer of her desk. If a woman turned out to be only testing the waters—not a strong lead, as they said in the business—or ghosted, disappearing from the site without explanation, she'd crumple up the photograph and toss it in a garbage can during her run the next morning. Leading on his potential mates had been her only hobby outside of running and yoga as the season wound down.

There had been days when Lucille considered removing the account, wiping the slate clean and giving Frat Boy another chance, but then someone would remind her of the degree of idiocy with which she was surrounded. Just yesterday, Hal, the production manager who snacked on hard-boiled eggs and pepperoni slices all morning long in some vain attempt to quickly shed the fifty pounds he had stress-eaten into his 5' 9" frame, cornered her in the break room to tell her about his dentist's new assistant and suggest that she pursue a human-interest story on her and the practice. It was obvious he was smitten with her, but there was something in the way Hal pursed and smacked his lips as he chewed the odorous deli meat while mispronouncing the woman's profession as "hygentist" that made Lucille want to grab the glass carafe from the nearby coffee station and smash it into Hal's face. She imagined the brown liquid scalding his flesh, the glass shards embedding themselves in his cheeks and eyes, and she twisted her hands together behind her back to keep from acting on her impulse.

Then, Frat Boy appeared in the doorway. He raised an eyebrow at Hal's back, then sauntered, peacock-like, into the room and up to Lucille. "Listen, Lucy," he began. "Chi and I did this awesome piece on kindergartners and technology in Oakland. Hal says we don't have time for it in the broadcast, but since it's Friday, we don't want to let it get buried in the weekend show. So, we're bumping your cancer screening piece to Monday. Cool?" He added this last word not as a question but more as a halfhearted attempt to pretend to include Lucille in the decision. Chi was the newest acquisition by the network, a kid named Norman Chiganski who was straight out of college and sported a man-bun and black-framed glasses he didn't need for vision adjustment.

It was fruitless to put up a fight—it would be two against one, two hungry up-and-comers versus her. Lucille knew she'd never win the battle, so she smiled at Frat Boy and nodded her head. "Sounds good," she forced herself to say. She kept the same plastic grin suction-cupped to her face during her introduction of Frat and Chi's two-minute feature, maintained it even when the camera gave her a reprieve during the piece's run, and was still wearing it when the show signed off at one p.m. It was the realization of what she would do that weekend that sealed her expression in place. It would be the final act of her long con on Frat Boy and his smarminess.

Lucille clicked the OFF button on the remote control, and the smiling brunette anchor was absorbed by a black screen. She padded soundlessly into their second bedroom, a small guest room crammed with a futon couch and two small desks that Dave and Lucille used mostly as a study. She opened her laptop, logged into Frat Boy's adultery profile, and downloaded the conversations she'd archived on the website, including the occasional naked photo a woman or two would send along. Then, she screen-shot Frat Boy's profile page, including the photographs she'd uploaded, and opened a new private window. From there, she created a fake Instagram account using the name of the latest pen pal of Frat Boy's, a particularly raunchy gal named Lisa who listed her hometown as Dallas, Texas. Then, carefully and methodically, she uploaded first the screenshot of Frat Boy's account, then each and every lascivious chat conversation between Lucille posing as her colleague and the women who had responded to his ad. Below every photo, she hashtagged each employee of Channel 8, from the managing producer and each of her co-anchors to all of the camera operators and the pimply-faced college intern who had spoken less than ten words the entire semester she'd been stationed there. At the very end of the list, she included her own, real Instagram account and, of course, Frat Boy's wife's account.

When she was done, she sat back in her chair and folded her arms behind her head. This time, the smile on her face was genuine.

Two days later, and Lucille lay wide awake in bed as the first wisps of sunlight peeked hesitantly from along the sides of the drawn shades. She hadn't slept well all weekend and despite her restlessness, wasn't in the mood for a run, but she pushed herself to climb out of bed, pull on her sweatshirt and shorts, and stuff her feet into her worn sneakers. She returned home just as Dan was turning on the coffeemaker.

"You're up early," he said, reaching inside of his bathrobe to scratch an itch somewhere on his upper chest. "What time are you in this morning?"

Lucille pushed her shoes off and peeled her socks from her feet. "I'm going to try to make it in as soon as possible," she said. "There's a piece I've been working on that I'd like to see wrapped up today." She could hardly contain her smile. She knew that her millennial generation co-workers were vapid narcissists without exception and that meant they would have posted on and checked their social media accounts multiple times over the past two days. She had restrained herself from opening her Instagram feed all weekend: she wanted it to seem genuine when she feigned surprise at the posts when she opened them at work. She didn't know what to expect from Frat Boy: humiliation, social withdrawal, perhaps even resignation, but she knew it would be satisfying.

Sure enough, when she arrived at the station, the atmosphere was eerily quiet, especially for a Monday morning. Lucille wandered into the newsroom, tucked her purse into her desk drawer, and clicked on her desktop computer. The peppy brunette morning anchor with the vintage hairstyle entered the room, and without a word, sat down hard on the chair of the desk beside her and slumped her shoulders. Then she folded her arms on the desk and buried her face inside of them. Lucille glanced around the room. No one was talking. No one was moving quickly. No one was smiling.

She leaned sideways, toward the brunette woman's pile of bee-hived hair, and put on her anchor voice, evoking as much concern in her tone as she could muster. "Hey, hey…" she began, "are you okay?"

The woman lifted her head and looked at Lucille. Her eyes were red and her mascara was running in thin grey rivers down the side of her nose. "It's so horrible," she stammered. "Oh my goodness. It's so horrible, don't you think?"

Lucille frowned at her. "What are you talking about?" she asked. She had read the national news on her phone during her commute; she didn't recall any terrorist attacks, mass shootings, or serial molestations.

"Carter. And his family. The baby boy…" The anchor began to cry, the words sputtering from her mouth like exhaust from an old car engine. "He… he…" she stopped and buried her face back in her arms.

Carter. Frat Boy. Lucille stood up from her desk and walked carefully into Hal's office. The production manager was leaning back in his chair, shoveling pieces of spicy cracker cheese into his mouth with abandon. He chewed hastily and spun his chair to face his desk when Lucille entered. "Hal, what is going on? I've been out of the loop all weekend: what happened to Carter?" she asked. She felt her heart race in her chest; whether it was from fear or excitement, she could not tell.

Hal swallowed and took a deep breath. As he let it out with a sigh, Lucille smelled the sour pepper jack and pepperoni odor coming from his mouth and took a step backwards on instinct. "Oh god. Well," Hal said, his face blank, "They are pegging it as a murder-suicide. Apparently, Carter's wife shot him and their son and then herself yesterday. Neighbors heard the noise and called the police, discovered the bodies in the morning. Just about breakfast time, I reckon."

Lucille did her best not to raise an eyebrow. It was just like Hal to equate a crime scene with food.

Hal continued. "There wasn't a note, but I think we all know what prevoked this."

He means provoked, *not* prevoked, Lucille thought, cringing a little. She shook the annoyance from her head and put her hand on her face, an attempt at wide-eyed astonishment. "I'm sorry: did I miss something?"

Hal looked down at his computer and began to type quickly. "You must have seen it… I swear, I thought I saw your name on the tag list…" He swiveled his computer screen around so Lucille could see it. It was Hal's Instagram feed, his bulbous face smiling down at the two of them from a headshot in the top corner. "Just look at this shit."

Lucille leaned over the desk, grabbed the mouse, and scanned down the posts. It was exactly as she had uploaded, but somehow, seeing the posts from another person's perspective made her stomach churn. She swallowed hard and kept her composure. There was Frat Boy Carter in his Chargers t-shirt, smiling like the cat that ate the canary juxtaposed with a bulleted list of his sexual preferences and fantasies. As Hal's screen sailed upward, Lucille scanned over the array of witty banter and flirtations she had exchanged with women over the past months. Expletives and phrases jumped from the page like water droplets on a hot frying pan: *suck, God I want you, my wife won't, last night was, let's meet up, I wish, if only, fuck me please, fuck yeah, FUCK!*

Lucille backed away from the screen. Hal interpreted this action as one of shock or horror. "I know: crazy, right?" He tossed a square of cheese onto his tongue and continued to speak as he chewed. "I mean, guys are guys, right? But shit, I'm surprised Carter had time to sleep!" Hal emitted a laugh that was half-chuckle, half-hacking-cough. Then he cleared his throat. "'Course, it's a shame one of his lady friends had to out him. He must have pissed that one off good for her to place all of those conversations for the world to see. He must have been sharing them with her maybe, some kinda sexual hunting partner or something. That's what a lot of people here are theorizing." He fingered the sleeve of cheese slices pensively. "Or a damn good hacker."

Lucille smiled slightly and folded her hands together behind her back. "Okay, well, thanks, Hal, for letting me know." She paused, imagining Frat Boy's wife wielding a shotgun, pointing it at her husband, and pulling the trigger, his brain matter splattering all over white wainscoting like a tantruming toddler had thrown his bowl of tomato soup. "What a terrible tragedy." She started to back out of the office when Hal spoke again.

"Yeah…" he sighed. "Poor kid. He was a rising star that one. He was being promoted to the evening edition next week. 'Kept it a secret until the move was official. Boss likes, er, liked his initiative and screen presence." He returned his stare to the computer screen. "'Guess they'll be looking outside for a replacement."

Lucille's heart dropped into her stomach, and she swallowed hard to keep her composure. As she walked back to her desk, she clenched and unclenched her fists, whispering to herself under her breath. They had promoted Frat Boy? She'd been there three times longer than him, produced twice as many human-interest stories, and she had a journalism degree from Boston University, for Christ's sake. Where did Frat Boy go to school? Some Mid-West state college with a heavy focus on Greek life and football? The idiot had managed a final *Fuck You* to Lucille, even from the grave.

When she reached her desk, she kicked one leg of it in frustration, then, realizing how childish she appeared, she sank into her chair and booted up her computer. The brunette anchor was still sitting at the neighboring desk. "I know it's frustrating," she said to Lucille. "I mean, who could have known he had this secret life?" She rested her head in her fist and continued talking to her colleague, even though the latter had expressed no interest in pursuing a conversation. "Cute shoes, by the way," she said. "You shouldn't scuff them up with kicks like that: you'd be cutting off your nose to spite your face."

Lucille flashed her a polite smile and turned to her computer screen, pretending to be engaged in work. For the rest of the day, she did her best to keep her mind occupied, though at night, she wondered when the police would be knocking on her door once they traced the Instagram account back to her IP address.

Two weeks passed, and no one came to inquire about Lucille's involvement in Frat Boy's death. The network had hired a new talking head for the midday show, a chortling young man who seemed to be such a carbon copy of her previous three co-anchors that Lucille began to suspect there was a Frat Boy mimeograph machine hidden somewhere on the border of the Bay area, churning out clean cut morons with superiority complexes annually. On a Sunday, Lucille woke at her usual time, climbed out of bed, pulled on her sweatshirt and shorts, and stuffed her feet into her worn sneakers. She ran her usual route around The Castro as usual, passing the baby boomer biker and the dreadlocked hipster along the way. A beat-up Chevy with a bumper sticker reading *Get busy livin'* nearly side-swiped her on Collingwood Street, so she removed her earbuds and paid extra attention as she ran up 18th and across the Rainbow Crosswalk, scanning her surroundings for any moment towards her.

It was then that she saw it: a plain, USPS mailing box with a red postmark and meticulously typed recipient address, leaning against the wall beneath one of the windows at the corner Starbucks. Curious, Lucille ambled up to the package and picked it up. The box had been opened on one side, but the contents were still inside, stuffed hastily as if the recipient had opened the package, unfolded the packing paper, and disappointed at the items, replaced them and discarded the whole bundle without a second thought.

Lucille glanced around, and since it was so early, the only other people on the street were runners like herself, lost in their own thoughts and audiobooks. According to the address, the owner lived in Nob Hill, a posh neighborhood far to the north of the Castro. She fished her hand inside the box and pulled out the bundle, tossing the cardboard frame aside. It was a small box wrapped messily with what looked and felt like butcher paper. She pulled away the wrapping to find a plain white box, the kind a piece of jewelry might be housed, and a folded note. She opened the note first and read the four lines inside.

A girl whose status is unknown
Pieces sent to a chosen few
Action is yours; her destiny own
You're the only one who nose what to do.

A poem? Lucille was confused. She shoved the note into the slim pocket in the back of her compression shorts and looked around cautiously. *Whatever it is, it's fair game,* she thought. *Someone threw it away. It's not like a box that big could've fallen out of someone's grasp without them realizing it. And if it's worth something, well, fuck the fool who was stupid enough to leave it on the street.* She pulled open the top of the white box and delicately moved the cotton batting on top aside.

There, resting like an infant Messiah in a tiny white cotton bassinet, was a hunk of pale flesh stained red and slightly bluish. Lucille poked at the piece with her finger. It felt like real skin. On the edges of the strange gift was dried brown blood coagulated and caked to a crispy pulp. It was then that Lucille realized what she was looking at; it was a human nose, severed from the face.

She jumped, pushing the box from her grasp and watching it sail to the ground, spilling its contents onto the cement. The white cotton it had laid in sailed away with the sudden breeze of warm wind that blew pleasantly down Castro Street. As her eyes followed its journey down the street, she spotted the blonde woman with the knee brace a block away; she was running toward her. Quickly, Lucille snatched the body part from the sidewalk and ran in the opposite direction, toward Harvey Milk Plaza. It felt damp and gelatin-like in her grasp, like a dead mouse. She didn't know why she was running, why she needed to hide the strange object, but when she spotted what she was looking for just twenty paces ahead, she sped up, her toes only grazing the pavement as she maneuvered closer and closer to it.

When she reached the silver trash receptacle, she pulled the crumpled note from her pocket with her free hand. As she passed, she stretched her arms and reached both palms into the trash barrel to deposit their contents inside. She never stopped running, not until she faced the doorway of her green and grey apartment building on Eureka. She wiped the dried blood and sour smell from her hands on her shorts. A little bit of perfumed soap and water, and they'd be clean again. They'd be clean of everything.

The Bat

A mere six days after Jax received the first letter, fifteen body parts had been found and the national media was starting to dig into the story hard. One of the big three started calling the killer *The Hangman* because pieces were showing up one by one like the children's pen and paper guessing game. The nickname caught on quickly, with almost all of the networks using the title themselves within days of the moniker being created. An online encyclopedia page even popped up under that designation as some sick serial killer fan added it (Jax figured it was Connor), hoping to have a new legendary killer akin to the likes of John Wayne Gacy that they could talk about for years. Jax's name came up a few times in articles, but thankfully it was brief and only fleeting, really. It was just rumors and murmurs that the killer sent a letter to a "once famed reporter" that couldn't be confirmed as the investigation was ongoing.

The day after his meeting with Connor, which Jax, in hindsight, found surprisingly enjoyable yet terrifying (he had no clue how advanced technology was), he started driving cross country. It took a total of two days, with lots of stops and text messages from Connor (the damn kid wouldn't just call him, even when Jax insisted that he was driving and couldn't text), but Jax finally arrived in upstate New York, one of the locations that Connor had "narrowed" down as a possible home base for a suspect.

The night before, in a cheap motel two hundred miles from his destination, Jax had logged onto the "secure, dark" site that Connor showed him how to access and read the files on the man he was going to investigate, Hugh Tillman. Documents showed he was thirty-nine, an ex-soldier in the Army, dishonorably discharged for assault on a female officer. Jax was a bit leery that the kid's software could pick out potential serial killers based on digital footprints, but after reading Tillman's background, he'd be surprised if the guy wasn't on the path to either raping, killing, or mass shooting, if he hadn't already done one of them already.

Jax didn't bother asking how Connor got the man's

confidential military records or his sealed juvenile cases; he didn't want to know and even if he did, he wouldn't understand the complex layers of digital manipulation. He felt the same about Connor's "algorithm" that took "over sixty-one common psychopathic and criminal tendencies" and compiled them to determine if a person of interest had the potential to kill. It fascinated Jax, and if he had plans on staying a reporter, this would make one hell of an article. Jax pushed the ideas out of his head as he crossed into the small town of Ashland.

The southeastern suburb of Albany boasted a population of under two-thousand people. As Jax drove around its oddly still streets, the small shops and municipal buildings, his mind wandered to the case of Arthur Shawcross, The Genesee River Killer, who had enacted his reign of terror just an hour away. That man had raped and killed a ten-year-old boy and an eight-year-old girl and only served fourteen years for the hideous crimes. Once paroled, within days he was killing again—twelve more people before he was caught—never mind the burglary, arson, and other crimes he dabbled in along the way after being deemed "no longer dangerous." Jax's knowledge of this killer was extensive because he had been hired by a cable network at the peak of his career to be a "seasoned reporter" on a documentary series about the serial killer, The Midwest Mangler. As the expert, he had to discuss the crimes, go on investigations, and look into the case. The show flopped and was pulled after only two episodes even though they had filmed ten. While the gig didn't work out, Jax had loved the freedom and budget the show offered him to do research. He had learned everything there was to know about Shawcross, as well as other multiple murderers, because their crimes were similar in nature to the subject of the show. Arthur had received sexual enjoyment from starting fires. It was a thought that always stuck in Jax's head: *How could someone get off by burning things?* It was these kinds of questions that stuck in his head and created a rabbit hole of reading about serial killers.

For years, Jax read every book written on serial killers; he performed his own research, wrote articles, and even interviewed a few killers on death row. While the subject made his stomach turn, he found it fascinating at the same time, as he himself couldn't imagine hurting anyone, let alone eating someone or making lamp shades out of human skin. The research made Jax establish a series of mantras for himself, ones he often passed along to young journalists: *Never be shocked by what horrors a human is capable of; you never know what secrets a person might hold.* After encountering innumerable incidents of what he liked to call the "He was so nice" phenomenon, the one where after a serial killer is caught, everyone is shocked because their friendly neighbor was "so nice," he came to the understanding that there is horror everywhere in the world: some is well hidden, while some we just choose not to see. People have no clue if the soccer mom at the park is sticking things in her nine-year-old's rectum while giving him oral sex daily, a horror Arthur claimed his own mother performed. *There is darkness inside all of us,* Jax was known to say, *and more people choose to act upon it than any of us care to admit.* While the Hangman had not yet been classified as a serial killer, Jax's headful of killer facts told him Julie Piedmont had not been his first victim.

Turning down Tillman's street, Jax felt a bubble of excitement and nerves flow through his entire body. When he saw the dilapidated house, covered in trash, broken-down vehicles, and indescribable junk, Jax shook his head and wished Tillman could have been one of the "He was so nice" sort of types. A homemade sign made of plywood and red spray paint that read *Stay The Fuck Away* hung prominently from a fencepost; Jax thought there should be another that added, *Yup, I'm a Murder Suspect.*

With an over-the-top sigh that was befitting of a child looking for attention, Jax pulled over across the street from the house and turned off his engine. He pulled out his phone and took several pictures of the house, a few of which he zoomed in on various items. He sent the pictures to Connor in a text with a note saying, "Fuck you, *you* go up to this guy's door!" Part of it was in jest, but the other part knew knocking on this guy's door likely would encourage a news story on its own. Putting his head back against the headrest, he closed his eyes and slowly rubbed them, trying to release the stress of the situation. The drive had wearied him. He wanted to check into a hotel and freshen up before staking out some nut job's house, but it was too early for most check-ins and he had figured that a quick look would kill some time. Now, seeing a preview of the shit-show he was going to investigate, he was regretting this whole trip. And then, just as he was removing his fingers from his eyes, the explosion happened.

At least, it had seemed like an explosion. The noise was deafening and shards of glass sprayed his face. Jax froze at first, then dove across to the passenger seat and put his hands over his head. Not a second later there was another loud noise, though this one was more metallic in nature, and Jax thought he heard a grunt mingle alongside it. Jax peeked cautiously out from behind his fingers and looked up to see a filthy, crazed man wearing a white tank top and camouflage pants, swinging a baseball bat. *Really, could you be more stereotypical?* Jax thought to himself, but his snide self-commentary was immediately interrupted by raucous screams of the bat wielder.

"Taking fucking pictures of my house!? You think you can report me, make me clean, try to get me kicked out of my own home? You fucks didn't win last time, you won't this time, you mutha fucka!" The man slammed the bat over and over again into the car to punctuate his threats, creating flying glass and three thousand dollar dents. After hearing him, Jax knew it was a scare tactic and the man wouldn't hurt him if he wasn't provoked. Sitting up, a shower of glimmering glass scintillating then raining down from his jacket and onto the car's floor mats, Jax raised his hands to indicate he was not armed. He shouted out of the window.

"I'm a reporter, a reporter! I'm doing an article about how as Americans, we should be able to keep our yard however the hell we want. That no fucking neighbor or town committee can tell us how to take care of our own damn land; it's ours and we'll do what we want with it. I want to interview you and show the world it's your damn right to do as you please." Jax paused and held his breath. The batting cage was still. Jax put his hands down a little and looked out at the man whose chest was heaving up and down, the dog chains around his neck jittering slightly with each breath.

The man rested the tip of the bat on the pavement and leaned against the stick. He looked confused and almost disappointed that he couldn't be angry anymore. "Show me some ID, so I know you ain't lying."

Jax quickly pulled out his wallet and press ID for the newspaper. The man glared at it as if it was something that could hurt him and Jax wondered if he could read or needed glasses.

"Alright, get out of the car then," the man barked as if ordering him. He hadn't noticed that the press ID was for a newspaper half a country away, and this made Jax suspect that he had not in fact read the card, for whatever reason. Jax pushed open the car door with his knee and climbed out, slowly and cautiously, making a mental note to keep the keys in the ignition. Once Jax stood straight and planted both feet solidly on the asphalt, the man's shoulders slumped a bit.

"I'm… sorry about the car," he mumbled as if he were a child apologizing for spilling milk. In that moment, Jax knew that this man was not capable of The Hangman's crimes. Yes, this man was unstable; yes, this man would probably go on to kill and rape someone at some point, but he did not dismember and mail off pieces of a young woman along with poems. This man couldn't even read. Jax trusted his gut on this--he didn't need evidence to cross him off the list—but he was now in a situation he had to carefully disengage from in order to not wind up with his head split open like a melon on a side road in the middle of backcountry, New York.

"Don't worry about the car, it's a rental. I'll just say some kids did it," Jax said, but the man wasn't looking at him any longer: he was looking at his feet again, like a child. Both his bashful posture and the sadness in his face that had replaced the blind rage made Jax almost feel sympathy for the man, but he quickly reminded himself that he had raped a woman in the Army, so he pushed that feeling aside and spoke to him again, knowing that he now had an upper hand.

"Your house, how long have you lived there?" Jax said, stalling as he tried to figure out what to do. The man sucked his teeth for a second.

"Besides when I was in the Army, my whole life. It was Mom's, I got it when she died. She used to take care of it more, but fuck that, it's mine now and I can do what I want with it, I don't care what the asshole neighbors say, it's my land." Jax could see the rage starting to build in the man's face again.

"Hey, got any beer? Maybe we could have beer, sit in those chairs there in your yard and just shoot the shit for a bit. You can tell me about yourself and I'll write an article that will show your neighbors that you are a true American hero and don't deserve their shit. What do you say?"

A smile spread across the man's face. "Do I have beer? Does a bear shit in the woods?" Jax forced a laugh at hearing such a stupid line and put out his hand to make introductions. The last thing he wanted to do was share a beer with some unstable lunatic, but he figured he could close the case on eliminating this guy as a suspect and at the same time, possibly find a way to get him locked up for a crime he did commit so he didn't hurt anyone else. He knew he could use his car and the man attacking it as a crime, but he didn't want to get himself personally involved. He much preferred leaving the police an anonymous tip, and he enjoyed the thought of ensuring this first stop had not been a waste.

An hour and nine minutes later, Jax was leaving Tillman's house. The poor man thought he had a new friend and was going to be a local hero after Jax tricked him into a tour of his home and into telling him stories. Jax talked up the fact that he wrote for some "underground" sites that loved the same shit he did, so the man began to relax, bragging about having committed over twenty rapes and showing off his extensive illegal gun collection as well as an arsenal of homemade pipe bombs he had amassed, in case any of those "fuckers" from "over there" tried to move in near him. The idiot even let Jax take numerous pictures; hell, Tillman happily posed next to his gun collection with a giant shit-eating smile plastered across his face. It was too easy, but Jax felt good about it. After the local police received the photographs attached to an anonymous email, Tillman would be off the streets.

Feeling proud, Jax walked across the street to his car, which was beat to shit, and opened the door. He had to brush off all the glass before he could get in, so he carefully started to scoop it up with an old roadmap he found tucked into the door cubby. As he was methodically picking away shards, his phone rang. Looking at the caller ID he saw it was a rerouted call from his editor. Jax didn't want to answer it, but the man had obeyed Jax's strict rules to not call him unless it was life threatening, so the journalist stood next to the car, answered the phone, and picked at some of the gray paint peeling off in a dent. Before they exchanged any pleasantries, he could tell Declan was panicking, as his voice was four octaves higher and trembling. "Jax, Jax, I, well…the…there."

Jax felt his gut sink as he listened to Declan's voice; he had never heard the man stammer this badly before. "Deep breath, Declan: relax and explain to me what is wrong." Jax felt his legs getting a bit weak. He sat down in the driver's seat, and a few errant shards pricked through his pants, sending tiny shots of pain into his skin. He ignored it, knowing the pain to come might be much worse.

"Ok, ok. We have been gathering your fan mail and like you said, we have documented the letters and emails and filed them away. But this one, this one is too personal. I thought you needed to know. Want me to send a scan of it?" Declan asked. Jax could tell the man desperately wanted to be anywhere but on the phone with him.

"No, read it to me. Now," Jax said. Declan started to protest, but Jax repeated the word *Now* three more times and the editor acquiesced.

Jax,

I have faith that this letter finds you healthy and hungry for a good story. I was surprised to see you forgo the fame train on this scoop, Jackson. You should know: you were chosen for a reason; please don't disappoint me. If you do, you will have to be driving all over the country to pick up the pieces of your dear Maggie. The sad part is, I know where she is and you don't, so when she doesn't answer her phone, I know that it will take you days to find her. Meanwhile, I'll be starting a new game.

As of now, a mere fifteen pieces have been turned in, at least according to the news reports I've seen. I can't fathom what could possibly be going through a person's mind when they get a part of a body in the mail, can you? Why have some of my special deliveries not been reported? Surely the FBI has kept a shoulder secret or a pancreas under wraps, you know, just to try to keep some cards close to the vest, but the rest…it makes you wonder, doesn't it? I hope it makes you wonder enough to write an article, because if I don't see you post one—a damn good one, not one of those old fluff things, but a hard-hitting piece on The Hangman (not the name I would have chosen, but I like it)—Maggie's gallbladder just might be in Wyoming by the end of next week.

I look forward to reading it!

Get the facts, Jax. Don't forget what made your career.

Your Biggest Fan,

The Hangman

"He doesn't write the word 'Hangman'; he drew this kind of stick figure suspended by the neck on this T-shaped thing," Declan explained.

Jax swallowed hard. Declan's voice was drifting further and further away until he could barely hear the editor ask if he was still there. Eventually, Jax rubbed his jaw and swallowed. "Yeah," he said finally, then he thanked Declan and told him to send the scan along.

For the first time in his career, Jax felt faint and the need to vomit came upon his lips, but he swallowed again and it subsided. He glanced back at Tillman's house and wondered if the man would be interested in selling any of the illegal items he had.

Piece #30
Pittsburgh, PA

Marge hated her job, just as much as she hated her name and her hair and the ample layer of fat that covered every inch of her body. Marge pretty much hated everything. Someone once told her (ok, it wasn't a person, but an infomercial at two in the morning), if you don't like something, change it. It was a great concept and Marge tried desperately to change things the next day; she ate healthier, went for a walk, and researched schools to where she could return and finish her degree. But the quote stuck in her head longer than its inspiration lasted, which was about one and a half days. At eleven-thirty on the second day, she broke down and ate two bags of M&Ms ("*sharable size*, my ass"), cried in a bathroom stall at work, and went right back to her pathetic life, choosing to ignore her pain and misery until another low point cycled around, surrendering to the emotional merry-go-round that seemed to be revolving more and more quickly as of late.

It was during another one of those low points that Marge signed up for her latest weight loss gimmick, believing that losing just a few pounds would shed all the years of sadness with them. Marge saw the ad for Pound It! weight loss program on one of the worst days of her life. That morning, her car, which was almost the same age she was (and thus, harbored as much sex appeal), broke down in the Fort Pitt Tunnel. Every day for seventeen years, Marge had driven that tunnel. The long tube that burrowed through the mountain for nearly a mile was illuminated by only sickening yellow lights that made Marge tighten her stomach and hold onto the steering wheel with two hands; her knuckles whitened each and every one of the thousands of times she drove through it. Never did it occur to her how awful it would be to break down in the middle.

Almost exactly halfway through, her car sputtered, its interior lights flashed, and the engine died with one loud, farting gasp. Smoke billowed from under its scratched and sun-faded hood and the old machine stopped working. Worst of all, she was in the left lane and no one would let her over to the right as she coasted to a full stop. Fear set in when the first car almost hit her and honked obnoxiously as if the driver really thought she just wanted to stop and admire the beauty of the tunnel walls. It took less than three minutes for the entire tunnel to clog up as she sat in the driver's seat having no clue what to do.

Being in the dead center of the tunnel, Marge had no cell service and there was nowhere to push the car to so that she might get out of the way. Car after car honked, people screamed at her, and she just sat there. At one point, she got out and stood behind the car to try and wave people around her, doing her best to be the people-pleaser she'd always tried to be. The exhaust fumes and heat of the tunnel were overpowering, and she broke out in a sweat as she made her best apologetic face and waved cars by.

Not a single person stopped and offered to help. Most still honked, a few yelled, and then one middle aged, balding and chubby man rolled down his window as he moved slowly around her. Her heart momentarily swelled with joy as she believed he intended to offer help, but instead, his face scrunched up and turned a sickly reddish purple, and he screamed at her in a rough guttural yell, "I'm fucking late for work because of you, you disgusting, fat fucking cunt." Before Marge could attempt a reply, a large, very full, very hot, Pumpkin Spice coffee from Dunkin' Donuts slammed into her chest. It burst into such a brilliant explosion that it perfectly coated her entire face and torso. The smell wafted to her nose, and she briefly thought it was too early in the season to be enjoying such a flavor, but then the scalding started and the thought disappeared from her mind.

For the next twenty minutes, Marge sat sobbing in her car, her head down and her wet shirt sticking to her rolls of fat; she wanted to die. When the police officer arrived, she was, at first, relieved. But then he turned out to be a dick who seemed genuinely annoyed that he had to help her. In fact, he didn't help her at all: he merely gave her a three-hundred-dollar ticket for causing traffic and not moving her car. Marge didn't bother to argue with him; she was too relieved that he called for a tow truck, which arrived ten minutes after that. She could have been wrong, but she could have sworn she heard the cop tell the driver, "If she was a hundred pounds lighter and twenty years younger, someone would have helped her and I wouldn't have to be dealing with this shit."

The tow truck driver didn't talk to her the entire drive other than to gather her information. When they emerged from the tunnel, an hour after she was supposed to be at her desk job, she had enough service to get the three messages from her boss that said if she wasn't there in thirty minutes she was going to be fired. When she called to explain her situation, he instructed her to take the day off and to come in the next day "to discuss her future at the company." Between the ticket and the tow and the disposing of her vehicle because it was beyond repair, the day cost her over a thousand dollars and she worried that she would soon be losing her job on top of having to finance a new car.

By early afternoon she was heading back to her apartment on the PGH; she hadn't ridden the bus since she was a teen, yet the faint potpourri of piss and disinfectant hadn't changed in all those years. As the bus made its many stops, Marge did her best to blend in and disappear, which was difficult, as she smelled like she had bathed in a pumpkin spiced frappe and looked as if she'd thrown up on herself. As her fellow passengers avoided her, Marge thought of ways to kill herself. The thought of ending it all had always been there, but typically, it had resided in the far reaches of her mind, like a secret escape plan to be used only in an emergency. That day was that emergency. She was humiliated and without a car, and now broke and possibly without a job: what the fuck did she have left? That was when she saw the advertisement, pasted brightly and beautifully on the back of a bus stop bench.

At first, it didn't look any different than any of the millions of weight loss ads she had seen and fell for in her life. It featured a fat woman looking sad, standing next to the smiling, skinny version of herself, the number of pounds she lost proudly proclaimed in big, excited letters. *118!* The logo for Pound It! ran next to the two versions of the woman along with the slogan, *A Unique and Different Way to Lose Weight!!!* There were not one but three exclamations points, so it had to be important. What made this display stand out from the millions of other ads was that Marge knew the woman. It was her old roommate, someone who had always been fatter and more pathetic then her. Truth be told, that was why Marge had found her to be a good roommate: Carol's misery made Marge feel better. The "after" picture of Carol was shocking. The woman who never had weighed less than two hundred and fifty pounds in the four years she had lived with Marge now looked like a damn fitness model.

With haste, Marge pulled out her old flip phone, opened her camera, and took a photo of the ad. Marge didn't want to wait until she got home to look up Carol on Facebook, but she was already over her data plan for the month and her ancient phone, which was likely to die like her car any day, was awful at surfing the web. The rest of the thirty-minute ride, Marge forgot about the day's tribulations and instead thought about Carol. If Carol could do it, *she* could too.

That night, after three showers (she couldn't get that goddamn pumpkin smell out of her nose) and a load of laundry, Marge logged onto her computer. While she needed to book a rental car and figure out her finances to see if she even could afford a car, she found herself googling Carol before anything else. Sure enough, there on Carol's Facebook page was a gleaming shot of her once fat friend's new-found abs. For over an hour, Marge poured over every picture and a post of Carol's for the past two years. She learned that her former roommate had lost the weight in the past year and adamantly praised Pound It! for her success. After a while, Marge decided to email Carol. It took her fourteen drafts—some were pages long, others just a paragraph or two—but finally, she settled on a simple email that praised her weight loss and said how proud she was of her. It made Marge nervous sending it, but by dinner time, she had hit Send.

Before she'd finished microwaving that night's meal, a Hungry Man Salisbury Steak Dinner (two of them, actually), she received a reply from a very excited Carol. After six emails back and forth, Marge agreed to meet with Carol for lunch on the weekend to catch up, but mostly to talk about getting on the program; as luck would have it, Carol was now a recruiter for Pound It!. The rest of that night, Marge spent debating her car situation and making sure to put her mind in the right place for work the next day; she was going to have to play the pity card and suck up to her boss. Despite dreading this certain humiliation, Marge went to bed happy: the thoughts of the razor knife in the back of her medicine cabinet and how she could use it had disappeared.

The next day, Marge picked up her rental car and got to work early. Her boss was "on the fence" about firing her, but he gave her a second chance; she would have to stay late for the next two weeks to make up for the hours she missed. The thought of answering calls from angry customers who couldn't get their cable working for an extra ten hours made her stomach turn, but at least she still had a job. Getting a new car was going to screw her financially, but having no job would have been the end of it all, even if she did hate the fucking thing.

The next few days were slow and monotonous, but every free second she had, she looked up Carol's pictures and imagined embodying her physique. If she had a new body, she'd have more confidence, she could get a better job, find a man, and finally, not be the hag who lived in the shitty apartment. Maybe her life wouldn't end sad and pathetic without anyone in the world even knowing she was gone; maybe this was going to be her second chance. Just in case she would be starting the diet that weekend, Marge doubled her intake of junk food for a few days, making her stomach hurt and her need for a bathroom break more frequent, but in her mind, just like before every diet, she needed to have "one last hoorah."

In her and Carol's relationship, Marge always had been the leader. She was the one who wasn't as shy, the one who pushed Carol to do things, and the one who acted with confidence, yet seeing her friend now, simply because Carol had lost weight, Marge was terrified. However, after the long hug Carol gave her at the Vegan House—a restaurant Carol had chosen—Marge felt at ease and in awe of the woman she once considered a sister. They caught up quickly, laughing uproariously at their reminiscences, and Marge was happy for the first time in ages and wondered why she had shut out all her old friends over the past few years. When their salads, which looked like plates of garnish to Marge, came out, it was time to talk about the diet and Carol's transformation. Marge was hesitant, but Carol put her at ease as if she sensed what Marge was thinking.

Reaching across the table, Carol took Marge's hand and spoke. "You know, I understand everything you are thinking and feeling right now. I was you, but bigger and more ashamed, until a year ago. Look, you are doing this, I will coach you and in a few months, you and I will take our new sexy bodies to Vegas to get laid and party. I promise you *can* do this and you *will* do this."

Marge instantly blushed and started to tear up. "I want that more than anything… I, I can't be like this anymore. I just can't, but, how much does it cost? I hate to admit it, but I'm broke, so broke I'm going to have to charge this lunch."

Carol smiled and shook her head back and forth. "It will cost you nothing, not a dime. In fact, you will save money as the program will provide you food. Normally, it costs a shitload of money—it's very intensive—but twice a year, they take someone like you or me to use for their ads and they cover the price."

Marge had no words. She didn't know how to respond.

"Trust me," Carol continued. "I thought it was a gimmick too, but look at me. I'm proof and you know what, all that shit we think about losing weight changing our lives, like we always talked about: it's true. I have a boyfriend for the first time in years, I got a raise at work, and I'm a spokesman for the company which gives me a few thousand extra a month. I never thought I'd be this happy."

Marge smiled and a tear spilled out of her eye. She was the happiest she'd been in over a year.

That night, Marge sat at her kitchen table and read the extensive paperwork. In order to sign up and to become a spokesperson, she had to sign an eighty-seven-page contract, ninety percent of which she did not read. It was extensive and confusing, but she trusted Carol and did what she was told; it was going to be worth it. The basic principles of the program scared her a bit, though: they seemed a bit intrusive and really, Pound It! reminded her of a story she had read when she was young. She knew it was by Stephen King, but she couldn't recall the title; in it was a man who wanted to quit smoking, and the company he hired followed him and threatened to beat up his son or torture his wife or something if he picked up a cigarette. Carol had said they would follow her and make sure she didn't eat, and that made her think that maybe the methods of Pound It! were based off King's story, but in the end, she didn't care from where they'd received their inspiration, as long as the program worked.

The orientation the next day was five hours long and intense. She learned that someone would show up at her door and force her to work out, twice a day, every day for the next year. If she refused one work out, she would get a bill from the company; with each additional missed workout, the bill would increase. If she didn't pay, they would garnish her wages at work—she had signed to allow this in the contract. This level of commitment scared Marge a little: working out was something she had always been too tired or depressed to do, but since she was broke, the financial incentive might overpower any of those negative feelings: she would be too scared to ever miss a day.

Pound It! would also search every inch of her apartment to make sure there was no fattening food hiding anywhere; they would remove everything edible on the first day of the program and she would only be allowed to eat what they sent to her house from that day forward. They promised to visit unannounced to spot check for unauthorized food in the house and to watch her when she was in public and again, if they found anything or spotted her eating anything outside of what they had shipped to her, they'd bill her. Marge thought it was genius, really. People pay for gyms and diet pills, equipment and fad food, but that doesn't push anyone to *use* them; a punishment definitely would. Besides, the amount she'd spent over the years on diet crap would probably be less than any fines she did amass should she backslide.

The only thing that seemed odd to Marge was the clause about the "motivational" surprises she would receive. Carol was very vague about this, saying it was best to keep them secret, but she did state that it was possible that out of nowhere, someone would take her on a life-changing experience or she might receive a gift that would make her second guess why she ate bad all of her life. Whatever was going to happen, Marge was excited, more excited than she had been in decades. For the first time in her adult life, she had something to look forward to and a goal to work towards. Day one hadn't even begun, but already, her mood was better than it had been in ages.

Three weeks later, Marge had never felt so tired, sore, or happy in her life. She had already lost fourteen pounds and people were noticing her transformation left and right. Pound It! was documenting her progress with pictures and video diaries and the online presence made her feel like a star; she had never received such attention. It was hard not eating her usual stuff, but the positive comments she received more than made up for her cravings. Her dreams were coming true, just like Carol promised. Sure, there were a few scary moments and weak times, but she had yet to earn a fine and the lack of privacy had been worth the results. So far, they had surprised her three times. Once, when she was walking out of work, two people showed up: one to take her car home for her and the other to ride a bike next to her as they made her walk the twenty miles home. She thought she was going to die, but every five miles, they held a mini-celebration with other Pound It! members cheering her on and balloons and all sorts of fun things. When she finished, she had never cried so much or had been as proud as she was. The second time, a woman jumped out at her on her morning walk and quizzed her about nutrition for an hour straight. The third time, in the middle of the night, her room suddenly filled with light and three people came into her room (she was required to give the company a key) and woke her up to watch a movie about heart attacks. The film was graphic and scary, and, if Marge were honest, this incident was the only time she seriously considered quitting, but after the representatives left and let her go back to sleep, she realized how much the film made her never want to eat bad shit again and she reclaimed her motivation.

The food that arrived daily wasn't bad, either. Sure, it was boring like any health food, but she got used to it quickly and it was nice not having to worry about what to eat when. Every other day, an extra package would arrive with some sort of motivational thing: a stress ball, a scale for food, a book, a motivational sign, all sorts of stuff. It was exciting and Marge loved every minute of it, but one of the packages confused her more than anything else. Although she was initially confused about its meaning, she maintained faith that Pound It! had sent it for a very special reason.

Unlike the other packages, this one arrived in a plain white box, not in the bright green with the Pound It! logo printed on the side, but it had to be from them: it was sitting right on top of her daily meal box when she opened her door that morning. After she carried the boxes inside, she quickly opened the food ones and stacked the containers in the refrigerator, leaving her morning meal on the counter. That day's selection was her least favorite, a "breakfast salad," two words Marge thought should never go together. After that, she turned her attention back to the white box.

Using a butter knife, she cut the packing tape and opened the mysterious delivery. It was such a small box that she knew it wasn't a poster or book like she'd received in the past: *Maybe a necklace?* she hoped. Whatever the gift was, it was surrounded by white, waxy paper, and taped to its top was a note. Marge's stomach tightened a bit with excitement. Perhaps it was a reward for hitting twenty-five pounds! She unfolded the note and saw that it contained only an odd poem of only four lines in length.

> A girl whose status is unknown
> Pieces sent to a chosen few
> Action is yours; her destiny own
> One of ten digits to count, it's now up to you.

Marge hated poetry and couldn't decipher the short verse's meaning, but she assumed it made sense to whoever had written it or to someone who had taken more English classes than her. Three more times she read it, trying to discern the connection it had to her weight loss. Obviously, a digit had to do with the numbers on her scale, but if that was the case, she had lost more than ten. Letting the mystery wash over her a bit more, she waited to unwrap the paper until the poem started to hurt her head. Finally, she shrugged and grabbed the waxy paper and began to unroll it. It felt cool, but that could have been because it had been sitting on top of the cold box of food on her doorstep. After unwinding three layers and opening the even smaller box inside, she let out a scream and then laughed loudly at what she saw sitting on a bed of cotton batting: a big, human toe painted with bright pink nail polish.

Marge looked around the room and waited for the punchline. It was as if any moment, someone was going to barge in and let her in on the joke. Squinting, she pulled the toe closer to her face to get a better look at it. The appendage looked so real, she couldn't believe it. The toe's nail polish was slightly chipped and there were even a few tiny imperfections in the skin.

Marge laughed out loud to herself, realizing where they must have gotten the toe: Tom Savini, the legendary special effects make-up artist, lived on the other side of the city and had owned a world-renowned make-up school nearby. Pound It! must have had one of the students make it. She had driven by Tom's house as a teenager because a boyfriend of hers had been obsessed with him; she considered the memory, then shook it out of her mind and tried again to deconstruct the nebulous poem and figure out what she was supposed to do with the toe.

A girl whose status is unknown.

That must refer to her; the status of her weight loss and whether she would keep it up could be considered unknown. But what does the "pieces sent to a chosen few" mean? *Wait*, she thought. In the King story, the wife lost a finger to motivate the husband to stay on his healthy path. The toe delivery had to be connected to that; after all, she *had* thought their company's methodology was inspired by the story.

Marge set the toe on the counter and began to eat her salad absentmindedly. *Action is yours; her destiny own.* That made sense; her destiny was her own and the actions she did were her choice. Ten digits… ten chances? Marge finished her salad, cleaned the counter and picked up the toe with her fingers. Christ, it felt real. She was going to have to post on Facebook about how amazing Tom's students were later.

It's now up to you.

The last line echoed in her head. It was up to her to change her own life and she needed to be selfless about it. Like the wife in the King story who had sacrificed a finger to help her husband, Marge had to help inspire someone and be selfless before she could ever truly help herself. That had to be it. Marge felt a wave of pride and empowerment come over her as she realized what she had to do.

She got dressed and started to head out the door but stopped in her tracks. She returned to the kitchen where she opened the junk drawer and dug around until she found an old key chain ring and a thin piece of cloth ribbon she'd saved from some forgotten gift. She grabbed the toe and the string, carefully tied a tight knot around the toe, then tied the other end of the ribbon to the key chain. After a few seconds of finagling, the toe successfully hung from her key chain. Finally, she attached her own house keys to the new charm.

Marge's smile spread across her face. Sure, it was morbid, but hell, people carried rabbits' feet on their keys. What mattered most was that she knew it would serve as a reminder to always give a part of herself to everyone else, because she was worth it.

The Visitor

Thirteen years earlier

Dennis stretched his legs as far as he could, pointing his toes so that his feet dipped below the seat in front of him. Usually, he appreciated Professor Habermehl's classes; he had enrolled in the course, Critical Analysis of Western Mythology and Folklore, his senior year because he had a few electives to burn, and even though he'd already fulfilled his Humanities requirement, he enjoyed the instructor. Besides, it would be an easy A. He'd grown up hearing—perhaps, being terrorized by would be a better description—a number of the stories from Karen.

"*Rub-a-dub, three maids in a tub. And who do you think were there? The butcher, the baker, the candlestick maker, and all of them going to the fair*," Professor Habermehl was saying. "This version of the rhyme dates back to the fourteenth century. If we can agree that many nursery rhymes are reflections of some of the unclean truths present in their origin's time periods, what is this little ditty describing? Who are these men? What class level do they represent?"

Dennis could feel eyes on him from across the lecture hall. He had been dating Claire, a sophomore English major who lived on the third floor of his dorm, for a few weeks. She, too, was taking the class, but that was just a coincidence; he hadn't even known they had this in common until he had spied the textbook on her nightstand the previous evening. It was that night, last night, that she had finally sent him the signal that she was ready to be physical. Usually, Dennis was clueless about social cues, at least those that lent themselves to naked dalliances; he had jumped the gun on slipping out a condom so many times that finally, he had resolved to waiting for the other party to make the first move.

Yesterday, he and Claire had gone to the movies—there was an art film theater at the center of town, the kind that served wine and microbrew beer as well as used real, organic butter on its popcorn—and saw something featuring Tilda Swinton, an actress who had always fascinated Dennis, although he couldn't tell if it was because she seemed to slip effortlessly between quirky supporting roles and gender-fluid powerhouse ones or because she didn't always appear to have eyebrows. Afterwards, they walked together across the green to Garman House. On the way, Claire slipped her hand around Dennis's, and the two of them stepped gingerly through the lush grass that appeared slightly bluish, almost bruised, in the waxy illumination of the streetlights. Despite urgent dissuading from his mother, he had opted to attend a small but prestigious college in Massachusetts, and even after four years of living there, he appreciated the quaint details associated with New England small towns: the vivid colors of the rolling hills, the incongruous blending of staunch tradition with liberal activism. He liked being able to walk just a few streets from campus and smell the earth below his feet, the deterioration of old maple and oak trees, and the nearby farmland. He didn't miss the big city at all. Most of all, he didn't miss Karen.

When they reached the porch of one of the sprawling homes the college used as a dormitory, Claire removed her hand and began to fumble in her jacket pocket for her keycard, but Dennis held his hand up, signaling her to wait. A moment later, the front door opened, and two girls bounded out and down the steps, not bothering to acknowledge either of them, and as the door began to close behind them, Dennis grabbed the knob and motioned for Claire to enter.

From there, it had seemed more like a movie than the one the two of them had watched just a few minutes earlier. Claire led the way, walking slowly but purposefully up the hardwood staircase to the second floor, Dennis trailing immediately behind. When they passed the entrance to his room, she grasped his hand again, continued around to the next staircase, and led him wordlessly to the third floor.

Their silent agreement remained unbroken until Claire once again fumbled in her jacket pockets to find her keys. "Joy went home for the weekend, so we can be alone," she said, her hand finally locating what it had been fishing for. She turned the key in the lock and pushed open her door. Once the two of them were inside, she shut it quickly, as if trapping a feral animal. Dennis walked to the bed on the right side of the room and sat down.

"No," Claire said sharply. "That's Joy's bed. Don't sit there." She pushed to the floor the few articles of clothing that were strewn along the room's other bed and patted the comforter. "She gets mad if people touch her stuff," she explained, then removed her coat and draped it over a nearby desk chair.

Dennis walked to Claire's bed and sat down hesitantly. He didn't want any misunderstandings. He was going to let Claire take the lead. Sure enough, after waiting less than a minute, Claire stepped in front of him and peeled her light green cardigan from her shoulders. Underneath, she was wearing a frilly, off-white sleeveless blouse, the kind Dennis equated with mid-nineties grunge girl bands: androgynously shapeless yet nostalgically feminine. He didn't have time to consider the top for long, though, for after she unzipped and pushed her jeans to the floor, she pulled the blouse over her head and stepped toward him wearing only her underwear. When she leaned down and kissed him, her tongue flicking this way and that along his teeth, and he could taste a hint of popcorn salt on her lips.

She pulled back and looked at Dennis in the eyes. "Take your jacket off, okay?"

He obliged, pushing his hooded sweatshirt from his shoulders and onto the floor. She unbuttoned his shirt and began to kiss his neck, running her lips from his collarbone to his earlobe. He held her tight to him. Her skin was soft and warm; her body, somehow comforting as his arms engulfed it. She leaned sideways and sprawled onto her back across the comforter, resting her feet, still covered in small, white socks, on her pillow.

Dennis stood up and removed his shirt, then his pants. It felt cold in the room, especially since he was wearing only a pair of plaid flannel boxers, and he longed to press his skin against Claire's again so that he would be warm again. He climbed on top of her and their two bodies moved insistently until Claire reached back, and unbuttoned her bra and pushed her panties downward.

Dennis ran his hand along her bare chest and kissed her mouth and neck, desperately willing his body to cooperate. No matter how many times he touched her, he could not get more than partially erect. He reached between her legs and felt a scratch of stubble. She had shaved herself nearly bald save for the thin landing strip of hair Dennis always equated with Adolf Hitler's mustache. He never had liked porn where the women were completely shaved. It made him feel quasi-pedophiliac, watching satyrs of small girls who wore masks and cloaks of grown women.

He removed his hand and concentrated on envisioning the last woman he'd had sex with, a stranger he'd met accidentally after leaving his friends at the Moan and Dove, the nearby hipster brew bar, and hitching a ride down the long strip of route 116 back to campus. She'd picked him up in her gray Kia four-door and asked him if he wanted to smoke a joint with her in a nearby parking lot. When they climbed into the back seat, however, they'd ended up fucking: him, half-sitting, half-lying down with his head against the back windshield while she straddled him, her skirt pushed up and her panties in a damp ball on the floor. Her pussy had been covered in hair; not thick hair, but a light and even, downy layer. It felt liked brushed cotton against his lower stomach as it swept urgently against it. Afterwards, she had kissed him gently on the mouth, pulled her underwear back on, and driven him to Garman House, then without a word, sped away. She had never even told him her name, but in his mind, he had named her Linda because she had reminded him of a younger Linda Lavin, the actress on that seventies sitcom *Alice*. Even with the image of Linda's face, the feel of her bouncing on top of him, fresh in his memory, he could not get hard with Claire.

She reached her hand inside of his shorts and squeezed gently. "What's wrong?" she whispered. "Are you okay?" she asked.

Her concern only made him feel more inadequate. He pushed his groin hard against hers and she jerked her hand away and placed her palm on his chest. He thrust harder, then reached down, pushed his boxers to his thighs, and awkwardly entered her as best he could manage. Claire moved her hand to his face and cradled it lovingly, encouraging him to continue. Dennis continued to shove his body forward, and the force of his movement nudged both of them higher and higher towards the foot of the bed.

Finally, Claire's shoulders touched the end of the mattress;

her head hovered parallel to the floor. She craned her neck backwards so that it was nearly upside down, and Dennis repositioned his forearm over her throat to balance himself. It was then that he saw it. With his arm obscuring Claire's face, the body below him now appeared to be decapitated. This idea flooded his mind, raced through his body, and filled his cock, swelling it until he thought it might burst. He pounded himself in and out of Claire excitedly, the sound of his grunting growing louder and louder, until the orgasm undulated over his body like a steamroller and he bowed his torso back to ride its wave, grasping one of her breasts with his free hand. He had never cum so intensely, and his body jerked a few times in aftershocks before he withdrew and rolled onto his side beside her.

Claire shimmied downward so that her face was even with his. "You didn't even wait to make sure I came," she said disapprovingly. "What the fuck?"

He closed one of his eyes, an extended wink, and her face blurred a bit. He was suddenly tired, but he didn't want to sleep in someone else's bed. He wanted to sleep in his own bed. When Claire rolled off of her bed, snatched a red robe from a nearby wall hook, and covered her naked body with it, he wasted no time getting dressed.

"I think you need to leave," she said, though the statement seemed pointless. Dennis had already finished tying his shoes.

As he lay on his back in bed that night, he did not replay the sex with Claire in his mind. Instead, he thought of Linda. He imagined her naked, sitting spread eagle on top of him, her soft whisper of pubic hair barely a shadow in the near darkness. He was grasping her hips and bouncing her torso up and down on his cock.

Her arms and head were missing.

"Mr. Sweeney, what are the implications of this?"

Professor Habermehl's voice jostled Dennis out of his reverie. "Implications?" he repeated in an attempt to buy himself a moment to form a response. He glanced self-consciously around the room, finally meeting Claire's stare from five rows away. She was frowning.

The instructor continued. "Here we have three

tradesmen—honest, hard-working men—spying on a bevy of maidens as they bathe together—"

"It illustrates Laura Mulvey's film theory on the patriarchal gaze, that women serve as objects for men," Dennis interrupted. "I mean, yeah, this isn't cinema, but aren't rhymes that are passed down through cultures in some ways a form of that culture's entertainment? They might as well be watching Janet Leigh take a shower," he said.

"Interesting," answered the instructor, turning his body to face the other side of the lecture hall. "And how should we feel about these tradesmen? Are we cheering them on, or are they embroiled in scandal, being caught engaging in such lurid voyeurism?" Professor Habermehl moved on to another student. "Miss Evanston?"

Dennis collected his things and bolted from the lecture hall as soon as the class ended. He didn't think Claire wanted to speak to him, but he didn't want to take the chance. There was nothing to say, really.

He had three hours to kill before his afternoon lab, and since he'd missed breakfast, he decided the best thing to do would be to drop his book back in his room and head to The Black Sheep, a local deli, for a quick bite. Although he managed to get in and out of Garman House without any sighting of Claire, he continued to rush. He wanted to get into town and away from any confrontation, at least until dinner. Had he been more careful, he might not have knocked down the woman standing at the bottom of the dormitory steps as he exited.

He stopped to help her up, apologizing profusely as he did. "Ma'am, are you alright? I'm so sorry. I was rushing, and I… I don't have any excuse. I'm a jerk. I hope you're okay," he said, searching her expression for any clue as to how she was feeling. He assumed she was a professor although he hadn't seen her on campus before; she was dressed impeccably in an expensive-looking suit and simple handbag. She may have been a trustee or some other kind of big wig for the school. He had spied the red soles on her shoes when she pushed herself back to a standing position, and he knew that meant they belonged to a big-name designer, though he couldn't think of the name off-hand.

The woman smoothed the sides of her jacket and smiled, her lips pressed tightly together. She had large, brown eyes and dark, wavy hair. The shift in her expression drew crackles of lines along the sides of her eyes and mouth. There was something eerily familiar about her, something in her face that made Dennis uneasy.

"Well, isn't this a fortuitous accident?" The woman's voice was flat and measured, the kind of tone Dennis equated with old New England money. "I believe you are exactly who I came to see." She paused and stared at him for a moment. "You *are* Dennis Sweeney, aren't you?"

Dennis frowned. Why would this woman be coming to see him? Was she a dean at the college? Had his scholarship been cancelled? Had Karen missed a tuition payment? His mind raced with paranoia. "I am," he answered cautiously. "Did I do something wrong? I mean, besides semi-tackling you on my way down the stairs." He offered a half-hearted grin.

Her expression did not change. "Am I catching you at a bad time?" she asked. "Are you on your way to class?"

Dennis considered lying but he believed that somehow, this woman would see right through a facade. "No, I have a lab from two to five. I was just going for something to eat."

The woman paused again and stared at Dennis, then offered her hand. "My name is Elizabeth Becker," she said. He grasped her hand and they shook. Her skin was cool but tight. "Do you mind if I join you? I'd like to talk to you about something, if you don't mind."

His eyes darted quickly along the street. He didn't see a car parked nearby. No one seemed to be watching them, and Claire was nowhere in sight. He shrugged. "Sure, why not? Is it okay if we walk?" He turned his body to face the sidewalk.

Elizabeth Becker brushed the sides of her suit again. Dennis guessed it was more of an ingrained tick than a compulsion to remove any stray lint or dirt. "Walking sounds fine. And I promise to return you in plenty of time for your lab class."

That evening, Dennis sat on his bed, trying to focus on writing his lab report, when his cell phone rang. He knew without checking the screen that it was Karen. She called every

Monday evening without fail, and most of the time, it was to complain incessantly about a co-worker, supervisor, or case she was working on, to criticize him for his choice in school, major, or pastime, or simply to harangue him about some minor infraction or another from months earlier. He'd gotten into the habit of putting her on speakerphone after more than one call had left his ear red from pressing his phone against it for more than three hours. He wasn't ashamed to admit that he had grown to dread these weekly marathons in masochism, but he had always been too weak to stand up to Karen and put an end to the psychological torture. This week, however, he looked forward to her phone call. This week, he realized, would be the beginning of something delicious.

"Hello," he said flatly into the phone.

"Hello, Denny." Karen's voice snapped from the speaker like a lizard's tongue.

He didn't wait for her to say anything else. "Mom, you'll never guess who I met today."

There was silence on the other end of the line, something that never happened when he was speaking to Karen. He could hear her breathing, however, and he knew she was listening and continued. "My grandmother. Funny… she looked awfully good for someone who'd been gunned down by muggers nearly forty years ago."

Piece #29
Wilmington, NC

Allie dropped her parents off at the airport like she was picking up dinner from a fast-food drive-thru in reverse. She didn't even bother to shift into PARK.

"Oh, sweetie," her mother leaned over the center console and planted her fuchsia lips on Allie's cheek. "I am so glad we did this. Your home is as beautiful as always. We'll see you and Patricia at the holidays, yes?" She withdrew her face from her daughter's, and Allie could not help running her eyes along the cakes of makeup dried here and there along her mother's dehydrated skin. Even her lips were like two rotted raisins, hard and crispy with a line of congealed spittle tracing the place where they met.

She forced a smile and patted the gearshift nervously. Her step-father, Steve, was pulling the couple's bags out of the open trunk and when he was finished, he slammed the hatchback hard and began to pile the luggage onto a nearby silver cart. "Let's go, Eudora," Steve sighed impatiently. "I'm sure there's a line at security. We don't want to miss our flight."

Eudora put her palm on the side of her daughter's face and stared at her silently for a long minute. It was as if she was trying to commit every detail of her only child's image to memory. If Allie were kidnapped or opted to stop at a local bank and hold it up—you know, just for some *walking around money*, as Steve called it—she could provide an excellent description for the feds. At last, she removed her hand, patted Allie's arm, and climbed out of the car. This took some effort, as Allie's mother was not a slight woman by anyone's standard. But, she was a strong woman, built like her own father, with tree-trunks for legs and broad shoulders like an Olympic swimmer. Once she had pushed herself upright and had smoothed her dress and readjusted her hem, she was right as rain.

Allie ducked her head and leaned sideways to peer out of the driver's-side window. "I love you, Mom," she said quietly. "I'll call you next weekend."

Eudora cast her a small wave, then wrapped her wrist

around her husband's upper arm, not for support but out of habit. She was a Southern lady, through and through: Alabama born and raised. Allie had never seen her without her hair done or her clothes neatly pressed. Come to think of it, she could probably count on two hands the number of times she had seen her mother wear pants instead of a dress, and Allie was thirty-seven.

Allie, too, was Southern, but not in the way Eudora was. She was born and raised in Monroeville, Alabama, home of authors Harper Lee and Truman Capote. One of her earliest memories was of seeing Lee at the Winn-Dixie while food shopping with her mother. Standing in line ahead of them at the cashier, the author wore a simple blouse and faded blue jeans with a pack of cigarettes sticking out of the back pocket. When she turned to look at Allie sitting in the carriage alongside the handful of items Eudora had tossed inside, a last-minute gathering for dinner that evening, Lee smiled softly at the girl. "Please," she said, looking at Eudora and stepping aside to allow Allie's mother to move ahead of her in line, "I'm in no hurry. You go on ahead."

Grateful for the favor, Eudora nodded her head and thanked the woman for her graciousness. As she pushed the cart through the small parking lot to the family car, Eudora spoke to her daughter. "That woman is an award-winning writer, my love. It just goes to show you, if you're brought up right, you never lose those manners, no matter how famous you become. She is a true Southerner. You remember that, Allison." She stopped to load the grocery bag into the backseat of the car. Allie climbed out of the carriage and sat obediently in the seat next to the parcel, and Eudora leaned down and buckled her seatbelt. "Don't ever let the madness of the world pull your poise out from under you," she added, and shut the door tight.

And yet, here Allie was, too lazy and wrapped up in her own selfish shit to help her own mother out of the car or remove the suitcases from her trunk for her family. So much for Southern gentility. She had fled Alabama as soon as she was out of high school, joining a group of migrant farm workers traveling up the East coast as the growing seasons rotated, until, at the age of twenty-two, she met Patricia while on a short break between stops in Delaware. Patricia, a tall, square-jawed woman with a mop of thick, auburn hair and long, elegant fingers, was four years her senior and worked as a public defender at the New Hanover City Courthouse in Wilmington, North Carolina. She, too, had grown up in the South—in Rocky Mount, a few hours east of Wilmington— but had chosen to stay. Although Allie savored the freedom she'd enjoyed as a nomad, after two years of long-distance phone calls and hastily-planned quickies when the two's schedules aligned, she happily planted herself for good alongside Patricia in the latter's three-bedroom, two-bath ranch home just thirty minutes from Kure Beach. The two had lived there thirteen years.

With only a high school education, Allie's career prospects were slim. Patricia made more than enough to maintain their modest abode, and the pair rarely traveled or desired anything extravagant, but Allie missed the autonomy she'd enjoyed as a self-supporting gypsy. Patricia granting her an allowance made her feel like a child, so she took a part-time job as a maintenance worker at a local plant farm, one that specialized in the carnivorous plants native to the state. On her breaks, she'd often visit the greenhouse to gaze at the Venus fly-traps, sundews, and butterworts; even after years of employment there, she was still morbidly fascinated with the primal doom and danger the plants seemed to emit. When she was under stress, more often than not, her nightmares would feature the plants in some menacing or foreboding way.

Two weeks earlier, as she dreaded the arrival of her mother and her husband, she hardly slept more than three hours a night. When she finally nodded off, she dreamed she was walking out of the front door of her house and onto the small porch surrounded by flower beds. When she looked down, however, instead of brightly colored blooms, she stared directly into tall cylinders of pitcher plants, a hundred of them, their long, tubular green and red necks swaying and curving upwards toward Allie like a nest of sinewy snakes, heads cocked forward and following Allie's every movement. As her body stiffened, unable to move, the fleshy flaps of their tops folded backward to reveal gaping maws of darkness, and in unison, they began to growl a low, guttural cry, a sound Allie was certain was a command to one another to attack. Sure enough, as Allie's heart dropped into her stomach, her feet cemented to the paint-flaked wood floor, the cavernous mouths sprouted teeth like sewing needles, and the tube necks stretched and elongated and pointed at Allie, reaching and growing until they could touch her frozen body, and one by one, planted their sharp fangs into her flesh, furiously tearing it from her bones like rabid animals. She could only watch in horror as chunks of red and brown and black fell like confetti around her feet. And then the pitcher plants snatched at her eyes, and the world went black.

Allie awoke from this dream screaming, startling Patricia and likely concerning their neighbors on both sides. From that night on, she swallowed two of Patricia's Klonopin before climbing under the sheets. During the week her mother slept in the guest room, she chased the pills with two shots of vodka.

It wasn't that she didn't love her mother—she did—just like it wasn't that she didn't love Patricia—she did—but there was something, something deep and dark and empty inside of Allie, something like the dark, ominous tubes of the pitcher plants, that was unhappy. She had loved traveling; having no tethers, living hand to mouth like a boy on an adventure, had satiated Allie, and without that freedom, she was always wanting seconds. Seeing Eudora pulled the regret Allie felt to the surface, her presence poked at the open wound, made it bleed and dribble pus. Her silence reminded her that when she was a teenager, she had had her whole life, the whole world, in front of her. Now, she was relegated to being a housewife in a Southern town, maintaining a job out of boredom rather than necessity. Without intending it, she had become her mother.

When the package arrived on her front porch two days after her departure, she opened it without a second thought. It had been addressed to Patricia, but they were beyond the point of maintaining separate identities. Nothing was a secret anymore, nothing a surprise or anticipation. Allie had drawn the line at using the toilet with the bathroom door open, however—it was alright if the mystery had dissipated, but the loss didn't need to balloon to that degree of distaste. From there, it would be only a matter of time before one of them didn't bother to brush her teeth before coming to bed or keep up with basic genital hair trimming, and then they might as well buy separate twin beds and change their designation to siblings instead of partners. She liked fucking Patricia, even after fifteen years, and although the frequency and spontaneity had severely lessened over the past year, Allie had no cause to look elsewhere for attention.

The package was large, a plain, white Postal Service box at least a foot and a half long and nearly a foot wide. There was no return address, and Patricia's information had been typed neatly across the label so Allie was unable to discern any clue about the sender's identity. The box was heavy, too, which only piqued Allie's interest further. When she pulled the contents out onto the dining room table, she was further intrigued. Whatever the gift was, it was wrapped in plain, off-white paper, the kind in which their steaks were bundled by the butcher Allie visited every week on food shopping day.

She placed the oddly-shaped item on the table and picked up the small, white sheet of paper that had fallen out after the box spilled its secrets. It was a note. Allie's heart dropped slightly. Was it a love note? It couldn't have been a shipping invoice: it was much too small. She opened the paper and read the tiny, typed words arranged in four neat lines in the middle of the page.

> A girl whose status is unknown
> Pieces sent to a chosen few
> Action is yours; her destiny own
> Naked without a boot or shoe.

Allie paused. *Naked without a boot or shoe?* What did that mean? Who was naked? And what was this object that had been sent without the sender's name? Allie pawed the butcher paper, pressing here and there as if assessing the mysterious item for lumps. Was it a statue? A priceless heirloom? An original work of stone or marble art? She turned the piece over and found the edge of the paper and began to unroll it. When the floor was awash with an endless wave of discarded paper, Allie was left holding what was inside.

It was a foot. No, not just a foot, but a foot and lower leg, cut somewhere just below the knee. The foot itself was missing one of its digits: the big toe; this was particularly relevant because when Allie tried to stand it up, it toppled over onto its side, the absent extremity devastatingly missed by its neighbors. So, Allie let it play possum while she stared at the lump of flesh on the dining room table. It was a slim leg, free of spider veins or bruises. The tiniest trickle of hair was sprouting from its pores, but otherwise, it was perfectly smooth. The toes that remained were painted with a garish bright pink polish, the color Allie imagined a small child would wear, but the leg didn't belong to a child. It was as long as a full-grown adult's.

Allie sat in one of the high-back chairs at the table and took stock of the situation. Patricia was sent a leg. And most of a foot. And a bizarre poem. And the package had no return address. She poked the ankle bone hesitantly with her index finger. The flesh was tepid and clammy, but soft. She was surprised it hardly had a smell: the weather had been unseasonably warm that week. She wondered how long the package had been in the postal system. Certainly, whoever sent it must have frozen the leg, then shipped it solid as a rock, allowing its travels to thaw it along the way. The thought reminded Allie of the commercial for kids' yogurt she'd seen last week, the one where the mom snatches a stick of sugar-saturated goo from the freezer and tosses it into her son's lunch bag. Whoever had mailed this piece to her wife wanted it to be fresh on arrival. *Well, Bravo*, thought Allie. *Mission accomplished.*

As she continued to stare at the strange delivery on her table, Allie caught a shape sailing upwards out of the corner of her eye. She jerked her head toward the wall of the small foyer outside of the guest bath. A wide, brown feather, pasted flat against the paint, was slowly creeping upwards toward the ceiling. Confused, Allie stood and padded cautiously toward the strange object. As she ventured closer, she realized that is wasn't a feather at all, but an unsettlingly large bug of some sort. It was light brown with two long black stripes down its length. It seemed impossibly long, but the body itself measured only about an inch and a half. Each of its legs, however—and there were fifteen pairs of them splayed outward on all sides of the creature—was nearly as long as its body. Its tiny black eyes were immobile atop of its bug head. Allie could see that each of the thirty legs were black and brown; from afar, they had appeared as one solid fan of stripes.

She was leaning closer to get a better look when the vile-looking critter suddenly scurried up the wall, its swift pace sending involuntary shivers up Allie's spine. She watched in horror as the mammoth centipede reached the top of the wall and, instead of stopping, continued onto the ceiling and toward Allie. When it was almost above her, Allie slowly lifted her foot to slide sideways, but that is when it happened. The centipede let go of the ceiling and dead-dropped toward the floor, landing on Allie's shoulder and immediately resuming its breakneck velocity.

It crawled quickly toward her back, and Allie jumped and began swatting the back of her shoulder with her opposite hand, evoking a very helpless squeal of terror from her own throat in the process. She felt its hard, worm-like body scrape the tops of her fingernails and the spindle-like legs tickle her skin as she brushed the wicked thing from her shirt and onto the floor. She said a silent prayer of thanks that she was wearing her flat-bottomed loafers that afternoon as she ran after the creature, who, for its part, was high-tailing it out of the room like a party guest who realized too soon that the silent fart he emitted smelled like a cross between a garbage truck in the dead of summer and a platter of rotten meat. Despite her shoe's thick sole, Allie could feel the bug's body crush beneath her weight—a racing car in a compactor—and before she lifted her foot again, she spied three small legs peeking out from under her loafer; they emitted a tiny spasm, then lay crooked and still on the hardwood floor.

As she wiped the carcass from the bottom of her shoe and off the floor with a wet paper towel, her phone rang. Allie dumped the cloth in the kitchen trash and answered; it was Patricia.

"Hey, babes," Patricia's booming voice called playfully through the receiver. "How's your day going?"

Allie's eyes drifted from the spot where the bug had first appeared to the corpse leg still lying prostrate on the table. She laughed a little. "Yeah, it's been interesting," she answered. "Yours?"

"Same ol' story. A lot of driving offenses today. Two DUIs

in one morning. Must be the season," she said, then shifted gears. "Do we have anything planned tonight? Did I forget a dinner party or date night?"

Allie put her hand on her hip and looked toward the kitchen. She hadn't even thought about starting dinner. She glanced at the clock. It was nearly five. Maybe sandwiches would suffice. "No... no, not that I'm aware of," Allie said. "Why? You running late?"

Patricia paused as the sound of a truck roared by in the background. "No, but Tim has an extra ticket to UNCW's soccer kickoff: do you mind if I go? I'll be home right after."

"Of course not. I'll find something here to munch on." She paused, torn between which news to bring up first. "So, I just killed a very scary-looking bug in the dining room."

"Scary-looking? What do you mean? Like a Palmetto?" Patricia asked.

Allie had grown up in the South: she'd seen her share of Palmetto bugs. This was nothing like it. "Oh, no, it was different. Not a roach or anything. More like a... well, I thought it was a feather from a distance, to be perfectly honest. Then I saw it up close and realized it had about a zillion legs. And it ran fast as a mother-fucker. Creeped the hell outta me." She glanced at the trash barrel, second-guessing for a moment if the vermin were really dead.

Patricia chuckled. "You've never seen a feather bug before?" she asked. "That's what they call them around here. House centipede, right? Really long legs and kind of striped? Light brown in color?"

Allie thought of the bug in her head and immediately became squeamish. "Yeah, that's it. Super creepy."

"I can't believe in all your years working up and down the coast that you never encountered one. I used to see them every now and then when I was a kid. Mostly in the cellar, though. My family was one of the few in our neighborhood who had a cellar. It was always damp and dark, and it had that smell, that mildewy smell to it, so we didn't go down there much, but whenever I had to fetch a can or jar of something for my mom, I'd see one on the wall or in a corner." Another truck roared by, then Patricia continued. "They're beneficial, actually. They eat other bugs. Think of the little guy as your own private

Orkin man."

Allie replayed the action of squashing the centipede in her head. "Yeah, well, it's too late for that. He's moved on to chow down on that flea circus in the sky, I'm afraid."

There was a rustling sound in the background and a sprinkling of different voices overlapping. "Hey, I gotta go, babe," Patricia said, the chorus of conversation growing louder. "I'll see you tonight."

"Ok," Allie responded, glancing over at the dining room table. "And you got a package today in the mail…"

"What?" Patricia's voice grew staticky and far away, then the call dropped.

Allie put the screen on her phone to sleep and walked over to the pale body part. It was her secret alone for now. Maybe it was a threat from one of Patricia's former clients. Maybe it was evidence that a client wanted her wife to hide. Hell, the postmark on the delivery box was smudged: Patricia would never be able to tell what day it had arrived. Allie could repack the entire business and reseal the box and pretend she'd never seen the thing, allow her spouse to deal with the strangeness.

No, she'd leave it out for Patricia to freak out about when she got home. Let *her* get a bit of a scare in the dining room. Fair is fair. *Beneficial feather bug, huh?* she thought. She shrugged her shoulders and wandered back into the kitchen to make herself a sandwich.

That evening, as the sun made its getaway into the western hills, Allie kicked her loafers off and curled up on the couch, pulling a faux fur throw over her legs. She clicked a few buttons on the remote control and the room filled with the other-worldly glow of the oversized television. When Patricia had first brought home the monstrosity, Allie had asked her to return it, as its presence dwarfed nearly every other object in the wide room shared by the dining and living areas, even the sofa. However, it was a battle lost before it had started: they had always wanted to host the annual Super Bowl party, and certainly, a giant T.V. was a base requirement. Soon, Allie grew to appreciate its existence. When she switched it on in the evening, she often lit a few scented candles and relied merely on the glow of those along with the radiance of the mammoth screen to illuminate the house. There was no longer a need for a lamp.

Allie rested her head on a throw pillow, took a deep breath, and closed her eyes for a moment. If she fell asleep, Patricia would be home soon and would wake her. Sure enough, when she opened her eyes again, the show on the screen had changed. No longer was Kyra Sedgwick sporting her terribly tacky sweaters in a police procedural: now, some sort of law and order reality show had taken her place. Allie had to admit—she was intrigued by these types of shows, the forensic science and grimy details of each malfeasance in particular. If she could do it over again, she would have gone to college to be a crime scene technician. She watched in earnest as a coroner told the interviewer where and how each bone on the victim had been snapped and found herself wondering if there were any bags of potato chips in the kitchen for snacking.

I really need to vacuum more often, she thought. *And move the damn furniture to grab all the dust bunnies that collect there.* She saw a soft brown tumbleweed of hair dance across the white carpet a foot in front of the coroner's milky white face whose countenance was two feet wide in the frame's tight headshot. Allie blinked. Neither she nor Patricia shed much hair, and they didn't own a pet. Where was the…

It wasn't a dust bunny.

Allie sat straight up on the couch and pulled her feet closer to her thighs. Running across the width of the rug was another house centipede, this one larger and somehow faster than the first. The pale glow of the television seemed to strobe along its powerful legs, blurring them into one terrifying ripple of velocity. Allie looked frantically around her body for a weapon of some sort. She grabbed the box of tissue from the side table and taking her best aim, hurled it at the creature. It hit its mark but did not stop its target. A half second later, a clump of legs emerged from under the box and the bug continued its frantic pace across the room and toward, toward…

Allie looked sideways. Approaching the first centipede was a second one; this one was the same size as the one Allie had killed earlier in the day, but its black stripes were wider, seemed darker. Allie wondered if these bugs were purposefully camouflaged to blend into poorly lit crevices. She certainly hadn't seen any of the them before that day—where were they coming from?

She swung her legs slowly over the edge of the couch and slipped them carefully into the discarded loafers. As she did so, she felt a tickle on the front of her ankle, and when she looked down, she saw a third centipede crawl from the shoe and scurry up her shin. Allie leaped from her seat in horror and shook her leg like it was on fire. She felt the bug sail to the floor, its thirty legs scraping delicately against her skin.

Allie ran to the light switch on the opposite wall of the room and flicked it on. When she returned her gaze to the living room, the bugs were nowhere in sight. She slowly wandered back in front of the sofa. No centipedes anywhere. She must have been dreaming, and yet, the experience had felt different than the one with the pitcher plants.

She glanced at the clock; it was nearly eleven: Patricia would be home soon. Allie toddled into the guest bathroom off the great room to splash water on her face. She was taken aback when she caught her reflection in the mirror: her face was sweaty and pale, her eyes puffy and bloodshot, and her hair stood out in all directions. It had been, certainly, an unnerving dream. She closed the door most of the way, peeled her clothes from her body, and turned on the shower; she would feel better once she scrubbed the day's events from her body and refocused.

When she was done, she stepped onto the bathmat and wiped her face. The mirror was fogged and the heavy air of the bathroom was steamy and thick. Allie blotted the skin on her arms and legs and hanged her towel back on the rack as neatly as she could. She grabbed her waffle-knit bathrobe from the hook on the back of the door and slid one of her arms inside. It was only then that she saw it.

Where the robe had been stretched an enormous, dark brown centipede, one so long it more than doubled any of the ones she'd spied previously. It had arranged itself vertically, as if it were staring humbly at the floor, and its body formed a thin S shape; the endless rack of legs splayed wide, like the thing was preparing to give the white wood a big bear hug.

Seeing Allie standing there, staring in horror, the creature began to shift a little, shaking its bug head in disappointment.

Oh Allie, it seemed to be saying, *don't you know we are your own private Orkin men? How could you be so afraaaaaaaid?* As if punctuating this declaration, the centipede began a mad dash down the door in a rocket pace. Allie shook the robe from her arm and jumped sideways; before the monstrous bug reached the floor, Allie had flung open the door and bolted into the great room, her damp bare feet leaving ephemeral prints on the shiny floor.

On the edge of the living room, she skidded to a halt. The three creatures from her dream were back. They spilled from the edge of the rug and onto the hardwood floor of the dining room, making their way in a unified pack toward the kitchen. Toward Allie. Toward Allie's bare feet.

She rushed to the dining room table in a vain attempt to beat the speed demons in their spontaneous race. When she stopped in front of the first chair, the centipedes had shifted their destination. They had reprogrammed their GPS, it seemed, to the table. Without thinking, Allie grabbed the nearest object closest to a weapon: the detached leg. Holding it firmly by the ankle, she slammed the bottom of the foot down onto the nearest bug, squashing its tiny black eyes into its head. As its remaining torso and legs flailed in panic, Allie picked up the leg and slammed it down again: this time, on the second centipede, the one with the darker, thicker stripes. This one she nabbed spot-on, blanketing the bug's full body with the dead extremity.

When she pulled the leg back, she saw that the heel and upper pads of the foot had made contact with the bug, but the middle portion had been spared. The centipede's middle pulsed and throbbed in anger, its legs waving in unison like a drowning bat. Allie glanced at the first centipede; it had stopped moving. She checked the bottom of the foot in her hand: it was dented, slightly smooshed, the dead flesh having begun to decay and soften.

The third centipede crawled onto her foot again, but this time, it dug its tiny fangs into Allie's flesh, sending a sharp sting up her leg. On instinct, Allie slapped the area with her free hand, but the creature was too wily for its victim; it scurried around behind Allie and stung her again on the heel. Allie hopped in a semi-circle, raised the leg weapon as high as she could, and slammed the thing directly onto the creature over and over, a game of Whack-a-mole with only one target, until the bug was just a brown smudge on the floor with no distinguishable body or legs.

Allie felt beads of sweat drizzle down her naked body. She wiped the wetness from her forehead with her free hand, then, still wielding the leg weapon, walked calmly back to the bathroom. The mother centipede was no longer on the back of the door but had made her way during the frenzy to the bathtub. As Allie entered, she froze on the lip of the tub.

Allie did not hesitate in her approach. When she was within arm's reach, she held the ankle tighter and smashed the bottom of the foot onto the centipede, splitting the bug in half. Its top portion fell into the tub, its legs wriggling madly in the drops of water left from the shower. The bottom half stayed planted on the edge, and Allie slammed the foot onto this portion again and again and again. The corpse's extremity began to split as well, the heel ripping from the rest of the foot, coagulated blood, decomposed musculature, and liquefied fat deposits oozing from the wound and down Allie's arm each time she raised it. The centipede was no longer identifiable, just a brown and black mucous-like goo on the porcelain.

"Al!" Patricia's voice boomed behind Allie. "Al! What are you doing? What the fuck is that in your hand?!"

Allie stopped her obsessive ramming and turned to face her spouse. "The centipedes were everywhere," she stated, as if this statement explained everything, including the indiscernible, bloodied hunk of flesh and bone that remained clutched in her hand.

Patricia put her hands on her hips. "The feather bugs? I told you: they are nothing to be scared of; they are just bugs, okay?"

Allie focused on her grip of the ankle bone in her hand. Then, with all of her might, she chucked the carcass at Patricia. It hit her stomach and fell to the floor, leaving a red splotch across the belly of her Calvin Klein dress shirt. Allie laughed and wiped the sweat from her left cheek.

"Oh, and that came for you today," she said.

The Impasse

There was a song on the radio, one Jax knew by heart because he used to sing it to Maggie when he needed a break from his sculptures; in a way, it was their "goofy" song: the song that made them get up and act silly. That, of course, usually led to them laughing then hugging, then kissing, and more often than not, pawing each other naked in the studio, or if they had the patience that day, back to the bedroom. They'd usually shower after and leave the work for another day; sometimes, Jax would go back to the studio and smile and hum the song as he finished up whatever piece he was making that night in the garage. That night, as he drove down a dark, long and silent highway in his new rental, he didn't even notice that their song was on the radio. If he had, he probably would have taken it as some sort of sign or simply cried.

The hours immediately following hearing Declan read the letter were a blur; Jax could hardly recall what happened. He remembered some sort of fight at the rental place about the damage to his car and having to take a taxi to a different rental facility, but before he was consciously thinking again, he was back on the road.

When he tried reaching Maggie six times on the burner cell to no avail, he started to break down: his entire body was shaking, his head was throbbing, and his intestines turned to liquid. Cramps bubbled up inside of him to the point where he had to find a restroom immediately, and the closest one was in the back of some seedy road stop halfway outside of Albany. After the watery nerves poured from his rectum, he started to feel better, but when he noticed there was no toilet paper, he finally broke. By the time his tantrum had run its course, he had broken two stalls and scared the shit out of a young man who was taking a piss. He cleaned himself with paper towels, washed his face, and looked in the mirror. The image staring back at him resembled a drug addict going through a violent withdrawal.

A bit calmer and somewhat sedate after expending so much energy in worry and physical sickness, Jax was heading back to the car when his cell rang; he prayed it was not Connor, and it wasn't: it was Maggie. His heart dropped when he saw the caller ID. On one hand, he was relieved she was calling; on the other, he feared that it wouldn't be her on the other end. With a dry, scratching swallow, he hit the answer button and quickly put it to his ear.

"Jax? Jax are you ok?" Maggie's voice drifted into his ear, caressing his face. The tears came fast and he didn't care that half a dozen people were walking past him into the rest stop.

It took him a few hard seconds to form a response, and even then, it was choked and he could tell by her silence that it scared Maggie. After a few sentences, he stumbled to an old bench and fell into it. Resting his palm on the seat he felt the tiny green flecks of paint sticking into his skin, and they reminded him he was alive and that Maggie was as well. It took him a while, but he composed himself and was able to explain to her that he needed her to completely disappear for a while, to not call him for one week exactly unless she was in danger.

It broke his heart to hear Maggie crying softly on the other end, but it was necessary. Before getting off the phone, Jax told her how much he loved her. He always did that, but he never had felt it more than in that moment. Saying it made his entire body tremble. When their conversation was over, he put the cell in his pocket and brushed the paint flecks from his palms. He told himself to take ten minutes to breathe. After that, he would go back into the rest room and freshen up, get some food, and call Connor to figure out where to go next. Even though he had been an atheist since the age of twelve, he said a small prayer in his head, asking whoever or whatever was listening to make sure Maggie got far enough away from everything...fast.

An hour later, cleaner and with food in his belly, Jax read over the information Connor had sent him. The next stop on his "Meet America's Psychos" tour was in Vermont, just over the border from New York, about another hour from where he was. This time, it was a man in his late fifties named Maxwell Simmons who was bald, short and tubby. Simmons was a shop teacher at the local high school and had a wife and two kids in college, both at the University of Vermont. Moreover, the man had a cleaner record than Jax himself.

When Jax questioned why he was looking into this man, Connor simply said, "His browser history and chat room records." When Jax pressed him for more, Connor assured him, "Trust me: the shit this guy is looking up…if hasn't killed yet, he will soon." Jax felt a bit dumb not understanding how what a man looked at on the internet could be so damning, but again, he blindly trusted Connor and started to drive.

As he entered The Green Mountain State, a breaking news flash interrupted the CNN feed he was listening to on satellite radio. Montpelier police were reporting an active situation: several people had been killed by a man using what authorities believed was a sword. Jax thought for a moment; he was pretty sure that U of V was in Montpelier, where Simmons' children were. Jax's heart started to race. Maybe Connor's instincts had been on the money: perhaps Simmons had suffered a breakdown and had starting killing out in the open. It seemed like too much of a coincidence that it would be happening the same moment he was heading across the border, but he was more than hopeful that The Hangman situation might wrap up before he ever had to get more involved.

His hopes were crushed, however, when he was able to pull over and get a CNN feed on his phone. When he saw live video of the crazed man in front of the Capitol building, he instantly knew it was not the short, balding man he was looking for. Jax shook his head and got back on the road to finish up the last thirty minutes of the drive.

As his car followed the long stretches of asphalt winding through forest and hills, Jax's mind began to wander. He began to suspect that what he was doing was ridiculous: a computer was not going to just hand him a killer on a silver platter. He should stop, find a hotel, and do old school research: make phone calls, hit the pavement, and select his interviewees on instinct, but without an incident or location, where the hell would he start? He suddenly found himself in front of a very neat but average-looking suburban house. The yard was immaculate, the white siding was clean, and fresh chrysanthemums grew everywhere. If a monster was inside, he was well hidden.

Jax parked across the street, happy to not feel like a maniac with a baseball bat was going to come out and begin smashing his windows. He wished he could call Maggie, he wished he felt more in control and most of all, he wished he understood why he had been chosen. *Your Biggest Fan. Don't forget who made your career.* Jax mulled those two lines over and over in his head.

A shiny, black SUV pulled into the house he was watching. It parked in front of the garage and out jumped a man who looked like he would need to use a step stool to get inside. Jax grabbed his clipboard and half-heartedly jogged across the street to stop the man before he went inside.

"Mr. Simmons!" he said, plastering his widest grin across his face. "Sorry to bother you, but I work for the teachers' union. Do you mind if I talk to you for a moment?" Simmons jumped a bit and stiffened when he turned to face Jax. That didn't make him guilty, Jax told himself. It just made him a man with a nervous demeanor. Simmons moved to his left hand the small lunchbox he'd been holding and offered his right to shake. Jax immediately accepted it and added, "I'm Nick, from the state office. I was sent out to ask you a few questions."

Simmons eyed him suspiciously. "What is this about?"

Jax smiled again and glanced at his clipboard, pretending to organize his thoughts. "This isn't really a conversation I like having with a fellow union member, Mr. Simmons, but with the investigation opened, I'm sure you know: I'm the first line of your defense." Jax swallowed and flashed the man a bashful look meant to put him at ease. "Basically, I need to ask some questions to see if there is any validity to the claims and decide what to do. Hopefully we can clear up this matter and close it now."

There was an uncomfortable pause, and then Simmons started to fidget nervously, his face swelling a bit and turning a reddish, purple color that was familiar to Jax from the time he had spent in Irish bars working contacts back in his Chicago days. "What? I am not aware of any reason I'd need a union rep. This is preposterous. Why wasn't this brought up at the school?" Simmons' hands moved quickly around his jacket and pants pockets as if feeling for an answer in them.

"Well, it's a serious matter, sir, and I am your union rep," Jax explained, keeping his voice even. "No charges have been filed, but the claim has, and I'd like to go over it in detail. Maybe we can go over it inside and straighten it out."

Simmons' face had darkened to a beet red at this point, and Jax could see he was building up his voice to fight back and tell him no. "Tell me what this is about first. I'm not letting some stranger into my house without any information." Simmons had begun to gasp between words. Beads of sweat began to blossom on his forehead, and one after another, they popped up like flower buds starting to bloom.

"Well, let's start with your browser history. Do you use your school laptop at home by any chance?" Jax stared at Simmons, holding his breath. His bluff worked: the man's eyes started to flutter, and Jax reached out to keep him from fainting. After a few sloppy and uncomfortable minutes, Jax was inside Simmons' house and getting the man a drink of water from the sink.

"Just breathe, calm down," Jax said. The journalist covertly scanned first the home's modest decor, then his subject, who was blubbering into a handful of tissues. Jax knew without a doubt that this man was not The Hangman; he might have some dark urges deep down that he tried to satisfy with some online searches, but this man certainly could not handle the fear and pressure of kidnapping and killing someone. And he honestly doubted the man would ever act upon his urges if he couldn't handle a stranger simply asking about his online activity.

After ten minutes of faking his way through a conversation about how using his school laptop for his searches could lead to a lot of trouble, Jax glanced at his watch. "You know, I am running late as it is." Jax stood up and gathered his clipboard and jacket from the kitchen.

Simmons did not look up. "What's going to happen to me?" he cried, his voice slightly muffled by his hand. "None of the girls were underage…that I know of. I just—I just—there's nothing illegal about bondage and—"

Jax held his hand up, a motion lost on his companion as the man still wasn't looking at him. "Listen, Mr. Simmons, I think we've talked about this enough for now. You need to remember that the laptop belongs to the district. Anything you use it for is subject to their search and view. My advice is, invest in your own computer. Visit your sites on your own Wi-Fi, and as far as the other clips, the snuff…" Jax pretended to glance down at his clipboard.

Simmons lifted his head from his hand and looked at his visitor. "They aren't real. I know: they are just fantasy." He cleared his throat nervously. "I mean, not *my* fantasy, per se. I don't think about killing women or anything. I just—I just—" He began to cry again. "I was just curious, I guess. You hear about that stuff, and then when you find it…I don't know…"

Jax patted the man softly on the shoulder, feeling awkward and slightly repulsed at the same time. For a moment, the photographs of Julie Piedmont flashed in his head. More than anything, however, he was angry: angry at Connor for sending him to another dead end.

As Jax climbed back into his car, he glanced back at the house; Simmons was standing in the doorway, clutching another wad of tissues in his hand. His face was puffy and pink, but his expression was blank. For a split second, Jax wondered if he had just been played, but he pushed that feeling down along with the gas pedal and drove away.

Five minutes later, Jax found himself in a supermarket parking lot, angrily calling Connor. He didn't answer. Jax called twice more and received no answer each time. Two seconds later, he received a text from the kid that read, *How did it go?* Jax almost threw his phone across the dashboard, but he calmed himself. Jax texted back: *Answer your FUCKING phone.* This time, the phone rang for only a millisecond before Connor answered. Jax immediately proceeded to spew his anger in a hot, jabbing rant.

"Look, your software is impressive in its scope and detail, but as far as its ability to catch criminals, it's crap. The guy had issues, but he has not committed a crime and probably never will. You keep me on this wild goose chase and I'll be driving and talking to internet pervs and nut jobs until I'm sixty. But it won't solve this fucking case. I'm going back to my ways, what I *know* works. Thanks, kid, but I think I've got it from here." Jax opened his mouth wide to crack his jaw. He sniffed, trying to take a deep breath and calm himself again. He felt slightly guilty about how angrily he had spoken, but when he heard the taps of Connor's fingers on a keyboard in the background, the kid apparently ignoring him, his annoyance bubbled up once more.

"Alright," said Connor finally. "I see where you are. There is a hotel two miles down the street on the left. You have a reservation waiting for you. Check in, do whatever research you need and I'll be there in the morning with a new plan. Trust me: we are close. We can't lose momentum now."

The thought of the kid being able to pinpoint exactly where he was made Jax feel uncomfortable, dirty and watched, so much so that he started the car and began to drive. "You don't need to come here, kid," he said into the receiver. "I appreciate what you have tried to do and I bet you'll make millions on your software…" Jax had a weird feeling of déjà vu, like when he had broken up with his girlfriend senior year of high school. He was trying to let Connor down easily, end the relationship. but the kid quickly cut him off.

"Jackson, I said I'll see you in the morning." The phone suddenly went dead. No one called him Jackson, not since early interviews on the news. In fact, most people didn't even know that it was his legal name. What the fuck was going on with this kid?

The Blog

TERRY'S TALES OF TRUE TERROR

Your inside source for mass and multiple murder trivia, in Wichita and the world

RSS Subscribe 🔍

New Entry!
The Hangman Hits Home in Kansas
October 13 by Ruth Estabrook — 5 comments

It was a sunny, typical Saturday in the Sunflower State when Erin Zwirn, a visiting professor at Wichita State University, received a small, seemingly nondescript package in her College Hill apartment's mailbox. Zwirn, who joined WSU's mechanical engineering faculty just this past August, had assumed the plain, white box contained a care package from her family in Bangor, Maine.

She could not have been more wrong.

Upon opening the box, Zwirn discovered that she had been sent not one but two severed human ears. She immediately contacted the police, who dispatched the State crime lab to her residence. Within the hour, technicians had retrieved the white USPS box and its contents, which included a short, unsigned note. Although the package displayed a clear postmark, the forensic team also dusted Zwirn's mailbox and requested that Zwirn be fingerprinted, presumably to eliminate her prints from any retrieved from the grotesque delivery.

Zwirn told the *Wichita Eagle*, "I thought it was an early Halloween prank at first. I mean, I was just talking to a colleague yesterday about news reports about The Hangman. It seemed a little too much like a coincidence that

I should receive one of the packages myself."

Reports of anonymous deliveries of other body parts have surfaced in the last 48 hours all over the country. Most recently, an upper arm was delivered to a widowed father of four in Portland, Oregon and a thigh to a recently retired public schoolteacher in Omaha, Nebraska. On Tuesday, a postal carrier in neighboring Leavenworth visited a hospital emergency room carrying a box containing a human torso. Officials placed the man in custody and questioned him for nearly eight hours before accepting the mailman's report that he had become suspicious of the package after it had been accidentally crushed in his delivery truck and began to leak a putrid-smelling brown fluid.

According to Kill-Tracker.com, the torso belonged to a female and was missing nearly all of its organs. The arms, legs, and head had been separated from the body and were not included in the box. Although this remains unconfirmed, one initial report lists the torso as missing one of its breasts. Police spokesperson David Tilley confirmed in a press conference this morning that Zwirn's package appears to have been sent by the nation's most talked-about murderer on the loose, The Hangman.

Targets of these horrific deliveries appear to have been chosen at random, with no connection established between recipients. Not since the cryptic messages of Northern California's Zodiac Killer have so many statisticians and amateur crime sleuths been working full-time in an attempt to decipher The Hangman's pattern. Postal offices around the United States have been placed on high alert following these reports and have been cautioned to separate suspicious packages from regular deliveries until local authorities can evaluate them, but a lack of sufficient staffing, especially in smaller towns and rural routes, may prohibit such action.

FBI officials remain tight-lipped about whether these body parts belong to missing Massachusetts college student Julie Piedmont as was first reported on Kill-Tracker.com, if they belong to another individual, or if the parts originate from a variety of victims. A report of human teeth being delivered to a former *Juggs* magazine model last week in Tulsa, Oklahoma was found to be fraudulent when it was learned that the woman in question had stolen a container of recently pulled choppers from the lab of the dentist's office where she works as a receptionist. She had contacted a local newspaper to report that she had received the pieces in a delivery the previous day.

Wichitans seem baffled by the run of grotesque misfortune their city has experienced over the past few decades. Infamous serial killer and former Park City resident Dennis Rader, also known as BTK, was arrested in 2005 in connection with a series of murders spanning nearly twenty years. He is currently serving ten consecutive life sentences in the El Dorado Correctional Facility and will not be eligible for parole for 175 years.

Not since the anthrax terror scare of 2001 have Americans been so wary of opening snail mail from unknown senders. Check back tomorrow for a link to more exclusive crime scene photos and top secret documents from Kill-Tracker.com. In the meantime, feel free to leave your thoughts on what The Hangman's end game is and to place bets on where his gruesome gifts will turn up next!

5 Comments

Marie, San Antonio, TX

It's really kind of sad that people want to make up getting body parts just for attention. I mean, it's scary enough actually GETTING that stuff, never mind why would y'all want to fantasize about it??

Danny, Wichita, KS

I am Erin's neighbor. Totally can't believe one of those packages came to our building. I know they say that the people chosen were totally at random, but I mean, wtf? Why her? Why didn't I get chosen?

Sean, Wichita, KS

I saw on Kill-Tracker that the postmarks originate in New England or upstate New York or Penn or something. Definitely Northeast. It's about time those guys got their share of wackadoos. I'm so tired of hearing about these crazy killers hailing from the Midwest or South or whatever. Gacy was from Chicago, Dahmer was from Milwaukee. And don't get me started with all the shitshows in Florida and Texas.

Jesus, Holyoke, MA

@Sean, Wichita, KS   Dude, Bundy was born in Vermont. We got our share. Trust me on that!

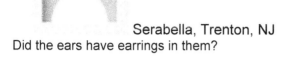 Serabella, Trenton, NJ
Did the ears have earrings in them?

Piece #17
Montpelier, VT

While he had shed his birth name of Michael years ago, Adriel still turned his head to respond when he heard people say his old moniker. It had been seven years since he went to the courthouse and stood in front of the judge to petition for the name change. "Michael means *like a God*, your honor. I am a mere man, not like a God. I am a follower of God, therefore I have chosen to give myself the name of Adriel, which means *follower of God*. It is a much more suitable name for me. Please, let me honor the Lord by making this change." The speech he had rehearsed a thousand times rang still in his head every now and then as if it were a comforting chant that reminded him he was making the right decision. His name change had been the first step in his decision to forgo everything earthly he ever owned, in order to spread the word of the Lord.

Every morning for almost seven years, Adriel got up at five a.m., said his prayers, went to church and prayed again, then took his flyers and headed to the Vermont State House where he stood on the corner in front of the vast lawn and massive building. Hour after hour, he would spout his memorized Gospel and hand out flyers one after another. That is, he *tried* to hand out flyers. Over ninety-seven percent of the people who walked by refused to take one. The other two percent would toss in the trash before they were even out of his sight. The trouble was, Montpelier was small. The vast majority of people he saw during the day were the same business people, politicians, and locals on their daily walks; this meant that after a month, everyone in town had seen him and didn't care what he was handing out. Everything in his fiber, or more so, the old Michael that still resided in the back of his brain, screamed at him to leave the town, to go spread the Word in a large metropolis like Boston or New York, but his initial vision had told him he had to stay here. The only question was *why*.

God had come to him on his fortieth birthday. He was drunk; really, really drunk. The four friends that had taken him out were embarrassed by his slurring and slobbering, and they apologized to the other patrons in the bar, explaining that it was his *Big Four-Oh* and everyone nodded as if they understood. Though in reality, this was a normal Tuesday for their companion; this day, he just happened to have friends with him. Michael, as he was known back then, was a hardcore alcoholic, the type of drunk that had lost his job and his wife the year before but continued, full-speed ahead, on his journey of self-destruction. By the time his fortieth birthday came around, he was couch surfing with the last of the friends that would put up with him and getting by with the little cash his mother could afford to give him. Support groups didn't work, neither did rehab or losing everything he had; nothing cured him. The sweet escape that whisky provided (his favorite drink, but when there was no money, anything that would scratch the itch, including vanilla extract tossed in a bottle of cooking sherry a few times) was worth more than everyone and anything. At the time of his party, he had long past given up trying to figure out why.

By the time he blacked out, two of his four friends had left, disgusted and needing to get back to their families and normal lives at a decent time. The two that stayed did so because they didn't want to be responsible for Michael's death; they dragged him back to his mother's house (both refusing to let him crash at their homes when he was this drunk) and vowed out loud that they would not see him again unless he cleaned his act up.

Michael didn't remember his friends' pact or how he had gotten to his mother's couch; in fact, he didn't even remember it was his birthday. It was as he stood in the shower, lathering, peeing, and vomiting all at once, that he first heard the voice. It was deep, so deep he couldn't understand the words. It wasn't his mother's voice, and his father had died when he was nine. At first, he ignored the sound and continued his shower multi-tasking, knocking a bottle of shampoo and a blue and white striped bar of soap from the caddy as he did so, leaving them to swirl around in the brown-tinted suds circling the drain.

When the water began to turn cold, Michael turned off the faucet and half-stepped, half-stumbled onto the pink-tiled porcelain floor, and as another wave of nausea pushed him onto his knees, he slid himself inch by inch across the cold squares, attempting to make it to the toilet unsuccessfully. He puked on the small bathroom mat and urinated on himself. He thought, for a brief moment, of his mother having to clean up the mess, but he didn't much care: he just wanted to feel the coolness of the tile against his skin and sleep, and that's when it happened. From his vantage point on the floor, the room began to shake with such force that Michael believed an earthquake had incongruously struck New England. Admittedly, he smiled as he thought of the walls collapsing onto him and ending his misery, but his countenance changed as the walls broke away and room suddenly opened, exposing a light so brilliant, Michael had to close his eyes and put his hands in front of his face. His last thought as he began to scream was of alien creatures invading the planet, but then the voice came back and he passed out cold.

When he awoke the next day, Michael had no memory of what happened after that moment. All he knew was he was never allowed to drink again and that God had chosen him. There were no specific instructions that he could recall, just a deep-seated need to clean his act up and spread the Word of the Lord. He had not one second of doubt of his destiny, no matter how much everyone laughed at him. He was absolutely certain that God had chosen him for a mission. After another shower later that day, he kissed his mother, asked for forty dollars, and headed to the bus station to buy a ride to Montpelier, a few hours' journey from his home in New Hampshire. Until the name of the city came out of his mouth, he didn't even know where he was going. God had placed his destination onto his tongue as he approached the ticket window.

A few days later, he was sleeping in Hubbard Park in the capital of Vermont. It took him two months to secure a job cleaning the kitchens at the local culinary school after hours. A few weeks after that, he had earned enough to move into an efficiency apartment on Main Street. Four months later, he changed his name and his pilgrimage began. His days were spent handing out flyers, no matter the weather, and his nights were spent cleaning the kitchens. Before he knew it, seven years had passed.

The last two years, Adriel started to question his mission— not his faith: no, he would never question that. But why the voice in his head told him he had to stand in the same place, which was not busy at all, day after day, no matter the weather, was beyond his understanding. He liked to fantasize that one day he would hand a flyer to someone who would be so changed by the Lord's Word that they went on to become a great preacher and change the world. The days when he stood in the heat, sweating and burning or shivering and freezing, he meditated on that idea or another, like maybe one day he would be standing there and save the life of a child in the street, right there in front of the Capitol building. It would be a huge spectacle caught on someone's cell phone camera—a miracle some would say—and that miracle would inspire millions to go back to their faith. He did his best to focus on the positive outcome his sacrifice would surely bring, but after seven years of nothing but being ignored and called crazy, he began to suspect that his vision might have been wrong.

Before the package arrived during that seventh year, things were darkest they'd ever been for Adriel. He prayed, hard, hard as anyone could, day and night. He prayed so much that the minister of the church actually asked him to take a break and leave on more than one occasion. His crisis of belief started to take a toll on Adriel: he didn't shower as much, he no longer shaved, adding to his frail frame a long beard that made him look like a homeless Jesus Christ, and worst of all, he began to crave a drink for the first time since the vision—and that scared him.

On two occasions, while walking back the short half-mile to his apartment from the State House, he found himself stopping at the local bars to look in the windows. He wouldn't let himself enter, though one time he had an incident at the Capital Plaza Hotel, where they were always kind enough to let him use the bathroom. Adriel always loved the ancient, period décor of the tiny lobby, so much so that on bad weather days, he would linger there to warm up, cool off, or stay dry until the manager gave him a nod that he had worn out his welcome. That particular morning, after making his way down the skinny hall to the bathroom near the back entrance, he stopped at the open door to the banquet hall, which was propped open, as it was being cleaned. There, parked directly in the entrance, was a large brown waiter tray covered in empty bottles and glasses,

glasses half full of wine and beer and…whisky. He stood there, stiff and achy with desire for the amber liquid-—hell, any high octane liquid. In his head, he pictured himself downing one glass after another. Licking his chapped lips, he debated grabbing the small rocks glass that held a watered-down centimeter of liquid and tossing it back. But then, out of nowhere, a chubby waitress walked over, smiled at him, and grabbed the tray. What he remembered the most about that moment was the woman was wearing a gold cross around her neck. It was then that he knew: God was *still* speaking to him, telling him to continue to fight temptation in service of Him.

After work that night, he went to the church and was not surprised to find it locked up; it was after two o'clock, after all. Instead of going home to sleep, he fell to his knees in front of the dingy gray steps and prayed. Over and over again, he recited every prayer he knew and pledged his love for God and Jesus, kissing the cement and offering his eternal worship and faith. Most of all, he begged God for a sign that he was in the right place, doing the work He wanted Adriel to do, for he was a warrior for God and would do anything. He held his arms to the sky and yelled into the air, explaining he could no longer continue, begging to be put to better use, but nothing happened.

The next day, the package arrived.

Returning home after six hours of trying to hand out flyers, Adriel trotted up the stairs at the same time he always did, an hour before he was due to begin his evening job. This left him just enough time to eat and take a break before cleaning all night. When he reached the top of his crooked steps, he was confused to see a long, skinny white box resting against the chipped red door. In the seven years he had been there, this was the first time he had ever received a package. He picked it up, figuring it must have been a mistake, but then he saw his name typed neatly on the label. There was no return address. Immediately his heart started to thud excitedly. *He had asked for a sign. Could God have been that literal and sent something to him?*

Rushing inside, he took the package and set it on the table. He was starting to sweat. He snatched a kitchen knife and with trembling hands, he cut the tape on each side, then sliced down the long seam on top. The package was nearly two feet long, but only four inches wide. His mind started to race, wondering what it could be. Sitting down at the one chair he had in the kitchen, he took a moment to pray and thank God for whatever he was about to receive, even if it wasn't from the Lord himself. He said this, but deep inside, he knew it was from God. He kissed the cross that hung around his neck then used both hands to open the package.

Inside was a swaddling of white butcher paper wrapped around something long and thin, like a stick. He ran his fingers lightly along the object, the waxy paper reminded him of twine, like the butcher had always used on the slabs of meat his mother had purchased from the market when he was a child. With this thought, Adriel let out a gasp, recalling the verse in the Bible where the word *twine* was used:

Job 8:17-19

Their roots twine around the stoneheap;
they live among the rocks.

If they are destroyed from their place,
then it will deny them, saying, "I have never seen you."

See, these are their happy ways,
and out of the earth still others will spring.

He had known that learning every word of the Good Book, all versions, would come in handy one day. God was trying to tell him something and His making Adriel remember the twine was the first of his messages. He held the package in both of his hands like a sacred relic; the object inside of the paper was solid, but not too heavy. He gingerly pulled back the butcher paper, and as he peeled back the final layer, what he saw made him fall to his knees. He was holding a human rib. It wasn't cleaned and bleached like one would see in a museum; no, this rib looked as if it had been recently cut from a body and scraped clean by a hunter: the same way it would have looked when God took the rib from Adam.

Genesis 2:21-22

So the Lord God caused a deep sleep to fall upon the
man, and while he slept took
one of his ribs and closed up its place with flesh.
And the rib that the Lord God
had taken from the man he made into a woman
and brought her to the man.

Adriel prayed, his hands flat on the ground, his forehead touching the old dirty linoleum, and he sobbed, thanking God over and over again for the gift He had bestowed upon him. His body was weak from both excitement and the new understanding that the past seven years had not been a waste. When he was able to stand and look upon the rib again, he leaned over and kissed it gently. After his lips left the cold bone, he spotted a small piece of paper he had not seen before. There was more! He grabbed it excitedly, hoping and wondering if it would be clear instructions this time.

```
A girl whose status is unknown
    Pieces sent to a chosen few
  Action is yours; her destiny own
A rib or a fib, it's now up to you.
```

All of these years, all of the people who had called him crazy, those who laughed at and walked past him without a second glance…they had been the crazy ones all along. He was the one laughing now, because there in his hands was physical proof that God, the Lord himself, had chosen HIM. Adriel laughed out loud, tears still pouring from his eyes. He raised the bone above his head with both hands and screamed into the air. *I serve you Lord, I serve you. I shall not fail you!*

It took almost a solid hour of crying and praying before Adriel realized he was late for work. Part of him wanted to forget the job completely, but the other part didn't know if he had to keep the job—God hadn't told him that yet—so he called his boss and called out of work for the first time since he had started there, saying he had a cold. Immediately after the words left his mouth, a sharp jab of pain shot through his gut. He had just told a *fib*. The word replayed over and over in his head: *fib, fib, fib.* God had known he would lie. What did He want Adriel to do now? There was so much to figure out. For the next fifteen hours, Adriel highlighted verses in his Bible, wrote down scripture and quotes, and theorized what his new mission would be. The one thing he did not do was ask or pray for more information. God had given him a sign, one more palpable than most in the Bible. When new scripture was written, he would likely appear in the pages as one of God's chosen disciples. People would worship and follow his actions, and wear pendants with his name on them. He had been selected as a true vessel for the Lord. This thought spread such joy over his body he had to sit and hug his arms around his shoulders several times. The ecstasy of having been chosen was beyond any pleasure the physical world had ever given him.

The next morning, after more than twenty-four hours of no sleep, no food, and no shower, Adriel realized he needed a break. He couldn't carry on his mission, after all, if he could not function. He rewrapped the rib and the note, carefully stuffed them into his jacket pocket, making sure they sat snugly against his own ribs, grabbed his Good Book and headed downstairs to the only restaurant he ate at, Down Home. The place was located on Main Street, a mere minute walk from his apartment door. Once inside, he sat at a booth and buried his nose in the Bible as the waitress poured coffee into the clean cup on the table. He absentmindedly asked for his standard breakfast of eggs, toast, and hash browns, and after a few sips of coffee, he looked up from his scripture and rubbed his eyes. It was then that the TV in the corner caught his attention.

The Today Show was playing; he couldn't hear the words but he saw the pretty hosts introduce a packaged segment on a celebrity family, the kind of people who were famous only for being famous. Adriel couldn't look away: it disgusted him to no end. Their life was pure greed and excess. The segment was short and ended with three of the heavily-made-up, collagen-injected daughters doing a photo shoot with diamonds. *Greed,* Adriel thought. As the program shifted its focus to something more serious, terrorists in some foreign country, a number flashed on the screen, over a thousand dead in the name of a different God. *Blasphemy*. The word flashed in Adriel's mind. Again, the segment was short and soon evolved into the next story. This third one was an outdoor cooking segment on how to prepare for a football game party.

Gluttony.

As the flash news program pummeled its audience with one segment after another, Adriel glanced about the restaurant. The other patrons watched the screen with glazed eyes, unemotional, unaffected. The people consumed the information like hogs in front of a trough. Even outside of the idiot box, Adriel realized, the world was full of sin. Certainly, he had always known this, but the extent was beyond what he had ever imagined. Everyone was sinning, constantly, and there was no end to the sacrilege in sight.

God had created life with a rib, and now, he wanted Adriel to destroy life with it so that it could start over clean. It was just like the floods and Noah, only this time, humans needed to learn in a much more violent way. After all, how else could they wake from their trances and understand? There had been floods and earthquakes and natural disasters daily, yet no one had changed. It had to be him, it had to be by his hand, with the very weapon God had provided: the rib. It was finally clear.

If they are destroyed from their place,
then it will deny them, saying, "I have never seen you."

See, these are their happy ways,
and out of the earth still others will spring.

If he destroyed the sinners, they will not enter heaven, it will be as if God had never seen them. Then others would spring forward to create a new paradise. Adriel placed his hand on his chest. The rib felt warm as if it were emanating heat to assure him he was right: this was his mission. This was what he'd been waiting for.

it's now up to you.

The line in the poem resonated in his head. The thought of killing another human had never crossed his mind before. At first, he thought he'd be disgusted, repulsed by the idea of destroying one of God's children, but now that he had his mission, he was excited to rid the earth of sin. After he finished his breakfast, Adriel headed a few storefronts down to Aubuchon Hardware, one of the last Mom and Pop businesses in upper New England, and purchased a few tools to assist in his holy crusade. Twenty minutes later, he was back in his apartment, the rib and a small arsenal spread out on his table.

Carving the rib into a point was harder than he thought it would be. At first, he used a knife, then he switched to a sander, then he went back to the knife. In the end, it was not nearly as sharp as he would have liked, but it definitely would penetrate skin as long as he put enough force behind it. If it didn't, he had a small axe that fit in his waist of his pants and a hunting knife that strapped to his leg. The last thing he did in his preparation, the step most important to Adriel, was to carve 15:13 into the flattest part of the rib. It represented the verse in the Bible that he now understood he was responsible for.

Chronicles 15:13
But that whoever would not seek the Lord, the God of Israel,
should be put to death, whether young or old, man or woman.

It was at ten in the morning, as the news and police reports would later state, that Adriel took his flyers and walked out of his apartment for the last time. On the short walk over to the Capitol lawn, Adriel was happier than he had been in his entire life: he finally had his purpose. The thought of dying that day did not cross his mind, for he knew the Lord would not allow a disciple to die until His work was complete. He had to kill the sinners and the non-believers, for as long and as hard as he could muster. He would not rest until God told him he could rest.

When he arrived in front of the wide building with its rounded gold roof, Adriel began his normal routine of handing out flyers. He savored these last moments because he knew they were leading up to his *real* work. He was struck with divine inspiration when the fourth sinner in less than a minute ignored his hand offering the flyer. He had to preach, had to say one last thing, to give sinners a chance to repent. Without hesitation, Adriel jumped onto a nearby park bench and started to scream, "Attention, please, I need your attention." No one stopped; only a handful of passers-by even glanced.

Adriel was crestfallen, but he understood that the time of reckoning had arrived. As he looked around for a crowd, he spotted the art class setting up on the long walkway that led to the front entrance of the building. There were twenty or so people with easels set up; most were elderly people, some were middle-aged women, and a few were twenty-year-olds, but all were opening up paint sets as a plump woman dressed like a forgotten hippie stood in front of them, apparently attempting to deliver instructions as she adamantly pointed to the golden dome. He instantly knew it was the library's free weekly art class as he had seen the attendees around the Capitol grounds many times. Part of his gut twisted as they seemed like good, normal people who would worship, but then it eased because he knew God would not allow him to kill any of the true believers.

Adriel jumped off the bench and slowly made his way over to the artists. As he circled the crowd, he got a good look at their faces as they stared at the dome, their skin appearing golden in the reflection of the sun. The glow told him that they were the ones God selected for him; He had sent His light onto them like a divine spotlight. Adriel smiled, walked into the middle of their gathering, pulled out the rib, and held it above his head like a magic wand. Only a few people looked at him, but no one seemed to care or even know what he was holding. Then he said, in a calm, but stern voice, "Matthew 10:34: *Do not think that I have come to bring peace to the earth. I have not come to bring peace, but a sword.*" Out of the corner of his eye, he could see the teacher approaching on his left. Before she could ask him to leave, he swung down his hand and planted the tip of the rib right into her belly.

Adriel held the rib deep inside of the woman, enjoying the warm sensation of blood flowing over his knuckles. As he looked into her shocked and pained face contorting with confusion, he whispered *Sinner* into her ear. As he removed the rib he thought about plunging it back into her body once more, but he knew she would die and he had many more sinners to go, so he moved onto the next one, a woman who looked to have been in her late eighties.

This woman stared at him with shock but did not move. Just as he was about to swing the rib at her, he saw the cross on her neck. "Do you really believe, child?" Adriel asked, and the woman nodded vigorously. "Then drop to your knees and pray for the other sinners who will die today." The woman, who probably suffered from severe arthritis and hadn't been on her knees in decades, dropped like a stone and began to pray.

At this point, the chaos had begun. The younger artists were already fifty or so yards away, running at full speed, not once glancing behind to their abandoned easels. Others hobbled away, a few were hiding, and still others stood frozen in shock. Adrenaline was starting to pump in Adriel's veins and it made him move faster. The next sinner was a man in his mid-fifties with an ear ring in his left ear and a rainbow pinned to his shirt. The man was backing away, but he had been trembling so much that his leg muscle control seemed to dislodge from his brain. Adriel took this opportunity and pounced on the man, bringing the rib down into the crook of his neck. It plunged into his artery, spraying blood in a theatrical and almost comical manner, covering both of the men in a sticky, red wave. Again, Adriel whispered the one word to his victim, though this one said two words back: *Fuck you.*

Adriel ran to the next sinner, a thirty-something-year-old woman who was rather attractive and wearing workout clothing. She must have been jogging by when the melee started but tripped and broke her ankle as it was bent in an unnatural way. She couldn't get up and was crawling, dragging her left leg behind her, into the middle of the road. Using two hands he swung the rib down with such force he thought it would crack the woman's own ribs, but she was young and in shape and rolled out of the way of the incoming bone. The rib hit the pavement with such speed it splintered into four large, sharp pieces. Bringing up his bloody hands, Adriel was furious. The gift from the Lord was broken.

Without hesitation, Adriel pulled the small axe from his belt, turned and swung it down at the woman; this time, her reflexes were not fast enough and the blade caught her in her bare shoulder, splitting the skin open and exposing her musculature for the world to see. Instinctively, she brought her hand to the wound as Adriel removed the axe. The woman screamed and tried to use her good leg to kick at him, but Adriel was in full vengeance mode and would not be stopped.

"An eye for an eye, a rib for a rib," he screamed as he brought down the axe, once, twice, then three times. The first swing split her face open, killing her instantly; the second one made contact with her chest and cracked her sternum with ease. The third broke open her chest cavity, exposing the intricate inner workings God had created on the sixth day. With his left hand, Adriel stuck his fingers inside of the woman's chest cavity and pulled up on her rib cage. His hand felt warm and pleasant inside of her as if he could feel God's love still pulsing inside of the sinner. As he raised the axe to come down on the other side of her chest to free the rib he would use in place of the one she had destroyed, he heard three loud popping noises. They were instantly followed by three searing bolts of pain through his own chest.

As he fell to the ground, he remembered that the fire station was a mere fifty yards away from where he started his mission. It was probably a bad idea, but God was going to protect him. The noises, screams, and sirens in the air started to echo and distort in his ears. Absentmindedly, he reached around for the axe but he could not find it; it must have slid away after he fell. A second later, two men, both in firefighter uniforms, were above him, holding some weird crowbar-looking things with deadly-looking hooks. Adriel took a deep breath and despite the blinding flashes of agony, laughed as he realized his own ribs had been shattered by bullets. While his vision was blurry, he saw one man lower his weapon as he bent over to secure him. At the same time, the other man looked over at the woman lying in the puddle of blood a few feet away. Adriel used this split second to reach for the hunting knife strapped to his leg. It was a quick and painful struggle, but like he thought, God was on his side. The lieutenant who held the bar at him swung, trying to stop Adriel, but the other fireman whose knees were now on his chest got in the way; he caught the nasty-looking hook right in the neck and fell off of

Adriel like a brick falling from the sky. The first man pulled back the bar, blood dripping from it. A firefighter's instincts are to rescue, so without a second thought, the man dropped the bar and started to help his brother-in-arms, ignoring Adriel, who was getting to his knees with the knife.

It was difficult, but Adriel was able to get the knife deep inside of the fireman's ribs from behind. After a few twists of Adriel's hand, the man fell on top of his co-worker. Standing once again, despite the immense pain, Adriel held the knife to the sky and started to preach once more. "Man shall be restored in that time, namely, in the days of the Messiah, to that state in which he was before the first man sinned…"

He did not notice the Capitol security guards running toward him, their guns drawn. He didn't even hear the shots they fired, nor did he have time to realize he was going to die or that God had finally forsaken him. His head merely erupted in a pulpy, red explosion.

The Fraud

Karen threw her rocks glass—scotch, ice cubes, and all—as hard as she could muster at the television. Both she and Dennis were amazed to see that neither object, the glass nor the set, had sustained major damage; the glass fell to the carpet in a muffled clatter and the broad screen showed only a small circle where the object had made contact. Behind that circle and the splattering of liquid that had jumped ship during the scuffle was the image of a cable news reporter with blonde hair and severe eye makeup. The headline *Punisher Proven to be Fraud* scrolled across the news ticker.

"…our sources tell Court Channel that Ms. Sweeney made the formal name change from Becker after passing the bar exam in New York State, although it's unclear what prompted this decision."

The screen changed to frame another talking head, this one a slim man in his mid-forties with silvering hair. "Bette, we tried to confirm these facts with District Attorney Sweeney but her office has declined comment. According to our sources, Karen Sweeney grew up in an affluent household, and her parents were not, in fact, mugged and murdered by an unknown assailant. Both attended her graduation ceremony at Harvard Law. Ms. Sweeney was raised in Lexington, a suburb of Boston, Massachusetts, and attended private schooling in New England until completing her law degree. A source close to the Becker family indicates that at that point, Ms. Sweeney wished to do some traveling, but her father insisted she find employment and would no longer be supporting her financially." The pundit squinted into the camera as if listening to a question on his earpiece, then continued. "Mr. Becker passed away about a month after that declaration. His death was ruled an accident, though we were unable to glean more specifics."

Karen stood motionless with one hand resting on her breastbone, staring at the screen. She began to finger the thin, gold necklace that she never removed from her neck. Dennis could tell that she wished she hadn't thrown away her alcohol. She stayed facing the television as she spoke. "I was in the middle of moving out of my apartment in Cambridge. My lease was up at the end of August, and I wanted to move to New York City, but I didn't have the cash saved up. My parents had paid for everything, even my housing, so it never occurred to me to get a job. Besides, going to school had been my job: isn't that what they say to kids?" Karen smirked. "So, you could say it was his fault... he *enabled* me, that's what my parents' friends said. Enabled. Like I was some sort of alleyway alcoholic or something."

Dennis shifted his weight from foot to foot. He could always sense when his mother was about to explode, and even at the age of twenty-four, with a good fifty or sixty pounds on her, Dennis felt his heart race in fight or flight preparation.

"So, I had no choice but to store most of my belongings at my parents' home. Lord knows they had plenty of room. I slipped home in the middle of a weekday. I thought no one would be there except the help, and the security cameras and alarms would be turned off." She bit her lip again, not to keep from crying, but to prevent herself from clenching her jaw, a painful habit she'd developed recently. "I mean, she didn't ever wear most of the fucking jewelry anyway, and he scared the bejesus out of me, lurking at the top of the stairs, his arms crossed in front of him, just waiting to catch me in the act or something."

On the television, the silver-haired reporter was interviewing some lackey from the mayor's office. Both men were frowning. Dennis held his breath.

"You see, Denny, it's like the lullabies and nursery rhymes I told you as a child. The real ones. Nothing is ever as flawlessly beautiful as it seems. There is always ugliness underneath," Karen said, still facing the screen. "Those silly tales are all there to teach you one essential truth in life: survival of the fittest. Natural selection. Sometimes, the only way to not be the prey is to be the predator."

The blonde anchorwoman's image returned to the screen. "Given that much of Sweeney's fame came from her active crusade to 'find' the perpetrators of her parents' nonexistent death, critics are wondering if she is fit to serve as district attorney with two years left on her second term. While the office isn't a popularity contest, city officials are concerned that blatant dishonesty could fall under the umbrella of moral turpitude.

Do we know what prompted her to engage in this charade? Perhaps our guest tonight can shed some light on this. Jax Matthews had been a reporter at the *Post* for two years when he broke the story of what some are calling 'The Media Molester.' Last week, the paper debuted a weekly column devoted solely to his investigative journalism. Jax, welcome to the program."

"Arrrgggh!" Karen suddenly yelled out in frustration and stomped her foot like a two-year old having a tantrum. "That piece of shit asshole." She stomped her foot one more time, and as she did, the cell phone tucked in the back pocket of her jeans began to trill. "These fucking vultures are ripping me into pieces. It's like everyone wants a mouthful for themselves to tear to bits," she yelled. She pulled out her device, looked at the screen, turned, and walked quickly down the hall and into the kitchen as she answered the call. Dennis stayed put. Once he knew his mother was out of sight, he allowed the smile that had been bubbling beneath his skin to spill onto his face. He picked up the remote control and raised the volume a few notches.

"…reveal a source, Bette. My readers trust me, and I won't betray them. All I can say is that everything in the letter checked out, and then some." Jax grinned like a canary-filled cat. "You gotta get the facts, Bette." He turned and looked into the camera's lens. "But, I will say this to my pen pal: thank you for your courage in coming forward with this chicanery. America is a better place because of people like you."

Dennis pressed the OFF button but stood watching the screen as it turned empty and black. He could hear glasses and plates breaking, one by one, in the kitchen sink, interspaced with primal screams of frustration from Karen. "Trust me, Jax," Dennis said out loud, still smiling. "The pleasure was all mine."

Present day

The woman at the sandwich counter was becoming

annoyed. "I said NO onions. It's written there right on the slip," she said, tapping her foot slightly and issuing a dramatic sigh.

Dennis was sitting at a high-top table at the local coffee and sandwich restaurant, a Christian-themed knock-off of Panera that decorated the bottom of its wall menus with the phrase *God Bless All of Us*. There were four of these shops within a twenty-mile radius, a mini-chain of sorts, and Dennis had visited each of them over the past two weeks, scarfing up the free and unfettered Wi-Fi while treating himself to dinner each time. Although the sign that was posted prominently on each of the front doors, *We are closed on Sundays in recognition of the Lord's decree*, had irritated him to no end—religious sentiment of any kind had always done so—he had to admit, the paninis were awfully tasty. Besides, the company had not been savvy enough to implement a firewall on their public internet. He needed to be able to browse newsfeeds and social media hysteria unfiltered.

The customer paid a second employee who was stationed at the register, then pocketed her change, ignoring the prominent tip jar nearby, much to a lack of surprise from the blank-faced college student who'd assembled her order. "Seriously. Is this job really that hard?" she said to him as a final send-off.

When the woman turned to locate an open table, Dennis pretended to adjust his prescription-less eyeglasses and be engrossed in his screen read. Much to his chagrin, he caught the woman out of the corner of his eye sliding into a booth immediately across the aisle from him. She continued to speak, as if Dennis had been part of the conversation all along. "I mean, what are these kids going to do when they have to work a *real* job? No Child Left Behind, my ass. They seem to get stupider every year."

Dennis pretended not to hear her. Not only did he not want to be interrupted, he had always made it a habit not to irritate or offend individuals who had access to his food or drink: he didn't want to appear sympathetic and the next time he visited, find a used Band-Aid pressed into his sandwich. He subtly tilted his screen away from the woman and clicked on an entry in the True Crime Reddit with the heading *The Hangman's noose reached all the way to St. Pete's, FL: my neighbor opened his package and threw up all over our lawn!* from the previous evening.

⬆
⬇ BieberliciousCasey 5 points • 1 day ago
I've been following this story since they reported the part in Montana. I think there's gotta be, like, multiple killers, right? I mean IMHO it seems like a shitload of work to get all those parts mailed to people.
Share   Report   Save

⬆
⬇ bigleaguechaw 1 point • 1 day ago
What part did your neighbor get? I didn't see anything about a Florida piece
Share   Report   Save

⬆
⬇ MurderINO6598 3 points • within hours
It was on tampabay.com this morning. The heart. I'd ralph too.
It is probably one guy but more than one victim. My roommates and I are keeping track as the parts get reported. So far, they don't make a whole body. Lots of missing pieces. Wonder what he did with those?
Share   Report   Save

⬆
⬇ kushballer80 1 point • just now
Hundred bucks says he ate them. Sick fahk.
Share   Report   Save

With this, Dennis stuffed the last bite of his dinner into his mouth and unfolded and refolded his napkin, trying to find a clean spot. He closed the private Safari window, packed up his laptop, picked up his tray, and got up to leave. The irate customer was watching him from her seat in the booth next door. When he looked at her briefly, she smiled, a look that said, *I'm just like you. We have to stick together.* He was careful not to register any emotion on his face at all and walked nonchalantly to the waste barrel to dump his trash.

He wasn't looking forward to doing the laundry, but he had let his work clothes pile up in the hamper next to his shower for far too long, and he had a busy weekend planned and would be nowhere near home. He could probably cram all of the clothes into two loads and be done before it was time to shower and complete his routine for bed. In the meantime, he could go for a run while the machines were plugging along. He was considering this plan when he turned the corner onto his street and spotted the police cruiser parked at the other end. As he pulled into his driveway, he saw the uniformed officer place a business card in his neighbor's screen door and turn and trot down the four front steps.

Dennis shoved his fake eyeglasses into the console tray, picked up his jacket and Macbook from the passenger seat, and casually climbed out of the car. He turned toward the officer, who was walking down the sidewalk in Dennis's direction, and purposefully fixed a mild frown on his forehead, a look that he believed said, *Hmmm… this is curious. I hope nothing is amiss in my staid, picturesque neighborhood that a policeman should be wandering about.* What he said out loud was, "Evening," and he gave a small nod of his head and began to stroll blithely up his walk to his porch entrance.

"Hey there," the officer said, giving a friendly wave. He looked down at a small notepad in his left hand. "Mr., uh, Sweeney? Mr. Sweeney, do you have a moment to talk?"

Dennis fixed a pleasant smile across his face and shellacked it with quick-drying adhesive. Without missing a beat, he said, "Sure, no problem. Do you mind coming inside while I drop these things off?" He gestured to his coat and computer case.

"Not at all."

"Great."

The two men walked in what seemed like a long period of silence. Dennis concentrated on slowing his breath. He told himself that the man was not there for The Hangman: he couldn't be. Wouldn't the FBI or the riot squad or something along those lines have come instead? This was a beat cop, and he was alone at that, unless his partner was busy inside another house on his street. Interviewing his neighbors about Dennis. Inquiring about Dennis's comings and goings. Asking if they ever saw anything strange going on in Dennis's home. Questioning Dennis's—

"I'm Officer David Gallup," the cop said, thrusting a business card in Dennis' direction once they were standing in the kitchen. "I'm investigating a series of break-ins on your street over the past two months. Are you aware that a number of your neighbors have had their cars stolen?"

Dennis accepted the card and placed it in his shirt pocket without looking at it. "Yes, I've heard that. Made me much more conscientious about turning my alarm on, that's for sure." He paused. "Can I get you anything to drink? Coffee? Tea? A couple of bottles of water for you and your partner?" He picked up the iron tea kettle on the stove, an antique Karen had brought with her when she had invaded his home; he had kept it there more as decoration than anything else.

Officer Gallup looked flustered, but not with Dennis. "That's kind of you, but you're my last stop. I've tried all of your neighbors' doors and only got one answer. I didn't think anyone would still be at work at this hour. I'll try again after my dinner break, which is where I'm going right after I leave here." He patted the slight pooch in his abdomen and grinned. "In any case," he began again, clicking the end of a pen and positioning it over the paper. "Have you seen anyone hanging around the neighborhood who doesn't live here or who seemed suspicious?"

Dennis took a purposeful pause and stared out into space, as if searching his memory. "No… no one I can think of."

"Any damage to your car or anything gone missing around your property?"

Again, Dennis paused and pretended to think. "No, nothing. I guess I've been lucky."

Officer Gallup made another notation in his book. "Okay then. Well, you have my card. If anything comes to you or if you do see something suspicious, please report it. We've had more reports of theft on this street in the past month than in the whole east side combined."

"Wow… well, then yeah, of course. And I'll keep my eyes open," said Dennis. He started to walk toward the door to escort the cop outside.

"Hey, do you mind if I use your facilities while I'm here?" Officer Gallup asked, looking around the room, letting his eyes rest on each and every object. *Is he looking for a toilet in the kitchen?* Dennis thought. And then he saw it. The envelope containing the next letter he planned to mail to Jax Matthews was hanging from a magnetic bag-clip on the front of his refrigerator; he had placed it there to keep it safe until he could drive to the coast that weekend and slip it into a mailbox. Dennis could read the address from where he stood, two feet further away than Officer Gallup.

"Of course, no problem. Bathroom's down the hall, first door on the right," Dennis said.

The policeman tipped his head, checked his notebook quickly, and started toward the doorway. "Say, is a Karen Sweeney still at this address by any chance? Census says she lives here too... your... er, mother?" He turned into the hallway and continued to speak with his back turned to Dennis. "I'd like to talk to—"

He never saw the teakettle. It came down, hard, on the back of his head. He hadn't heard Dennis as he darted, quick as a mouse, back to the stove and then behind him. And by the time he had hit the floor and Dennis had rolled him onto his back, he mercifully had passed out cold, so he didn't feel the blows that followed as Dennis brought the kettle down over and over onto his nose and jaw, his teeth cracking and spraying from his mouth like jumping beans.

Piece #19
Boston, MA

Cory stared out of the window of her fourth-floor dorm room. Below, cars whizzed by on Storrow Drive, bobbing and weaving like prize fighters circling their opponents; beyond that, a crew team moved in unison along the Charles River, arms and oars waving, a graceful millipede gliding along the deep green water.

Her roommate since freshman year, Meghan, had gone home for the weekend, so she could relax in peace. She didn't have to hide in the stacks at the library until eleven P.M. under the ruse of having a social life. When she returned to the University after summer break, she'd smuggled a small bottle of Jameson whiskey in her duffle bag, and two weeks later, she'd binge-drunk it, spilling a sprinkle of it here and there on her sweater for good measure so that she could return to their tiny double reeking of booze, pretending to have attended a fraternity kegger at nearby Northeastern. It was a full-time job pretending to be well-adjusted. She'd savor the three-day reprieve.

College had been a tough adjustment, notwithstanding the move to a big city five hours from her small-town home, but not as academically difficult as she had worried it would be. She thought the classes would be hard, and while she was challenged with new ideas and fascinated by many of the lectures her professors delivered, she didn't have to study much to earn straight A's on exams. She wrote her papers weeks before their due dates and used the rest of her library camouflage act to read about absurd medical anomalies and rare psychological disorders. Last week, while nibbling the edge of the steaming burrito from Qdoba she'd smuggled into the fifth-floor stacks, she fingered the edge of the medical reference book's page with her pinky.

Trimethylaminuria, or Fish Odor Syndrome, was first discovered in 1970. It causes the sufferer to emit a foul body odor akin to rotten eggs, dead fish, or garbage.

Cory swallowed, then sniffed her food suspiciously. She leaned her head toward her shoulder and inhaled deeply through her nose. Did she have Trimethylaminuria? She didn't think so, but how would she know, really? I mean, how did people know if they smelled foul unless someone told them? What if people had been too embarrassed—or even worse, too nauseated—to give her a heads-up? She returned the mammoth tome to the shelf and removed another one, then quickly flipped to a random page with her left hand, still clutching her clandestine dinner in her right. In the middle of the article was a black and white photograph of a small toddler wearing a pair of frilly white bloomers and a badly stained bib. It was hard to determine what had caused the stain; to Cory, it looked to be gravy or spaghetti sauce of some sort. She read the adjacent text.

Cyclic Vomiting Syndrome affects children ages three to seven, producing waves of sustained nausea and vomiting every few months, weeks, or even days.

Cory hated to throw up. Terrified of experiencing this unpleasant symptom of food poisoning, she rarely ate leftovers, had never taken even a bite of cold pizza, and when she prepared Ramen noodle soup or EasyMac canisters using the microwave she shared with Meghan in their dorm room, she added an additional 30 to 45 seconds of cook time for good measure, content that the resulting boil-over mess or tacky consistency was worth certain obliteration of any harmful bacteria. She wondered what she would do if she had a child with this cyclic vomiting disorder. More than likely, she'd drag the tot to Walmart and "accidentally" leave him behind in an abandoned grocery aisle.

Of course, a distaste for throwing up wasn't a mental disorder; if anything, it would prevent her from ever becoming a successful bulimic, but she did admit to having her share of mental illnesses. It was the twenty-first century, for Christ's sake: if you didn't have at least one bout of loony tunes before the age of thirty, you were probably a robot, or at the very least, in denial. Cory chalked it up to an after-effect of 9/11. Although she had been only a toddler at the time of the terrorist attacks, it was her own personal theory that everyone in the country, maybe even the world, had contracted a shared post-traumatic stress disorder, the collective unconscious breaking out in epidemics of depression, anxiety, and psychosis like children with lice in a daycare. Her own mother, a former pageant queen turned nail salon receptionist, had been treated for pica when Cory was a freshman in high school.

Individuals with Pica suffer from a compulsive urge to eat non-food items. This disorder can originate with a change in the body's equilibrium such as iron deficiency or pregnancy. Other times, it is triggered by stress. Sufferers have been known to consume rocks, chalk, and glass, paint, wood, and even body parts. This patient (see photo above) had ingested more than 1,000 metal items, including nails, tacks, and salt shaker tops, before dying during the surgery to remove the items.

One day, when Cory returned home after tennis practice, she stumbled upon her mother eating a bar of soap in the guest bathroom. As her daughter stood wide-eyed and mouth agape, Cory's mom took a big bite of the swirled-pink bar, chewed it into small bits, and swallowed. By the time his wife returned from the treatment facility a few months later, Cory's father had replaced all of the bars in the house with pump dispensers, and everyone used liquid body wash in the shower, although from then on, each time she squeezed a healthy glob of the liquid into a washcloth, Cory imagined her mother tipping back her head and chugging the substance in secret.

Cory had two disorders that she knew of, even though she had never shared this information with anyone and certainly had never sought treatment for either of them. The first, she'd determined, was kleptomania. She and Meghan shared a mailbox in the lobby of their building; each dorm room was assigned one box, but it was large enough to accommodate moderately sized care packages from home. Cory didn't receive care packages. It wasn't that her parents didn't love her—they did—but rather, they simply didn't think she needed any TLC or cheerleading from the sidelines. Their Cory had been a straight-A student, editor of the school newspaper, captain of the tennis team, and runner-up for Homecoming Queen both her junior and senior year. She didn't need a shoebox full of

Hershey's with Almonds and Little Debbie Nutty bars: their girl was *a-okay* on her own. Meghan's parents, on the other hand, sent a cornucopia of sugary sweets and carb-happy snack bags every thirty days. Cory's roommate always shared the bounty with her, leaving each box open atop of their small refrigerator for anyone to peruse, but there was something about the monthly arrival that gnawed at Cory's psyche. It, along with Meghan's seemingly endless holiday deliveries, greeting cards, and even discount coupons and personalized invitations to customer appreciation extravaganzas from area restaurants and clothing stores, chipped away at Cory's self-esteem. Her roommate's excessive snail mail, juxtaposed with Cory's impersonal bank statement, made her feel small, unimportant. It made her feel forgotten.

And so, by the time their first fall semester together was winding down, when it was her turn to retrieve the mail from their shared box, Cory began to take some of the letters and packages addressed to Meghan. She'd smuggle them up to their room and tuck them deep inside the bottom drawer of her dresser until she was sure Meghan had left for her night class or was certain to be away for a good two or three hours. Then, surreptitiously, she'd pull the loot from its hiding place and savor opening each piece. She'd pretend the pastel envelopes and boxes addressed in swirly cursive were addressed to her, soak in the well-wishes and juicy bits of gossip sprinkled here and there in personal notes from the senders. On the invitation to a post-Christmas party back in Meghan's hometown, the host hand-wrote, *Jason will be there: I know he's dying to go with you! Totally text him when you get a chance: he will freak!* Nestled within the small box of conversation heart candies and cherry Lifesaver lollipops, Meghan's mom's simple note read, *Sending you hugs and kisses, Valentine. Be safe! xxx Love you.* Inside of the folded postcard from Sephora, a typed message declared, *Happy Birthday, Beauty Insider!* and included a coupon for a free vanilla cake-scented hand lotion.

After a few months of this, Cory finally had opened her laptop and googled "stealing mail disorder." Nearly all of the results provided overviews of general kleptomania, but Cory had no impulse to steal anything else: she had a specific compulsion to swipe Meghan's mail. Certainly, there had to be some definition of the illness she'd contracted. On page three of her results, *Weekly World View* featured a faux news story on a postman charged with a federal offense of pilfering his route's mail after he was admitted to a hospital with an intestinal blockage; apparently, he hadn't just been stealing the mail, he'd been consuming it in obscene amounts. The accompanying photograph showed a man with a bloated belly being led away in handcuffs, a gaggle of uniformed police officers surrounding him on all sides. Cory had laughed, then quickly covered her mouth in shame, hoping any library patrons wandering the upper stacks hadn't heard her.

She finished the last bite of the burrito, wiped her mouth with the waxy wrapper, then placed the crumpled paper into her jeans pocket. There were far worse things to suffer from than kleptomania, she'd decided, and it had been to reassure herself of that fact that Cory had begun browsing the medical textbooks on the fifth floor. Somehow reading about these bizarre medical anomalies placated her anxiety. However, every once in a while, she'd feel a slight pang of paranoia that perhaps she did, in fact, suffer from the disorder she'd discover within the pages.

Mucus fishing syndrome causes the sufferer to compulsively "fish" pieces of mucus from his or her eye. Unfortunately for the sufferer, the more mucus is pulled from the tear duct, the more mucus the body produces, creating an endless cycle of removal and resurgence. For this reason, mucus fishing syndrome is classified as a body-focused repetitive behavior (BFRB).

On instinct, Cory touched the inside corner of her right eye with her finger, then yanked it away. One BFRB was enough for one person, she decided. She willed herself to avoid reading about the other body-focused disorders, pulled herself up from the floor using a nearby shelf as leverage, and returned the book to its place.

The time on her phone read 9:40. She could take her time walking home from the library, even dawdle in the downstairs lounge of their building, and return to her dorm room at a respectable 10:15. It was a Thursday, after all, a week away from a three-day weekend, and people were scrambling to get their semester papers and research proposals done ahead of the holiday. No one wanted to lug work home if they could help it. Most of the people on her floor were certain to be locked away in their rooms, madly typing away on their laptops and guzzling bad coffee.

She clutched her jacket closed rather than zipping it up and strolled casually out of Mugar Library and took a left. The sprawling, grey-bricked buildings of the Colleges of Arts and Sciences and Law School cast ominous shadows behind them and over the expanse of green lawn overlooking the expressway that students nicknamed "The Beach." On a sunny day, people stretched out on the grass and closed their eyes, and with very little suspension of disbelief, pretended the whizzing traffic was the crashing of ocean waves. Cory ducked toward the streetlights and into the glare of Commonwealth Avenue just as the above-ground green line train heading towards west campus click-clacked past her.

The air was cool with a slight dampness hovering expectantly. Before long, Cory turned left and made her way down the one-way side street, then turned right onto Bay State Road. Six months from then, the street would be awash with blooming cherry blossom trees, the slightest of breezes sending pink petals dancing along the sidewalks and brownstones. Two blocks up, the front door of her dormitory would come into view. Before then, however, two dark shadows staggered and stumbled down the sidewalk toward her, their unnecessarily loud voices slightly slurred and slowed, reminding Cory of a battery-operated CD player her mother sometimes used when she walked on her treadmill.

Patients diagnosed with Auto-Brewery Syndrome will often fail a breathalyzer test, their alcohol levels registering several points over the permissible limit for operating a motor vehicle, even when they have not imbibed. In this disorder, the sufferer's digestive system produces a type of yeast that ferments carbohydrates, producing ethanol. This ethanol, in turn, intoxicates the sufferer.

The unsteady men had come from the direction of the MIT frat house and seemed harmless enough, but Cory put her hand in her jacket pocket and felt for the sharp cuticle scissors she always carried there anyway. Having a keycard instead of metal keys placed vulnerable college students at a disadvantage: it was tough to jam the corner of a plastic card into an assailant's eyes or throat, and the one metal contraption she did have in her possession, the tiny key for the mailbox, was barely longer than her fingernail. At least, that's what she would tell security if they ever discovered the scissors in her pocket. The two men slid to the right, forming a misshapen single-file line as they sailed by her, and both parties were silent as they passed.

When she arrived at the door of her dorm room at last, she saw that her roommate had left a note on the whiteboard on their door. *Headed down to Bentley for networking thing with Mark. May not be home until tomorrow afternoon. Heart you- M.* Bentley College was nine miles away in Waltham, and Meghan had begun dating a senior business major there at the beginning of the term. Said boyfriend was president of his fraternity and was always hosting some event or another; he rarely if ever visited Meghan on her own turf as he was too busy planning rush week or alumni visits or posh dinners with the college's administration. Meghan's formal invitation to the faculty-centered social had arrived two weeks ago.

Cory still had it tucked away in her drawer.

That morning, she continued to stare at the cars and rowers from her vantage point four stories up. Sandwiched between them in her field of vision was the occasional jogger keeping pace with the small, steady waves of the river. It was Saturday, and the warm sun streaked through the oversized, though drafty, window, caressing Cory's face and neck. Her eyes drifted to the pane of glass and antiquated lock on the sill. They were old windows, their trim painted many times, with rickety metal screens neither Meghan nor Cory had ever touched. The dormitory's rooms were temperature-controlled for both heat and air-conditioning, so they never had a reason to open the double-paned frames.

Cory tried the lock and found that it flipped over surprisingly easily; she then pushed the heavy window upwards, and once she had pushed it as far as it would go, she crouched and pressed her face up to the screen, breathing in the crisp smells of both dry leaves and automobile exhaust. She focused her vision downward, along the brick side of the building, and felt her stomach dip a bit as she realized how far up she really was.

Sufferers of the neurological condition Alice in Wonderland Syndrome report incidences of skewed perception. AIWS is a rare psychological disorder that usually affects children and typically, as they age, patients appear to grow out of it. Researchers have discovered that the condition is caused by an excess of electrical activity followed by abnormal blood flow in areas of the brain that control vision and monitor texture or size processing. In turn, sufferers interpret objects as being much larger or smaller than they actually are. Such episodes cause the patient to become disoriented. Differential diagnoses include dementia and ingestion of a psychoactive alkaloid.

Cory wondered if anyone had ever jumped from a dorm window in desperation, a sad suicide attempt, or misbegotten drug adventure. She glanced at her cell phone sitting in the charger on her dresser nearby. It was nearly noon. She had spent the morning relaxing languidly in her bed, falling down the rabbit hole of YouTube movie trailer videos and social media posts on her laptop. Meghan had left the previous afternoon, before the weekday delivery of mail at four p.m.; on weekends, the mail arrived by eleven in the morning. Cory decided she would collect their two-day's worth of mail, then smuggle out a pile of pizza slices from the dining hall; she could nuke them until the cheese boiled and have lunch quietly in bed.

In the mailroom, the clerk had just finished sorting the items and was closing the master door on the boxes. She didn't look at Cory and briskly carried her empty mail bin out of the room. Cory slipped the small key into the box and opened the metal door. A long, thin box, just over a foot in length, filled most of the space; alongside it, a handful of envelopes and a glossy postcard stood pressed against the side of the metal wall. Cory pulled the smaller items out first and looked at each addressee. All of the envelopes were for Meghan, of course. Even the postcard promoting an event at Toscanini's ice cream shoppe in Cambridge's Central Square bore her name. Unsurprised yet disappointed just the same, Cory removed the final object, the white cardboard box, and closed the small door. She glanced at the mailing information. This was for her roommate as well, but unlike previous care packages and occasional orders from Poshmark and ModCloth, this delivery had no return address, no company insignia, no personal markings at all: just Meghan's name and address. Their box number was listed nowhere; it had been a miracle the carrier had known where to place it. On the other hand, Meghan was a popular girl; she had received hundreds of pieces of mail that school year alone, so of course the clerk knew which box was hers. If it had been addressed to Cory, it may never have reached its recipient.

Cory piled the stack of pizza slices she'd wrapped in napkins on top of the white box and covered her contraband with a fan of envelopes. The monitor near the door looked quickly at her and her bundles, then moved her eyes to the other students hovering nearby. Cory jumped quickly into the waiting elevator, and upon returning to the room, placed the slices neatly in the refrigerator to be heated later. As she did so, her phone's ringtone blared cacophonously from the top of the dresser. She could see by the caller ID that it was her mother, and she sat on the edge of her bed, the mail key still in her hand, and hit the green answer button.

"Cory, sweetheart," her mother's voice cooed from the speaker. "How are you?" For some unknown reason, her mom always sounded extremely content when she called Cory, like she had just received an hour-long massage or ingested a small dose of Ecstasy.

Cory tossed the pile of envelopes and the postcard onto the foot of Meghan's bed, then placed the box, upside-down, on her lap. "Good, Mom, really good," she said. It was her pat response. She could have been expelled from school, had her foot run over by a train, or spent the week in a Turkish prison, and she'd still say the same thing. Cory was counted on to be good. She wouldn't let them down. "What's up?"

Her mother began to talk about the weather back home, which, since it was only a state away, was not much different than the weather at school, but Cory listened and added a verbal nodding of "um-hmm" each time it was appropriate. As her mother's voice lilted musically in her ear, Cory ran her finger along the seam of the box. She carefully inserted the tip of the mail key into the seam on one end and dragged it meticulously along to the bottom of the box, splitting the cardboard in two. Then she turned the box sideways and did the same to the seams on the sides. She'd performed this ritual many times with assorted boxes addressed to her roommate. She was extra cautious not to tear or peel the box in any way, as on two occasions, she'd changed her mind and decided not to pilfer Meghan's treasures and had carefully resealed the boxes good as new. Whatever was inside of this one was relatively dense, and though she was certain it wasn't typical care package fare or something edible at all, she was intrigued to discover what it could be.

"So, do you think you'll be joining us?" her mother was asking. Cory had been so focused on cutting open the seals, she had missed the change in topic.

"I'm sorry, what?" she asked. "Where again?"

Her mother emitted a barely audible sigh, but her voice returned to its pleasant tone. "To Cape May. With me and your father and your brothers and the Marrinans," she repeated. "In July. Will you be home or will you be in Boston for the summer?"

Cory had considered staying in the city for the summer. She could sublet an apartment, maybe get a job at a Dunkin' Donuts or waitressing somewhere touristy, like near the whale watch boats at Rose Wharf. The important thing is, she'd be alone. She'd have the privacy to do whatever she wanted, whenever she wanted. "I don't know, Mom," she finally answered, picking up the butcher-paper wrapped object from the white box and examining it. "I'm going to try to get an internship maybe. You know, it might help my chances at getting into grad school. Build up my resume." She found the edge of the waxy paper and began to unfurl the mysterious object from its wrapping.

"Well, if you don't stay the month, you could at least pop down for the Fourth. Corinne's just been promoted at the studio, you know, and Edward and his new wife are expecting their first child. It would be nice if you made an appearance, expressed your well wishes. I know you don't like sitting on the beach or at the pool, but no internship is going to have you working on the holiday, darling," her mother noted. With this last sentence, her cadence became frothy, her voice slightly muffled, like she had placed a spoonful of mashed potatoes into her mouth. Cory thought of the afternoon with the bar of soap, then shrugged the memory from her mind. She had unraveled the packing to its final layer and peeled back the paper to reveal the contents at last.

Sufferers of Capgras Delusion become convinced that acquaintances and loved ones, including family members and friends, have been replaced by imposters. Although its focus is generally restricted to individuals, this skewed belief can expand to objects and familiar locations, such as the patient's residence or workplace.

"Cory, sweetheart, are you there?" her mother was practically yelling into the receiver now. Cory felt a sense of unreality washing over her. She needed the voice on the other end of the line to stop talking. She wanted it to be quiet so she could process what was happening. She was staring at a disembodied arm and hand lying prone on top of the pile of discarded butcher paper. A small folded note rested neatly on the wrist. Cory picked up the paper and opened it. The meticulously typed text mirrored the one on the address label.

A girl whose status is unknown
Pieces sent to a chosen few
You can lend the poor gal a hand
And offer some help if you know what to do

"Mom, my phone is almost dead," Cory finally managed to say. "I gotta call you back later, okay?" She could hear the voice respond before she tapped the red END button on her phone screen, but she didn't know what it had said. It didn't matter anyway. What was the point? She had a severed arm, hand still attached, sitting in her dorm room, right there next to her.

Body Integrity Identity Disorder causes the sufferers to believe that one or more parts of their bodies are foreign and should not be attached. Patients with BIID are legally sane but possess a dysfunction in their brain's body map: the part that the sufferer believes is not part of his or her body is not correctly connected to the corresponding region of the brain. At this time, amputation of the part perceived to be foreign is the only successful treatment for this malady.

She poked at the edge of the arm with two fingers. The flesh was cool but gelatin-like and felt denser than she had anticipated. The side of the arm, where the detachment had occurred, looked like a photograph from her Human Biology online textbook; upon closer inspection, she could see the rings of skin, fat, and muscle circling the bone. The separation had not been done cleanly at the elbow but an inch or two closer toward the wrist. A spongey, dark brown substance was stuffed in the hollow spaces of the bone. *It must be marrow,* she thought. She felt her stomach lurch. *Don't vomit don't vomit don't vomit don't vomit don't don't DON'T*

Cory closed her eyes and took slow breaths in and out of her mouth until she felt her body settle. Then, she jumped from the bed, quickly and officiously rewrapped the hand and arm in the butcher paper, placed it back in the box, and re-taped the package exactly as she had found it. It wasn't until she had fixed her last piece of adhesive that she noticed the typed note lying face down on the floor. She picked it up, tore it into tiny pieces and showered the confetti into the trash can.

She wrestled her coat onto her body and shoved her socked feet into her sneakers, wincing for a moment as the tightness of the shoes prodded the newest wounds on her skin, before sticking her keycard ID into her jeans pocket and stuffing the package into the sturdy backpack she had brought to Boston but rarely used.

Congenital Insensitivity To Pain, or CIP, is a genetic mutation that often results in the early death of the sufferer. Patients with this condition cannot feel pain, and thus, injuries that require treatment are often ignored and may cause greater damage: foreign objects in the eyes can tear corneas, gashes that are not cleaned and covered may progress into infection and sepsis, and eating, talking, or even crying may result in sufferers biting off the tips of their own tongues.

Her backpack slung around her shoulder, she didn't wait for the elevator but instead raced down the stairs and out onto Bay State Road. She didn't stop her urgent pace until she had reached the door of the library and saw the sign warning students that all bags would be inspected upon entry. She'd walked through the door a thousand times and had never noticed this proclamation. Then again, she hadn't been carrying a severed body part with her before.

However, it was Saturday morning on a long weekend, and the facility was nearly empty, and because of this, the security guard who usually sat at his post just beyond the turnstile was serendipitously absent. As calmly as she could, Cory walked to the elevator and rode it to the fifth floor. She walked silently to her regular place in the stacks and looked closely at the shelves. There were seven levels on each shelf, and the top of the highest book nearly grazed the ceiling.

She unzipped her backpack but kept it hanging over her shoulder, then pushed a few of the books forward on their shelves, creating a makeshift ladder. After testing the sturdiness of the metal frame, she stepped carefully on the lowest shelf and positioned her hand on a higher one for balance. Pulling and stepping at the same time, she slowly made her way upward until she could touch the beige plaster ceiling with her fingertips. Then, she reached back, slid the box from her bag, and wedged it between two books on the highest shelf. When she had aligned it so that it matched the surrounding spines, she climbed carefully back down, replacing the repositioned books as she went. Once she was safely on the ground, she inspected her work. The white box appeared to be a book at quick glance, and since the shelf was so high off the ground, only someone looking for a title near it would look at the spine closely enough to realize there was no label attached.

Her hands felt greasy. Cory looked at her fingertips; they were covered in dusty soot. No one had moved these books in some time. The box would be safe there, at least for the near future.

That evening, Cory sat on her bed in front of her laptop, binge-watching a popular science fiction series on Netflix she'd heard some of her classmates discuss. She could not stop thinking about the box and its contents. Why hadn't she just turned the box into campus police? Then again, how would she explain opening her roommate's mail? She could lie and say that Meghan had asked her to open any packages that arrived, but surely, as she was the intended recipient, they would interview her at length and uncover the truth. She could say that she opened it by mistake, that she had believed the delivery had been for her, but no, that wouldn't work either. No one would believe that Cory, who had never received a package the entire time she'd been a college student, assumed the box was for her. Finally, she could have replaced the package and the rest of her roommate's mail in the mailbox, pretended that she had forgotten to empty the box all weekend, let Meghan discover and deal with the delivery on her own.

Why hadn't she done that?

She made a resolution to return to the fifth floor stacks the next morning and do just that. Except… except they searched bags upon entry and exit. What if they confiscated her package? Opened it to see what she was carrying? How could she explain herself?

She began to take inventory of her current situation. Her disorders had spiraled out of control. This kleptomania, or whatever pushed her compulsion to steal Meghan's mail, had gotten her into quite the jam, and her other issue, the one she didn't dare research, the one she had taken great pains to conceal since she was an adolescent: it, too, had been spiraling off of the deep end as of late.

Cory removed the sock from her right foot and crossed it onto her left thigh, exposing the bottom. She ran her fingers along the bloodied, jagged pads below her toes and under her heel. She reached into the pocket of her jacket that was hanging off of her desk chair and pulled out her cuticle scissors.

With the precise eye of a trained surgeon, Cory examined the flesh on the bottom of her foot. Nearly every inch was raw, the skin peeled away in strips, the last dermal layer visible in some areas, the translucent membrane appearing a deep red from the layer of muscle beneath. In other areas, where Cory had cut down and through this layer, dried blood filled the cracks and crevices. Everything stung, like when she had accidentally dripped lemon juice into a freshly torn cuticle, but instead of the pain being pinpointed, it pulsed along her entire foot pad, shooting up her leg when she pressed down on the most tender areas.

She was used to the pain. It had haunted her since she was thirteen. Her friends and family thought she avoided summertime activities because she wanted to protect her fair skin. Really, she simply could not engage in any diversion that might expose her wounds to public scrutiny.

She felt for any ribbons of flesh she hadn't peeled and when she found a strip of skin she had begun to rip the previous night, she gripped it between her thumb and forefinger and pulled it slowly, the sharp sting seizing her movement for a second. Bright red capillary blood dribbled from beneath the flap still attached to her foot. It was like a hangnail, she always rationalized. She had to snip it in order to even off the surface of her skin. She had to pick at anything hard, anything that jutted out. Each stabbing pain was followed with a rush of endorphins, pushing her to continue.

Excoriation Disorder compels the sufferer to pick, peel, and/or cut at their skin a few times throughout the day or continuously over a period of several hours. A mental illness akin to Obsessive-Compulsive Disorder, it falls within the category of body-focused repetitive behavior (BFRB). Sufferers may perceive imperfections in their skin that they attempt to correct, but their constant excoriation results in scabbing, scarring, and sometimes, infection that can develop into sepsis. Patients will often avoid activities that expose their wounds to the view of others. Unlike cutting, excoriation is not performed to release pain or as a cry for help; rather, it is a compulsion and almost always done in secret.

The box was safe in its new home, lost in the forgotten stacks of the library. Cory reassured herself that it was likely that no one would ever discover its secret. She took a deep breath and positioned her cuticle scissors, the tips dripping crimson, along a hard scab beneath her big toe.

She would make everything perfect again.

The Betrayal

Against his better judgement, Jax checked into the hotel Connor booked for him; it was a room at the Ramada Suites and rather comfortable with a kitchen, living room, and bedroom. Jax took a long shower, shaved off three days of stubble, and lay on the bed for what he expected was to be a quick nap, but he woke up six hours later at 11:00 at night. Confused, with sleep still clouding his head, he sat up and looked about the room as if he were in a foreign, scary place. It took him a second to remember where he was. Then, instead of relief, worry set in. He had wasted a significant amount of time; now he couldn't make phone calls to the few sources he had left. The internet, the one thing Connor could control, was Jax's only option.

As he turned on his Macbook and logged into the free Wi-Fi, Jax wondered if Connor was watching everything he did on his computer. He probably was and the idea of it creeped him out, but he couldn't do anything about it that night. Tomorrow though, he would go buy a new laptop and phone so he could make a clean break from Connor's spying eyes. With Connor on his mind, he decided he should see what the kid had been posting on his website. He had to look up the name again, and when he finally landed on Kill-Tracker.com, he was mad at himself for forgetting such a simple name. At first, he typed it in without the dash and got some techno music website, but when he added the dash and the site popped up, his heart fell out of him, rolled onto the floor, and stopped dead.

There, right on the front page, taking up almost three quarters of the screen was the photo of Julie Piedmont's arm lying next to her mutilated body, the goriest parts blurred out. A sleek watermark of the site's logo ran across the picture so no that other site could steal it. Large red print above the photo read *See ALL of the Exclusive, Uncensored Pics of the Hangman's First Kill!* For a brief moment, Jax wished he could report Connor and get the site taken down, but he knew the kid probably was running it through fifty routers in various countries, keeping any government agency from touching its content.

The ticker on the bottom showed that 234,556 people had seen the photo already. Jax felt ill and wanted to cry. He wanted to cry because he was so stupid; he wanted to cry because the poor parents of this kid were likely going to see the photos; he wanted to cry because society was so fucking sick that people were flocking to see a young girl's murdered remains get butchered. He wanted to cry because he was exhausted and had wanted nothing to do with this; he wanted to cry because he didn't know why the killer wanted him to play a part; most of all, he wanted to cry for Julie, the girl everyone seemed to have forgotten was dead and dismembered. He just wanted to cry. Instead, the rage that was bubbling inside of him overcame his sadness, pushed the tears back down, and flushed his cheeks with scarlet anger.

Jax had to stand up and pace. In all of his years as a reporter, he had kept his cool. He had never flipped out on a source, not even when a five-time rapist spat in his face during an interview, saying he'd fuck his mother. To that, he had simply wiped his face, smiled, and nodded. That was part of what made him a great reporter: he could remain calm, even when someone was shoveling bullshit all over him or accusing him or attacking him; no matter what, he could just stay cool, get the facts, and be the better person. The fact that he had trashed a bathroom stall the night before and now wanted to do the same with this hotel room was not him. This was someone different, and he did not like him. He wanted to examine why this case was hurting so much, why it was pushing him over the edge to the point of making bad decisions, but he also wanted to feel this rage, to let it wash over him and destroy all the nerves and fear he had.

Just as he was about to flip his bed mattress and stand it against the wall to hit repeatedly, his text alert dinged. Picking up the phone, he felt more rage than ever reading the words. *Jax, just calm down*, the text read. *I can explain. I'll be at your room in two minutes.* Jax took a deep breath; the realization that Connor had been watching him through his computer and likely watching his web browsing so he knew Jax had checked the site, was sending him over the edge. The fact that Connor knew at that moment he was pissed and that he was already in the hotel when he told Jax he wouldn't make it down until the next day, made his mind explode.

With one sharp and hard flick of his wrists, Jax snapped his phone in half. Shards of glass stuck into the palm; tiny beads of blood started to form at the edges of the glass. Seeing this, he threw the halves down in disgust. One piece softly thudded on the carpet while the other clattered and skidded onto the bathroom tile. As it slowed to a stop, the glint of the tiny camera reflected the bathroom light into Jax's eyes, and the sight flooded a memory into his head. He only had a few minutes to prepare, so he hurried.

The knock on the door was soft, almost like someone was trying to see if the resident was sleeping without really bothering him. Jax wiped the tiny dots of blood off his palms on his jeans—the bleeding was finally stopping—slowly got up from his seat, looked around the room, and walked towards the door, doing his best to remain calm. Part of him wanted to swing the door open like in some dramatic movie scene, but instead, he calmly opened it. Connor stood before him, wearing a t-shirt with his *Kill-Tracker.com* logo on it and jeans that Jax couldn't tell if they were dirty or just designed to look that way. Connor did not look at Jax in the face; he merely put one hand up in a half-hearted wave as the other clutched a laptop to his chest. Jax nodded for the kid to come in. Connor looked around as if scared, but he reluctantly entered and stopped in the middle of the living room, then turned to face Jax who was shutting the door.

"Jax, Jax, Jax, please, please hear me out. I know you have to be mad. But look: our site was being crushed by the damn copycat site and our investors were threatening to shut us down if we could not show them something substantial. I had to give them something big, and it's working: the numbers are going through the roof, the retweets and the shares are insane…we are going fucking viral, Jax!"

The reporter wanted to punch the kid in the face more than anything, but he knew without a doubt, Connor was the type to not fight back and just press charges and sue, so he just clenched his fists instead. He walked up to Connor who instantly took a step back.

"She is a kid, Connor. A real human, not some story in a

movie. Her parents are going to have those images burned into their memories forever now: do you understand what that will do to them?"

Connor sighed as if what Jax said was silly and pointless. "The public has the right to see crime scene photos, it's part of what——"

"Listen to me, you little shit. You don't get it," Jax said, pointing a sharp finger into the kid's chest.

In response, Connor jumped back and tripped on the coffee table, his arms swinging comically, dropped his laptop on the carpet, and continued to stumble backward before landing on his ass. As he did, something small and black fell from his belt; he quickly grabbed at it and stuffed it under his shirt, but Jax knew what it was: a Taser. He used to carry one himself.

"Did you bring that to use on me?" Jax said, stifling a laugh at the outlandish idea.

"I, I didn't know how you would react. It's just a safety precaution." Connor got up and straightened himself but maintained a palpable distance between them.

"Look, I talked to the board and gave up ten percent of my ownership in the site: that portion will be in your name starting tomorrow. You'll get a cut of the profits, and we are thinking they are going to be huge, especially if we can continue to get exclusive details. That is why we need to go to this guy's house tomorrow in Western Massachusetts: I really think he could be our guy. He is a forens——"

Jax was having a hard time breathing, but he managed to yell loud enough to stop Connor from talking. "Stop! You will not put anything in my name. I'm done with you, I'm done with your site, and I want you out of here. You mention my name or do anything else again and I will kick your ass, then sue your ass for invasion of privacy and whatever other shit I can find. You got that?"

At this threat, Connor grinned, he smiled so broadly that Jax thought his face might split open and a monster would spill out. The kid clapped his hands together twice loudly and sat down in the chair that was behind him. He leaned back in it and crossed his legs, a bit too dramatically to show he was comfortable and had the power. Jax was not afraid of the little shit, but he did know Connor was more than capable of casting some strange voodoo on the internet, so he was hesitant to just grab him and throw him out of the door.

"Jax, look, I have been trying to help you, trying to get you back on the national spotlight again, but you are fighting against it so much. Look, there is one thing I won't put up with, and that is being threatened. My father threatened my mother once…" Connor froze for a second and looked off into space, then lightly shook his head and pulled out his cell phone.

"Never mind that," he continued. "The point is, no one threatens me. Jax, I want you—*you*—to get the fame, but you don't want it. I was your biggest fan, man. All you had to do was follow what I said. If I push this button, your life is destroyed." Jax watched as Connor pointed to a purple blinking button on his phone screen. It looked like some comic detonator trigger, but instead of keeping Jax's attention, Connor's words echoed in his mind. *Your biggest fan.* If Jax had been a character in a movie, this would have been the moment when the camera would zoom in on him for the big twist, Jax thought, because, all of a sudden, it all made sense: Connor had been the killer all along and had been sending him on a wild goose chase for God knows whatever sick reason.

"I set this up as a sort of fail-safe. With one click of a button, your bank accounts will be depleted, you'll suddenly come up on terrorist watch lists, you'll have over two thousand articles hitting the web in ten minutes about how you stole your stories. And, as an added bonus, you'll be accused of sexually assaulting a few women on your way up the ladder of the Top Reporter Darling list. It will be a shit storm with solid digital evidence that will take you years to clear, and you and I both know: even if you are even able to do that, people will always believe the articles they read."

Jax wanted to laugh, yet he wanted to rip Connor apart. The fucking kid watched too many movies and thought he was some sort of evil villain revealing his master plan. Jax nodded to show he was listening, then responded. "So, you are blackmailing me with internet fraud? This after you stole police evidence and posted it online and hacked into government feeds and other shit?"

"Yes, yes, Jax: I'm blackmailing you. You saw how easy it was to hack into all of the government sites: you know I can do this shit, too," he paused. "Look, I don't want to have to do this, man: all you have to do is keep on the path I set you on. There is a purpose to it."

Jax shook his head and thought for a moment. His eyes drifted along the furniture of the room, and it was then that he saw it. There, on the far side of the coffee table, sat the laptop that Connor had dropped. It had landed, half-open, and a letter had fallen out, one that looked exactly like all of the letters he had received from The Hangman previously. Even from a distance, it was easy to see the familiar formatting: the same font size, the same font style, the same light gray coloring— even the paper stock appeared to be the same. Jax couldn't help but stare at it, and he couldn't hide his consternation from Connor.

"No, that…" Connor began, "That's not…oh, fuck. Jax, I was going to give that to you. You…you got another letter. We intercepted it before it got to the…the newspaper. Shit, sorry, I should have started with that. Let's start this conversation over, okay?" Connor said. Suddenly, he was sitting up and looking uncomfortable rather than calm and relaxed.

"You killed her," Jax said. It wasn't a question but a statement. "You killed her to save your company, didn't you? It had to be elaborate and grand to get national attention: a new serial killer that you could have exclusive access to. You needed me to break the story in order to glean attention for your dark website." Jax swiftly understood the reality of what he was saying. It had been a game all along. Connor had sent him the letters: that is the only way the kid knew to be at the newspaper that quickly. Jax felt like such a fool. A fucking fool.

"Jax…Jax…. I might be obsessed with serial killers, but I'm not one. My, my mother was killed by my father, and when he was arrested his DNA showed up in a database as having killed three other women. It fucked me up," Connor said, swallowing hard. "I…I looked up to you on the news when you took down that sex ring in Philly, the Sadistic Six…it was a huge story at the time when I was in foster care. I was only allowed to watch the news, so I saw the coverage all the time. You were so bad ass, I even wrote you a fan letter and you wrote back telling me to follow my dreams of being a reporter. That's why I'm your biggest fan, man. That's the whole truth, but I did not kill Julie or anyone. I swear to fucking god."

Jax started to approach Connor. The reporter wanted to call the police, but he had broken his cell phone, after all. He would have to take the kid down himself, then use the room's landline, which was located on the other side of the kid. "I was going along with everything, why threaten my fucking wife?" Jax asked, trying to buy himself some time. "Why torture me that way?"

He took another step closer only to watch Connor pull out his Taser. Jax jumped, trying to escape the four-foot gap between him and the kid before the weapon could be discharged, but he was not quick enough. Two tiny darts like harpoons in a massive whale stuck into his left shoulder, one scratching against his collar bone. The shock that followed was stunningly powerful, like nothing he had ever felt: his body clenched up and his mouth slammed shut. Thankfully, since he was in motion, his body kept going and landed on Connor, sending electrical waves through the both of them.

When he awoke four minutes later, Jax ached all over. It was as if his entire body had completed a ten-hour workout and was now feeling the pain. Connor was still underneath him, both of them slumped awkwardly in the chair like drowsy lovers. He searched the kid's face and was relieved to see he was still unconscious. Fighting the pain and the cloudiness of his mind, Jax stood up, grabbed Connor, and searched the room for some implement with which to restrain him, finally settling on the tie of the complimentary bathrobe. Just as he was finishing the final knots, Connor's eyes opened and the boy starting bawling like a child. Jax didn't know if it was from the pain or from the realization that he was caught, and he didn't care.

"Jax, I'm sorry I threatened you," Connor blubbered, his nose growing red and puffy. "I'm sorry. But you were my hero, man: you still are. I'm not good at interacting with people and I was scared you'd leave and I didn't know any other way of making you stay. I didn't kill Julie; I know nothing about the killer that you don't. *That* letter is fake. I was going to try and get you to think it was real so we could post it as an exclusive on our site." Jax ignored him as he double-checked the ties, then stood up. Walking over to the lamp, Jax leaned over and pulled off the tiny hidden camera he had placed on the edge of the lampshade. Then he walked to the side of the room and did the same from the wall painting and headed to the room phone. He had always kept surveillance pieces in his laptop bag, and today, he finally had needed them.

"You might not have admitted it outright, but I think I have enough stuff for the police to lock you up. They can figure out the details from there. Even if they can't pin the murder on you yet, they can charge you with at least fifteen years of crimes; impersonating an officer, stealing evidence, hacking systems, blackmailing me...I bet they will offer you a good plea deal for your telling them where all the body parts were sent."

Connor shook his head as he listened and made a final plea as Jax picked up the receiver. "You're making a mistake, Jax. Don't let your last story be that you let the real killer go. You turn me in and they will stop looking for the asshole and spend time trying to convince themselves I did it. This is a mistake. If another innocent girl dies, her blood is on your hands. Your hands, Jax."

Jax ignored him and dialed 911.

Piece #25
Cadillac, MI

If caught, Byron would face countless years behind bars, yet he still did it… weekly. And lately, daily. The justification in his mind was that yes, it was illegal, but no one was getting hurt and no harm was being done to anyone or anything, so why stop? His wife, Miranda, who left him years ago when she found out, thought he was nuts. Even Byron, at one point, thought he was and sought help through therapy, but it did nothing but cost him an exorbitant amount of money. In the end, the need to break into people's homes and look through their stuff won, and the marriage failed.

Byron had no clue where the desire, or rather, the *need* to break into people's homes came from. Really, it had nothing to do with breaking in: that part he actually hated and it was the one part that made him nervous as he never knew if there would be a dog, alarm, or someone sleeping that he wasn't counting on. The breaking-in stuff was just a necessity to get to the important part: looking through people's things. Walking through a house, where he was not supposed to be, where no one knew he was, gave him a high. Skulking about unmonitored taught him who people were. How did they decorate? Was the house clean or messy? Did they have pets? What did their environment smell like? What sorts of things were in their nightstand drawer? There was just so much magic about having an intimate, private look into people's lives without them knowing who he was.

Some nights, he would spend hours upon hours inside a house that was not his, examining every single picture hanging on the walls and going through every single drawer he could (though he stayed away from kitchen cabinets and drawers as they were boring and didn't reveal much about the people who lived there, though he *always* checked the fridge). Byron was never looking for anything in particular, he merely wanted to know the people in a way that was not possible in a normal friendship. Not that he had any friends. Night after night, sometimes two houses in one night, he would break in and make himself at home in other people's lives.

He first began his routine in his teens; the first time, it was to spy on a girl he had a crush on. He just wanted to see what she had in her room, what sort of posters she hung up and what sort of stuffed animals she cuddled to go to sleep. But when he was in her house, he ended up going through every room, not just hers but her brother's, her parents', even the guest room, and he found himself forgetting his fascination with the girl and instead became fascinated by the entire family. It was like taking a drug for the first time: it hit him so hard and fast that he cursed himself for never having done it before. Immediately, he wanted more, but soon the want turned to need.

As the need grew, Byron became really, really good at picking locks and breaking into pretty much any door (he almost always went for a door: windows were too risky—if anyone saw him climbing into one, they might call the cops. A stranger going through a door is merely a curious situation, not an alert). In fact, he got so good and did so much research, he could drive by houses at sixty miles an hour and rattle off the make of the door and the best way to get inside of it.

Security alarms were always a pain, so he avoided houses that had them. The good part was, as common as they seemed, fewer than twenty percent of homes had them. However, with the advent of internet-ready and wireless cameras came a new fear. They were popping up everywhere, and unlike security systems, the cameras were often not as easy to spot. One time, he broke into a dumpy little home outside of Detroit. It was so run down, he was positive there was no security system and there wasn't; instead, the owner had placed some sort of Alexa device on the kitchen counter. It heard him make noise, and within seconds, a voice, like God's, was talking to him, saying the police were on their way. He got out in plenty of time, but it taught him a valuable lesson: be silent, search the home, and unplug any voice command devices immediately...or just leave.

The reason Byron had never gotten caught, so his theory went, was because the people never knew he was there. He never forced his entry, never broke anything or stole anything of importance. Sure, the owners might think they left an item in a different place or be curious why their comforter had wrinkled, but since all the doors remained locked and nothing was missing, it was often rationalized as a brain fart.

Occasionally he would eat some food, take a dump in their bathroom or even jerk off (though not as often as you'd think), but he'd never leave evidence behind. Until every house had some sort of security system, Byron figured he could keep on doing this until he died and if he ever did get caught, he'd get a misdemeanor breaking and entering charge; at most, he'd face under a year of soft time in jail. With a clean record and evidence that he had no intent other than to "look," he would more likely be sentenced to community service and therapy. If that ever happened, he'd have to quit his hobby. Until then, he savored it.

For a long time, Byron thought about writing a book about his experiences. He was going to call it, "I Know Your Secrets: The True Story of a Serial Voyeur." In the book, he would reveal all of the crazy things he saw and experienced over the years: the time he got stuck in a closet for ten hours when he couldn't get out of a house in time, the time he found a dead body (an old lady who must have been dead for weeks; he anonymously reported it and it made him feel good), or the time he found a full blown drug den complete with more money in stacks than he had seen in his life (that one made him freak and run, but was too scared to call the cops—he had watched too many cartel movies and knew better). Once he had found a little girl captive in a cage, a dog collar around her neck. He put a pillowcase over his head to hide his identity, picked the lock on her prison, and instructed her to walk to a neighbor's house to call the police. It was a big news story and the proudest moment of his life. When he wrote about that story, he planned on talking about being a superhero of sorts, since he had stopped crime and saved lives through his illegal activities. There were also the filthy sex stories: those alone could fill a whole book, two even. The crazy items he'd find in drawers, the houses with full-blown sex dungeons, the home videos he'd pilfered and pictures he'd found: the list was endless. While he masturbated and enjoyed sex, when he came across things like spiked paddles and anal plugs bigger than a gerbil, he was shocked and mildly disgusted, but he knew if he wrote a book about it, it would sell like hotcakes.

What stopped him from writing this book was the

realization he could not write for shit. For the life of him, he could not pen any story that had any appeal, even if he used the juiciest of stories. Part of him wanted to hire a ghostwriter, but who would believe him? Even if the writer did, who was to say he or she wouldn't turn him in? So, the book stayed on the back shelf of his mind and the notes he kept tucked away in his journals. Maybe one day he would find a way to tell his story and let the thousands of people know that if they had lived in the outskirts of Detroit in the past twenty years, he had probably laid in their bed and pawed through their medicine cabinet.

The night it all happened, Byron was on autopilot. It was one of those nights where he wasn't heading out for desire; instead, he was heading out to fulfill the *need*. Yes, he could sit home and watch a movie or catch up on paperwork, but if he did that, there would be a tiny nag at the back of his head the entire evening, whispering in his ear, *Go! Go find their secrets!* There were very few nights when he regretted going out, but he *did* regret most nights that he stayed home as he viewed them as wasted opportunities. Most of those nights he would lie in bed and think of all of the secrets he could have unearthed had he ventured out. So, he went out that night, driven by necessity, running on the instinct of a thousand nights before.

In hindsight, he would wonder what made him pick *that* house on *that* night. However, it was a system that led him there; chance only determined what he would discover. Each night in a particular week, he would visit a different town near Detroit. If there were no incidents, he would return to the same town on the same night the next week. It was the same routine with streets. Locked in a hidden cabinet in his house he kept a detailed street map with a tiny little x marking each house he had visited. Each night, he'd make his way down the street, visiting all of the homes he could get into before moving onto the next street and so on. Thankfully, with over a million homes in the suburbs surrounding Detroit, he would never run out, even if he visited five a night, every day until he died. That night, he planned to visit the town of Cadillac, a street called Raymond Circle, house number seventy-seven.

The routine called for him to drive by the house three times, twenty minutes between each pass and from a different way each time (if possible). He'd then park at the end of the street and call the number he wrote down on the sticky note. If someone answered, he'd hang up and he'd move onto the next house on the list. When there was no answer, he'd call back twenty times exactly; that was the magic number—no one could take the phone ringing that many times. They would either answer with a scream or put the phone off the hook; both responses told him to go to the next house. If they did not have a listed landline, he skipped that house; unfortunately for Byron, this was happening more and more. The proliferation of cell phones was putting a serious damper on his hobby.

Seventy-seven Raymond Circle had a house phone and no one answered. The next step in his routine was to park one to two miles away, preferably at a store or restaurant where his car would not be noticed. For this house, the closest public lot was next to a CVS pharmacy just over a mile away. The walks he made each night kept him in shape, though they sucked in the winter. He'd always walk with a flashlight and water bottle and wore sweat pants, as it provided him the perfect alibi. *Sorry officer, just out for a jog!* Luckily, it was an excuse he'd only had to use a few times. *No officer, I don't take my ID with me when I run. I know it's stupid, but I'm always afraid I'll lose it.* If they checked his custom running suit for any other items, then he'd be screwed. But Byron knew a pat down would require a lot more suspicion than just being out for an evening run, because he always broke in between 7:00 and 10:00 p.m., any later and a family out for the night was bound to come home.

That evening, he followed his procedure as usual. After a quick stretch by the car, he started on his walk and enjoyed the seasonably warm weather and the clear night. There was something he loved about being out at night under the stars; it was both freeing and calming, just him and the air and the unknown galaxy. At least if anyone questioned him about why he was out, he would not be lying about that part.

As always, when he arrived at the top of the chosen street, he would start to jog. From the opposite side of the street, he'd survey the house, continue around the block, and return: this time, on the house's side of the street. Then, just as he approached the house, he'd take a sharp turn and run right into their backyard, always keeping his excuse ready. *Fucking skunk! I'm so sorry, I just really didn't want to get sprayed. I did not mean to cut through your yard, but I panicked!* He'd had to trot out that bullshit close to fifty times over the years when motion sensor lights snapped on and woke up a neighbor. If the lights didn't come on, he'd continue running to the back door and work his magic. The few times someone was actually home and awake, he'd run like hell, duck where there was cover, switch his reversible clothing and put on the baseball hat he kept in his pocket. The important thing was to continue jogging, like he knew nothing. While those nights were terrifying, they were also exhilarating.

There was no one home at 77 Raymond Circle. It was eight at night and the sun had just set, allowing a cloak of darkness to engulf the house. The back of the house had a small brown deck that looked as if it needed some fixes to keep it from collapsing during the next barbecue. Next to the grill was a Hampton Sky faux wood Nottingham sliding door. Byron laughed to himself; it was one of the easiest doors to open. He slid the thin metal rod he kept in his back pocket along the foot and side and the locks slipped open with a faint *click*. After sliding the door open, he slipped inside and shut it behind him.

The first thing he always did after making it inside was take a deep breath. The way a house smelled said a lot about a person. The owner could never sense it, but a visitor could instantly smell any odors foreign to his nose. Three quarters of the houses he invaded smelled heavily of fried food and pine needles—that made Byron's stomach turn. Sometimes, if the scent was bad, he'd only spend only half his normal time in a house; when a sour note hit his nose in addition to that greasy Christmas tree smell, he knew his visiting time was limited.

In his nightly process, he would typically do a speed check of each room to check for animals, humans, and any smart devices that could be listening. This house had none. Back in the kitchen, he relaxed and looked around. At first glance, it was clear the home had last been renovated in the same year as its house number. It was decently clean but a bit boring. The fridge told him it was an older couple who lived there; ancient magnets held smudgy crayon drawings *To GaGa and PaPa* on the door. Inside of the refrigerator hid the typical offerings of an elderly couple: half-finished cans of soda, tons of leftovers wrapped neatly with aluminum foil and Saran Wrap, and a few bottles of medications and eye drops stacked in the butter drawer. Typically, while it made him feel bad that he was an ageist, he didn't care much for the older people's homes. While sometimes they surprised him with great secrets, most of the time, they were just plain vanilla. While he always got a kick out of old photographs as a window into the lives that the people *had* lived, he was much more interested in the lives people *were* living.

Next, it was off to the long, carpeted hallway, one that emitted an orange hue in the beam of his flashlight; part of him cringed at the idea of people walking on it barefoot. He could go down the long hallway, back to the bedrooms and the good stuff, or look at the living room off to the right; he chose to get the boring part over first. He followed the pale beam of his flashlight (the lowest wattage possible so it wouldn't be noticeable from outside) across the same orange ratty carpet and found a couch that must have matched the carpet at some point but now looked like a beaten stack of pillows faded to a pale brown color instead of an orange. As he moved the beam around the room, he found the old people standard: TV trays covered in various letters, pills, and other necessities of people who did not leave their recliners often. It was then that something on the coffee table caught his eye, something he hadn't noticed on his walk through.

At first, he jumped backward slightly, thinking it was a snake (he had seen too many pet snakes in his life), but the color was off. Relaxing his shoulders a bit, he ventured a step closer and aimed the beam of light onto the white box and the contents that were spilling out of it. The box sat on the edge of the table, the flaps splayed open and a giant pile of thick, ropy, purplish-pink tubes sat coiled inside. One long length of the tubes crept out of the box and hung all the way to the ground, a stumpy end just barely kissing the decaying carpet fibers. Ideas of what it could be raced through his mind, but none of them made sense. No matter what rationalization jumped into his mind, he knew the truth; he *knew* it was a box full of intestines.

Byron's heart started to slam in his chest. Had he finally stumbled upon a serial killer? Just then, a possible explanation popped into his head: maybe, just maybe, they were materials for sausage making and the couple had simply forgotten to return the box to the fridge. But then he remembered the time his father tried to show him how to make homemade hotlinks; the skins of the intestines were dried and bleached, and they certainly were not this big.

Excitement and fear fought mercilessly in his brain, each trying to take control of the moment. Neither won. Byron stood there, scared to step closer but excited at the story he would have to tell later. After a few deep breaths, he realized he had to search the rest of the house better than he had earlier to make sure it was safe. There could be traps or kidnapped victims if he had indeed stumbled unluckily into a serial killer's den. He had to make certain nothing could harm or hinder his escape. Once he did that, he could take his time and examine what the hell was going on. He raced from room to room, around looking in each closet, under each bed, and finally, in the basement, where most people kept the darkest of secrets. 77 Raymond Circle was just a typical, old couple's home. While this reassurance calmed him, it also piqued his curiosity: why would anyone have a box of human intestines sitting on their coffee table if the rest of their house was normal?

Creeping closer to the mysterious body part, he shined the light downward and saw that there were two coils on the box-- one fatter and shorter, the other skinnier and four times the length this had to be both the small and large intestines. The skinny one was the one spilling out. Byron was so fascinated he broke his golden rule: he removed his thin "running" gloves and touched the knotty cords with his fingers. He had to be sure. He nodded his head; there was no doubt they were real. Despite the season, this was not some sort of Halloween decoration they were preparing; these came out of something once alive, and his gut told him that something was a human. Carefully kneeling down, he looked at the box and was shocked to find the intestines had been shipped to this house, it was not just a box the couple had stored them in. This changed everything. Perhaps the owners were not the evil killers he had previously imagined; instead, they were more likely the victims of something. That is when the panic set in.

As he stood up, he instantly saw what he had stupidly overlooked beforehand: the half-full glasses of soda on the TV trays next to the small plates of fried chicken half-eaten: dinner that had been interrupted. Old people don't like going out at night, and they certainly don't leave food on the plate half eaten and wasted. Moving the light around, Byron spotted the letter opener lying next to the box and the crumpled napkin next to that. The package must have come during dinner and the moment they opened it, they got up and rushed out. The energy-conscious husband must have snapped off the television and lights on instinct as they evacuated the house to get help.

As if on cue, like a dramatic scene in some police procedural or a climactic scene in a Hannibal Lector movie, three cop cars pulled up to the house, their blue and red lights flashing a strobe light around the living room. The police didn't screech to a halt and run out with guns aimed; they simply pulled up and parked neatly. Byron felt faint as a fourth car, a twenty-year-old Buick, pulled into the driveway. His mind screamed at his feet to run—he had plenty of time to make it out the back door and through the backyard—but they would not move, they did not listen. As one, then six car doors opened, they finally processed the message.

As Byron rushed through the house, he realized his light had been on the whole time; if anyone had spotted it, he was done for it. Snapping it off as he ran, he pushed his way through the kitchen, slid the door open, slipped outside, and carefully closed the door behind him. Unfortunately, he had to use the slim jim to lock it; otherwise, there would be a manhunt on in a matter of seconds when they discovered the back door was unlocked. Trembling in a way he had never experienced, he pulled out the thin metal, slid it into the door and heard the locks snap shut. Taking another deep breath, he turned and performed a quick reconnaissance of the yard. Of course there was a fence, a six foot one, and it was covered in vines. He would have to run and jump it. *Do that and you are free,* he told himself as he stood up and leaped from the deck.

In fifteen strides he had made it to the fence. Just as his

hands grasped the top of the wooden spikes, a light popped on, illuminating the painted brown wood. The light was intensely bright and focused just on him, and the voice that followed was loud and demanding. In that split second, he knew he had to make a decision: get arrested and try to claim it was a coincidence that he broke into a house that contained human organs, or run and try to get away, which would bring more charges.

Byron's choice to run became national news, as the first person of interest was arrested in the Hangman case.

The Sacrifice

Officer Gallup's body quivered a bit, then was still. The bottom of his face, now nearly unrecognizable as human, was a wet, sticky mass of jagged bone matter and red goo.

"This is what happens when people lose their tempers," Karen called from the basement stairs. "This is exactly the kind of quagmire you drown in when you make spontaneous decisions." Dennis was surprised to hear her voice; he hadn't been home very often over the past two weeks, and most nights, by the time he returned home, he had only enough time to shower and brush his teeth before getting into bed. They had barely talked at all.

He looked down at Officer Gallup. What remained of the skin on his face was already swelling to a blackish-blue color, the same hue as his uniform. A darker color was spreading along his crotch and upper thigh.

Dennis closed his eyes and inhaled slowly. When he opened them, he had slipped into his forensic technician persona. He eyed the walls and ceiling of the hallway with critical distain. No matter how meticulous he was in his cleaning, he would never catch all of the blood splatter.

He walked back into the kitchen, retrieved a handful of latex gloves from the box he had pilfered from work the previous year, and pulled a pair onto his hands. Then, he gingerly stepped over Officer Gallup, taking great care not to tread in any liquids that had dripped or splashed, and grabbed the man by the ankles. It took him some effort, but he was able to drag the corpse through the kitchen and over to the basement stairs, though he left a bright red streak behind, a fiery snail's trail speckled with the occasional purplish spot or beige piece of brain matter and bone. He pulled the policeman's legs onto the stairs so that his buttocks started to hang over the top step. Finally, he climbed over the body and flicked the light switch just inside the doorway.

As if he'd turned on a radio, the sound of Karen's voice spontaneously curled around the railing up to Dennis's ear.

London Bridge is falling down,
Falling down, falling down.
London Bridge is falling—

Dennis covered his ears, forgetting that he was still wearing the latex gloves. They made a soft crackling noise, like mice scurrying along newspaper. "Shut up," he whispered and closed his eyes. "Shut up shut up shut up shu—" When he opened them again and looked to the bottom of the stairs, all he could see was the cool, gray cement of the floor, the corner of John Boy's long abandoned litter box visible in the far corner of his field of vision. Karen was nowhere in sight.

"Do you remember the story of London Bridges?" Karen's disembodied voice asked from somewhere below. "Tell me. Prove to me you remember everything I taught you."

"No," said Dennis. "Just shut up and let me concentrate." He grabbed Officer Gallup by the shoulders and pushed him into a sitting position. His head, the lower half a misshapen mass of pulp, dripped quickly darkening liquid onto the cop's belly and thighs.

Ignoring him, Karen began to recite her monologue as if reading from a script. "Some historians believe that the bridges of the nursery rhyme refer to the many structures stretching across the Thames, beginning with the first wooden one erected by the Romans in 50 AD. The massive effort that bridge's construction entailed was for naught, as it was soon destroyed in Viking invasions, and its resurrections demolished by fire and weather in the eleventh, twelfth, and thirteenth centuries."

Dennis pushed on Officer Gallup's shoulder blades, believing that the policeman would tumble down the steps. *Ass over teakettle, as they say*, Dennis thought, without intending to be ironic. However, the policeman's corpse had another idea. Instead, his upper body folded forward until his forehead was touching his knees. He stopped in a position that looked as if he were trying to tie his shoes.

"From then until the mid-nineteenth centuries, many incarnations of the London Bridge were erected and replaced. The children's rhyme as we know it today surfaced during Victoria's reign," Karen continued, "around the same time the old superstition about bridge-building was at its height."

Dennis sat down on the floor behind Officer Gallup, bent his knees, and positioned his brown loafers on the policeman's back. As hard as he could, Dennis kicked his legs forward, and finally, the body toppled slightly sideways and thumped awkwardly down the stairs, landing with his head face-, or what was left of his face, down on the second step and his torso splayed in a slightly bowed position, arms flopped bizarrely on either side. From above, he appeared to be offering the floor a bear hug.

Dennis padded carefully after his ill-fated visitor and saw the brownish footprints he'd left on the dark uniform. He ran quickly back upstairs and snatched a box cutter he'd been keeping in his junk drawer, then bounded back to the basement. After he had rolled the body a few times as he sliced and removed the blood-soaked shirt, Officer Gallup arrived at his final destination next to the furnace, five feet from the bottom step, his eyes staring blankly at the ceiling of pipes and sub flooring. Karen began to sing loudly, sounding joyous and excited.

> *Bricks and mortar will not stay,*
> *Will not stay, will not stay,*
> *Bricks and mortar will not stay,*

"Stop it," Dennis commanded, turning towards the wall closest to the furnace. "I don't want to hear any more!" But the singing continued.

> *Suppose the man should fall asleep,*
> *Fall asleep, fall asleep,*
> *Suppose the man should fall asleep?*
> *My f—*

Dennis stopped his frisking of Officer Gallup, placed what he had collected on the bottom step, and walked angrily over to the abandoned oil tank that sat against the wall. The voice took on a hollow quality. It echoed slightly, then sounded strangely muffled, but its rhythm remained unchanged.

Give him a pipe to smoke all night,
Smoke all night, smoke all night,
Give him a pipe to smoke all night,
My fair lady!

He walked to the far side of the large, black tank and stared at its oval end for a moment. Then he positioned the box cutter over the multiple layers of duct tape that held the sheets of body bag material he'd brought home four years ago to cover the three-by-two-foot hole he'd cut into the steel. By the time he had sawed through the tape and rubberized fabric, his blade was dull and useless, and he tucked the instrument into his back pocket and peeled the hole's cover aside. A thick, musty, leathery odor poured from the tank's contents like a rancid tsunami, and Dennis did his best to hold his breath as he reached into the interior, grasped his mother's mummified shoulders, and pulled her body gently from the tank and onto the cement floor.

She was still wearing the bathrobe and pajamas she'd worn on the night he strangled her, though the fabric had become matted, brown, and translucent in places from oil and time. Her face was drawn and dehydrated, and her bottom teeth jutted forward in a perpetual grimace. The thin gold chain glinted incongruously against the waxy, dull skin of her throat.

Dennis dragged Karen over to Officer Gallup, then rolled her over to balance on top of his body so that the policeman now stared into her dry, empty eye sockets. "I do remember the rest of the story, Mom," Dennis said. "The seedier, grittier explanation for the children's rhyme. And you've given me a wonderful idea."

He picked up the pile of the policeman's belongings from the bottom step and ran upstairs to his bedroom closet. In the back, he'd hidden a getaway suitcase, complete with cash, clothing, and many of the disguise pieces he'd used when dropping off the packages at postal offices just a few weeks previous. He hadn't wanted to have to use his escape plan so soon—he had intended to stick around at least long enough to see Jax Matthews' return to media glory—but he guessed this day would be as good as any. He could call in sick from the road to buy himself a few days' head start, then ditch his cell for good.

He reopened the cabinet under his sink and fished around inside, finally emerging with a mostly-full bottle of turpentine and a forgotten grill lighter. He placed into the outside suitcase pocket the rest of the latex gloves he'd left on his sink, and before zipping up the compartment and removing the gloves he was still wearing, he grabbed the letter to Jax hanging on the front of his refrigerator. He unscrewed the top of the turpentine bottle and as he walked slowly back to the cellar, dribbled a thin river of the liquid along the stairs to form a pungent path all the way to the policeman's hip.

At last, he stood over his mother and Officer Gallup, still lying on the basement floor in a lascivious position. "The old superstition festered well into the latter half of the nineteenth century," Dennis told them. "Bridge builders would encase a person within the structure—a living, breathing person preferably—and with this sacrifice came the assurance that the bridge would hold." He carefully poured the remaining paint thinner evenly across the top of Karen's back. "True believers cited the fact that no bodies were ever found within the ruins of a fallen bridge as proof that the legend was true."

Dennis laughed, the sound resonating like a hollow, eerie echo in the stillness of the basement. "And don't you worry, District Attorney Sweeney: the sacrificial lamb couldn't be a common peasant or wayward child; no, it had to be a person of substance, royalty even. Take that as my final compliment to you." He crouched and wedged the empty bottle beneath Karen's skeletal hand. "It just goes to show: without sacrifice, everything falls apart, no matter how carefully constructed the plans."

He took one last, long look at his mother's thick, wavy hair that drooped over the side of Officer Gallup's mangled chin like black Spanish moss, then headed back up the stairs one final time. When he emerged at the top, he grabbed his keys from the hook next to the porch door, clicked the button on the grill lighter, and tossed the flaming plastic wand gently down toward the cellar floor. "Smoke all night, baby," he called down. The lighter landed on the back of Karen's thigh, and as soon as Dennis saw the flames begin to lick her shoulders and arms, he grabbed his suitcase, walked calmly out of the house and into his Subaru, and started the engine.

As he drove inconspicuously down the street, he spotted John Boy the cat sitting on his neighbor's stone front steps. His former friend watched the orange car until it disappeared around the corner and out of sight.

Early the next morning, Dennis took one final look around the Subaru. He didn't bother wiping down the car's interior: it was registered to him, and besides, he left no fingerprints and any DNA investigators might be searching for could be obtained from his work space or what he guessed was left of the house. As long as Officer Gallup's identity remained in flux for a few days, he had enough time to put some distance between himself and Massachusetts. He slid the faux eyeglasses on his face and placed his house and car keys under the visor before grabbing his suitcase and wheeling down the fourth aisle of LOT A, Long-term Parking, at Hartford's Bradley International Airport. After only five minutes, the shuttle arrived, and he joined two other people in the back of the mini-bus, his suitcase stored safely in the rack beside him.

The young couple, a man with curly brown hair and a tiny woman with glasses, nuzzled happily across from him as the vehicle bounced and wove its way to the terminal. Dennis realized he must have looked at them a moment too long, as the woman smiled and nodded to Dennis's suitcase. "You going anywhere fun?" she asked.

Dennis grinned, mimicking the inclusive smile the woman in the sandwich shop had given him. "Miami: South Beach. Bachelor party for my brother. You?"

The woman smiled back. "Oh! We have a layover there: we're probably on the same flight! My name's Bridget, and this is Chris. American nonstop, right?"

Dennis froze his face in place and tapped the side of his eyeglasses. He knew from his criminal justice studies that witnesses tended to best remember physical characteristics that their eyes were drawn to. If his face ever appeared on the national news, he wanted the woman not to recognize him without glasses. "Yep, that's the one. I'll probably see you on there," he said.

"Awesome," said the woman, and she sounded like she

meant it.

"American," called the driver, and the bus slowed to a stop. Dennis allowed the couple to exit first and as he stood on the curb next to his suitcase, he rifled through his laptop bag as if searching for his boarding pass and ID. As soon as the bus pulled away and the couple disappeared inside the terminal, he crossed the street and lined up in the taxi line. A cab pulled up and Dennis climbed inside.

"Bushnell Park, please," he told the driver. He knew that from there, the Amtrak train station going south was a quick walk. He might take the train to Philly, or Washington, D.C., or even New York City, and after that, well…

The possibilities were endless.

Piece #11
Atlanta, GA

They were all snakes, as far as he was concerned. And not your average garden snakes, either, but long, predatory serpents with darting black eyes and slithering, sinewy bodies that wrapped themselves around their victims, squeezing until their prey's eyes bulged like a cartoon character.

Mark thought of this while his eyes bounced between the muted closed-circuit screen and his fellow guests in the green room. There were three of them that morning, each awaiting his or her turn on stage, freakish eye-candy performers in a traveling sideshow. The woman, a too-thin brunette with some sort of European accent—Scottish, maybe?—paced back and forth along the side wall, whispering to herself. Mark wondered if she'd prepared a monologue for her appearance. It was supposed to be all ad-lib, being a talk show and all, but he assumed she was one of those Type A movie stars, now past her prime and heading quickly toward washed-up, who had made it a full-time job climbing back onto the media darling horse. He eyed her, trying not to seem too obvious in his perusal. Her eye make-up was heavy but flawless, and he was certain she'd received a fresh injection or two of Botox in the past week. Although her mouth was in constant motion, none of the skin above her eyebrows moved an inch. This was the first time Mark had met her in person, though he remembered her clearly being in some action movie with Jason Statham or Bruce Willis or someone like that ten or so years back, and surely, they'd been at the same premieres and after-awards parties a decade previous. She was older now, it was clear. Her fuckable days were far behind her, and no mid-morning show, no matter how high the daytime ratings, would change that.

The woman stopped suddenly and put one hand on a hip. Mark sipped a ginger ale and watched curiously as her countenance morphed from happy to delighted to quizzical to serious, an emotional flip chart. *She's even practicing her expressions*, he thought. He glanced over at the third guest, a twenty-something year old pop star whose last Billboard hit had been when the singer had still been in his teens. This guest was sitting in one of the other low-back easy chairs, his head tilted back, resting on the cushion, and his bent knees spread wide. Soon after his heyday—according to the tabloids, at least—the singer had acquired a wicked drug addiction that volleyed him back and forth between rehab and jail for a number of years. *He's here to prove to the world that he's put all of that behind him*, Mark thought. *Look at me, fans! I may have sold my Grammy to pay for a bag of crack cocaine, but I'm back in fighting shape and ready for the ring!* Mark chuckled under his breath. *Pathetic*, he thought. *Both of them.* He could smell the desperation streaming through their pores. They emitted it in noxious waves with every exhale. They were both junkies, addicted to the adoration fame and fortune had brought them once upon a time, both jonesing for another hit.

Mark wasn't like them.

Sure, he hadn't worked in seven years, and seven years was a lifetime in show business, especially after being a Nielsen darling for three years straight. He had starred on a hit sitcom. Well, *starred* might have been too strong of a term; his name had been in the opening credits, anyway, and he had been part of the ensemble nominated for the SAG award. They hadn't won, but a nomination was something. And then, all of a sudden, the show was canceled, and within six months, no one was taking his calls, not even his own mother. He'd lived on residuals for a time, when the show had gone into syndication then developed a bit of a cult following on Hulu. However, that well had dried, and Mark had been faced with the decision to either find a job outside of the entertainment industry or reinvent himself and resuscitate his career.

It had been Charmaine, his former agent, who had suggested the talk show; this was after he'd followed her home, scaled her wrought iron fence, and refused to leave her patio until she gave him five minutes of her time. He'd have to travel, she said, because a lot of the trendier shows weren't filming in L. A. or New York anymore. "Whatever exceeds the stipend you can deduct it off your taxes. A business expense," she said, as if that softened the $700 credit card charge to upgrade the round-trip flight to Atlanta. The show was paying for an economy class seat, of course, but Mark didn't want to be trapped next to some trashy family with a screaming kid or two kicking his seat back. It was first-class or nothing, and luckily, American offered a nonstop flight that dropped him off just as night was falling on Georgia two days prior to the taping. He could return to Los Angeles two hours after leaving the show.

He'd selected a hotel outside of downtown and rationalized he would take an Uber to the studio when the time came. He didn't want to risk being mobbed by a wave of angry haters or the press—he'd fought that battle much too often for his comfort—so he reserved a suite in an unassuming hotel within walking distance of Little Five Points, which according to Google maps, was an artsy neighborhood with a plethora of bars where he could disappear. The first night he was in Georgia, he'd been too exhausted to go out: the three-hour time difference, combined with the stifling heat, suffocated him. He'd seen a liquor store just a few streets from his lodging on the ride from the airport, and once he'd dropped his bag and placed the special package he'd brought in the small refrigerator next to the bed, he'd wandered off to procure a bottle of tequila and a cold, pre-made sandwich from Starbucks for his dinner. The next morning, after scarfing down a bagel from the hotel's continental breakfast, he'd walked a few blocks, through Freedom Park and down Moreland Avenue, to poke around a small gathering of shops, keeping his aviator sunglasses on to avoid being recognized. From a head shop, he bought a patchouli-scented sachet for his travel bag—by the time he'd unpacked, a fetid, rotting smell was wafting from its lining—window-shopped in the bohemian clothing and trinket stores along the strip, and surveyed the area restaurants and bars, deciding on a Mexican cantina for dinner later that evening.

When he returned to the hotel, he attempted to check for publicity on his upcoming show appearance, but the hotel's Wi-Fi was painfully slow, and after a few minutes of refreshing the search results, he gave up and curled up on the firm queen-sized bed and took a nap. When he awoke, the sky was darkening and his stomach rumbled with hunger. He splashed cold water on his face and swished some mouthwash in his mouth before returning to the street where he'd spotted the Mexican joint.

Despite its enormous size, the restaurant was nearly empty, and rather than sit alone at the bar, Mark opted to take a table on the patio. At a nearby table sat a borderline-chubby woman with bobbed blonde hair. Mark placed her as mid-to-late twenties, although admittedly, his age register was rusty from having lived in Hollywood for so long. She sipped a blue margarita and smiled shyly at him as he sat down, and when the waiter brought him his drink, a house margarita with a double shot of top-shelf tequila, he motioned to her to join him. Her name was Barbara, she said, and she was visiting the area with her roommate and her roommate's boyfriend; they had traveled from Arkansas to watch the taping of some television show about zombies that the three were crazy about.

"Jen and Carl," Barbara explained, "are having some *alone time*." She raised her hands in the air and made an air quote motion with her fingers. "That's what they call it. Jen and I have an agreement. Once a week, I make myself scarce until at least eleven o'clock so that she and Carl can have alone time. We've already been here a few days, and we spent a couple a'days before that in the car, so I figured, this is the night." She took a long sip of her drink from a wide straw.

Her eyes are too small for her face, Mark thought. *Beady. That's what's wrong with her. She's got beady eyes.* He was always finding the faults in the women he met, and he hadn't ever met a girl who didn't have at least one. Even the plastic surgery addicts had an oddly shaped eyebrow, a slight lisp, or unfortunately ruddy skin. All women were flawed. Only the savvy ones camouflaged their blemishes with grace.

Barbara was not a savvy girl. She blinked her lashes at him as she spoke and often positioned her head so that it tilted downward, forcing her to look slightly up at him. These motions only exacerbated the incongruence of her tiny eyes. To make matters worse, she stared at him almost constantly. Even when their plate of guacamole arrived and the two of them began dipping into it with salty tortilla chips, she continued to stare at him. She reminded him of a ball python one of his neighbors used to own who'd fix its gaze on him as he sat on the couch across from its tank. It had appeared to be stalking him, tempting fate to dissolve the glass barrier between them so that it could sink its fangs into his neck and swallow him whole.

For the moment, he allowed Barbara to think she was the one doing the stalking. But she hadn't recognized him, even after he'd removed his sunglasses and told her what he did for a living. "Were you on network T.V.?" she asked, keeping her eyes fixed on his face. "'Cuz we only stream stuff. When Jen finally moves in with Carl, she'll probably take the T.V. anyway, and I'll have to watch my shows on my laptop like most of my friends."

Mark flagged down the waiter and ordered them more drinks, plus a round of shots. "You're not driving, are you?" he asked playfully. He knew she wasn't. She had told him that the three of them were staying at an AirBnB down the road, in the opposite direction of his hotel.

When they had finished their latest round and Barbara began to slur her words a bit, Mark quickly paid the bill and glanced at his phone. It was only ten o'clock. Barbara couldn't return to the room yet, he explained to her, so why shouldn't she accompany him back to his place for a nightcap? He'd get her a cab in an hour. Barbara smiled shyly just as she had when she first saw him. The skin on her neck, chest, and cheeks blushed bright pink. *Alcohol flush*, Mark thought. *Another flaw.* But, she didn't talk too much, and when it came down to it, she was a warm body in a city he'd never have to see again, and she hadn't recognized him, so the likelihood of a level five clinger was relatively low.

When they arrived at the door to his room, Barbara leaned against the hallway wall and lifted one of her calves so that it crossed over her opposite knee. She began to fidget with the buckle on her platform sandals. "Sorry… my feet are absolutely killing me. I have to take these off for a bit. You don't mind, do you?" she asked, continuing to remove her shoes without waiting for a response.

Mark opened the door and gestured for her to enter. "Of course not," he said.

Once she had removed both of her sandals, Barbara scooped them up by the straps with her left hand and padded into the hotel room. Just as she had in the restaurant, she kept her eyes fixed on Mark's as she passed him, breaking eye contact only when she'd walked too far ahead to see her host without turning her head all the way around. "This is cute," she remarked, glancing about the simply furnished room. She tossed her handbag on a nearby chair. "What show did you say you'd be filming tomor—"

When she had been within falling distance of the bed, Mark punched the side of Barbara's head as hard as he could, silencing her speech as efficiently as disconnecting a speaker from an MP3 player. He saw her head tilt awkwardly sideways, then recover, and for a moment, the woman seemed to be swaying. Then her body fell forward onto the quilt-covered mattress and began to slide backward.

"Oh, no you don't," Mark said quickly, grabbing Barbara's shoulders and pushing her firmly onto the bed. He hadn't planned to hit her. He had planned to maybe fuck her, maybe score a Bible-belt blow job out of the deal and kick her trailer trash ass to the curb, but her constant staring had unnerved something inside of him. He rolled her onto her back. She was passed out cold. Breathing, but definitely unconscious. Her eyelids were closed. Finally, the snake had stopped sizing up its prey. He pushed down on her shoulders, hard, half-expecting the woman to start wriggling below him, but her body made no movement except the slight rising and falling of her chest.

Mark felt Barbara's teal-colored blouse. It was soft, some sort of fluid, man-made fabric: rayon, perhaps? Mark assumed it was one of Barbara's nicest pieces of clothing, one she'd brought especially for a special night out on the town in the big city. He pulled hard on the button placket and the blouse ripped open, revealing pale, blotchy skin. She wasn't wearing a bra, and her breasts were small, almost prepubescent. Mark had dated a professional dancer in New York City back when he was first trying to break into the business. She had had a boyish chest like Barbara's, but she'd also been tall, lithe, gazelle-like. Next to her, Barbara would be considered stocky, borderline obese even. By Los Angeles standards, she was downright fat. Fat, and yet no boobs to show for it. The irony.

"Hey Barbie," Mark said out loud, his voice echoing slightly in the silent room. "Ever wonder what you'd look like with a pair of decent sized tits?" He reached over the side of the bed to the refrigerator and pulled the door open, removing a wad of butcher paper about two inches high. He unwrapped the paper and pulled a round, flesh-colored object from inside. It was slightly slimy, oozing brownish liquid from where it had been severed from its original owner. Mark slapped the disarticulated breast onto Barbara's bare chest, covering one of her nipples. A dark, watery substance dripped from beneath the foreign body part and dribbled down the side of Barbara's torso and onto the bedspread. "How about that? Half a boob job." He adjusted the breast so that it aligned with the rest of her chest and squinted his eyes to try to envision what it would look like attached. For a moment, he wished he'd brought his travel sewing kit so that he could hand-stitch the object to Barbara's skin.

After a few minutes, the game had lost its novelty, and Mark was starting to sober up. He fished the half-empty bottle of tequila from the nightstand, unscrewed the cap, and took a long swig. He folded his legs underneath his body and sat there, on the bed, staring at Barbara and her exposed torso, the yarmulke of bluish-peach skin and brownish-pink nipple still lying atop. The edges of the extra part were dark red, almost black, and ragged. Mark sat there and stared a long time, until his eyelids began to weaken and he placed the almost-empty bottle on the nightstand, curled up next to Barbara, and fell into a deep sleep.

The next morning, he woke to the tinny music of his phone's alarm clock. Barbara was nowhere in sight, and neither was the breast. All that remained of it was a small pile of discarded butcher paper on the worn carpet. Mark rubbed his eyes, took a long, cold shower, and opened his Uber app to reserve a ride to the studio.

Mark leaned back in one of the two easy chairs in the green room and watched the monitor with interest. The brunette with the foreign accent was laughing dramatically alongside the show's host, an athletically-built woman who had the ridiculous name of Tara Tooley and huge brown eyes and big white teeth. The two were assembling an appetizer of spicy edamame. Charmaine had told him: the show was a hybrid of topical chat and instructional cooking, the newest chimera in the onslaught of mindless daytime drivel. Mark didn't know anyone who watched it—thank God for that—and no one but Charmaine knew he'd be appearing on it. He had been assigned the middle spot and would be co-chefing the main dish, cellophane noodles with pork and Thai basil.

If the assistant didn't appear at the door, his cue to start walking backstage was when the host invited audience members to sample the completed appetizer. Then, they'd break for what would be the commercial, the host would chatter on about some ridiculousness, and there would be Mark, schmoozing and making a general ass of himself while he tried his best to appear charming and hirable.

Mark glanced sideways at the pop star, who was still lounging in the opposite chair, holding one hand in the other and cracking each individual knuckle. The door opened quickly and a small blonde woman with severe, black-rimmed glasses trotted inside. "Mr. Petersham, it's time," she said quickly, and pushed the door open wider like she was preparing to shoo a herd of cats into a barn.

Mark stood up and stretched. He placed his ginger ale on the coffee table then thought better of it, bringing the can to his mouth and gulping the remaining liquid. He wordlessly flashed a finger-gun hand signal at the pop star and walked toward the door, handing the empty can to the assistant on his way out.

The back hall to the stage seemed to be filled with people, but no one was doing anything important, at least not from what Mark could see. Most were standing around, chatting in low voices, drinking their chai lattes and pretending to listen to their colleagues as they thumbed their phones. One corner was so congested, Mark had to turn his body sideways to squeeze between two small groups of people. When the front of his thighs brushed up against the ass of a young redhead who was nodding excitedly to her co-worker, he felt his groin swell and he reached his palm out ever so slightly so that it drifted along her pantyline as he passed. Normally, he would do his best to not tentpole his trousers before stepping in front of the camera, but he knew he'd be given a long apron to wear before he stepped into the lights, and besides, his head was still swimming with hangover: any modicum of pleasure could only help.

The lights were brighter than he remembered. The stage's

pastel decor seemed to be screaming at him from the very second he stepped in front of the audience. His head pounded. For a moment, he blinked furiously at the people while they clapped like robots on cue from the stage manager. He knew he looked like a deer in the headlights, so he covered for his momentary awkwardness with a friendly wave of his hand and a half-skip up to the host, his arm stretched to shake her hand vigorously.

Tara Tooley flashed him a wide grin and invited him to join her behind the kitchen island to begin preparation of their meal. Suddenly, the room was hot, too hot for Mark's comfort. He felt beads of sweat pool on his forehead and wondered if the camera would pick them up. He handed Tara the red chili and minced garlic on cue and watched as she tossed the spices effortlessly into the hot oil in the wok. They exchanged meaningless conversation, the host talking a mile a minute while Mark struggled to keep up. His head was really throbbing now, and he had to watch Tara's lips move in order to comprehend what she was saying.

Tara gathered the ground pork from her cutting board and tossed handfuls of it in the pan; it sizzled as she stirred it officiously with a wooden spoon. Mark stared at her blankly. Her breasts jiggled slightly when she made quick movements, and Mark followed her right nipple with his eyes like a cat with a laser toy. "Now that I'm broiling, Mark, I'd like it if you smoked some pot," she said to him.

Confused, Mark froze. The audience was silent for what seemed like a full minute.

"Now that the water is boiling, Mark, place the cellophane noodles into the pot," she repeated.

Mark snatched the delicate, milk-colored noodles from the counter and dumped them gently into the bubbling water. He watched, mesmerized, as the starch softened and relaxed, and the individual noodles broke free of the bunch and began to swim around the pot. His eyes were burning, but he resisted the urge to rub them as he knew his makeup would smear, leaving him to look like a demented hobo.

Tara was saying something to him. He looked up and, to his horror, watched as a long, cellophane snake slithered out from between two of her teeth and wound its way down her neck and over her shoulder. Panicked, Mark looked to the stage manager, who was staring back at him, but instead of eyes, sinewy pale serpents slithered from his sockets, their heads swaying back and forth to a silent charmer's tune.

Mark closed his eyes and took two deep breaths. He was hungover. He was overheating. He had to keep it together. *Breathe*, he told himself. *Don't fuck this up. Breathe.* He thought of the morning of his flight, of the package he'd received in the mail.

There had been a woman standing outside of his gate; Mark could see her from his vantage point at the corner, but she hadn't seen him yet. She was tall, and her wavy, light brown hair bobbed around her shoulders as she leaned against the fence post, bouncing her leg nervously. Mark retreated down the side street and walked around the block. He knew how to cut through his neighbor's yard without notice. He'd had plenty of practice in the past year, ever since the damn #metoo movement got fiery. All of a sudden, women were confronting him in the supermarket, leaving snide messages on his voicemail. He'd even dodged a civil suit, thanks to an old buddy who was having an affair with a seedy lawyer on Wilshire Boulevard who specialized in trumped-up lawsuits. He should really just move, find a new place, start fresh. After all, his career was going to be rejuvenated, why shouldn't his abode?

Luckily for Mark, his front door was sheltered from the street by a large arborvitae bush. His visitor surely would get bored soon and leave. He paused to pick up the square white box in front of his door and keyed himself inside.

There was no return address on the package. It wasn't a script: those were delivered by messenger, and he didn't recall ordering anything online recently. Still, he slit open the box at the seam using a kitchen knife and pulled out the small object wrapped securely with rolls of butcher paper. When he recognized the piece as a human breast, his stomach lurched and he felt nauseous. After a moment, though, the queasiness passed, and he shifted gears and immediately tried to figure out who had sent it to him.

Was it an ex-girlfriend? No, most of his women had

implants. This was all human flesh. It had been a while since he'd touched a natural tit, but he knew one when he felt it. Could it have been the bitch he'd fucked in the make-up trailer a few weeks before the show had been canceled, the one who made all the fuss after about feeling pressured by him to take her clothes off? The one who'd claimed she hadn't liked it rough, just the way he'd given it to her? That fucking press. They'd crucified him, stomped on him when he was down. They were like starving lions entering the Colosseum: one drop of blood and they were on him, mercilessly.

He held the breast in his hand and lifted it up and down, pretending to gauge its weight like a jeweler. He guessed it was the left breast. Was it a symbol of some sort? Could it be a message from one of the show runners, maybe the director? Those hacks liked to think they were creating great art with even greater meanings, but it was all a load of crap. A dive into their depth always ended with a broken neck.

He shook the wrapping paper, wondering if he had missed something. A small square of white paper tumbled out, and Mark put down the breast to unfold the note and read it.

> A girl whose status is unknown
> Pieces sent to a chosen few
> Action is—

"What the fuck is this trash?" Mark asked the silence. He crumpled the note with his hand and tossed it into the wastepaper basket without even bothering to finish it. Everyone thought he or she was an Oscar-winning screenwriter these days, yet most of the dialogue he heard on television was crap. This new generation of writers, they were raised on standardized testing and participation trophies. They had self-esteems the size of skyscrapers but they could barely put a believable sentence together, and now they were writing cryptic poetry. Fuck that.

The body part, however: that was something of value. He carefully rewrapped the breast in the original paper, then laid it carefully in his suitcase, beneath his toiletry bag. *TSA is gonna have a field day with this if it shows up on screening*, he laughed. He wasn't worried. Good-looking people like Mark were never pulled aside for extra checks, and as the body part did not resemble a weapon, he doubted anyone would give it a second look.

His Uber was due to arrive any minute. Before he took a long look out of his window toward the street to see if the woman had left, he tossed the cryptic note in the toilet and flushed.

Mark opened his eyes and forced himself to look at the host. He did his best to look calm and friendly; he thought of puppy dogs and kittens frolicking on a king-sized bed— it was a trick taught to him by one of his acting professors back in school. *Pleasant thoughts breed pleasant expressions*, he thought, repeating the instructor's mantra in his head. Tara Tooley was giving him a strange look. No one was speaking. As the front lights dimmed, Mark felt yellow vomit force itself up from his stomach and out of his mouth; he watched as it splattered the countertop, leaving a splash or two on the pot of boiling noodles and on Tara herself. The show paused for commercial, and Mark was grateful for the reprieve from the glare of the lights.

When it was clear the cameras had stopped rolling, Tara leaned over to her guest. "I never wanted your rapist ass on the show in the first place, you prick," she muttered under her breath to him. "I hope this stunt ruins you for good." As she turned to walk backstage and clean up, the stage manager and a security guard marched toward him on stage. Each placed a hand in his underarm, and before Mark knew it, they were whisking him off stage and back to the green room to collect his belongings. As he walked from the building, he glimpsed the rehab resident pop star on the muted television screen: he was standing where Mark had been on stage as a cleaning crew worked furiously to mop up the mess.

By the time he reached Atlanta's airport, his whole body ached. He couldn't remember being this hungover in his life. A nice, quiet day of rest alone in his apartment was just what the doctor ordered. After sailing through security, Mark climbed onto a barstool in one of the gate-adjacent bars and ordered a Bloody Mary.

He was halfway through the glass when a middle-aged

woman slipped onto the chair next to him. She was plain-looking but pleasant enough, and she smiled at him while he dunked the celery garnish into the tomato juice. She ordered a water and gulped down most of it in under sixty seconds, then turned her body to face Mark's.

"Aren't you Mark Petersham?" she asked, the Southern drawl oozing from her lips.

Mark shook his celery stump and dropped it on the napkin next to his glass. "I am, little lady," he said, brushing his hands together. "You a fan? If you can locate a pen, I'd love to give you an autograph."

The woman laughed slightly and slipped back off the chair. She stood next to Mark, then reached toward her waist. When she brought her hand back up, it was holding a police badge. "Mark Petersham, Atlanta PD. You're under arrest for assault in the first degree. Stand up, please, and put your hands behind your back." From the other side of the bar approached a white-haired man wearing a taupe-colored suit. "Sergeant Amaral," the woman continued, "would you cuff Mr. Petersham and read him his rights?" She bent down and grabbed the handle of his carry-on suitcase. "I'll take care of this for you: don't you worry."

Unable to speak, Mark did as he was told. As the three of them made their way out of the airport and to a waiting squad car, Sergeant Amaral spoke up. "And rest assured: we've been in contact with the Los Angeles police department. They are very interested in that body part you had in your hotel room." He shut the back door and Mark's world was silent for a full minute.

Then, he swore he heard hissing.

Excerpt from the final chapter of

All of the Pieces:
The Hangman Killing
by
Jackson Matthews

The progression from arrest to trial was one of the quickest I had ever seen. The Feds wanted the "package hysteria" over with and they needed a win according to an inside source, so they blindly accepted a few of the inconsistencies and raced towards the finish line without looking back.

They didn't have enough to convict Connor for the murder, no DNA and no physical evidence, and there was no record of Connor being near when Julie was kidnapped. The loophole they utilized was that while Connor had no alibi for the time Julie had gone missing, records showed that his cell phone was over four hours away. The DA claimed it was easy to leave a phone in a location and drive four hours to kidnap someone—hell, the killer drove for countless hours to ship all the packages—but it was a stretch.

The last "fake" letter that Connor had on him that night, the one that made me snap and jump him, was the key piece of evidence the DA tried to use in the trial. It was their "slam dunk" evidence that proved Connor had been writing the notes all along. Forensics even said that the ink and paper "could" have been from the same printer as the others I received previously. They also stressed the fact that I no longer received any letters after Connor was put in jail. In the end, they did not have enough evidence to convict him for the murder of Julie Piedmont, though the DA has stated that they still feel they have the right man and will attempt to try him again when more evidence comes to light.

They did, however, convict Connor on numerous

"internet crimes" and for all of the other crimes I told him he would get charged. He received a sentence of forty years. The kid, a serial killer fanatic who watched his own mother be murdered, was now in jail with real killers and would be until he was past the age of retirement.

When the sentencing came down, I was in the courtroom. I carefully watched Connor's face and I saw that he truly was crushed. He cried soft, steady, silent tears. I've always made it a point to never feel bad for a criminal as I believe everyone makes their own choices, but this verdict hit my gut hard. I felt sick, to the point where I had to leave the courtroom.

Right now, you have read over four hundred pages of an exhaustively researched story about a poor girl, a crazed killer, a messed-up kid, and a reporter who got caught in the middle. You learned of the plight of poor Julie Piedmont's family, who never buried their daughter, not all of her anyway; The Hangman claimed to have mailed all of the pieces of his victim to locations all over the country, and yet, not all of her body parts were turned in to police. What happened to those missing pieces? I can't fathom what would possess someone to hold onto a body part that had been mailed to them anonymously, and I've seen just about every kind of psychopathy and mental instability there is.

You read my personal thoughts on how and why I thought Connor was the killer, how I was positive he was the one who did it. Hell, I even testified and was a key reason he got convicted. So why would I feel bad about him going away, when he was probably a murderer? Because, I *no longer* believe Connor killed Julie.

It's rare that I change my mind without shocking evidence, but after going through every detail for months, looking at every word I wrote and every note

I took over and over again, something doesn't add up. I can't put my finger on it. There have not been any other murders, no new letters, and almost a year has gone by, but I truly feel now that some sadistic killer is out there, planning a new murder and laughing that he got away with Julie's. For the first time in my career, I hope to God I am wrong...

The Gallery
Seventeen months later
Brooklyn, New York City

Jax had a seventy-eight-dollar glass of wine in his left hand and Maggie's soft, warm fingers nestled between the fingers of his other. The excitement of the opening was palpable. It had been a long journey, but they finally had arrived at their dream. Looking around the gallery and its stark white walls and harsh spotlights highlighting the rich woods and stains of his pieces resting on heavy pedestals, Jax, for the first time in his life, thought he would feel complete. But his brain would not settle. His art was his world and his life now, but this—being featured on a showcase to be critiqued and praised—was not what he wanted; it was not why he created his pieces. Regardless, he was still as happy as he had ever been. There were just a few tiny strings sticking on the back of his coat that he just could not cut away.

The Hangman killing should have been a million miles away. Jax had moved on, but the murder-obsessed culture of America had not. Instead of just enjoying the party, Jax was worried that the press would show up and ask him questions about the case and not his art, that the crazed serial killer fans would come out of the woodwork to ask him questions or try to get his autograph. The worst part was the uncertainty: Jax truly didn't know if the people who were there had shown up for his work or because he was "that famous reporter who wrote the best-selling book about the Hangman Killings." It was something he would always struggle with; if he succeeded as an artist, would it be only because of his previous fame?

Jax tried to shake these ideas out of his mind and enjoy the party, but the suit he had on was killing him. If Maggie hadn't chosen it, he would not have worn it. It was tight: too tight and yet it was probably the fanciest thing he had ever worn. He had plenty of suits, but not a tuxedo and not one that had a sheen to it, with sharp cuts and a bow tie that looked like Freddy Krueger had used it as an emery board. It looked ridiculous, but the various "consultants" and experts in the field told him he needed to stand out, that at a gallery opening, attendees should be able to walk in and instantly be able to point out the artist, even if they had never seen him before or did not know his work. While Jax absolutely hated the idea, he understood it and trusted his "team," which Maggie was in charge of, so he wore the damn thing even though he felt stupid as hell.

As the night progressed, more and more people showed up. Jax was introduced to all of them one at a time. People fawned over him, asking questions about his art that he truly couldn't answer, but he was a master bullshit artist and returned answers that went over well, or at least people faked the fact that they liked them. He grew more and more edgy with every patron, beginning to believe each was a poser and was just there to be at an "event"; these were rich people with too much money who bought up new artists' work as investments on a gamble in the event the starving painter or sculptor would evolve into the next "It boy." Years later, they could brag that they were some of the first to buy the work and that they had an original piece before the artist rose to fame.

Blah, blah, blah.

One wrinkled old woman droned on about how Jax reminded her of Andy Warhol (which was really just a way for her to drop the fact that she knew "Andy"). Jax tuned her out and stole glances about the room. When he heard the lady mention The Hangman, his heart dropped.

"Darling, your book: it was fabulous," she drawled. "It amazes me one man can be so talented: a writer, a journalist, *and* an artist. How do you do it?"

Jax swallowed hard and simply nodded before changing the subject back to "Andy." He asked her how she knew him, and as he suspected, she took the opportunity to gush on about it. Jax smiled and let his mind wander as he pretended to listen.

The fact that the book he wrote on The Hangman paid for his new career ate at him ferociously. It made him feel like he hadn't earned the studio, that he had bought it simply by cashing in on one last "big story." At that moment, Maggie squeezed his arm; she could tell he was thinking about it. They had discussed his feelings about the book and the studio a thousand times, but in the end, Jax had written the book because writing it meant freedom. It had been their way of owning the place and not involving an investor. It had been a hard choice, but Jax reminded himself that it was his last story and that he had no intention of writing another word in his life, other than love letters to Maggie and art piece descriptions. The book had allowed him to make that choice. Squeezing his eyes shut for a second, Jax tried to tell himself that he wasn't a sell-out, but no matter what he did, the moniker *Hangman's Gallery* whispered in the back of his mind. He knew, deep down, what and who had really paid for that opening.

Pushing the thoughts of Connor and The Hangman out of his head, Jax had tried to focus on the party. He had tried his best to accept this new sort of attention, one that wasn't for some other person's story but for his own talent. It was a strange feeling. The sculptures had always been just his, in his garage, shared only with Maggie, and now, there were hundreds of people staring and pointing and critiquing each piece, talking to dealers and buying them up like they were the last pies in the bakery before Thanksgiving. Jax didn't know how to handle this new attention, but he did his best to keep a smile on his face and to answer questions he never thought he would get. The most frequent by far had been "What is your inspiration?" to which Jax wanted to answer, *I don't know, I just make things I like*, but he couldn't. He was expected to say things that had deep meaning, like, *the wood, it talks to me, it tells me what it wants to be.* He hated the pantomime of it all. Jax started to wonder if he could change his mind about public appearances and become one of those "reclusive" artists that never showed up in public, making their work even more valuable. Was it too late to become that?

After a few too many questions, Jax needed a break so he excused himself. Not wanting to have an awkward bathroom conversation, he did not use the public one, but rather the private one that was connected to the back office. After taking a quick leak and thinking to himself that hundred-bucks-a-glass champagne looked exactly the same as two-dollar-a-glass champagne coming out, he looked around the tiny room that was just a sink and toilet and took a breath. He still needed some time, so he went to the office and sat at his desk, a pointless piece of furniture now, since he never used it and any paperwork that was required for the gallery was handled by the staff he had hired.

Sitting down, he rubbed his eyes and looked at the picture of Maggie on the desk. He had taken the picture of her years ago on the Atlantic City Boardwalk on a particularly windy day. It was their first trip away after the book came out and they were truly happy. Looking at her red hair flying about her face and the laughing, easy smile as she squatted down to pet a Boardwalk cat, Jax felt his lips turn up on the sides. Maggie was all he needed. He began to stand up and make his way back into the cacophony of the opening when a small stack of mail on the edge of the desk caught his eye. A familiar-looking envelope peeked out from the center of the pile, and all at once, a rope lassoed Jax's heart at lighting speed and squeezed it hard.

On instinct, Jax pulled open the top drawer of the desk to snatch a pair of gloves, then realized: this wasn't his old journalism desk. He wasn't that reporter anymore. And yet, he couldn't help it: he had to see what was inside. Wrapping a tissue around his fingers, he grabbed the corner of the envelope, carefully slid it from the stack, and examined it. From the weight and density, Jax could tell what was inside, and it made him take a deep breath.

He slowly slid a letter opener through the flap. The paper ripped with a noise like a sinister serpent cackling. The sound sent chills down his back, right into his balls, which instantly tightened up with fear. He glimpsed the edge of the first polaroid inside. This time, he was unaware of the smile that crossed his lips.

Epilogue
Three months after that
An unnamed suburb in America

Dennis tapped the steering wheel in tandem with the twittering of Bad Company's "Ready for Love" streaming softly from his car speakers. He was still getting used to the car he'd picked up in West Virginia, a cranky '88 Chevy Nova with a faded red and white racing stripe painted down the side. He made a mental note to stop at AutoZone later that afternoon and buy some touch-up paint to cover up the marking completely.

Without an MP4 jack or even a CD player, the music options were limited, but Dennis didn't plan on driving across multiple states in it again; at least, not for a while. He'd surely have upgraded his transportation options by that point. The song ended, and Dennis pushed the tiny white button on the side of the stereo, ejected the ancient cassette tape, and turned the knob to OFF. From his vantage point in the parking lot, he could see the children playing on the hot stretch of playground adjacent to the town's nursery school. Some gathered in groups, breaking into spontaneous games of tag or a splattering of uncoordinated dance steps as they giggled and whispered to one another; still others ran aimlessly around the lot, sometimes tripping over their own feet and sailing painfully onto the hot tar or gawkily kicking a tired-looking soccer ball back and forth. One small but vocal cluster held hands in a circle and sang and danced. Dennis rolled down the driver's side window using the manual crank handle on the lower half of the door and listened.

"Awww… aren't they sweet?" cooed Karen's voice sarcastically from the back seat. Dennis imagined her body propped up against the black cloth interior, her taut skin the same brownish-gray hue of an old, forgotten crayon, one of those New Age colors labeled Hazy Shade of Winter or Pastoral Sunset or some other ridiculousness. He almost tilted the rearview mirror so that he could see her but stopped himself. *She's not there*, he reminded himself. But sometimes, he wondered.

Milling about the children were three adult women: teachers, Dennis supposed, although he doubted the sum of their ages would qualify for social security. Two of them moved very slowly; one held her hand in a permanent salute in front of her forehead in an attempt to shield her eyes from the early summer sun. The third woman, a tall, pale, gazelle-like figure with long, spiral-curled hair tied back in a long ponytail, eagerly rushed about the recess area alongside her wards, smiling and laughing despite the visible sweat stains forming under her arms and below her breasts.

It had been a hot spring, and although it was only early June, it looked to be an even hotter summer. The Northeast had seen its share of heat waves, but Dennis was far away from there now and still acclimating to his new location and identity. He knew he'd never work in forensics again—that was a given—but he had managed to land a position as a veterinary assistant at a Mom and Pop clinic. The doctor there moonlighted performing bullet-removal and other minor surgeries for organized crime members on the downlow, and Dennis had agreed to assist him when an extra set of hands was required. In exchange, the veterinarian paid Dennis under the table for his day job. Although he'd vanished suspiciously from New England, there would be no new tax records, no fresh social security transactions, and no record of him having started the fire or The Hangman mystery whatsoever.

He'd left no trace behind, like a printless fingertip.

Dennis ran his palm over the top of his closely shaved head. He was still adjusting to this change as well, though he had to admit, he rather enjoyed the eerie feeling of having installed an air conditioning unit on his noggin. He still jumped a bit when he caught his own reflection in the mirror; a purposeful weight gain of thirty pounds and loss of nearly all of his hair altered his appearance even more than he had hoped.

The soccer ball came sailing by his open window and landed, bouncing wildly, on the hood of the unmanned car behind him. The spiral-haired teacher frantically unlatched the gate to the schoolyard and rushed through the parking lot after the ball. She passed the window of the Chevy without giving its occupant a second glance. Dennis readied the policeman's badge he'd pocketed after knocking Officer Gallup down the cellar stairs; he'd checked the cop's pockets and had taken his notepad and badge holder with him in his getaway suitcase. At the time, he'd kept the credentials to avoid leaving any evidence but soon realized their additional benefits. Now, he kept the wallet with him whenever he hunted. If anyone asked why he was parked, watching a troop of five-year old children run about the playground, he'd flash the badge and say he was investigating one of the employees for drug trafficking and *since the case is on-going, would you mind not mentioning my presence to anyone?*

He spotted the teacher in his sideview mirror, returning with the wayward ball clutched against her chest. The sound of the children who were gathered in a circle grew louder; they were singing, their tiny falsettos tinkling like sleigh bells in the hot sun.

Ring around the Rosie

As her image grew larger in the reflection, he swore he could smell her. Her perfume was reminiscent of lily of the valley, a spring scent. Young. Clean. She was almost to his car door. He could see she was smiling. She was even prettier close up. She had pale blue eyes, just like the R.E.M. song.

Pocket full of posies

Her body whooshed past the Chevy like a gust of wind. She never even looked his way. Just like all of the others, she was oblivious to her surroundings.

"What did I always tell you?" Karen's voice wafted from behind him. "You have to look out for yourself because no one is going to look after you."

Ashes, ashes

Dennis started up the car and put the shifter in reverse. He would return that afternoon and follow the pretty, unassuming schoolteacher home. He would return to watch her again tomorrow. By the weekend, he would know where she lived, when she came and went, and who would miss her the most.

Survival of the fittest. People think it's Darwin's law, Dennis thought to himself, *but it was Herbert Spencer's long before that.*

He checked the rearview mirror before taking his foot off of the brake.

We all fall d—